LO
1/10

The Long Division

ALSO BY DEREK NIKITAS

Pyres

The Long Division

Derek Nikitas

MINOTAUR BOOKS ⚘ NEW YORK

THE LONG DIVISION Copyright © 2009 by Derek Nikitas. All rights reserved. Printed in the United States of America. For information, address St. Martin's Press, 175 Fifth Avenue, New York, N.Y. 10010.

www.minotaurbooks.com

"Long Division." Words and Music by Benjamin Gibbard, Nicholas Harmer, and Christopher Walla. © 2008 EMI Blackwood Music Inc., Where I'm Calling from Music, Shove It Up Your Songs, and Please Pass This Song. All Rights Controlled and Administered by EMI Blackwood Music Inc. All Rights Reserved. International Copyright Secured. Used by Permission.

Book design by Jonathan Bennett

Library of Congress Cataloging-in-Publication Data

Nikitas, Derek.
    The long division / Derek Nikitas.—1st ed.
        p. cm.
    ISBN 978-0-312-36398-7
    1. Mothers and sons—Fiction.   2. Murder—Investigation—Fiction.   I. Title.
    PS3614.I54L66 2009
    813'.6—dc22

                                                                      2009012743

First Edition: November 2009

10 9 8 7 6 5 4 3 2 1

For my teacher and mentor,
Wendy Brenner

and they carried on like long division
'cause it was clear with every page
that they were further away
from a solution that would play
without a remain, remain, remain, remainder

—DEATH CAB FOR CUTIE, "*Long Division*"

The Long Division

Last house on a Friday, and Jodie's body ached for weekend. In the master bath she scrubbed soap scum and toothpaste and coiled hair from the sink basin with cleanser wipes. *No water* was the rule—chemicals only. No using the client's toilets, either. Even if she had to pee, Kwik Kleen rules forbade her. Jodie was owed nothing by the world, and the rules applied to her.

In the mirror she caught sight of her ruddy face, the freckles all leaked together. The uniform was a button-down shirt with the fake front of a maid's apron printed on it. Her hands, inside rubber gloves, she kept moist with lilac-scented lotion. Hair the color of Cheetos, tied back with a plastic clip, although one spiral strand of her bangs came down to irk her face.

Out in the hallway the vacuum cleaner yawned again and again, Inez pushing. Five women in the house including Jodie, all scattered to different rooms. The place was three floors, seven bedrooms with as many bathrooms. It was a three-hour scrub-and-shine job. Such lonesome hours Jodie spent in these bathrooms, they seemed almost a comfort. In here was a mounted flatscreen TV and a Jacuzzi tub with ten gold jet valves she had to keep the lime and rust away from with her scrubbing.

The people were never home when the Kwik Kleen van pulled up. In their portraits, they were a family of four with rich brown skin. Their decorating taste was for earthy oranges and yellows, for weird stilt-leg carvings of giraffes and bushmen with large heads. Wicker disks on the walls that Jodie didn't know what they were.

But wondering slowed her work, which was bad because wages were for hours estimated, not actual. Told herself she could dream about strangers' bathrooms later, off-clock, over a tumbler of wine on ice and the television mutter and the chug of her radiator. Still, she wondered if they wondered about her when they came home and saw this room readied for them.

When the tiles shined, Jodie tossed the soiled rag into her bucket. She lifted the handle and stood stoop-shouldered, eyeing the bathroom for what she might've overlooked. She followed the plan, top to bottom, clockwise, no water. She sighed at this, the finish of a fifty-hour workweek, as if it were something.

Back through the master suite with potted palms and a four-poster bed, sunburst carvings on the headboard, matching armoires and nightstands. Her tennis shoes sank into the carpet. Outside a window, wet February blew a drizzle with dead leaves in the mix. By rote she glanced around for any missed tasks. She didn't care to check, but the tic was fixed after two months on this job. Atop one nightstand, a clay bowl not larger than an ashtray sat with its lid tilted askew. With her free hand in a rubber glove she reached out to straighten the lid.

Inside the bowl was an inch-thick stack of folded money. The lid was propped such that she couldn't see the whole stack, just a corner of the topmost hundred-dollar bill. Jodie inched the lid further off the bowl and the doubled-over money stack began to unfold itself. She touched her thumb to the blooming bills, and they were all hundreds, maybe fifty of them. More than she ever saw in one place, even back when she worked grocery store checkout.

Just outside the room Inez still vacuumed the hallway with her back to the bedroom. The vacuum cleaner's headlight doused the hallway walls like a search beam. The bed beside Jodie had a tropical-themed duvet cover folded over goosedown pillows, tan corduroy throws fanned out across the fold. The owners of this cash slept here last night. They dreamed of a redhead maid in blue gloves and wet-kneed jeans and sneakers a size too big. Her fingers on their money.

She still held the bathroom bucket. She smelled of her own armpits and bleach. If these people dreamed Jodie here, what did they dream would happen now? Another static weekend, more Monday-to-Friday toil, hours like empty baggies she filled one after another with expired leftovers? Unfair, how they baited her. Casting off enough money to throw her life wide apart for weeks, maybe months. It all turned unbearable when she looked inside the bowl. Her spirit was inside there, long-lost but suddenly—

—van's back passenger side, crammed against another maid's lumpy ass. Jodie clutched a Hardee's cup with nothing inside it but melting ice. Pressed her head against the windshield and watched Chick-fil-A and Cartoon Network billboards. Five o'clock Friday on seven lanes pushing northbound from Atlanta. A thousand slow-motion cars and trucks stewed in a river of exhaust. Soundtrack on the radio was some Mexican polka, accordions and horns, ten-man mariachi sing-alongs. The van smelled of chemicals and dust, but Jodie guessed now she'd never have to catch a migraine off the Kwik Kleen bleach fumes again. The stolen cash was stuffed in her left pocket against her thigh.

Traffic at a crawl meant cops would beat them to the Kwik Kleen office, handcuffs ready for her wrists. Jump out now and run, down the embankment into the scrub where the kudzu melted down the trees like burning candles. But the law could nab you easy, drag you out squirming with twigs in your hair and your shins muddied.

"¿Qué pasa, Roja?" Inez said from the shotgun seat. With her cheek glued to a cell phone, she eyed Jodie in the rearview mirror.

"Nada," Jodie said.

Inez twisted herself around and said to Jodie, "My boyfriend's cousin is having a party. You should come." Inez was nineteen and engaged to this boyfriend named Hector who sprayed paint on walls for work. She was the only other maid who spoke fluent English, the only other legal worker.

"I don't feel too great," Jodie said.

"Aw, come on. Everybody's going," said Inez.

"I don't know," Jodie said. Almost every weekend Inez dropped these invitations. Jodie would smirk and mutter until the question went away. It seemed like a joke, the idea of a whitegirl thirty-two years old at a Chicano all-night fiesta. Instead, Jodie was planning how she might hop a taxi back down to Buckhead and offer up the loot to those she stole it from, get on her knees and beg mercy. She'd lose her job for sure but maybe skirt jail time.

Couldn't figure how it happened in the first place, how this plan to steal first stabbed into her head. She could've resisted the urge easy enough. She could've walked off and slumped into this van like usual, gone on as before. The worry chilled her deep. Body tremors made her grip her plastic cup too hard and the lid popped askew. Thought she needed money but what she needed—

—Kwik Kleen storefront shared with a Korean dry cleaner. They parked the van in the sidelot and Jodie slid the door, stumbled out into the cold, fought to keep her breath slow. The rubbery muscle threads in her back were primed to snap. Overhead droned the fat transport planes in patterns over Dobbins ARB. Across the street, taxis and busses idled at the station, drifters loitered, everyone on watch duty.

Boss shoved through the store's aluminum side door with a huff so hard it misted in the air. He was Cuban, a refugee going on twenty years, a sweetheart for illegals and the minimum wage he could pay them. He hired natural-born Jodie Larkin at the same rate and promised raises after a first-month probational period. Raises never came. Soon enough she might've quit. She might've done a lot of things.

"Where you ladies been at?" Boss said.

4

"Traffic," Inez said. "Always traffic."

"I got crap to settle and don't need to be waiting all night," Boss said. He eyed each gal in his housekeeping harem like he meant to pick one for the night. Soon as he squinted at Jodie, she dropped her glance into the topmost bucket in the pile she held. The inside was lined with black grit and smelled like fake pine.

The maids lugged supplies into the storeroom, where the busted overhead light forced them to grope around in the dark for the shelves where things went. When they came into the office, Boss rolled his swivel chair from behind his desk and waved a stack of envelopes. Calling names: Mariana, Raquel, Inez, Haida. No Jodie Larkin. The others took their paychecks.

"Jodie, stick around a minute, will you?" Boss said. They were all shoulder-to-shoulder in that office cluttered with bulk boxes of cleaning solutions. The computer keyboard keys and the telephone buttons were filmed with the grease that time collected. "I said Jodie," he told the others, shooing them out.

She wanted to pull the money out of her pocket and toss it in his lap.

"Problems," Boss said after they were alone. "Issues."

Jodie slumped down onto a sturdy box of solvents. She couldn't take it standing.

He said, "I don't got your money, Jode. It ain't here, I'm sorry to tell you. Sons of bitches at the money place screwed it up. Clerical error, they claim, but they're a bunch—"

Jodie put her face in her hands.

"Aw, cripes," he said. "Don't bawl on me here."

The bell inside the phone unit clanged, and the shock of it made Jodie cry out. The ligaments in her throat were strained. The other maids were just outside the door, Inez cackling a laugh about something. Jodie slipped somehow completely out of the world where you could just be alive without anguish. Kept going back to the moment, the nightstand, the bowl, her hand on so much money.

"No—I didn't—" Boss said into the phone. "—where? Hold on a sec." He put his hand over the mouthpiece and nodded at her. He said, "It'll only be till Monday, Jode. First thing Monday they'll have it over here. That's what they said, all right? You need me to front you something for the weekend?"

"Front?" She could hardly hear what he was saying to her.

"Twenty? Forty? Forty's about all I can spare right now."

"No, no—I'm okay."

"You sure? Serious?" He took the phone away from his ear and reached into his breast pocket, peeled out a twenty between his middle and index fingers. Fluttered it at her. "Take it," he said. "Pay me back come Monday."

"I'll manage," Jodie lied. She didn't know how. SWAT team breaking down her wall, plainclothes detectives knocking calmly at her door, Boss on a rampage. She just couldn't dare go home with what amounted to six months of wages, two years of Georgia HCV–subsidized rent. Her apartment was cramped and dark, a trap to keep her cornered. It wasn't anyplace she could trust, but no place was.

Outside Inez leaned against the store's brick façade. She craned her neck forward to see into a compact mirror she held while she primped her hair. A cigarette dangled from her glossy lips and the smoke was making her squint. When Jodie came out, Inez grabbed her by the elbow and said, "You're coming with us tonight to this party, *Roja*. No excuses."

"My check didn't come in."

Inez snapped her compact shut. "*Puta madre*. You need cash? I can ask Hector."

Inez's boyfriend Hector was there across the lot in the driver's seat of his Toyota Celica GT convertible. Faded red paint and flaking canvas top, spoiler, *No Fear* decal on the tinted strip across the top of the windshield. Hector had one arm laid across the open window frame, hand slapping the outside of the door to the Dem Bow beat of the reggaeton coming from his radio.

"Let me get the address," Inez said. "Or, no—you need a ride anyways, right?"

"I'm a mess. I smell like bleach."

"So don't I, right? You ain't getting out of this. That *cabrón* ain't gonna ruin your weekend with his no-check bullshit. There's gonna be some badass music, some dancing."

"I'm in my uniform—"

"Yo, *Roja*, what else you gonna do on a Friday? You live by yourself, right?"

"And my cat," Jodie said.

"Pobrecita." Inez pursed her lips and blew a fake kiss at the sky. Hector honked his horn and Inez rolled her eyes, gave another kiss to the tip of her cig—

—night with strangers, four margaritas poured into the same plastic cup, mostly tequila. She sat on the steps leading down from the back door, sipped her drink and smoked a Kool. More reggaeton pulsed from stereo speakers propped in the open windows behind her. Backyard of a brick ranch that somebody's relative of somebody rented. A dozen kids chased a soccer ball, scurried behind men who sat in lawn chairs circled around a fire pit. The men spoke low and burst out laughing, slapped shoulders, stomped their boots in the dust. Faces golden in the firelight—all unfamiliar, all Mexican, like Jodie had somehow finagled an escape across the border and hid herself among the natives.

"¿Qué honda?" said a squat Latino with a black T-shirt too tight across his gut. He leaned on the rail beside her head, put his face inches from hers, and grinned like he'd already stuffed his whole evening in the bag. He gulped from his bottle of Sol, lime wedge fizzling inside. He was maybe twenty years old.

"*No español,*" Jodie said.

"*Qué lástima,*" he said, pursing his lips at her. "*Calor de mi corazón.*"

"Something about your heart?" Jodie guessed.

"*Heat,*" he said, "yes. Javier ease my name."

"Everybody's name starts with—" She hocked phlegm in the back of her throat.

Toothy Javier imitated the sound, like it was some surefire mating call. He said, "*Su cabello es muy bonita.*" He brushed his fingers along a red curl that sprang away from her scalp.

"*¿Gracias?*" Jodie said, and shrugged.

A couple screaming kids barreled up the steps into the house, almost knocked Jodie's margarita from her hand. The men around the fire muttered and nudged one another while they watched Javier flirt. They ruined her buzz with their leering. They dragged her back down into her tired body and her worry. Even this place wasn't—

—heater warmed her chilled skin. In another life years ago, Jodie withstood western New York winters, but Atlanta thinned out her blood. Now at the slightest cold snap she shivered like a stray pup in a sewer pipe.

Javier drove Hector's Celica with headlights spotlighting southbound I-75, an empty splay of pavement this time of night. He wore only his black T-shirt and jeans, as if to prove he could fight the cold with nothing but machismo. How Jodie agreed to this ride, she couldn't remember. Only that Inez had whispered "watch out for him" and winked, like she was giving her blessing. Whitegirl trophy for the stumpy farm boy from Chihuahua or wherever. She knew what they had all thought, and she let them think, because what did it matter compared to what she knew about herself?

She was in a tequila drowse. Panic worn down after hours on watch, but still throbbing low and constant like the bleep of a forgotten alarm clock in the next apartment over. She watched each exit, afraid a cruiser lurked full of cops itching to take her down and hound her till she cracked. Kool pack in her purse, maybe ten menthols left for her to burn. She took one and scorched its tip with the bright orange spool of the dashboard lighter. The radio played something sweet for once— old Selena, or a J. Lo ballad, or slo-mo Shakira giving her hips a rest.

"This exit," she told Javier. She was crouched down low in her seat, shoulder strap across her neck. She cracked her window and ashed through the slit, readied herself to lie. She said, "*Yo necesito—mas*, uh, *cigarrillos*—from—*el estación?*—"

"We find a gas station for cigarettes?" Javier said.

"*Sí, sí*—but first—my *apartamento*."

"*Apartamento*," he mused, like she'd named some fine wine he was hankering for.

"*Aquí*," she said, signaling the turn into her complex. Every parked car, even those familiar, looked like an unmarked with cops inside it. Seemed stupid that they'd post officers to catch a petty thief, but Jodie knew jack about the law or how she might avoid its snare, especially full of this much booze. Amazing she didn't somehow steer Javier off the face of the planet.

She pointed out her unit and he pulled the Celica into the spot that abutted her door. He twisted the key in the ignition and the headlamps tucked back down into the hood. She touched him on the shoulder. He wore his eagerness like a child promised candy for dessert. The caterpillar mustache above his lip glistened.

"We get inside?" Javier said.

"No, no," she said. "Please—a *momento*, okay?"

"*Discúlpeme*." He slipped his hand off her thigh and hitched it on his own gaudy silver belt buckle instead. An eagle chewing on a snake, or something like that.

Jodie said, "No, I mean—one *momento* and—*nosotros vamanos* to, uh, *tu casa?*"

Javier leaned back against the driver door and grinned like he maybe later still had a shot at romance. When Jodie pushed open the door her purse dropped onto the pavement, spilled her cigarette pack, tampons, loose change. She cursed and crouched and scooped it all up. The booze swirled in her head like a toilet flush. She wobbled and righted herself against the Celica's hood, glanced down through the windshield. Poor slob Javier gave her a thumbs-up with both hands, and damned if it didn't somehow help steady her footing.

She laid one ear against her apartment door and inched the knob to see if it was loose. The sonogram pump of blood in her ear sounded like footsteps. Men waiting in the dark, flexing fingers inside stiff gloves, thugs hired by the man she stole this dirty drug money from.

Damn it, stifle your wild mobster thoughts. Just twist the key, push open the door, click the light switch, put your paranoia to rest.

There was nobody inside but Nero, curled on her bed in the corner. He raised his head and watched her over the curve of his back, squinted at the sudden light. Jodie tugged the money wad from her pocket and started laying it out in piles of five on her bedspread. All hundreds. Nero stretched himself out with a yawn that upturned his tongue and flashed his harmless fangs. He eased across the bed to sniff the bill stacks. Purred like he knew the value of this take. Jodie slapped the last bill down. Ten piles. A total of five thousand even.

"Don't purr," she told Nero. "I just ruined your life, too."

The bathroom was a walk-in closet with a sagging floor. She yanked the string for the overhead bulb, popped the shower stall door. Nobody there. No hands over her mouth or knives to her neck. She snatched her shampoo, conditioner, toothpaste, pill bottles, stacked them in the crook of her arm and then piled them on the bed for Nero to tap his nose at. His hackles were raised.

Jodie took to her knees bedside, retrieved a vinyl duffel bag she'd bought years ago for a Florida vacation that never happened. She unzipped the bag and loaded in the toiletries, threw open her dresser drawers, groped handfuls of underwear and socks and stuffed them in. Jeans and some skirts, T-shirts, pairs of sneakers. The bag fattened full.

The folded slip of paper on top of the dresser she slid into the back pocket of her pants.

A lone red-light blip on the answering machine. Tapped the button and the robot said *one new message, today, seven P.M.* Whatever time it was now, Jodie had no clue. On the recording, Boss clears his throat to talk: "Yeah, uh, Jodie. Something weird, just after you left, so I'm calling around. Appreciate if you'd shoot me back tonight, don't matter how late—"

His canned voice was enough to knock her seated on the bed. She pressed her face between her hands and Boss rushed toward her through hours and miles until he was there in the room huffing hot blame down her spine. She wanted to tell him, Stop, I confess, here's what's owed with interest, and here's my sad magnetic nametag, *Jody*, spelled wrong.

The windows in this place were three missing cinderblocks with glass, all too high to look through. The money spread out beside her seemed just enough to buy a plot in hell, but it could do something else. It could carry her to her son. She could see him again, and for the first time in five years. What made sense was what she had heaped inside the bag and where she planned to take it, and a man stood in the doorway with his fingers looped into the waistband of his pants.

It was only Javier. No deadbolt on her door, just a rinkydink chain lock she installed herself last month after a drunk man, a stranger, bashed on her door and screamed "Queenie, come out with your hands up! I'm gone wrap a staircase round your neck." But here, unthinking, she left the door wide open for Javier to mosey through.

"Okay? Problems?" Javier sang, as if problems were a delight.

"No problem," she said. She clawed the money back into a single pile, blocked his view of it with her body. If Javier saw, his grin didn't wiggle even for a second. He crouched down when Nero trotted over to greet him. The cat slid his flank along the lip of Javier's left cowboy boot. While Nero distracted him, Jodie crammed the money back into her pocket.

She squeezed the flaps of her duffel bag together and zipped it up tight, hoisted it into her arms. "My overnight bag," she told Javier. "Could you put it in the car, *por favor?*"

The weight of her luggage nearly knocked him flat. She worried she'd finally scared him off, but he kept up the grin as he lugged the bag back through the door.

Nero eyed the open escape route, pivoted his ears at the clap of a car door, but he showed no urge to flee. He was content with his limited space. He twined himself around her ankle and she lifted him to her chest. He rubbed his face along her chin. She propped him on her shoulder and hurried to the kitchen counter and laid down her purse. Slid inside it three cans of 9 Lives from the cupboard. She decided to leave without locking up. Let them come, let them sift through the meager leftovers, let them wait in the dark, let them—

—circled her lap, fretting and mewling. Nero propped his front paws on the window frame and peered with wide pupils at the night. Javier drove with one stiff arm, wrist hung on the steering wheel at twelve o'clock. Veering out of the complex he cranked through gears and he asked, "Eh, why is you carry the pussy?"

"Are you allergic?" Jodie quipped.

"I keep, eh, dog. Pete-bull dog. He's mouth ease angry?"

"It's fine. We can put *el gato* in *el baño.*"

"My house ease small."

"That's okay, too."

Nero howled nonstop, no matter how fast Jodie's petting. He emitted that fruity stench of animal fear. Jodie inhaled and it infected her, tuned her senses too high. She blurted at Javier, "They're spraying, is why." She gestured a nozzle squeeze to illustrate. "In *la mañana*—the exterminators—will spray—my *apartamento* for cockroaches—*cucarachas*, right? The spray *no es bueno por el gato. Comprende?*"

Javier scratched his matted black hair and sneered. He stopped at the red-lit corner of Route 41 and Roswell: gas stations, Los Reyes bakery, Title Pawn, and that KFC with the red-and-white steel Big Chicken landmark, sixty feet tall with moving beak and slow-spin eyes. Its lazy silent squawk seemed like mocking meant all for Jodie.

"Cigarillos, por favor," she reminded Javier.

He grunted and cut a hard left into a fluorescent BP, squealed the wheels to show off his mood. Jodie fished a wrinkled hundred from her pocket while he jerked up the handbrake. He propped his elbow on the window frame, pressed his fist into his cheek. The Latina on the radio was pitched too high and climbing.

But Jodie brushed the hundred along his forearm and sighed, *"Por favor."* He gnashed his teeth, she arched her eyebrows, and their music was the last stiff twist of a guitar tuner before the string snapped.

Javier slid the cash from her hand. He said, "Hundred?"

"Sorry, it's all I got."

"¿Qué tipo?"

"Ti—oh, type? What type? Newport 100's."

When Javier popped the door open Nero lunged for the exit, but Jodie hooked her fingers under his flea collar. She poured the cat into the backseat where he went on meowing beside her duffel bag.

Javier pushed through into the convenience store. He might've refused her, might've snatched the key, might've pegged her scheme—but Jodie bumbled past these tripwires. It was too much guilt to bear, like some dream she sometimes had of choking an infant blue with her hands and when you wake you think, Christ, who am I in my sleep?

She hoisted herself into the driver's seat, popped the handbrake and cranked the gearshift toward reverse, but nothing budged. Nero slinked across her lap again and she *shooed,* but he anchored his claws to her jeans. The transmission rattled its distress. Javier, just inside the store exit, stopped short with a hundred in his hand, no cigarettes. They watched each other through two sets of glass, and Jodie saw her ugliness dawn on him.

Her left foot kicked the clutch and she realized it was a stick shift. She floored the clutch and dropped the stick down into the R slot by mistake. Too much weight on the gas pedal and the car barreled backward with a hard right crank that swerved it a half-circle around. The Celica stalled dead.

Javier came out from the store like any odd bystander. He seemed resigned to do nothing—no jumping the hood or wrenching door handles. Jodie kept her clutch step hard and fired the starter key, thrust the stick into first. The car lurched forward. The cat in her lap swayed and almost tumbled but she caught him by the scruff. Last second she grabbed the wheel and aimed for the road. Sharp left and she shut her eyes and tough luck to oncoming traffic. Crossed two lanes clear but on instinct stopped short of the red light.

The red light stared her down and dared her and she was not its equal.

"Turn," she pleaded. In the rearview Javier sprinted over grass patch and street.

Still in first, Jodie braved a gas-and-clutch combo. The car heaved through the intersection. Momentum took shape as she glided into second. Javier was farther gone behind her with nothing but his hundred-dollar payoff. Heat from the vents and heat in her gut where the hard tequila simmered, and Nero howl-howling at the glass. She knew for sure which turn—

Cape Fear's Wright Beach in mid-January never had its own picture postcard. Calvin was here at three in the afternoon to meet in person for the first time his Internet friend Freez, his anonymous confidant since the day after Christmas. Cal was fifteen. Freez said he was twenty, a surfer and software designer and sponge for the delirious shame that Cal withheld from everyone else. Cal waited just short of the shoreline as wave crests surged from some depth to break on the beach in mere bucketfuls.

Alone with shut-up boardwalk shops, parking meter heads removed for the season, Johnny Mercer Raw Bar boarded, the pier arcade padlocked. Nobody to drive Calvin out here because they'd ask why, and no fake explanation flew. An hour back, Cal caught the bus instead, rode it as far as it would go. This time of year the last stop was Lumina Center, two miles inland. He'd trekked the extra mileage through wind that mashed his bangs into his eyes. He wore his adoptive grandfather's navy peacoat and tan corduroys, duct-taped Converse high-tops. Can of Mace in his pocket. His iPod lifted a mix of wistful Britrock up white wires into earbuds.

Expectation wrenched at his throat. To draw a live bone-and-blood Freez-man from binary code and wireless routers and IM windows—this plan now seemed to Cal more awful a creation than any mad doctor's monster. Cal's cell phone read 3:10, and he began to think Freez duped him after all. No real-life meet. It was almost a relief.

But then a red hatchback pulled into the beachfront parking lot. Cal turned down his iPod and squinted. It could've been anyone, but it was Freez for sure. Cal had envisioned him revving onto the beach in a jeep with surfboards on the roof, shirtless in the driver's seat. Or maybe he'd come swaggering out of the waves in his wetsuit and they'd build a bonfire on the sand like in those glittery MySpace photo shows that usually sickened Cal's sensibilities.

But Cal came here to be overwhelmed. He was already in the riptide throes. The only way he'd let himself succumb was full tilt because he was immune to doubt by now. Doubt sedated him for too long, years. You need to kiss a girl, then *wham!*, you're healed. You need faith. You need to reconnect with your bio-mom before you'll know yourself for sure—as if she were some consultation oracle.

Cal walked onto the lot. The hatchback driver who emerged was maybe thirty or more, scalp exposed under thin and uncombed hair. He wore an aqua-colored vinyl parka, drank Aquafina from a plastic bottle, eyed the locale like he expected somebody to charge out and drop him with a net.

The guy said, "Hey there—are you Reece, by any chance?" His voice cracked on *Reece*.

Cal gripped his own throat to hold back the revulsion. This guy who was supposed to be Freez, he took quick water sips, barely enough to wet his mouth. His bloated gut pushed against his parka, though he was scrawny otherwise. Sneakers that looked just out of the box. Some unvoiced promise was reneged, and it felt to Cal like the batteries went dead in the center of the best song he ever heard.

"Of course you're Reece. I recognize you from—from your avatar," the guy said.

Cal squeezed the mace canister in his pocket.

"You're here alone? You didn't bring anybody with you?" the guy said.

Cal said, "You're not Freez."

"Gene in real life, but yes. That's a great jacket. You look great wearing it."

"But you're not the same guy as the picture you e-mailed me."

"Oh—that—right. Listen, I didn't mean to give you the wrong idea. It's just, you know, I'm a little self-conscious about—about myself. I didn't know what to expect, so I'm just relieved you're really—I don't know—you're not here to cause me some kind of trouble." Knuckle hair and a pale strip on his finger where his wedding ring should be. Pungent cologne, something discount. He looked like somebody's father and probably was. He said, "You're kind of pale there, kiddo. You all right?"

"I feel light-headed. I don't know what I was thinking."

Like a valet, Gene hurried to open his car's passenger door. Nobody'd ever treated Cal this way, so servile—certainly not a type like Gene, the kind of person who you just knew humiliated servers at Burger King because somebody in the prep area forgot to hold the pickles.

But Cal refused to go home in the same skin he'd left with, so he sat down inside the car. Gene stood against the open passenger door and pushed his thumb though Cal's loose hair. The car smelled like stale cigarettes and that mannish cologne and fake pine air freshener and Big Red chewing gum.

"Your hair is so bizarrely orange. Is it natural?" Gene said.

"I don't know what's natural about me and what isn't," Cal said.

"Aw, don't say that." Gene eased the door shut and scurried around toward the driver's side, hopped into the seat, shut the door, shoved the water bottle between his legs, and rubbed his hands together. He turned over the engine and the heat came on, stale and dry. It made Cal feel feverish. On the speakers was the music Cal file-shared with Gene a few nights back.

"Flaming Lips," Cal said.

"What?"

"This music I ripped for you."

"Oh, right. I thought I'd—you know, I'm trying to wrap my head around it. Weird stuff. Hey, I got you something in return." Gene pulled a brown paper bag from his parka. Cal could see it was a DVD, and he worried it was smut and how he could possibly be expected to react. But what slipped out was the first season of *Cape Twilight Blues*. On the cover, all the major characters were mashed together in a dorky late-90s group photo taken downtown by the Cape Fear River. The show was Cape Fear's big claim to fame, an international cable network hit, taped on location in a Carolina coastline town that was meant to substitute for Maine.

"That one's the real Reece, right?" Gene pointed out the trouble-making outlaw with the leather jacket and the gloomy smirk. The actor's name was Bobby Keene-Parker, and Cal met him once on-set at the state college where they filmed the high school scenes, got his autograph on a black-and-white publicity headshot.

"Yeah," Cal said. "He looks like a thug in this picture. It isn't until the third season you find out he's gay. And his girlfriend's not only homeless but imaginary."

"Double-whammy. You probably have this season already, right?"

"No, I don't have any of them. I don't really watch it much anymore."

"I thought you were a big fan. Didn't you say you guest-starred on it?"

"Just as an extra. A couple times. I just walked by in the background, took books out of a locker. No big deal. You see these actors out around town, at grocery stores and cafés and stuff. It's like normal everyday. Sometimes it's like some gleam is over everything in this town. Even though you know it's all fake. It screws with your head."

Gene said, "You're pretty perceptive—and mature, I think. You're really only fifteen?"

"Really only," Cal said.

Gene put both his hands on the steering wheel and grimaced at the windshield as if they were driving somewhere in the dark without headlights. A drizzle started to wet the sandy pavement and the glass. With all the boarded-up stores, the place was like an empty film set.

Cal never really believed it anyway—that he'd be allowed some kind of gauzy reverie out here on the shore with another boy, groping those parts of someone else that he was ashamed to touch even on his own body. Flashes of obscene text on a computer screen, catalogs of violations that seemed so deliciously sinful back when Cal thought they were poetry. Now that he saw what head those words had spewed from, he knew he'd banked his lust on toilet-stall scrawl.

Cal dreamed only to lure himself out here. He knew that now. Unknown pleasures bore no relation to his real life. He was closeted good and tight—no limp-wristed, lispy obviousness for his few school friends to speculate about. Even his best friend, Burt, who moved to Akron two years ago, never supposed, not aloud, not once.

This Freez, this real one named Gene, was like a hundred men Cal saw every day. Just some jerk in the doughy flesh. The sense of threat kept waxing and waning like tides, but such panics Cal found too familiar. He was fed up with false alarms. He was bitter enough now to strike a match and make it real.

Gene said, "You want a drink?" He slid the water bottle out from between his legs.

"No thanks."

"It's vodka. It'll help."

"I really don't feel too hot. We were cool, right? Our online puppet show?"

"I worried you'd be a sting operation," Gene said. "Before I got here."

"Then why?"

"Good question. Why'd you?"

"I have too vivid an imagination," Cal said.

"Look, I'm sorry I misrepresented myself. I didn't think—"

"If we kept it going anonymous—I don't know. I'm sorry."

"Don't be sorry. I'm the one who agreed to it, knowing. You've been genuine."

"I don't even understand what that means."

"We can't backtrack now. I'm sitting here in a car with a minor. I'm already here."

"I guess I'll take a drink, I guess."

Gene passed Cal the bottle and Cal circled it under his nose, poured some onto his tongue and shuddered. The burn in his throat was a warning that he'd headed beyond the breakers into the deep where all the world's unknown things still dwelled. He took another gulp and shuddered and passed the bottle back.

"It's not just you," Gene explained. "I don't recognize myself." His lips were dry and pale and not any lips you'd desire, but Cal's whims kept rousing him to kiss. It was an urge as whacked as those he had to lick men's-room urinal cakes, or touch his hands to both electrodes on the old car battery in the garage.

"I keep thinking—you're the only one who knows about me, but who are you?" Cal said.

"My intentions . . . I have to go back to my family after this."

"We can just pretend—"

"We've been pretending, Reece—"

"My name's not—"

"This is the shitty truth: Neither one of us wants to be here. You didn't want to find out I'm some old slouch. So here we are, for what? I'm such a joke. Right now there's some young buck—like one of these assholes from *Cape Blue Whatever*—beautiful, prime—and why does he deserve it? The sun shines from his ass. You and me are stuck here tortured because of our fucking needs—fuck! I know how you see me, all right? I make you sick right now in person, but everything else about me you loved. Admit it. I gushed and you lapped it up and vice versa, right? So the only problem is me, the physical—what I can't do jack about. If I was really him in the picture I sent—. Instead I'm junk. I make you sick."

"I don't even know you," Cal said.

"I'm sorry but that's bullshit, too. That's the thing. We've talked for hours. I haven't slept for days because we talk. I sicken everybody, and what'd I do to earn that? Nothing. I was born and I got old. So let me ask you how it's fair I should be judged on that? That the fucking law should judge me? Say it's a man who wants a woman—they call him a stalker if he fails, or if he's successful, well, then he's a—I don't know— *ladies' man.* Based on what? Based on shit you can't control. One you go to jail for, the other you're golden. Why should a person always lose? How's that fair?"

"It's human nature," Cal muttered.

"Human nature? You're a minor, but in the Dark Ages? You'd be half-dead by now, or in some other culture somewhere. Ancient Greece? Don't even get me started there."

The CD music was churning into a frenzy while Gene squirmed in his seat. He slapped the power button, and in the new quiet Cal heard the low groan from Gene's throat. The man's eyes were yellowish moist. Never in Cal's life had he seen a grown person so pent up, not even his own adoptive parents—his father who sulked and hid behind book spines, or his mother who jogged five miles daily to keep her chemistry calm. It was like standing on the edge of a volcano.

"Just get the hell out of my car," Gene said.

"It's raining."

Heavier now, it thrummed against the car roof. The coming clouds were even darker. Cal had been through hurricanes—the school cancellations and flooded streets and debris. Violent weather thrilled him because it was news from some elsewhere sweeping in to stir the sediment that lay dormant too long. Like when three months back a tropical storm knocked power out for a day, the first thing after Internet access returned, Cal tracked down his birth mom again and wrote her an e-mail. The wind and the lightning spurred him, somehow. He felt charged for weeks, even though she never wrote him back.

"Get out of my car," Gene demanded again.

"What are you afraid of?" Cal asked.

Gene struck Cal across the cheek with his open palm. The impact cracked Cal's head against the doorframe and tottered the axis of the globe. His jaw went heavy and a cicada sang inside his skull. A sharp liquidy sting inside his nose. Cal put his fingertips against his nostrils and they came away bloody. Hadn't seen this much of his own blood in years. A popped zit, a paper cut, a bite on his tongue—nothing more than that.

Gene said, "You see now, you little faggot? Get out of here."

"Look," Cal said, and he showed Gene his blood. It contained the compounds of his pedigree, chemistries both latent and active. It bore no relation to the people who raised him.

"Get that shit away from me," Gene said. He grappled Cal by the wrist.

With his free hand Cal produced the mace canister he'd stolen from his mother's key ring. It was the size of a Magic Marker, with a hair-spray dispenser that he covered with his thumb. Gene released his wrist and fumbled for the door latch, spilled himself out onto the pavement and rabbit-kicked his own door shut. He howled out there like he'd been doused, but the spray went untriggered.

Cal leaned across the vacated driver's seat and pressed the doorlock down. The keys were in the ignition. Blood dripped from Cal's nose onto the DVD case in his lap. He sniffled it back, wiped his upper lip with the sleeve of his jacket. The pain still cut across his face. It was the closest thing to the daydream he hoped to prove true.

Gene was already hunched beside the driver's window, peering in at Cal. He didn't slap the glass or rattle the door handle. He said, "What if somebody drives by, Reece? You're the one who—"

Cal cranked his seat into full recline so he could tilt back his head and pinch his nostrils shut. He drummed up a power he didn't know he had, and Gene stood soaked outside the car.

"I'm sorry I hit you," Gene said through the glass barrier between them.

Cal turned the car music back on. Gene pressed his hands against the window and pleaded, but he might as well have been a netted fish, mouth gaping and shutting and gaping for nothing. When the song finally died down, Cal heard him say "—drive you home, all right?"

"No way you're getting near where I live."

"Your parents? How are you going to explain this?"

"They don't know me any more than you," Cal shouted, still pressing his nostrils shut.

"Tell me what's going to happen," Gene said.

Cal didn't want to talk anymore. He opened his door and stepped out into the rain and locked it shut behind him. When he released his nose, he couldn't tell if what ran down his face was blood or rainwater or both. The bloody DVD case in his hand was diluting pink and washing clean. On the driver's side of the car Gene was bent over, hugging himself and staring at the ocean as if deciding whether he should stroll over there and drown.

"Don't follow me," Cal said.

"How could I? You locked me out of my car."

"Let's just forget it."

Gene nodded, then raised his cell phone to his ear.

"Who are you calling?" Cal said.

"Triple A."

"Don't follow me."

"I said I wouldn't," Gene said, then into the phone, "Yeah, I'm locked out of my car."

Cal walked away, tossed the DVD in a public trash can, thumbed through files on his iPod. He'd be drenched within minutes. The rainwater beaded on the glowing LCD screen, cutting colors apart like sunlight on spilled motor oil. Like his flatscreen monitor at home, how it rippled out spectrums when you touched your fingers against the bare-chested JPEG named Freez.

Cal wondered what source Gene swiped that image from. A real person somewhere, though Cal would never meet him. Freez was empty like this parking lot and these boarded shops. Freez could be deleted, but in that space Cal's desire still brewed and frothed and spread. He felt the pulse of far-off lightning headed—

They were locked inside a moving car with the heat vents gushing, but still the cold was a killer. Midair clusters of snowflakes recurred like fractals, then liquefied on the windshield. Roadside snowbanks stood as tall as the mailboxes they nearly buried. One box had its red flag raised: I surrender, Winter. The plastic medallion Scotch-taped to the rearview mirror showed St. Christopher hunched in pain with the Christ child albatross on his back.

Dwight drove. He followed the tracks of the last car that passed maybe five minutes ahead. Wynn sat in the passenger seat with his knees hiked up to his chin. The heater did all it could, which was jack. A fresh long-stem rose was laid across Dwight's dashboard, thorns and all. Wynn didn't know why, or where it came from. Seemed like something Dwight didn't want to be asked about.

Dwight was skull-eyed and two weeks unshaven, smelled like formaldehyde. Wynn hated the look and the sniff of him, but they were best friends since grade school. When Dwight said get in, Wynn got in. Dwight was wearing leather gloves with the knuckles cut out. His hands creaked and groaned against the steering wheel.

"Why're you driving so fast?" Wynn said.

"I'm going twenty."

"You're going twenty but where are you going?"

"To meet a man about my sister."

"I don't want to meet a man."

"Stop wigging out, bro. He's gonna get us to Cecelia."

They were two miles out of town, nothing but pines and phone-wires and lonely houses lost in the drifts, nothing here to hold them down. It was Thursday. Tomorrow morning Wynn had a first unit math quiz he couldn't miss, not this early in the term. But Wynn suffered chronic love for Dwight's kid sister, Cecelia. And she'd been missing for a month. Wynn had no choice but to come along.

Dwight said, "When we find her, you'll talk. You'll get her to listen."

"I haven't seen her in months. I feel like we've gone inside some vortex."

"Cut it out. You're freaking. You're talking bullshit, man. You're too keyed up."

"Explain something to me. What are we doing? She's not going to listen to me, Dwight. Why did you think she would? Why didn't you tell me she was lost?"

"When? You and me don't talk. You didn't even know my voice on the phone."

"Who has she gone to, Dwight?"

"I don't know, or I don't want to say. Some fucking crackheads."

"I'm supposed to be asleep right now. This is why I'm going to college—you get it?"

"Forget about me all you want," Dwight said. "But you want Ce-ce to see you this way?"

Wynn had cut a whole new patch for himself these last couple years, but that patch was contained in the palm of Cecelia's hand. She could crush it all in an instant if it pleased her, even from a distance and through her brother by proxy, even if it was months since they talked last. To cope, Wynn pined over old JPEGs of her on his laptop, left halting messages on her expired TracFone. She was nineteen and didn't sing much for old friends anymore, especially those of her brother Dwight's sorry posse—meaning Wynn himself and a couple random phantoms and fuck-all else.

A red beam glinted in the rearview, spread across the walls of white. A color so strong it seemed to short-circuit Dwight's car engine. Gone was that purr of snow that kicked against the underbelly. The things that had been holding together were shivering apart.

"Don't gab," Dwight said. His face hardened. He veered toward the white ice embankment on the shoulder. A siren yelped behind them, and it seemed that this red whorl was emitted from a lightbar on a prowler roof. A floodlight came on, a pure punch straight through Wynn's skull. It made him yearn for the soft of his bed.

"I told you not to speed," he said. "Shit, Dwight, I told you."

"Wynn, *chill*."

The county sheriff's deputy in his badged fur trapper hat loomed outside the driver's door. Dwight unrolled his window, but it was hard labor with the ice caked onto the outside of the glass. The cigarette in Dwight's lips bobbed to indicate his steady pulse. Wynn held his breath and corralled the wild grazing of his mind for a minute.

"Evening, officer," Dwight deadpanned.

"All right, already," the deputy said as he aimed a Maglite into the cab. The beam hit their feet, their laps. Dwight wasn't wearing his seat belt. There were drugs in the car somewhere for certain. Old roaches and resin stuffed between the seats, a lingering odor of pot.

The cop shined his torch on Wynn's face and said, "Who's this?"

"My friend," Dwight said. "He's my best friend since grade school."

"What's he doing with you?"

"He's gonna help me get my sister," Dwight said.

"Why him?"

"Because they're in love. He's in love."

"I don't want any blowback on this," the deputy said. "It's my ass more than you. I'm doing my part here." His voice quivered like a glitch in an automated phone operator's spiel.

"Appreciated. You're a saint with a badge," Dwight said. He dug into his coat pocket, unveiled a clear sandwich bag with a stack of cash inside, slipped it through the crack in the window. The cop's hand took it. His face was part of the night. A dispatcher on his radio receiver crackled some number code. The cop said, "Well, it looks like they're in a trailer park called Willow Bend, in Unit Eight. The park's three miles up on the left."

Dwight shook his head and said, "I drive past there twice a week."

"Looks like they set camp there just a few days ago. Three guys and your sister, mostly."

Wynn's seat belt was crushing the air from his lungs. An hour back he was brooding on a mathematics text in his dorm lounge, then his cell phone spasmed in his pocket, then Dwight revved up curbside, and now?—plotting payoffs with a cop in the snow-swept boondocks. Talking: *three guys mostly.* Guys with fists and worse.

But Wynn was just some dope wearing loafers and a ski jacket padded like a flotation device. Greasy hair strands hanging in his face. At least a year since he lifted a barbell or moved faster than brisk.

"Dwight, I need to know you've got this under control," the deputy said.

"Affirmative."

"Are you armed?"

"*Nyet,*" Dwight said. But he'd already shown Wynn the S&W .38 Chief's Special he was carrying in the inside breast pocket of his winter coat, his dad's revolver. Wynn had nothing for defense but his two hands so stiff with freeze they wouldn't close up.

"Anything goes wonky and I wash my hands. I wash anyway, right now, you hear?"

"Whatever wiggles your jowls, Deputy Dog," Dwight said.

"Cut the shit, Dwight. I'm doing you a serious favor. Please tell me you're just striking poses for your buddy here so I can shrug off your nauseating attitude."

Dwight bowed his head like the gravity of the evening finally seized him. He said, "Sorry, Sam. Deputy Hartwick. I'm grateful, in all seriousness." He smoothed down his disheveled hair and rolled up the window, cranked the engine. He snorted some phlegm and the cop outside the car watched them through the ice film. Finally the deputy moseyed back to his constant red-and-white beacon.

"How much was that you spent?" Wynn asked.

"Five huns." He jerked his head cockeyed, cracked bone somewhere in his neck.

"Sheesh. You know him? From where?"

"From a fortune cookie: 'Old rivalries will blossom into shared back-scratching.' He loaned me a pair of bracelets once, shiny silver. It was love at first frisk. Deputy Sam Hartwick."

"I go to school with a Hartwick. Erika."

"She's the Deputy Daughter."

"No shit?" Wynn said. "She's in my honor's World Lit class."

"Fucking fascinating."

"Why's this guy helping you? What's he know about Ce-ce?"

"He who helps others helps himself, grasshopper. Confusion says so."

"What, you hired him to find her?"

"I said if he keeps his eyes open, I'll make a donation to his favorite charity."

"Why doesn't he just come with us?"

"He'd have to arrest her for possession, probably. She'd never forgive me. Plus, Hartwick wants no part of our private family matter. This was an exclusive arrangement for me and him."

"Dwight, what trouble is Cecelia—

—back behind the trees and the bunker of plow-swept snow. Glints of yellow light, trailers huddled like frontier encampments, naked tree branches scraped siding and windows, thick roots jutted up to throw parked cars and pickups off-kilter, and every roof was doused with a clean dome of purifying snow.

In the car, Wynn gripped his loafers where his toes froze numb. He coughed against a crystalline chill that attacked the pink flesh of his lungs. A brain-thrum of doom like riding the unstoppable rail when you know the bridge ahead has buckled. Numbers kept him calm. He divided a fraction with an infinite remainder, pushed the total decimal places he could hold in his memory.

"Who are these people, Dwight?" Wynn asked.

"Pushers. They're dirty, whatever they are. They took my kid sis."

"What do you mean they *took* her?"

"I let them get too close, let them snort the scent of her. I let her leash lead out—"

"Don't denigrate her like that."

"Don't word-fuck me, bro." Dwight pressed his gloved index finger against Wynn's temple. Wynn slapped at the finger, but it was a flaccid display of nerve. Nerve was something inborn that fixed when the sperm stabbed the egg. Dwight and Cecelia had it, but none ran through the tender twists in Wynn's genetic strands.

"Dwight, are these people dangerous? I mean, what the fuck are we doing?"

"We're catching them up." He groped toward the backseat, rifled plastic bags and empty cans until he got what he wanted, slid it into view, long and solid—an aluminum baseball bat. "Take it," he said, offered it, handle-first.

The grip tape was sticky in Wynn's palm. It'd peeled away over years of use. In fact Wynn knew this particular bat, its dents and scuffs. With it, he'd slugged baseballs and rocks and water balloons. He'd been bruised in the shins by its bite.

Dwight bowed his head and pressed his hands together. He mouthed something with his eyes clamped shut, and Wynn remembered a rumor that his bad old buddy Dwight had been attending church most Sundays as of late. But prayer didn't juice Wynn's confidence as much as positive probabilities. Wynn camped with those who believed God was in the numbers—mathematic principles weren't invented, but discovered in the cosmos by limited man.

"Go in the glove box," Dwight said.

Wynn did, and the black wad of wool inside unfurled into a ski mask with a red yarn-tuft like a cherry on top. "Serious?" said Wynn, and, "Where's yours?"

"I go commando. Let them see, I give a shit. You can pull the pompon off, you want—

—arctic blast slapped his iced jeans against his calves. Dwight on the front stoop of Unit 8. Wynn two steps down. Wynn breathed into the rough weave stretched over his mouth, peered through lopsided eyeholes that scrunched his brow. His cargo: an aluminum bat, though he hid it behind his back. He'd been terribly miscast as the muscle here. His heart was flopping, fishlike.

Dwight's head was naked, not even a wool hat to keep the wind from scrambling up his hair. He knocked on the screen door. He held a full bottle of red wine he'd procured from the backseat dark, a local Finger Lakes brand. Also the single red long-stem rose pinched gingerly between index and thumb. Dwight, like somebody's sorry prom date come a-calling. It was a ploy designed to confound whoever answered the door, but to what aim Wynn didn't dare ask.

The trailer curtains were drawn, but thin enough to frame the furtive slide of shadows inside. The vinyl siding was dingy white set against the purer snow, networks of grime where vines had once crept. The storm door gave way to a broad-shouldered silhouette. Gush of hot air, wood-burn smoke. Their greeter was an animated slab of beef hulking behind the snow-splattered screen. Dwight dropped the rose and yanked the screendoor loose. It came sliding unhinged down the steps toward Wynn, and Wynn knocked it aside with his bat, over the rail. The bat leaped from his hands and sank along with the door into the silent snow.

The rose was already trampled on the stoop. Dwight flipped the wine bottle like he was a juggler, caught it quick by the neck, cracked it blunt across the doorman's face. Glass burst with a liquid red spatter that might've been grape or blood or both. Somebody grunted, but nobody talked. Wynn was not made for this. He was wrong from the start. The doorman tumbled backward with a hand pressed to his jaw. On that hand was a tattoo of torn flesh with cyborg metal underneath. The doorman reeled against a washing machine.

Dwight drew his blued carbon steel revolver. The bottle in his other hand was just a cone of jagged glass. He was chanting, "On the floor, on the floor, on the—"

So the doorman squatted in a dirty laundry pile.

Just inside the foyer, another man sat at a collapsible card table. Early twenties looking forty, sores on his lips, gaunt. He had a paper plate of crinkle-cut French fries for dinner, ketchup on his chin. Three place settings, three paper plates, three bottles of Molson Ice—but no third thug in sight, no Cecelia. Lip Sores showed both his palms and let his eyes phase wide. Dwight turned the gun on him. Lip Sores flinched, used his hands like a shield, like they'd stop speed-of-sound projectiles.

"Dwight—" Wynn said, but he couldn't say what worried him exactly.

"Where?" Dwight demanded. Held the gun cockeyed, like movies.

The open area beyond the kitchen cubicle was scattered with loose firewood. Sleeping bags lay strewn around a woodstove. A floor-bound TV with a tiny screen showed some mute cooking demo of scallops sizzling in a wok.

Dwight told Wynn, "Down there, bro. Go see." He gestured with the gun toward the hallway beyond—more dingy paneled walls, a retracted accordion room-divider. The wood smoke roiled in Wynn's lungs. The mask grew moist around his mouth. The black rims of the eyeholes tightened like sun-blinded pupils.

Wynn advanced. He kicked logs and bottles, stomped sooty slivers of aluminum foil lying around the carpet. Rank urine stench around this place. He pressed a hand against a wall to stop himself from swooning. Steam in the hallway and a dim slice of light beyond.

Cecelia was there just ahead of him in the hall. He knew her shape. At the sight of her, the pile of coal in his gut ignited. Commotion and curses behind him, but Wynn was beyond that squabble and harm. She was the only reason he'd come along.

"Ce-ce," Wynn said.

Cecelia cried out and stumbled away from him, crashed through a doorway at the end of the hall. Wynn peeled away the ski mask as he rushed toward her, pleading "Wait!" The room was a squalid little closet not wide enough to pitch a tent inside. Twin mattress on the floor with a ragged quilt and a pillow with no pillowcase. Familiar movie poster taped lonesome to the wall—Cecelia's favorite, *Almost Famous*.

One exposed lightbulb pulsed in the ceiling fixture. Cecelia crouched with her back to the door, rummaged a suitcase overstuffed with clothes. Her bare legs were tanned the color of iodine. Thick gray socks bunched around her ankles and thin metal bracelets cluttered up her wrists. Her head was bound in a white bath towel like a beehive hairstyle, and she was whimpering curses to herself. She turned on him with a little wood-gripped .22.

Wynn dropped the skimask like it was a skin he'd molted.

"Wynn," Cecelia said. "You're in the wrong place." She wore a man's extra large T-shirt hanging loose from her shoulders to her thighs. It had the print of some pro wrestler's furious face on the front of it.

"Your brother—he's here, in the kitchen."

"You let him drag you out here? Wynn, you trust too much. It eats you." Her voice was raw and her face was haggard, dry lines around her mouth and purplish flesh below her eyes.

"It's not Dwight," Wynn said. "I hate Dwight. I wanted to help find you."

"You can't find me—and Dwight and me are the same problem. God,

Wynn, you got away—so what the fuck are you doing? You got away from us and you turned back around."

"Remember the time I won you that Siamese fighting fish at the county fair?"

"No," she said. "Let's not remember nothing now. It ain't gonna help us."

"I have a girlfriend," Wynn lied. "Her name's Erika."

"Then I guess you should be ashamed of yourself."

"What are you doing here, Ce?"

"Forgetting," she said.

There was a rush in Wynn's left ear, a chorus of voice that merged into one voice as Dwight blundered through the door. Handguns and tumbling heartbeat and fiery fissures splitting down the contours of Wynn's gray brain. The swell of dark energy, the negation that filled the empty spaces between and forced all matter in one eternal slow-motion burst. It was three quarters of everything, that emptiness.

"Mom is sick in the hospital," Dwight blurted.

"You're the sick one! Get out of here!" Cecelia screamed.

They were stabbing their guns at each other. Wynn grappled Dwight's elbow and yanked his aim downward. Dwight teetered off balance and bellowed and crashed himself against the doorframe. Cecelia held her .22 at arm's length as she backed away and stood atop her mattress. Wynn slid his hands down Dwight's arm and clasped them over the leather glove and the gun. Dwight breathed quietly. He kept his free hand planted on the wall. One simple shove was all he'd need to wrest his hand back. He was bluffing, and Wynn knew it.

"You see what happens?" Cecelia demanded. Her gun discharged, barely a kick but she reeled backward from her own momentum, crashed into the room's sole window and brought down a set of venetian blinds. Black frigid night outside the window, like an old wound torn back open. She fell in shambles on the floor and flashed the sleek, flawless stretch of one thigh. Wynn's gut fluttered like he was in free fall.

Dwight was shot, so he surrendered his revolver with no more fight. His hand fell limp and he bowed forward and pressed his forehead into a clutter of Cecelia's clothes on the floor. It happened so fluidly that it seemed choreographed. Impossible that Dwight could actually be hurt, especially by a measly .22 round. If Dwight made any sound, a snigger to betray himself, Wynn heard nothing over the peal in his eardrums.

Cecelia gawked at her brother's collapse like it wasn't her doing. She pulled at her own face until it was grotesque. Even now Wynn ached to touch her, knowing she was ruined. When she was ten and he was thirteen, she kissed him inside the dugout beside the vacant baseball diamond near her house. She said "Look out" and brushed her lips against his mouth on purpose. Three years his junior and she taught him how to hunger like this forever.

Now, in this putrid place, she was showing him the tiny barrel of her gun like it was some new mouth for him to kiss. The round she fired stole away with the tip of his earlobe. He dabbed fingers against it. Warm blood streamed across his knuckles. He said, "Cecelia, what—"

"You stupid lemming," she said—and fired again.

Wynn couldn't track the bullet's path, but he knew she'd keep on punishing him with those bullets if he let her. He was wrong to come back here, he knew. He moaned into the bottomless desire she'd hollowed out in him those nine years back. He never saw her naked, but he built whole palaces around the notion. He'd hoped if Cecelia could love she'd love him, but instead she could only bruise herself against rough regrets. She could only make him hurt.

Wynn found his best friend's .38 Special caught in his own hand. The grip felt like a bootsole. It had weight and potential, but three quarters of that being was emptiness, three quarters of himself and Cecelia, everything. It seemed an illusion to use the gun, and she was trying to kill him, trying to force his consciousness blank. Wynn didn't want to be here anymore.

He aimed and pulled on the trigger and the hammer wavered and he pulled harder. He cried out at the awful force of it. The noise. Cecelia's head jerked, and her eyes locked on a sudden final truth she couldn't speak to reveal. On the towel wrapped over her head, a wet sphere began to darken outward. She let her arms with their dozens of bracelets collapse onto her legs.

"Oh, God," Wynn said.

The urgency slipped from her face. She went slack and dumbstruck like some rude wax model of herself. Wynn had done this somehow. He crawled closer to staunch the widening blood with his fingers but recoiled. He couldn't touch. If he reached out, the time and the distance would divide forever and he would never touch. She wasn't his to touch, not even now.

"You were shooting at me," he explained.

She slumped down onto the mattress and her eyes that had been pleading with him now looked toward somewhere invisible. They didn't blink. Her hiccupping breath went quiet. The leakage on her towel was saucer-sized and undeniably red.

Wynn had an urge to collect it all in his cupped hands—but the urge was pointless. The shock of what he'd done surged through him and amassed in his throat, too suffocating to expel. He lay beside her body on the mattress. He smelled the lingering green-apple scent of her shampoo. His bullet-torn earlobe spilled a galaxy of red starbursts over the mattress.

"Cecelia," he said. "Cecelia, wake up. Wake up—it was an accident. I'm sorry."

"What . . . she sleeping?" Dwight's voice reaching Wynn's muted ears in scattered pieces. Dwight was sitting on the floor in the doorway with his gray face and his jacket unzipped, pulled back from his shoulders. His blue button-down mechanic's shirt had a blotch of blood a few inches below where his name was stitched into his breast pocket. He pressed one hand against it like a pledge while he pulled the glove off the other with his teeth.

"You shouldn't have brought me here," Wynn said. "She didn't want me here, Dwight."

"Can't hear you. Shot a stupid twenty-two . . . stuck in my fucking ribs . . ." He coughed against his bare hand. He tried to lift himself up by the knob on the open bedroom door, but it was shoddy hardware and it snapped off in his hand. He slumped back down and dropped the chrome ball beside him.

"Your mother isn't sick," Wynn said. "You can't make anyone love you."

Dwight winced. "What? . . . wake her . . . tell her . . ."

Wynn didn't say what wouldn't be heard. He wanted to explain that nothing changed or would, that the laws of the universe remained intact, but Dwight wouldn't understand because he was too far behind already.

Only gestures mattered now, and Wynn's was to fire the .38 twice into Dwight's chest, there beside the bleeding that Cecelia already started. Two determined pulls that cocked the hammer and launched the bullet and revolved the cylinder. That was what Wynn had to say, to repeat, for her sake. Dwight howled a curse too faint for Wynn, and he craned his neck like a drowning man seeking the surface in vain.

Wynn stood and aimed into the hall beyond Dwight. Two bullets left in the five-round cylinder and two men down there who were—what? Live? Dead? Wounded? Armed? Gone? Imaginary? Worse than those men were Dwight and Cecelia here. These corpses Wynn couldn't believe, though he'd brought them to that state himself. He couldn't step across the boundary Dwight formed, which was wider than could be measured by the dimensions of this room.

He put the snubnosed gun to his wounded ear and squeezed the trigger not hard enough. The counterweighted hammer fought and his willpower fought and he did not want to die like them. This was not his whole life in ruins. They'd brought him here, they'd wagered his love for them and lost and they could bring him no farther now.

Wynn set the revolver in Dwight's open hand.

He shimmied the bedroom window upward with the flats of his hands until the ice surrendered. Then he slid out feet first and plunged into a snowdrift two feet deep. The cold struck him like a gut-punch. He staggered out into the squall, heard nothing but the tinnitus screech. If men followed, he didn't hear and didn't dare look. The blood from his ear had soaked across his neck and shoulder. He pressed on, though already his feet were numbed.

He'd find the hiking trail some half-mile south if the winter didn't kill him first. Knew these woods of his childhood and trusted them over Dwight's stranded getaway car. That car was target to whatever thugs or cops would overtake Wynn if he dared to pilot it back through the trailer park.

His worst tonight was done. He knew these woods and their paths that led not a mile off to his own parents' house on the county-line road, Dwight and Cecelia's another half mile on. But he wouldn't go back there. He'd trudge the miles instead, risking hypothermic death, back to campus and a morning math exam. He'd brave shivering oblivion to reclaim what he'd almost—

Red-eye getaway. Jodie's heart sought to punch through her throat. Slide the white lines and don't veer, hold your breath till the roadside cruisers fade from the rearview. Think what a miracle you went so long in check, years of lobotomy jobs—grocery clerk, deliveries, factory temp, even a volunteer week shoveling shit for animal control. No wonder it all wound tight inside you, sprung the instant you swiped the cash.

Route 85 pushed Atlanta backward and offered bright varieties of wholesale stores and electronic emporiums. Her eyes tightened to slits. Misty ghosts roiled just ahead of the headlight cones. Nero finally lay calm and curled. Hours passed and she crossed the South Carolina borderline when "low fuel" lit the dash so strong it made her flinch.

Stolen cars got reported, license plate numbers got logged on cop blotters, interstate flight was a probably a felony, and a stalled car on the highway would lure cops with questions, or lure worse, like backwoods prowlers out on the hunt for trouble. So find gas pronto, darling.

Jodie banked on a hunch: Hector and Javier, both illegals, wouldn't dare call the cops for help. She didn't know this for sure. Maybe they had green cards. Maybe the Celica was already posted to every cop-car laptop in a quad-state net. She didn't know. She'd never run from such trouble. Calculated crimes fit her like a choke collar, but there were higher morals to mind, the ones that belonged to her, the ones that concerned her fifteen-year-old son.

She exited. First on the rest-stop drag came the Speedway, a major chain too well lit and outfitted with security cams. Farther down was a local place with ads for moon pies and boiled peanuts etched in erasable marker on the windows. Nero was on alert again, front paws on the passenger windowsill and tail tucked down between his legs. She said, "We're stopping for a sec, babe. Don't go nuts on me." She peeled the lid off a Nine Lives can and put it on the seat beside him.

Outside the pumps had turn-dial numbers, and no options for credit or debit. A posted construction-paper sign wrapped in cellophane said PRE-PAY AFTER TEN P.M. Inside the store were dusty floors and shelves full of shitty prepackaged food and cheap CDs and ephedrine pills for truckers and a couple beer coolers and a porn magazine rack and an unkempt counter clerk who refused to take her hundred dollar bill until she spent at least eighty of it.

She bought two CDs at ten bucks a pop, Nirvana and Metallica to keep her awake and determined. Bottle of ephedrine for the same purpose, two bags of Lay's potato chips, a few cans of Red Bull. She kept lugging her spoils back to the counter for the clerk to ring up and bag. Some liter bottles of water, a travel tool kit with a couple screwdrivers and some wrenches, a carton of Kools and thirty bucks on the pump to round out her tab.

"Where you headed to tonight?" the clerk wondered.

"Jesus," Jodie sighed.

He was poised to scan a Red Bull. He said, "I'm Christian, ma'am. I sure can't appreciate being cursed for my curiosity."

"I'm sorry."

"I should boot you out, *Jody*," he said, leering at the name tag perched on her left boob.

Jodie said, "You're wearing a Judas Priest T-shirt and you sell porno magazines."

His scowl twisted into a grin. He said, "I'm just fucking."

"Just start the pump, please," she said. Too much attention already, and her fucking nametag still on her chest.

"Gladly, as I can guess how bone dry your tank is like to be—

* * *

—sucking Kools in the eighty-mile-per-hour dark. Kurt Cobain in the CD player moaning on about faults and apologies, and Jodie cringed to think what that man wound up doing to his own head. The highway was hers alone, hers and the wildlife corpses parading by on the roadside. She kept swerving mirages, chancing the edge of the center embankment. On a stretch blocked off for road repair she plowed down a string of orange traffic cones that blubbered the underbelly. An edge to her manner that'd been dull a decade now sharpened.

Jodie in the backseat at age ten while her father drives with his blooming red beard. Snow in the trees, and a Magic 8-Ball in her hands, shaken up, fortune pyramid inside the porthole swirling possible futures in an antifreeze bath. She let Dad drive till the ruts along the shoulder edge snapped her back awake with her own hands on the wheel. Came to her mind weird ideas that claimed she crashed the car and died long hours ago, and this endless asphalt was the curse of her afterlife.

Light drizzle, and the wipers shuddered dryly across the windshield. She found a Golden Biscuit, and backed into a slot flanked by two SUVs and a waist-high hedge that trailed along the roadside. The rain drummed the roof like impatient fingertips. Nero complained while she rummaged the paper grocery bags and found the travel-sized case of tiny ratchets and screwdrivers. Nero meowed for it.

"It ain't food," Jodie told him. "Besides, you just ate."

She smoked a cigarette with the window cracked. Radio news from Columbia spoke of various arrests, cancer patients scheming wild stunts to raise awareness, some state congressman indicted on fraud—but nothing on a redhead in a hot sports car with a wad of stolen cash. The cars and trucks hushed across the long stretch of highway, the people inside them all headed somewhere while ignoring the truth that this somewhere would be the same place for everyone eventually. Jodie coughed into her fist, popped open the driver door, flicked the cigarette. She crouched down low like a soldier, eased her door shut.

She moved along the edge of her car and crept into the path of grass between the Celica's back bumper and the hedgerow. Hidden, she hoped, from the parking lot and the diners at booths in the Golden Biscuit windows. A dull morning was telling the shape and color of things—things like Jodie. And the rain was spreading cold across the back of her shirt.

She worked fast to untwist the dual screws that held Hector's Georgia license plate. Stuck the screws between her lips, clamped the plate under her armpit, dragged her muddied knees across the grass. The SUV beside her was faced outward like she needed, North Carolina license plate. She eyed the other few cars in the lot to be sure there was a second North Carolina plate among them. Mercy, there was. She wound both screws out till she could pluck them free. She grabbed the plate and transferred it to the Celica. Her thighs ached from how she crouched as she worked. The rain matted down her hair and slipped her grip on the screwdriver handle.

Now the trick: put the Georgia plate on another North Carolina car, stick that third plate on the SUV. Two degrees of separation. Third driver catches the obvious interstate plate switch?—no catastrophe. Because cops would still need to track down the SUV before they could know the plate number Jodie was driving under. SUV driver probably wouldn't spot the switch for days, any luck. She'd seen this in a movie—didn't know if it worked for real or would be foiled by some police technology she knew nothing about.

Here she was like a cat squatting in a box, trying to bury the shit she'd made.

She finished the threeway switch, knowing her effort wouldn't matter if she got pulled over later. Nothing would matter then. And who knew what million ways there were to get caught—security cameras, databases, monitors, profiles, private eyes?

Her mind was off Nero when she opened the driver's door. She grabbed for him but he skittered under the car. Despite the damp she laid her hip on the wet ground and reached across the undercarriage for him. She couldn't see, but he was beyond her reach. She didn't want to lose him this easy. She'd whittled her whole life down to his purr. Gone—a roommate some months ago, a few stray boyfriends, a baby boy she donated like a bag of old clothes fifteen years ago. Just Nero, and here he was slinking away from her across the parking lot, his shadow arched by the light from the Golden Biscuit.

"Nero," she pleaded, clicked her tongue against her teeth the way she did when his dinner was ready. She followed behind as he disappeared around a dark corner of the building. Barely any light back there, just the orange sliver of a faraway morning out beyond a water tower. She kicked dead brush and debris and she shivered at the stinging cold of the rain. Uncoiled hair strands pressed against her face.

"Nero, please." But the cat was black and the dark was black and he never gave her a chance. She lurched for him and stumbled hard against the palms of her hands. Punctures in her skin from gravel and even broken glass and God knows what else.

She sat in the mud. She didn't care about how it soaked through her. Slapped her stinging hand against the brick façade and made it hurt much worse. She wanted to run off with Nero, get lost in the fields forever, but instead she leaned against the wall and sobbed from deep in her lungs. Turned her face to the sky and let the rain hit her eyes and asked "What the fuck are you doing?" of nobody but herself. A few coins and a pay-phone call would be all you'd need to end—

—grits, over-easy eggs, bacon. Coffee in a concave mug, hearty sips to smooth her throat. She sat on a stool at the counter. Fry cooks at the grills, waitress milled about the booths pouring caffeinated and orange-rimmed decaf. Jodie was soaked and muddied just minutes ago, but she took a towel and fresh clothes to the women's bathroom, dried her hair as best she could. Now she sat, looking clean yet still feeling grimy.

Other customers were staring her down. How she must've looked—
sleep-deprived, wild wet hair and rumpled clothes from her duffel bag.
Her own odors lingered thick enough to make her wince. Maybe they
were right to be wary of her. She sat with her empty fork in her fingers,
tines rattling against the plate edge. She fought nightmare visions of a
SWAT team bursting into the restaurant with guns drawn on her,
howling *down on the floor, arms spread!*

Some guy sitting catty-corner kept locking eyes with her, kept tug-
ging at his beard and adjusting his baseball cap like some hillbilly
mating dance. She folded open the damp paper slip she'd rescued from
her dresser back home, laid it flat on the counter. The ink-jet letters
had faded and streaked bluish. If it was ruined, she could replace this
printout—find Internet access, log into her old Yahoo! account. The
e-mail would be stored in her inbox still. She caught it late last year
while at the Cobb County library main branch searching job postings.
Almost deleted it because she didn't recognize the sender, *TwilightReece,*
and because her mail was never anything but spam, all of it.

Her son's message was already a month old by the time she read it.
She'd not heard from him in years, and then—boom, this e-mail. Clicked
reply but couldn't fill the blank box with even a single word, so the cur-
sor blinked in place for fifteen minutes. She wanted to say—say what?
The shock had crowded out everything she could think for a reply. So
she printed it, logged out, hadn't checked her mailbox again in the two
months since. Every time she read it was like giving birth all over again:

Dear Jodie Larkin,

*So I bet you didn't expect to hear from me. How are you? Long time no
see, but I guess you're still in Atlanta probably, right? I'm still in Cape Fear
NC. My dad's a professor at the college here, but you know that. I found this
email address so hopefully you still use it. Hopefully I'm not freaking you out
either, so just ignore me if I am. If not, maybe we could keep in touch? I'm in
tenth grade now and "my own person," as they say. My parents don't know I*

wrote to you if you're worried about that. Maybe someday you could even come
visit. Or I could go there. You don't need to answer now. Just something to
think about. Got to run, so take care.

> *Your son,*
> *Calvin*

"You remind me of Molly," the leering man said. He slipped one stool closer to her.

"I'm sure," Jodie said. "Her last name starts with O, right?"

"Oh, maybe. To my eternal disappointment, she turned nun. Catholic."

Jodie shoved a lump of scrambled eggs into her mouth and chewed it noisily.

"How about you? Do you accept Jesus Christ as your personal savior?" he asked.

"I don't know—do you?"

He rolled up his left sleeve to demonstrate. A green tattoo ran the full length of his forearm, so faded and smeared and covered with hair that Jodie couldn't tell what it was meant to prove. But she nodded anyway and sipped her orange juice. The guy hunched across the one empty stool between them, stale cigar and coffee stink caught in his breath.

"You traveling by yourself?" he asked.

"My boyfriend is asleep up at the motel," she said, and she kept her eyes hid from his.

He raised both his hands in fake surrender. "Hey, I catch your drift. We're total strangers, you and me. These people who get offended when you don't trust them straight away?—I'm not one of them. I get it. That's exactly how people get conned, right? So if you want to tell me you've got a boyfriend up at the motel, you go right ahead and say it. I'm just trying to be friendly, like the Monkees. The good news, missus, is you can, as a matter of fact, trust me."

"I'd rather just eat my breakfast," Jodie said.

"Cheer up," he said. "Your prodigal puss-in-boots will be back any minute."

Jodie tucked her chin against her chest. So he'd watched her through the windowpanes, watched her chase Nero around like she was vaudeville, maybe even spotted her switching license plates. His grin and his squint suggested he was willing to give her several options besides a call to police, but Jodie decided she'd choose arrest over whatever else this man had to offer.

He took a wallet from his back pocket and fished out a twenty, slapped it atop his breakfast bill. He seemed suddenly disappointed in the whole scheme of things, shook his head in slow-motion denial. Jodie reconsidered. Maybe he wasn't the highway rapist throat-slitter her instinct said he was.

"You saw my cat?" she asked.

"Saw you wandering around hunting for her."

"Him. His name's Nero. He just jumped out of the car when I stopped."

"He'll get fed up with the rain. Nero's Italian for black."

"I thought he was a king or something," she said.

"That, too. Emperor. Fiddled while Rome burned, had his own mother executed."

A fresh chill spread across Jodie's skin. She was convinced again that he saw her messing with the license plates. He had a cell phone clipped to his belt. Maybe he already called the state police and they told him to stall her with conversation. Or maybe he was a cop himself, making nice before he shoved her against the counter and twisted her arms behind her back. Or a bounty hunter like that TV mullet guy with the pro-wrestler wardrobe and the testosterone wife.

"Sorry," he said. "Useless storehouse of trivia. Take care of yourself, hear?"

Then suddenly he was leaving, good-byes to all the waitresses. Outside he hoisted himself into the same SUV Jodie had stolen the plate from. She held her breath until he turned onto the main road and drove out of sight.

"How much?" she asked. Gave her bill to the waitress, who impaled it on a receipt stand.

"Ma'am, that last gentleman paid y'all's bill. He didn't tell you?"

"Do you know who he is?" Jodie asked.

"Y'all's secret admirer, is all I know. Nice way to start a Saturday, huh?"

Jodie pressed her toweled ball of wet clothes against her chest and backed away from the counter. She didn't like the sheen of things in this restaurant, the way every comment and sightline was slanted toward her. She wished she'd taken pains to figure out the meaning of that man's tattoo. It had to be some key he meant for her to decode, some warning.

As soon as she shouldered the exit, a black cat crossed her path. His coat was doused and his ears tucked pitifully against his head. She scooped him up by his scruff and laid him in the crook of her arm. He shivered against her breast, and his mangy state put her in mind of a story she heard in a Baptist church she visited in Atlanta once or twice: how the dusty prophet returns from his trial in the wilderness with—

—blew eastward on the interstate while Nero cried, and five miles on she scoffed at herself. She didn't fucking believe in Bible prophets or voodoo tattoos or any black omens. She believed in this road and Calvin and maybe the sliver of mercy she deserved when the—

—tin roofs rusted. A used-auto dealership strung about with fluttering yellow pendants. She passed a pork barbecue joint with a pig mascot on its billboard, dressed in overalls and wielding his own fork and knife. Hinterlands, North Carolina, 1950s time warp. A farmhouse had hundreds of pairs of beach sandals nailed to its siding, just out on its own in a field. The pines towered roadside, but they were stripped naked until the topmost tufts.

On the radio was a self-help monologue on Jesus and Buddha and Thomas Jefferson. Overcome our self-pity and strive for our goals. Jodie listened and felt the same weird uplift you get from T V ads about long-distance family phone calls. She hadn't talked to Calvin in five years. When she cranked the dial and a news station hit, she listened for—

—drizzle on the windshield. Breeze whistled through the window slit like teapot steam, briny scent of the nearby sea. She crossed the Cape Fear bridge beneath twin lift towers coated industrial marine, high above the water and the riverfront span of old mills and wharfs converted to bars and boutiques. North among the trees the river widened, and there was a battleship docked, with guns and cannons spearing out of its deck in all directions. Jodie thought of men, of fire and death, but reminded herself to be hopeful because she was entering this city where her son lived. She was mere minutes from him.

Saturday morning meant he might be sleeping in, or working an early shift at some local grocery store. He might be checking his e-mail to find that the deadbeat who gave birth to him couldn't manage to write him back once again. Or he was answering the doorbell to a team of federal agents gathered on the stoop: "Your mother is on the lam, and we have reason—

—parked at La Quinta but lugged her bag and cat across the street to the Rest Easy Inn. Nero squirmed in her grip till she set him on the check-in counter. The clerk was behind a sheet of Plexiglas with a cluster of punctures in the center to talk through. Indian, Pakistani maybe—the one with the forehead dot. Seventy bucks for the room, three tens in change. Three hundreds gone already and only forty-seven left. Jodie could burn through this cash within a few days, and what

then? Thinking ahead was slitting your own wrists. Think only here
and now.

The clerk slid the tray toward her. Inside was a key attached to a
block of scrap wood. She said, "Checkout time is noon."

"Noon? It's—almost ten now? For seventy dollars I get two hours?"

The woman shrugged. "Wait two hours, then you can pay till tomorrow noon."

"Forget it. Just give me two nights," Jodie said. She pressed another
hundred—

—shower off the grime, dry sweat, the tequila reek, sea salt, cigarette. She used a pair of scissors to clip her hair down. The sink basin
was littered with wet orange coils and Jodie stood unfamiliar with herself in the bathroom mirror. Her hair was parted in the style of a German cross-dressing cabaret dancer.

From a L'Oreal box she lifted a bleach bottle and foldout directions
with plastic gloves attached. She doused her hair, then sat naked on
the edge of her bed and waited for the color to fade. Drank bottled water
with her gloves still on. The chemical stink kept her awake, kept Nero
hidden behind the TV stand like he was afraid she'd dye his lustrous
black. Because they'd be looking for a redhead with a black cat. She'd
even worried when she was at the store buying kitty litter and hair dye
that they'd flag her at the checkout.

Once rinsed and dried, her hair shocked almost white, New Wave
like her older sister's friends back in grade school. The dark crescents
under her eyes showed their weight, but otherwise she looked younger.

She drew the curtains so the room was dark at midday, sprawled on
the bed in pajamas, and tried to doze. But visions hit her eyelids of nonstop roads, and in her ears a tinnitus engine droned so bad she couldn't
sleep even as she was already sleeping. Nero curled in the crook of her
arm and purred. The purple TV cast flickered on the ceiling. A lady on a
soundstage called out lotto numbers with a microphone as Ping-Pong

balls tumbled and blew through a plastic shaft. She cooed about how this could be somebody's lucky—

—residential street off the north end of Market, a recent housing development with lawns pale and patchy in the sand, leafless trees transplanted from nurseries and held upright with twine and stakes. Sunday dusk fell and the front-yard lampposts all around the neighborhood clicked on. Jodie idled the Celica curbside in front of a house with no lit windows or cars in the driveway. She hoped nobody was home, nobody to get antsy about her loitering out front. The Nowaks' house was across the street and two lots down. Down the road, a kid circled his bike around a cul-de-sac. From a distance and in this light he looked the same age and size as the boy Jodie remembered from five years ago in Atlanta, but of course Calvin wasn't that boy anymore.

Her own head tricked her too much now, still groggy from sixteen straight hours' sleep in her motel room. And she was only awake and prowling now because of a nightmare of crashing her car through a pier barrier into the sea, water flooding through the window cracks as clusters of pink jellyfish tumbled onto her lap until she woke up gasping.

The heat in the car was on full blast but couldn't stop her shivering. This close, she saw the spanking white vinyl siding on Calvin's house, the blue shutters, the skateboard lying wheels-up on the lawn. Convinced herself if she drove any closer, federal agents in dark suits would rush out from behind bushes and picket fences, guns drawn. She didn't really believe her paranoia, but she couldn't trust her faith, either.

Nobody here would welcome her. Calvin's adoptive parents would see straight through her desperation like they always did, because the father was a professor of something having to do with psychology and the mother could catch it just by instinct. On their doorstep they'd gush sympathy and sorry at first, but they wouldn't actually let her come inside. They'd trick her into thinking the distance between Atlanta and Cape Fear was better for everybody, healthier for Calvin, for his sense of security. They'd ask if she trusted their advice, and what could she say but of course? She gave them her baby, for God's sake. She couldn't let herself brew bitterness about the couple who saved her son, people who surely now regretted that they agreed to an open-records adoption with a girl knocked up at age sixteen and already a wreck.

The rearview mirror showed a police cruiser drawing up. In a panic Jodie twisted down the heat dial and lifted her foot from the brake and popped the glove box open, not knowing why. She steered away from the curb and shifted into first. There were actual gloves in the glove box, workman's gloves spattered red, probably from Hector's paint-contracting job.

The cruiser's headlights glinted in all her mirrors and then swerved left into the vacant driveway behind where she'd parked. She pressed her molars together and took a slow loop around the cul-de-sac. The uniformed cop eased out of his car, yawning. He tapped a salute at someone across the street, a teen rolling a wheeled trash bin down his driveway. He was a boy with a mop of orange hair like the tips of campfire flames, his feet half in his sneakers with the heels crushed down like slippers. He squinted at Jodie as she passed, just a brush and she was out of sight with her mirrored backward view of Calvin already—

The trick was to stay anonymous. *Dep. S. Hartwick* etched on Sam's name tag, but nobody was out here tonight to read it. Gloves meant his fingerprints wouldn't oil the plastic baggie, and he never touched the five hundred bucks sealed inside it. He didn't even know for sure if the count was right or if Dwight stiffed him, but it didn't much matter when the cash wasn't Sam's to spend.

Off Rural Route 86, Sam parked his Cassadaga County Impala in the Free Methodist lot and left it to idle while he trudged on boot toward the church mail slot. An anonymous donation, dirty cash made clean the minute it dropped inside. He rolled his shoulders to loosen up the stress. Sure, Weymouth dispatch could track his car's location by GPS, but none of those computer jockeys would think much about it. They'd see him killing the last half hour of his shift, is all—avoiding poor road conditions. Whatever codes of conduct he'd botched tonight, he was covered by the Higher Law that brought him to his church.

The Free Methodist was a whitewashed chapel posted on the edge of a vineyard, just bare knotted vines and open ground where the wind gusts gained their momentum before they wracked him. Hand atop his quilted, faux-fur Bullwinkle cap to keep it from flight. He held a grit-teeth grimace and a low growl that somehow helped him cope with the cold on his three-to-eleven patrols. He slipped the bagged cash into the slot, offered up some of his soul ache with it. Paying penance deserved no congratulations.

This church was where Sam married Jill going twenty years back.

Married young, twenty and stupid. The same church christened their daughter, Erika, when she was a toddler. Same church baptized Sam himself two winters back, after he started attending more often than Christmas and Easter. Now the congregation prayed for Jill's ailing brain each Sunday and pooled tithes to help pay her prescription bills. The pastor called it *charity,* but that word hurt worse than Sam's testicles in a tourniquet. He considered it a debt that was already more than twice the five hundred he was repaying tonight by stealth.

He made haste back to his prowler. Padded with long johns, uniform, and an insulated duty jacket with a plush pile collar, but it was hardly enough in this weather. On the way, the receiver on his epaulette said, "Weymouth to eight-twenty-four." He dropped back into the driver's seat and snatched the transmitter from the dash, yanked at the tangled cord to get it up to his face, answered, "Eight-twenty-four."

"MDT transmission," the dispatcher said, and then the laptop mounted between the seats hailed him with a digital audio thump. Sam's bowels clenched even before he saw the readout. Nobody else on these roads except Sam and the two men he pulled over, fifteen minutes prior. Even the other four patrol deps were couched at substations awaiting calls. It was about them—Dwight Kopeck and that unexpected kid riding shotgun along with him.

I wash my hands of this, Sam had said, as if voicing a denial made it truth. Where to find Cecelia was all he had offered, and now that same address popped onto his laptop screen. Eight Willow Bend Road, marked with a digital pushpin on the GPS map. Neighbors had phoned 911 to report gunshots and yells.

This was called Judgment. Streetlights beat onto his cruiser, alone in a church parking lot, and the snowfall bent sinister. On the passenger seat was a travel guide to Costa Rica with a bursting bright snapshot of a flower that looked like a tropical bird, or vice versa. Inside were photos of beaches with big green coconuts dropped in the sand, shacks renting surfboards, sloths lounging in the treetops. He reached for the book to have another glance, but drew back his hand.

"I gave You the money," Sam complained. "Did You not just see me?"

He stomped the gas and the Impala fishtailed, brought him around to face the exit drive. The unplowed road smoothed its boundaries against the surrounding fields, but Sam knew the bends. He drove fast enough to ice skate into a ditch or a tree if he lost control. He was disinclined to latch his seat belt. The headlights split the night open ahead of him, and he punched the light-bar console into action. The siren wailed, though no one—

—been afraid like this in years. Sam would be the first responder here, after a jackknife swerve into the Willow Bend trailer park. He killed the lights and sirens and wedged the prowler into a hard snowbank. Might have to reel it out with a tow chain later, but Sam couldn't care.

Ten yards down from the trailer sat Dwight's Lincoln Town Car, the joyride of choice for geezers and the lowlife grandkids who stole the keys from grandma's purse. Its windows were all fogged from the clash between hot radiator and cold night. Sam lunged up from the Impala with his Maglite in hand, shined a crossbeam over the Lincoln.

Dispatch radioed, "Weymouth to eight-twenty-four."

"Eight-twenty-four," Sam said. He popped the driver's door on the Lincoln, flashed the light on an empty front seat. The glove box stood open, meaning somebody here might have a weapon in hand. The key was in the ignition and another dozen keys hung from the ring. Trashed backseat: beer cans, newspapers, plastic bottles. It was a recycling bin on wheels, just the same as Sam saw it a half-hour back, except now the aluminum baseball bat was missing. Add to that any firearms those Unit-8 drug mopes were packing, and what gets cooked is a heaping fubar soufflé.

"Idiot," Sam said. It was patently wrongheaded for Dwight to have carted that sidekick along, worse for Sam to let it slide. He should've zipped his mouth and walked, to hell with Dwight and his family reunion crusade. Not everybody's prayers get answered. But then, Dwight had no trigger-happy rapsheet. He was just a lowly hoodlum making recent headway into respectability, nursing an earnest wish to find his crackhead sister, talk some sense with her, maybe get her into rehab. And Sam put his faith in the project.

Dispatch said, "Eight-ninety-six en route, ten minutes."

Backup ten minutes to arrival. The single-wide trailer, ten yards ahead. A plump female silhouette appeared in the window of the trailer next door, probably the 911 caller taking a gander. Sam's quick flashlight arc revealed that Unit Eight's side entrance doorway was wide open, screen door torn away and abandoned against the porch staircase, half-buried in the snow. Forced entry if Sam ever saw it. Wild footprints fanned out from the bottom step toward the road, coming and going. Bright lights still burning inside, but there was no discernible movement.

Sam laid his palm on his holstered Beretta and approached, held his Maglite beside his head like it was a weight he had to shoulder. The wind tried to ward him off, but these were exigent circumstances. Whatever mess had gone down in there was his alone to clean.

He belt-clipped the flashlight when he hit the steps. He noted the broken rose stem, crushed petals on the landing. Incongruous. Glass shards in the foyer, laundry doused with red that wasn't blood. A whiff of fermented grape told him it was wine. Abandoned dinner plates and beers on the kitchen table, overturned chair, scent of burnt gunpowder. Sam drew his gun.

Piss-scented squalor in the main room. Sam kicked empty sleeping bags, aimed his gun down the hallway, sidestepped as he progressed. His eardrums ached with the silence and the swish of his pulse. Mind ablaze with the moment, the chance he could get killed. To the left a bathroom emanated shower steam, but Sam gave it a cursory glance. Set his squint instead on the corpse of Dwight Kopeck slumped in the doorway at the end of the hall.

"Aw, you stupid wipe," Sam said. He swiveled and aimed his gun at nothing. It was the hot-water heater kicking on inside the utility closet, and he'd nearly shot a hole through the slatted door. Two years or more since he needed to unholster his weapon on duty. Five years with the county and he never once fired it outside the gun range.

Dwight was slumped, chin against collarbone so tight he'd suffocate if he wasn't dead already. A chest wound soaked his shirt and his hands and dappled the threadbare carpet. The revolver in his right palm was clean of blood and loose in his grasp, none of his fingers through the trigger guard. The look of things announced that the gun was planted postmortem by someone stupid or panicked.

The dingy little room featured a window thrown wide, hemorrhaging the trailer's weak warmth. Blood spatter on a bare hanging lightbulb cast the room in a faint reddish haze and seeped a coppery odor like cooked liver. Lying on the mattress in the corner was a second body, Cecelia Kopeck, her bare legs on the floor, one stretched long and the other bent at the knee, her left foot laid across her opposite calf. The towel on her head was soaked through with blood. The .22 in her hand looked native to its place, like it was already there when she died.

The stench ushered bile into Sam's throat, and he lunged toward the open window. He hadn't puked in years, though he'd seen bodies ravaged by car wrecks, seen chum-strewn train tracks in a suicide's aftermath. But this carnage called his name and clung to him like an orphan claiming to be his child. He shoved his head into the night and the nausea passed because something else caught his attention, a disturbance in the snow just below the window. With his flashlight, he beamed a set of foot tracks headed into the woods.

He faced the corpses again, Dwight and Cecelia, dead together like siblings in a sick nursery rhyme. He wanted them still alive and still estranged. Dwight's fatal flaw was his desperation, and Sam knew that path like he'd blazed it himself. The likeness had made Sam too eager to help, and the end result was the first Cassadaga County murder in months, first double in years, with Sam in the center like a black hole. Any third party reading these circumstances would sure as hell judge Sam a cut-rate crooked bribe hound, no matter where the payoff landed.

He stepped over Dwight's corpse, nudged the bathroom door fully open with his steel shank instep. Nobody on the toilet or in the shower. He led with his gun back down the hallway, free hand on his shoulder-clipped transmitter. He said, "Eight-twenty-four to Weymouth. I've got two special deliveries here, request full package," and hoped the dispatcher on duty knew the departmental discretion code words for dead bodies and the cavalry call. The flat tone she took with "Copy, eight-twenty-four" meant she was apprised.

Sam pressed through to the last room beyond the kitchen. It was a larger bedroom with water-stained walls, waterlogged cardboard boxes, old lamps without bulbs or shades, a couch stripped of its cushioning. He pivoted through the room with his gun double-handed at arm's length, pointing it at shadows while it shuddered. But there was nobody hiding out, nobody dead.

It appeared that all living parties had fled the scene, at least one of them on foot. Given that the Lincoln was still on the premises, the runner was probably Dwight's sidekick, the kid who saw Sam at the traffic stop, saw the payoff, saw the clusterfuck that resulted.

Another matter was which offender put the bad postmortem gun plant in Dwight's dead hand in order to make this nightmare look like a simultaneous win-lose death match between brother and sister.

A distant siren wail meant two minutes max before backup. Sam holstered his gun, peeled the gloves from his hands, shoved them in his coat pocket. He took a pair of rubber gloves from a pouch on his belt, tugged them on while he rushed back down the hall and crouched beside Dwight. The kid's eyes were glass, now that his soul was gone from behind them.

Sam pushed his fingers in Dwight's jean pockets, then folded him over at the waist to get at the back ones. Took the battered wallet he found and pried it open. There was cash tucked inside, but Sam ignored it. He searched instead for slips of paper, anything bearing his own name or number, then he replaced the wallet and returned Dwight to his death pose. He tried the jacket pockets and the inside pouch. Retrieved a blood-soaked cigarette pack, searched inside it, found zilch but the expected smokes, slipped it back in place. Greasy daubs of blood stained Sam's gloved fingertips. He lifted the revolver from Dwight's hand and pressed it against the soiled carpet until it was slick with blood. Then he positioned the gun back into Dwight's grasp, squeezed the fingers around the checkered grip, looped the index through the trigger guard.

From outside came the crunch of tires on snow, carried through the open window. Car 896: Deputy Carmine Gello's light bar flashed red and white against the treetops. Sam pressed his fingers against dead Dwight's jugular. No question Dwight was gone onward to some other existence, but checking a pulse would be the excuse Sam needed for why he was wearing rubber gloves, and why they were bloody.

If Ballistics came back as Sam suspected—gun in Dwight's hand matching the bullets in his chest—then investigators would figure a ruse, and they'd be right. He was just delaying the truth, but to what end he didn't yet know. Just time and distance. In two weeks he'd be with Jill in a beachfront bungalow on the Pacific listening to howler monkeys rant in the trees, easing out the early finish of her life, and nothing much mattered after that, nothing except Erika.

Gello's boots hit the porch steps. The dead siblings had lost all their senses, but Sam's surged as if to compensate. All around him the stench and sight of their deaths begged to be scrubbed clean of what might implicate him. No, no, go not to—

—feign control was torture enough. Sam combed the living room while investigator and technicians smeared a path of sludge from the front steps to the murder room. The TV showed a furious red-faced chef berating his employees while throttling a handful of limp spaghetti. Bad enough that half the sworn officials on scene had contributed vacation days to cover Sam's pending offtime, had even offered money that Sam refused. They kept their distance, and when they passed him their glances were heavy with consolation, as if Jill were dead already and it was her body down the hall being prepped for the morgue. They were commemorating Sam's mistakes down in that room, and he wanted to rip the camera from the photo tech's grasp and smash it apart.

He tried to call Jill and his shift partner, Murph, let them both know he'd be late, but no cell phone bars would rise from this hinterland. He removed his trapper cap and wiped sweat from his bald-shaved head. The trailer was cold enough now that the techs huffed steam as they passed, but Sam was burning in his scalp, anxious for the county's snowmobile to arrive so he could chase those tracks leading out to the woods.

For now he kicked among the sleeping bags and uncovered a hazy glass crack pipe, picked it up between his rubber-gloved fingers. There was lipstick smeared on the mouthpiece and brown residue in the bowl. Sam sniffed it, and a guy in a padded flannel shirt, jeans, and unlaced electrician's boots came around the corner cursing like the chug of an oncoming train. His name was Royce and he was Narcotics, meaning his work was mostly secret, ostensibly undercover, and it knew few boundaries between county, city, and federal agencies.

"Nice souvenir," Royce said as he cocked his chin at Sam's glass pipe.

"I should start collecting. I'd have a whole garage full by now," Sam said.

Royce was haggard, days unshaven and months overdue on a haircut, but his eyes were hairtrigger alert, like a man on the lookout for one specific wasp in a swarm of them. He had a Tim Hortons coffee and a snarl. Sam knew squat about the guys in Narcotics, except that narcs were immersed in the criminal swamp up to their chins and almost never came over to pick at corpses, not unless the dead were tangled in their nets already. To Sam the very sight of Royce was like a courtroom sentencing.

"You Hartwick? You the FOS?" Royce asked.

"That's me," Sam said.

"I know your name. You're the guy they're doing the vacation pool for, right?"

"Yeah," Sam said. "Everybody's been amazingly generous."

"Right, and sorry to hear about your wife. It's a damn pointless shame, you know? Breast cancer took my oldest sister. So nobody was alive on scene when you got here?"

Sam's attention was snagged on Royce's casual misdiagnosis, so he took too long to recognize a question and answer it. "Uh, no—nobody. Just those tracks, which I'm hitting soon as the snowmobile unit shows up."

Royce karate-chopped the paneled wall and swore in Italian. The coffee in his cup sloshed, dribbled over his knuckles. He sucked the coffee off his fingers and said, "Two days, man. We were two days to a bust. We were set to knock down this whole fucking crypt."

"Them two deceased are your marks?" Sam said.

"The female, Cecelia Kopeck, but she was way low. User, honeypot for dealer dick. Turned snitch if we'd a nabbed her, but now she's nothing but Jehovah's eyewitness. Our real marks flew the coop, and meanwhile this other vic rides from no place with his pistol blazing. ID says he's *Dwight* Kopeck. Turns out he's her fucking brother. You believe it?"

Sam nodded weakly and said, "Actually, I know him. Knew him. He's been coming around our church lately. Free Methodist, on and off the last few Sundays." Sam finessed as best he could to make it look fresh out of his head. The church revelation was a serious risk, but he knew it would become a soft spot once the investigators and narcs asked around. Not a chance he could pull off pretending Dwight Kopeck was a stranger. He said, "Dwight mentioned his sister a few times during open celebration and concern, told us she was missing and that she was an addict. He asked us to pray for him to find her."

"No shit?" Royce said, chuckling. "Well, answered fucking prayers."

"Yeah," Sam said. He felt like he'd been stabbed in the throat and probably showed it in his face. Maybe Royce would read it as nothing more than a sour response to the sacrilege—which it was, in part.

"This exposition's in your report, I assume?" Royce asked.

"Will be," Sam said—just a pinch too servile.

"Tomorrow afternoon, right? A-sap."

Sam nodded and ventured to ask, "You think the two of them shot each other?"

"Looks it. All's I know is my marks are gone and my case is ass-fucked."

"Can't salvage it?" Sam asked.

"You know how it flies, Hartwick. Murder trumps all. I'm gonna need to open all my files, spread 'em wide for the probe. Six months of slow-burn recon gone. Just *whoosh*. You didn't see nobody split, right? Fuck, I should've had eyes on this place tonight." Royce swiped the crack pipe from Sam's grasp and pitched it side-hand against a foggy storm window, where it blasted into powdered glass.

"Fuck you," Royce told the crack pipe.

Sam was six inches taller than Royce, thirty more pounds of muscle, but he took a step back, like Royce was pure righteousness in the flesh.

An hour back Sam believed the same about himself, but now he just chewed at reasons to believe he wasn't at fault. None had any meat on them. A deputy named Sam Hartwick had loosed dealers and killers on the world, and here he was, forced to stand inside that guilty man's boots. If they knew his culpability—

—time is it?" Jill asked.

Sam was astride a snowmobile with the engine rumbling low and the mounted floodlight splashing the edge of a snowbank. Cell phone to his ear, enough clearance on this side of the woods to get a signal. The road he flanked was freshly plowed and salted, a path cut through all the way back to Weymouth.

"It's eleven-thirty," Sam told his wife. "You won't believe it, but there was a double murder, and I happened to be the one to catch it, twenty minutes before my shift wound up. Bad timing, as usual."

Jill said, "Then I'm alone here for a while, huh?"

"Not long now. Where's Erika?"

"Rehearsals, I guess. In college the theater never sleeps, sort of like criminals."

"She need a ride home?"

"She'll let you know, I'm sure."

"How you feeling?"

"Just dandy. I have Letterman here to keep me company," she said.

"That gap-toothed bastard," Sam said, though the joke was too weary, too mandatory. The phone transmitted Jill's long sigh, the shifting of bed sheets and the goose-down comforter Sam bought her for Christmas, the new plush pillows. They were the only thinkable gifts for a woman recently diagnosed with six months at most to live.

Sam told her, "I'm on a snowmobile."

"Hm, that doesn't sound like work. Just don't drive it into any ponds."

"It's bloodhound duty, following old tracks. In fact I just hit a dead end. Plowed road."

"Just be careful, all right?" Groggy, she sounded like a tape record-ing stretched from overuse. Her voice should be preserved somehow, Sam decided, but then he'd never listen to it after she was gone, for fear of ruining the recording, and himself. Out here the cold wound through the trees like the lash of a whip, too arctic even for wild ani-mals to prowl, and all the emptiness urged Sam to connect. Just Sam and Jill out in the wilderness, like those cross-country hikes they took in the fall, back before they knew about her brain.

"You need me to get you anything on the way home?" Sam asked.

"Why don't you pick me up a double-murderer with a side of hand-cuffs?"

"Hardee-har-har," Sam said.

"Where are you?"

"North Cross Road, about two miles from Weymouth."

"So what you're saying is you're talking to me at the same time you're supposed to be chasing somebody who killed two people?"

"He's long gone from here, Jill. Headed into the city."

"Jesus, Sam. Should I be worried? I mean, Erika's not home yet."

"I don't think they hang in the same crowd," Sam said, but the ques-tion jolted him with fresh anxiety—because he hadn't wondered on the same question himself, too preoccupied with his own stake. North Cross Road cut along the back end of the SUNY campus, and though Dwight himself was no college material, his passenger looked the type. At least, he didn't look built for heavy lifting and homicide. What that kid resembled most was one of Erika's group from high school—the vil-lage beatniks sixty years too late. Not really one of them, since Sam knew most of their names and parents, but of their ilk, someone Erika might know. The worst hitch was that Sam had a solid description of him, but no explanation for—

—twenty-minute rush to morph him from caterpillar to ar-mored knight. Backstage, Erika watched the stagehands help the

Caterpillar slide down from his massive foam mushroom. For a second he flailed, but his pit team unzipped the green cotton-stuffed abdomen segments to let him loose. He bolted toward Erika on his bare scrawny legs, top half still puffy and green. His feet pattered silently over the hardwood floor. The Mad Hatter, the March Hare, and the Dormouse filed past the Caterpillar into position. Onstage, Alice's high-pitched voice resounded in the rafters, curiouser and curiouser.

"Tear me apart," the Caterpillar told Erika. She pressed her arms up against her chest and recoiled from him. He laughed and spun himself around so she could get at the Velcro seam running down the back of his costume. She peeled it open and the actor emerged almost human, still wearing a green-painted face and a fez. In her ear he said, "I seriously think they put real dope in that hookah."

Erika smiled but she didn't talk. Couldn't say anything clever enough fast enough, especially not while she had to make the transformation in time to get him back onstage as the White Knight. She followed him past the greenroom to the dressing room where other crew members were outfitting Tweedledee and Tweedledum, costumes Erika had designed and sewn herself. The Mock Turtle sat in a makeup chair eating Doritos from a snack bag, calf's head on his lap and foam halfshell on the floor at his feet like a sandbox lid.

The wall-length mirror doubled this absurdity. Even Erika looked the part, with her makeup-stained seamstress apron, bright red beret tilted over one ear, raccoon eyeshadow. Typical Erika, trying too hard at hipster. While she sneered at herself the stage intercom fed Alice's voice into the dressing room:

"Dear, dear! How queer everything is today! I wonder if I've been changed in the night? Let me think. Was I the same when I got up this morning? I almost think I can remember feeling a little different. But if I'm not the same, the next question is 'Who am I?' Oh dear, how puzzling it all is! I'll try if I know the things I used to know. Let me see: four times five is twelve, and four times six is thirteen—"

The Caterpillar actor sat down in his chair and laughed at his reflection. Erika averted her eyes when she realized he could see her watching him in the glass. Stupid, feeding his ego like that. She opened the makeup case while he rubbed away his green makeup with a towel.

"Have you ever read the real books, the two Alice books?" he asked her.

Erika nodded. She said, "For the costumes. The descriptions of them."

"There's some seriously heady metaphysical stuff in there," he said.

"But this play cuts most of it out, and mixes the two books together," Erika said.

"Well, adaptations," he said. "You're invited to the cast party on Friday, you know."

"I know," Erika said. She pulled back his hair in preparation for the rubber scalp with tufted white fuzz that she would soon apply. Two years into stage makeup and costuming, and she still wasn't used to touching people, especially actors who seemed so unfazed. Her Caterpillar sat there in his boxer shorts and his Bright Eyes concert T-shirt, and Erika couldn't look anywhere except the precise spot where her hands were working. It was the only way she could keep from feeling like she couldn't breathe.

"Not much of a talker?" the Caterpillar said.

"Not much to say."

"Felicia said you designed like half the costumes yourself."

"Not any of yours," she said.

"But still, that's seriously something."

It was a necessary dance with these actors. They had to disarm her before she started daubing their faces with makeup. She painted wrinkles around this one's mouth and his eyes, wondering how she'd found herself here. For a while she'd considered majoring in English just to keep from having to touch people, but she was taking credits enough to double-major anyway.

"Who. Are. You?" the Caterpillar asked.

"What?"

"Just practicing my lines. One side will make you grow taller, and the other side will make you grow shorter. But actually, what was your name again?"

"Erika."

"Right—I heard your dad's a county cop? So maybe you shouldn't come to the party."

"I wasn't really planning to," she said, and snapped on his fake scalp a bit too hard.

He flinched and said, "Why not? You're not into drunken, naked debauchery?"

"Not really my scene," she said, because it seemed the right response for someone like her. She could at least show up and stand in a corner, take a mixed drink if somebody offered. She could at least spend a few hours watching how certain people shined from the inside and passed their various masks around. A roomful of people who had no idea her mother was slowly dying or that death even persisted past the end of a scene. Everybody gets back up off the floor and exits stage left, a consummation devoutly to be wished.

"Have you a beau?" the White Knight asked. He stood to be fitted with the Styrofoam armor that the two other crew members brought from the costume rack. Erika wasn't finished painting his face, and he was more than a foot taller than she was.

"He's in Iraq," she said. "Please hold still."

He kept wincing anyway. He said, "You hang with some serious alpha males."

"Five minutes to go," she reminded him. "He didn't want to go to Iraq, but he joined the marines because he thought that he grew up too pampered."

"What's wrong with pampering?"

"He wants to build character, he says."

"That's heavy," he sighed.

The actual truth was that the soldier and the reasons were real, but the relationship was just a few prom pictures and a goodnight kiss. The marine e-mailed her a few times from Fallujah, from Baghdad. She wrote him back because he understood real fear and could explain it to her, but he wasn't really someone she could ever—

—pressed her coat against her thighs and sat on the icy step, hunched into the glow of her cell phone like it was campfire warmth. Outside the fine arts building, night was starless gray sliced apart by black power lines and fat white snowflakes. No new texts or voicemails from Mom or anyone. With a fingernail she picked at the road salt crusted on her pant cuffs.

Actors loitered over in the parking lot under the streetlamp. They skidded across the ice on their sneakers, guffawed at themselves. Beyond them, on the southern border of the campus, something tumbled out from the wooded jogging path. A deer as usual, but as it came toward the edge of the road, Erika saw it was actually a human silhouette. A jogger, then—running through knee-high snowdrifts, past midnight, now cutting across the street toward the residence halls.

Curiouser and curiouser.

Dad took ten minutes getting through Weymouth to pick her up. She was frozen stiff by the time he pulled the prowler into the pickup lane. The loitering actors scattered at the sight of him. Erika stood and dragged her messenger bag down the steps toward his car. She'd intended to walk the three blocks home, but he'd called her on his way into the city and insisted on chauffeuring.

"I thought your shift ended like two hours ago," she said. She lifted a Costa Rica travel guide off her seat and held it in her lap when she sat.

Dad's headlights swept across the parking lot as he turned the car away. He said, "I got held up by a call. I'm going to drop you off and then trade off with Murph."

"You didn't have to go out of your way," she said.

"It's fine. I don't like you walking around at night by yourself anyhow."

"Dad, it's Weymouth. Not exactly Detroit."

"You'd be surprised."

"The gritty Weymouth underbelly, right. You know all about it," she said. The snide tone seemed to leak into everything she said to her father. Her New Year's resolution was to quell that tone, but she rarely succeeded. Her own attitudes were petty even to her, but they appeared nonetheless, forced her to spit them out.

The malignant tumor was in the core of her mother's brain, spanning both hemispheres. It was butterfly shaped and when the wings spread themselves wide enough, like emerging from a chrysalis, Mom would die. The radiation held the wingspread back only temporarily. Invisible waves like raygun blasts through the cancer-cell helixes, but that cellular split was relentless long division. Just after Christmas, Mom's doctors had explained that she would die before her August wedding anniversary, probably months sooner. They advised her to quit her paralegal job, reconnect with family, go on dream vacations—and all of it quickly.

At a stop sign Dad reached over, nudged the Costa Rica book in her lap, and said, "Thought any more about this? There's still time to buy you a plane ticket. Our passports even came in the mail today, all three of us."

"Dad—"

"I want you to know that we'd love to have you along."

"Dad, I have school."

"I know, but I'm sure they could grant you a leave of absence, or whatever."

"This is for Mom and you. It's not about dragging your kid along."

"It's not a honeymoon, either," he said. They were still at the stop sign, headed nowhere. A car pulled up behind them and filled the prowler with its headlight beams. In that light Dad's face was granite, his eyes black, but he wouldn't look away from her. "I'm not trying to force you to go. It's just an option, that's all."

"Dad, you need to drive," she said.

He nodded and moved them onward. Alone with her father, the dynamic of the two of them together. She imagined ways to make it fit, like how she hemmed secondhand clothes too large for her. But some sutures weren't easily stitched. To consider her mother gone, to follow Mom on a swan-song tour of a tropical Eden, Erika couldn't—

End of last period, Calvin pinched the copper-wire arm of a six-inch figurine just a slight twitch higher. Twenty identical statuettes stood on a tabletop covered in Easter basket grass. His Aesthetics partner, Cora, had made her wire men so thin, and with such big, heavy heads, that they sagged of their own volition. She and Cal were posing them in an improvised stop-motion dance, every figure bent slightly for successive single-frame video camera shots. This classroom was the gathering center for the Gifted & Talented eggheads—their brain-trust star chamber, their mental ward.

Cora smelled of vinegar and dough and sweated in her eye sockets and talked too much about Sylvia Plath, but such faults barely registered with Cal. He was still too preoccupied with his morning commute. A red sports car had followed his bus to school, *No Fear* on the windshield and the sun glinting on the glass so he couldn't see the driver inside. An itch of concern because he also saw the same car a few minutes earlier, idling a block down from his bus stop. And last night it passed him while he wheeled the weekly garbage to the curb.

The dismissal bell rang and Cora said, "Somebody's going to mess with these poses."

"We were just goofing around anyhow," Cal said.

"But it was becoming something," she whined.

Last night, the red sports car was nothing much to fuss about, nothing compared to his nosebleed run-in with predator Gene at Wright Beach. But again this morning? Cal mulled over what he saw of the driver, who was not Gene like Cal might've expected but instead a woman with wide, petrified eyes. She'd grimaced at him like she was bracing for a crash. Of course Cal recognized her, even with the chopped, bleached hair, but he wouldn't let himself believe it could be her until the next morning when the car reappeared.

With the flow of foot traffic, Cal exited College Model School as usual via the transportation loop, passed his designated bus, and walked along the edge of the visitor's parking lot. He wore his wool hat low over his ears, popped his peacoat collar up, and searched the lot for the red car. If he got too spooked, he could slice through the high school lot and the college campus quad and reach his father's office in Homler Hall, a one-minute sprint.

Straight away he sighted the car in a visitor slot. Almost threw himself behind some shrubbery for cover, but on second glance he saw the driver's seat was empty. He stepped off the curb, glanced around, saw only students milling about, a campus cop on bike patrol. Further off a preacher stood on a park bench and called to all the passing girls that they were "hell-bound who-ers." The wind gained speed and splayed the preacher's hair like some Old Testament hex. Across the quad, a fire drill in Homler Hall had people swarming out onto the lawn.

Cal peered through the driver's-side window, shielded his eyes with his hand. A bag of chips and a Nirvana *In Utero* jewel case on the passenger seat, Red Bull can in the cupholder, Taz air freshener hanging from the rearview mirror. Cal's skin was washed in a low electric aura he couldn't ignore, and then somebody behind him called his name.

She stood jacketless with her arms crossed over her chest. Sniffling, cheeks ruddy from the wind, and hair cut short and jagged and dyed, she stood just quivering on the edge of the curb. Before last night it had been five years since he saw her last. Even if he never met Jodie Larkin before, he could've picked her from a lineup, the cut of her face and her freckles so much like his own. He would've known somehow that she was the mother he came from.

"I saw you last night," Cal said.

"I know it," she said. "I'm really sorry about that."

"And I sent you an e-mail a couple months ago."

"Yes, I got it. I didn't know what to write back—"

"That's okay—"

"—so I decided to come see you. I decided."

"But—" Cal pulled off his hat and kneaded it between his hands. The Homler Hall fire alarm bleeped, and people kept spilling out into the courtyard, clogging it up. Professor Nowak of the psychology department would eventually be one of them.

"You look pretty freaked out," Jodie said. She tried to force a laugh, but the preacher standing tiptoe on his bench was damning them all to hell. She unlocked her arms and put her hands in her jeans pocket. Cal recognized the Atlanta Zoo sweatshirt she wore, bought years ago when they took a day trip there together, with his adoptive parents following along like court-appointed supervisors.

"Do my—do the Nowaks know you're here?" he asked.

The question made her smile stop. She said, "No, they don't know."

His father was now among those crammed in the courtyard outside Homler, just a city block's distance away. No mistaking his baggy jeans and corduroy blazer combo, the bald patches on his elbows and the back of his skull. Dad could simply turn around and spot them at any opportunity, Calvin and his bio-mom, desperately unchaperoned. What had seemed a vague danger five minutes before was a specific thrill now.

"Calvin, I'm—I'm sorry—" she stammered, eyes on the brick pathway underfoot.

"Let's go somewhere," Cal said. He reached out for her, but she backstepped. She sneered at the preacher as he recited God's horrors. It was the wrong soundtrack for this halting reunion. He said, "Mom," and the word was enough to lure her eyes back to him.

"Sorry," she said. "That man yelling over there—"

"He's always there. People just ignore him."

"How could you ignore—

—Market Street redlight traffic. Nirvana played barely audible from the speakers. Cal caught whiffs of fresh cigarette smoke and citrus shampoo. His mother's scent was strange to him, although he wished it wasn't. What features felt so brutal on Cal played more subtly on her face. On her he saw how his skin might look unblemished.

"You like Nirvana?" Cal said.

She was checking the rearview mirrors. She said, "Huh? Oh, right. Classic rock, right?"

"Not really. Cobain died the same year I was born."

"I remember that. Everybody went around moping, but I was kind of too busy with reality." The light turned green and they passed the Whitey's El Berta restaurant, then the strip mall and the antebellum stonewalled properties and the sunken graveyard. They drove under the lollipop palmettos and the dappled canopy of Southern live oaks, lush even in winter and draped with Spanish moss.

"How old were you—when you had me, I mean?"

"Seventeen," she said. "Not too much older than you."

His adoptive parents were both in their mid-fifties, old enough to be his grandparents by the standards Jodie set. But of course proper girls at age sixteen didn't generally get pregnant, not at his school, not those churchgoer suburbanites who dreamed of Disney World vacations and hoarded brochures for private Christian colleges. Nothing too depraved among the privileged classes, nothing but Cal's own queerbait Internet forays, his violent luncheon with a reject from *To Catch a Predator*.

Cal didn't know what to say. He guessed Jodie didn't want to be asked what she'd done with her weekend in Cape Fear. What she seemed to have done was fret over every hour, drive out to his house, and balk at the last minute. She devised ways to meet him without alerting the

Nowaks, who didn't know she was here, who'd be displeased and suspicious if—

—Water Street gift shops, bricked walkways and bars and starving-artist galleries, just as quaint in real life as they looked on *Cape Twilight Blues*. Jodie gave Cal a twenty and sent him inside Java Queen for a paper cup of gourmet coffee and whatever else he wanted. He didn't order anything for himself, but he slid a cardboard sleeve onto her coffee, added double cream and sugar like she asked.

Outside, they strolled the promenade. She was a full foot shorter than him, so he bent himself into a slouch to compensate. The stretch of brick edifices gave way to a view of the Cape Fear River Walk, the massive bollards on the pier where the tourist riverboat was moored, and far across on the opposite bank, the USS *North Carolina*.

"It's cold," Jodie said. "I don't think I can stay out here long."

"Can I ask you who my father is?" Cal blurted. The question was meant to cut past all the more delicate, more trivial things he could've asked. How do you like Water Street? What brings you to town? How've you been these last five years? Their afternoon felt tentative, like any second she'd toss her unfinished coffee into a trash can and announce that she had to run, had to check into her Myrtle Beach resort by nightfall.

"He lives in New York," she answered. "We, uh—we broke it off a long time ago."

"Were you married? I never asked you that before. I'm sorry if I'm being too—"

"No, it's okay. You got questions, right? I had to expect. But we weren't married, him and me. We weren't even—together, really. I was a teenager, like I said."

"Right. Dumb of me to ask 'Were you married.' Duh. Of course not."

"Calvin, you go ahead and ask me whatever."

"All right," he said. "What brings you out here?"

"Your letter."

"But that was a couple months ago," he said. He was grilling her, yes—and in truth he didn't much care why she waited so long, only that she was here now, like a timely diagnosis: *Here's your problem, Calvin, here's why you feel always unmoored from your dock, drifting, here she is*—she who flinched whenever anyone walked past them. A cringe and a sideward glance as if she expected a stranger to haul off and punch her in the throat.

"I don't get to a computer much. And I needed time—to get enough money."

"How long are you going to stick around?"

"I don't know. As long as you want me to. I got—I don't know—I got a week."

"I've got school all week."

"I know it," she said.

"If you came in the summertime—" he said.

Jodie said, "I know, I know. The summer'd be better, with the ocean. I don't even remember the last time I went to the ocean. But I had to come when I could get off of work."

"So we spend our afternoons after school, without my parents knowing."

"I ain't trying to cause—"

"No, it's fine. I know the drill, and I can keep a secret."

She nodded her consent to circumstances she herself had prompted. They were stopped in front of the army surplus store. The window displayed knives and bayonets, a faded American flag, old war-effort posters of the type reprinted in history textbooks—Rosie the Riveter patriotic hoopla. She said, "I just don't want to upset nobody. God, I'm cold."

"Let's go in here," Calvin said. When he pulled the entrance door, the overhead sleigh bells clanked a flat note on the glass.

"What's this?" she asked.

"It's just a cool store," Cal said. "Let's warm up a second. I want to show you."

Inside was musty and tinged with the smell of old leather and rubber, moldy canvas, and even a hint of burnt campfire wood. It conjured suffering and death, damp trenches, the sputter of machine gun fire. The racks were stocked with state-army uniforms from around the world, mostly European, black and green fatigue jackets. Shelves above displayed Kaiser helmets, WWI or 1960s biker vintage.

"This is seriously creepy," Jodie whispered.

"Yeah, I love it. Über-kitsch."

Cal pointed out a mannequin poised just behind his mother. She jerked away from it with a start, hand on her chest. It was wearing fatigues, combat boots, and a gas mask that seemed modeled after a horsefly's head. It was meant to unnerve, Cal supposed. Like the propaganda posters on the walls, mottoes in German with stark cubist figures and Teutonic motifs.

"This war stuff—are you into this?" Jodie asked. She was sifting through a circular rack of army jackets, feeling the fabrics and patches and oversized buttons.

"Morbid curiosity, I guess. My tastes are generally ironic," Cal said.

The salesgirl sniggered at Cal from the stool where she sat behind the counter, leafing through a magazine. She had each pigtail dyed a different color, multiple lip rings, a camouflage tank top, and tattoos all up her arms.

Cal slipped the gas mask off the dummy and urged it down over his own head. The straps yanked at his hair and the rubber was sticky against his face, but he got it all on while Jodie was distracted. People flitting by on the sidewalk outside captured her attention. Cal saw himself in an upright mirror. The eye sockets and exhale valve made three wide portholes of perpetual surprise. The corrugated rubber hose hung down from the mouthpiece like a dead tentacle.

"Looking sharp," the salesgirl said. She came out from behind the counter, grabbed him by both sides of his skull, and tilted the straps till they fit right on his head. "There," she said. "Mark Five General Service Respirator, standard issue for British troops during World War Two. Excellent condition, except it's missing the filter canister." She slapped his dangling tube to show that it was a lifeline to nowhere. With his limited vision, Cal couldn't see Jodie. She'd disappeared behind another rack of clothes somewhere. The salesgirl said, "You look like a sea monster, like the black lagoon."

Cal shimmied the mask off, flattened his hair with the palm of his hand.

"It goes for one-fifty," the salesgirl said. She had one of her eyebrows shaved off, but not the other. "Nobody else in your school has a gas mask, right?"

"Not at my school. Maybe some of those Slipknot kids at Cape Fear Central."

The salesgirl snorted like she was offended somehow. Cal sidestepped away from her, found Jodie studying an upright display case full of old medals, crosses, and stars, most of their engravings worn away or filled with grime. Jodie took the gas mask from Cal's hands and laid it down over her fist, held it at eye level and peered into the empty eyeholes.

"So you want to buy this?" she said.

"I was just messing. I really don't want it that bad."

"You sure? Well, what else do you want instead?"

"Really, I was just—"

"No, anything, Calvin. I've missed a bunch of birthdays and Christmases, right?"

Cal didn't want it to be so easy. He'd meant to spring this place on her like a practical joke, somewhere he'd never bring his parents. He wanted her to hate it so he could feel properly disappointed in her. Owing Jodie, or anyone, was the last thing he wanted. Except for that niggling sense of deserving. She'd abandoned him at birth, this woman, so if doling out gifts would help her feel atoned, well then, maybe she did owe—

—bowie knife with a six-inch blade, saw teeth on the top edge and diamond-grip rubber on the handle. Cal didn't jazz on knives, but it seemed like what a boy should want. The knife was in a blank paper bag along with the gas mask. He'd have to hide all this stuff, maybe ask Jodie to hold it at least as long as she was in town. If the Nowaks found this merchandise they'd confiscate it, then back to the counselor and the school watch list, the threats to put him on Ritalin or Zoloft, the pussyfooting. There'd be questions, accusations. But for now they were back in her car, driving homeward from downtown.

"Do you have any other kids?" Calvin asked.

"Me? No, I never even been married. I just—just never saw it in my plans."

"So you didn't want kids?"

"I just never was in a place where I could raise them right, you know? I mean, look at what I just bought you."

"Don't worry. I'll keep it hidden."

"So, I already got you keeping secrets from people."

"I was doing plenty of that already," he said, but Jodie didn't ask him to elaborate. In a way, he wanted her to grill him on his secrets just so he could refuse to talk about how he'd met a man on the Internet who turned out to be some potbellied freak who punched him in the nose, and how the whole shebang was like a voltage jolt, the kind that makes the hair on your arms stand up. It was their first afternoon together in years, mother and son. So many more knots to untwine before he pulled the toughest one loose.

She was driving Calvin to his subdivision inlet where she'd drop him roadside two blocks from his house, then head back to some dank motel where she'd gorge on talk shows until Tuesday school let out. And Cal would plod along to droning teacher's voices all day, bend the arms of copper figurines, and think about Jodie and Gene and the roughshod world that was urging him out of hiding. He didn't want that prison anymore.

Two years before, Cal and his best friend, Burt, made a pact that when they had driver's licenses and a reliable car and a summer off of school they'd road-trip out to California and cruise the coast from San Francisco to Tijuana. After Burt moved to Ohio, their plan turned all the more vital. It gave them something to dream over cell phone calls and e-mails, an escape to scheme. But Cal couldn't wait anymore.

Cal said to Jodie, "What do you say we go somewhere?"

"What do you mean?"

"Let's go somewhere for a few days, like on a mother-and-son vacation."

"You got school."

"I'm in the Gifted and Talented program. They let you take time for independent projects whenever you want. It's a specific privilege in light of our academic success."

She said, "I never heard of anything like that."

Cal sighed through his nose. He didn't want to look her in the face anymore, so he gazed out his window at the concrete buildings they passed. Here he was judging his mother no better than anyone else, insulting her with lies.

She said, "But I never had no gifts or talents, so what do I know?"

"Everybody has gifts," Cal said. "Everybody's *special*. All my counselors say so."

"Yeah, well. I guess being special needs proof, right?"

"So, I say we both have nerve, you and me. That's special, but we have to prove it."

"Run away, just on some lark? Why would we do that?"

"Show me the place you came from, and where I came from. Then I'll know."

"New York? You're talking about driving all the way up to New

York, in the middle of winter? Do you realize how much snow, and how cold it is, and the bad roads they got in Pennsylvania, and your parents? They'd never—they ain't even supposed to know I'm here."

"We could go skiing," Cal said.

"I don't know how to—"

"I'm just brainstorming, *Mom*." He stressed the endearment like the thrust of a knife, clean and sudden and painless at first. She pulled the car into a Coastal gas station lot and parked it alongside the air pump. Then she put her face in her hands and let loose.

"I'm sorry—really. Forget I even suggested," he said.

She smeared her fingers across her tear ducts. She said, "No, it's okay, Calvin. I want to take you wherever it is you want to go, but we can't just go and do something like that. Your parents won't let us."

"I don't think I love them," Cal said. "I respect them and appreciate them and all but—"

"Don't say that. They're good people and they do everything for you."

"What they'd do for any kid—whatever kid they adopted. It isn't about me, specifically. But look how you came all the way out here for me—not just any kid, you see what I'm saying?"

"I don't think it's like that. I mean, with your parents."

"I'll ask their permission to go away, all right? They know because I'm fifteen I can decide for myself—I can reflect, and judge, and whatever—and right now they're so eager to please me they'll agree, they'll let me. It isn't like with regular parents where the connection is natural. They'd want me to figure things out. I'll tell them I'm going to see my friend Burt up in Akron. That's not too far from where we're going."

"But I know them," Jodie said. "They won't let you go with me. They don't trust me."

"They know they're going to have to deal with this eventually. With you."

"Nobody's even supposed to know I'm here, Calvin."

"So I don't tell them about you. Simple. I just say I'm leaving on my own, on a bus."

"And they're just gonna let you go away by yourself? Fifteen years old? They'd need to be the worst parents in the world. Social Services would be on their case."

"Well, I can come live with you, then."

"Now you're talking crazy. I'm not gonna ruin your—you hardly know me."

"I want to. That's what I'm saying."

"We can do that here. I'll take you to wherever you want to go around town."

"But I'm saying you're only part of it. I want to know the rest, and that's not here."

She wrung the steering wheel with both hands, chewed on her lower lip. She was wrestling with Calvin's logic, which they both knew was shit logic, but it was gilded in such golden yearning that it looked undeniable. You put faith in what you want only because you want it. Cal kept quiet while his mother squirmed in the grip of some particular truths. He averted his eyes and watched a Jack Russell throw itself against every window inside an SUV while its owner filled the gas tank. Dog had faith that there was always an escape because that's what—

—nobody home. Dad was teaching an Abnormal Psych evening class, Mom probably running her twenty laps around the college track. Cal refused to hesitate and lose his resolve. He'd left Jodie waiting in the car three blocks away in a Harris Teeter parking lot, and if she waited too long, mused too much, she'd start to see the badly frayed edges of Cal's plan.

He knew damn well she didn't believe school would let him skip just for being gifted, or that the Nowaks would let him play emancipated minor for a week. But she faked it, the same way you clap and cheer after your kid's amateur magic trick. She had to indulge him because she'd come all the way from Atlanta, saved money for months.

He bounded up the staircase hitting every third step. He was wheezing for breath by the time he reached his room. For a makeshift suitcase he grabbed his vinyl laundry bag, widened the drawstring, dumped the dirty clothes on the floor, shoved fresh clothes inside: a week's worth of underwear and socks, the thickest hoodies he could find.

He dumped the peanut butter jar he used as a piggy bank for fifty bucks in fives and ones. Shut his laptop screen, threw the cell phone charger in the bag, and searched for whatever else he needed. His brain thrummed too hard to think straight. He felt like a cat burglar raiding somebody else's house. His getaway car was waiting.

Shelves stocked with books, the preteen horror series he relished years ago, the thick fantasy tomes. Action figures posed atop books and his dresser and his nightstand, some still in their boxes. TV and Playstation, game boxes and disks spread all over the floor. Posters on the wall of *Cape Twilight Blues* and his mopey folk-rock heroes and, just to be ironic, Pink and Avril. His own prizewinning watercolors of alien planet landscapes—some displayed on the angled ceiling and some stacked on the floor. He left all of this behind.

In the kitchen he grabbed a bottle of Coke from the fridge and tucked it into his peacoat pocket. The jacket was his grandfather's from his time in the Pacific Theater, his grandfather who was pushing ninety in a Florida retirement home, who was not actually his grandfather but any random old man. But he was still a man Cal loved, so Cal couldn't just strip off the coat and leave it behind like the rest of his life.

Cal found a pencil and an orange stick-up pad and he wrote: *going away for a week—don't worry—I'm safe—love you both.* Peeled the note from the pad and stuck it to the fridge next to a note reminding his father about a checkup at the eye doctor. Cal knew his mother would call his cell the minute she found the note. She'd insist he come home and explain himself in person. And if he failed to answer then she'd call the cops.

How long before they tied him to his birth mother, how far they'd get—Cal couldn't know. What he did know was this: If he could stir a wild-enough crisis, then the Nowaks would have to forgive him. They'd be too damned grateful just to see him safe again. They'd forgive Jodie, too—maybe blame themselves for breaking her connection to her only son. And if not, then both of them could go to hell.

Poised by the front door, glancing through the blinds, Cal spotted movement. His adoptive mother jogged up the drive in her bright red tracksuit and her matching red headband, face all ruddy from her cold-weather workout. He locked the deadbolt to keep her stalled a few seconds longer, then dragged the laundry bag back into the kitchen and exited through the sliding glass door. Across the deck, then down into the yard, he cut a wide arc around the winterized pool. He hoisted the bag over his shoulder for balance, but its swollen end trounced the backs of his knees with every stride. He rushed and he stumbled but he refused—

Wynn crouched as the showerhead pelted his body and steam filled his lungs. Pain sizzled in his toes, his thighs, along the curves of his face. Fingers swollen red from an hour-long march through the winter, impossible to curl into fists. A continuous blood thread ribboned away from his earlobe wound, the shock that had prompted him to fire a gun.

Without a conscious thought he had killed them both. Their zero was too crushingly simple, a two-minus-two finished in a second's infinitesimal span, but it kept compounding every instant the universe persisted without them. They joined the formless void that was most of everything but couldn't be conceived.

Shampoo bottles cluttered the floor by his feet, soap scum coating the tiles, long red ribbon that curled toward the drain, and he pulled on its thread to see how far it would unfurl. Back in that trailer amid the bodies of his friends, Wynn pulled the trigger on his head and it fired and he died into this purgatory, or he was dreaming it like everyone, or some other dreamer conceived it by proxy, or the bullet stalled inside the chamber because time did not exhibit the property of movement. Nobody was shot, and everything was right as always.

But the revolver belonged to Dwight and Cecelia's father, kept in the lowest drawer of his dresser underneath old pairs of pants, wrapped in an oil rag. Dwight knew how to load the bullets, how to cock the hammer, how to clean the gun. He stole a Johnny Depp poster from Cecelia's bedroom wall and taped it to the fence rail, blew a hole through Johnny's forehead, collapsed into the grass from an attack of laughter.

Wynn lifted himself from the tile and his head swooned wide. He breathed steam, and the potential refused to give way to the actual. He could make it disappear. Tonight was backward-gazing ruin, but tomorrow was an early-morning math exam. Functions and symbols drew him away from Cecelia's blank eyes and Dwight's last heave. They were not his life and he told them so. They crawled behind him, up from the buried earth, still clutching at his ankles.

His fingers ached and itched but they bent enough to drag his towel from the rail and mash his face with it. Even with all this heat he couldn't stop shivering. He swiped one hand across the mirror to cut a path through the steam, and his own ruddy face glared back at him. The raw wound where the earlobe should be, the dead crescents of meat beneath his eyes, lips shredded white by his teeth. His was a face plastered on a post office WANTED bulletin.

Deputy Hartwick didn't know Wynn's name or where to find him, but in a city as small as Weymouth, how long? Eyes in this town, even on the campus—eyes that bled red light in emergency swirls. They'd barge in like demons with their blue skin and sparking Taser hands. They'd throw the siren wail from their wide-open mouths.

He pressed a wad of toilet paper against his ear, unlocked the door, and turned toward the common room with his towel wrapped around his waist. The sudden temperature dive wracked his nerves like a seizure. His roommate, Parker, was sprawled on the futon with a textbook spread open on his lap, sipping from a glass of red wine. Parker wore corduroys, a long black scarf, a beard, and he was a human rarity— one of only five philosophy majors on campus. When he first called math the language of God, Wynn believed him without condition.

"What happened to your ear?" Parker asked.

"Something—ice—some asshole threw an ice ball at me, over near the library bridge."

"Probably somebody from the rugby team. Quick—the equation for Zeno's dichotomy."

"My head is—"

"Just answer!" Parker demanded, toasting Wynn with his wineglass.

"The distance between point A and point B divided by two to the nth power, forever."

"The glass can never reach the mouth," Parker said. "I guarantee it'll be on the test."

"Probably," Wynn said. He almost tripped over the mini fridge on his way into the bedroom. He closed the door, kept the lights out, dressed in a pair of sweatpants. Across the room, Parker's laptop ran a constant slideshow of bright green Buffalo suburbia with boys in tuxes and girls with corsages, fishing trips, chess matches, a family posed with Egypt's pyramids in the backdrop, in blue rain jackets on the *Maid of the Mist*. Parker kept his life outside of school. The house where Wynn was raised was five miles off campus, but he didn't come from anywhere, especially not there.

Wynn's docked iPod played Nine Inch Nails, Reznor begging a plaintive question—*are you sure what side of the glass you are on?* Wynn's hands and feet were alive with itching, his stomach like an empty cask, numbers and blood on his mind. He lay on his bed, positioned near the single window. It overlooked the snowy span of campus below him.

To Wynn's own perception, this was the eleventh floor of a residential highrise with a view straight down the campus walk, where the spotlighted belltower rose from its vanishing point. In one potential existence, no cold made him shudder and no revolver made him shoot and no cell phone call from Dwight disrupted his study, and it was no more or less true than the actual.

He dialed Cecelia's TracFone number. His heart heaved with each ring. Her phone could be in her suitcase, in a drawer at her parent's house, swept under a booth at a diner somewhere, bagged as evidence in a crime-scene van. They could track his call if they wanted. Maybe there was no phone at all, just a voice-mail service, a mausoleum for her messages.

A betta fish in a glass bowl, won in a county fair ring-toss game and given to Cecelia. She was fifteen that night, and so dizzy drunk she spilled the fish on the hay-strewn ground. That winter she sprained her ankle in volleyball, and Wynn drove her to school to save her the shame of limping onto the bus with crutches. In his mother's borrowed car she told him her family was slow poison to those that loved them, always.

Through Wynn's dorm window the lights glowed in the lower rooms of other halls, from street lamps and the dim blue glow of the emergency phone boxes stationed at points down the line. The distance between each blue outpost was an eternity of dark intervals caught inside each other in a vicious infinite regress. The bullet's path was the same, but still it reached Cecelia's head.

She was dead but he wanted her to answer his call. Her voice said, "Never take it seriously, you never get hurt," then the beep and the silence where Wynn was meant to speak. He hung up and tried to let that broken line be the end. But one summer Dwight fell from a tree and broke his arm on impact. Wynn was still in the tree, clinging to a branch that the wind kept tossing. Dwight begged him to come down but he couldn't move. He could see the Kopecks' house from that height, Cecelia's bedroom window. There was a storm coming on, and earlier that week Dwight got them kicked out of Boy Scouts for making prank calls from the office phone in the church where their meetings were held. He didn't want to move.

Tonight the dorm window was a sealed pane that kept the winter out and Wynn inside and trapped the heat stirring up from the radiator. With the lights out he saw no reflection of himself in the glass, so he escaped the riddle of which side of the window was—

*   *   *

—ashen light every morning till spring. Bookbag on his back and a wool hat pulled low to cover the ear he dressed with tissue and Scotch tape, throb still needling down his neck like a rabid dog bite. Edgerton Hall auditorium, ten minutes early, Wynn watched others file in drowsy, mouthing their coffee cups. The professor with the unpronounceable Nigerian name came in and distributed blank test books, then projected the exam onto the overhead screen.

Wynn squinted to read the first problem: Provide the possible permutations of the following symmetrical polynomial. Wynn's thoughts tapered with the clarity of an incantation, and then reflected with a madding gleam where his pencil hit paper. The algebra paralyzed the moment with strings of unknowns until solutions arrived, and the heartache hazed back in. He rushed, but the answers all broke down to simple things. In his mind he saw the textbook pages the problems hailed from, like photo files stored in his head, like cheating, almost.

Wynn brought the completed blue book down the auditorium slope to where his professor leaned on the podium, glaring out at the class with the fixity of a border guard. The professor asked, "Do you have a *question*?"

"No, I'm finished," Wynn said.

"You signed the aca*dem*ic honesty pledge?"

"Yessir."

Students gawked. One of them had more erasemarks than work. On his way out of the auditorium Wynn realized he'd burned another full minute without thinking about the ache in his ear, that trailer in the woods, Dwight, Cecelia. The realization brought them back unfinished in time. His swollen hands itched ferociously, but he didn't notice until he slipped the pencil back in his pocket. He shot Cecelia Kopeck. He took away her mind and her love.

In the men's room he hunched over the sink and vomited clear mucous. The retching made his ear throb, forced hot blood through his jugular. In the mirror the shape of his face had changed—higher cheekbones and a thicker brow, like he was taking on Kopeck genetics, twisting into some version of their lost sibling. He'd stolen their face, their memories, and now he remembered not a single theorem to distract him from his fugue.

He needed the razor of winter on him again. In the main foyer the ceiling opened over a second-floor mezzanine, and a wall of glass showed the expanse of snow and naked trees outside. Wynn passed a coffee kiosk, a few café tables, but nobody was there except the bored barista and one girl seated alone at a table. He exited through the main doorway, breathed the crisp air, and pressed his hands against the stairwell rail. The cold shocked him straight. That girl he'd passed in the café—she was Erika Hartwick, the Deputy Daughter.

He pressed his palm against the ache underneath his hat. He saw Erika on a mattress in a bedroom with a bloodstained towel wrapped around her head, but it was Cecelia, another girl, nothing like Erika Hartwick. He substituted the one for the other like he was solving for a variable, like neither of them were girls but just two arbitrary, temporal manifestations of the abstract form: *Girl*. This was the language in which God spoke.

Wynn barely knew Erika. He'd blurted the lie to Cecelia just before she died: *I have a girlfriend. Her name is Erika.* At instants he was convinced of lies, and other instants bred new truths, but these flared and fled and then Wynn was right again.

Back inside the building, he ordered a coffee. He could bring himself to talk with her, with Erika. She was a terrible risk because her father knew his face, but that was exactly what made him feel he couldn't possibly ignore her. She sat alone at her table wearing an army-surplus jacket too thin for February. Her hair was knotted on the back of her head, crossed through with a pair of chopsticks. Her skirt was made from paisley neckties, rainbow leg warmers on her calves, kid's Moon Boots jutting out from under the café table. She read with her book spread open, chin on her arms crossed before her.

Wynn took his coffee to the self-serve counter, peeled open three packets of raw sugar, and dumped them into the black, chased the sugar with cream. He counted the swirls of his stirring straw and the clean, whole numbers settled him. She didn't lift her eyebrows until Wynn's shadow moved between her book and the sunlight. Keats, their literature homework, "Ode on Melancholy." She'd underscored lines with a red pen.

"Mind if I sit here?" he asked.

She jolted upright and scowled around at the other empty tables. She pulled her textbook up to her chest. Already Wynn knew he'd made a mistake, but he set his coffee on the table because whatever guided him was not his own will. Up close, Erika was flush and sullen, no makeup except her overdrawn eyeshadow. Pale and auburn-haired and squirming with discomfort, she could've been a high-schooler taking college classes. She looked nothing like Cecelia, but the old emotion surged across an invisible divide like the firing of a synapse.

Wynn nodded at the book. "I'm in your World Lit. My name's Wynn."

"Okay," she said. She grappled her book. She might've been thinking she could toss the hot contents of her coffee mug at his face if he moved too suddenly.

"If I'm bothering you or anything—" he said.

She shook her head and dropped her shoulders a little.

"You're local, right? Weymouth High School?" he asked.

Her eyes were so averted from him that she seemed to be playing some game. She muttered, "Two years ago." A hostile snarl, and suddenly she was a cop's daughter after all.

"I'm county," he admitted. "Boondock school, Lyme. Three years ago."

She chewed at the inside of her cheek and read Keats. Wynn strung numbers together to keep himself focused. Everything around him but Erika blurred. She wore a red scarf around her neck, and it was the center of things. He didn't want the scarf to make him think of blood or the swish of police light bars. He didn't want her to read him right and know his heart. She was the worst girl to accost like this, the absolute worst.

"You like that stuff, Romantic poetry?" he asked.

"Why not?" she said, two full words.

"I don't know. I liked that Indian one from last week better."

"The *Bhagavad Gíta*," she said. She looked pleased to lord her precision over him. He was probably some stoner slouch in her estimation, a redneck blight from the cabbage fields well outside of the city. Wynn's gut cramped at the thought of what she thought of him.

"I'm sorry I bothered you," he said. He jerked backward and the chair scraped the tile floor. He was nauseated again, tasted blood on his tongue. There was too much suffocating heat.

"Why?" Erika asked. "Why did you bother me?"

"I don't know. I saw a face I knew from class. I should've kept walking, right?"

Her expression was impartial, but she was mousy and baby-faced, so stern didn't suit her.

"Sor—" Wynn tried to say. He stood, but white lightbulbs popped in his head. Braced himself one-handed against the brick wall. The pain burst afresh in his ear and shot down along his jawline. The barista was serving another customer but stopped to leer at him. Wynn squeezed his hand shut but there was no gun there like he expected.

In an instant he was outdoors again in the crystalline cold where the steps leading down to the quad unbalanced him. He gripped the rail and felt the ice slicks beneath his shoes, and he concentrated on random decimals.

"Wind," Erika said. She stood two steps above, offered the coffee he forgot.

"Wynn," he said. He took the coffee and thanked her.

"Oh, I thought you said Wind. You all right?"

"It's just these sudden migraines I get."

"Maybe it's the coffee."

"Maybe," he said. "I have to go lie down in a dark room with the shades drawn."

"Moody," she said. She touched the chopsticks in her hair as if to check that it hadn't let down without her consent. She said, "See you in World Lit, right?"

Wynn said, "No, no, go not to Lethe."

"'Ode on Melancholy.' Funny." Her eyes drew downward to the crusted snow. She cracked a grin but aimed it at the salted concrete. Wynn's heart was still off the rhythm of the dance in his head. This girl whose father could ruin his life, she didn't offer anything that would help reverse Deputy Hartwick's knowledge or intentions. She couldn't tell Wynn anything, either. He forced himself into her presence when he might've kept walking. He drew her out.

It was because he understood functions, the ratios between like properties. Erika was someone new, but attached to old values somehow, still. She wasn't that other girl who had been primed to kill him, firing rounds that tore away a piece of his flesh. She wasn't Cecelia, who would've turned him into nothing if he hadn't struck the thick black hatchmark across—

The sign on Interstate 40 out of Cape Fear told them Barstow, California, was twenty-five hundred miles off, a jagged cut across the U.S. from the Atlantic almost to the Pacific. Almost, but it died in the dry Mojave like a cowboy out of water, just a couple hours short of the shore. Lucky Jodie and Calvin weren't headed that far.

Once, the boy was inside her womb. For fifteen years he was mostly out of her reach. Now he sat in her passenger seat so pent up with talk that he didn't seem to know what to say first. He leaned toward the windshield and gazed at the marshes and the towering stripped pines and the chunks of shredded tire on the roadside. He looked about to levitate.

Nero wailed, so the volume was raised on Nirvana to drown him out. Jodie didn't want to think that she also cranked it up so not to have to talk just yet, but there was also that. The first few things you say to each other were the riskiest.

She wanted to watch Calvin instead of the road that kept coming at her each mile the same as the one before. She wanted to get somewhere that looked new, where the Celica could merge with real traffic. Five miles overspeed was her limit, and every car that stormed up behind her was a state police cruiser until it veered past and turned out to be just some regular car.

Cal sneezed and she blessed him and he asked if there were any tissues.

"Somewhere, maybe," she said.

He searched, lifted a CD case and said, "Looks like you're a fan of Shakira, too."

"Them CDs are my friend Hector's. This is Hector's car."

"Friend Hector—like a boyfriend?"

"Not like a boyfriend," she said. "He's the boyfriend of a friend from work."

"Nice guy to loan you his car," he said.

Her answer was some croak deep in her throat, and she touched her neck as if she could shift her vocal cords back into place. Cal was already past the snag, watching a billboard come into view. He was a version of her with an Adam's apple, a more rugged face, mop of hair hanging over his face like an oversized eyepatch. But he was still familiar as the bathroom mirror. The resemblance kept her believing this reunion was warranted by some law of nature. Told herself she had more claim to him than the Nowaks, but the worry lingered anyway.

From a distance the billboard said JESUS SAVES, but closer it said JÉSUS SAVES UP TO 35% WITH FARMER'S SECURITY INSURANCE. *Hey-Zeus* was a grinning Hispanic with a sombrero on his head and a fan of cash in his hand. She couldn't help but think of Javier abandoned at a BP with a hundred dollar bill, the moment he finally stopped grinning like that.

"I'm sorry, but that's about the funniest billboard I've ever seen," Cal said.

"Kind of offensive," Jodie said.

"On so many levels."

"So I take it you're not . . ." but she couldn't word her own question right.

"I'm not so proficient with the whole blind-faith thing," he said, "to be honest with you." He reared back his head and sneezed like a whiplash into his fist.

Jodie decided against blessing him again, considering his beliefs, or his nonbelief. It didn't matter to her. She just liked hearing him say words she didn't know the meaning of, hearing him talk, no matter what. It distracted her from the fear piling up in her gut. Somebody would've already searched her apartment by now, noticed her gone, questioned her coworker Inez, and learned about the stolen Toyota. Strangers turning over rocks, sniffing what clung to the other side. A miracle she wasn't nabbed already.

"So I've been wondering how you found me?" Cal asked, sniffling.

"I waited near the busses. I seen you come out, but I couldn't—"

"I mean, find me in town, where my house was."

"The phone book from my motel," she said.

"Right, duh. It's not like my whereabouts are some secret, right?"

"No, but I didn't want to make trouble. I wanted to hold on till . . ."

"I didn't mean it like that."

". . . till I knew you wanted to see me."

"It's okay," Cal said.

Jodie held her breath as another car reared up behind her, a white sedan that could be a cop. At the last minute it swerved into the passing lane and sped on ahead. Dark was coming on as the stars lighted up, and it was still another hour to 95 North. The headlights lifted up to meet the road rushing at them. Every joint that joined her bones ached from days of nonstop—

　　　　—how long their fugitive run would last. The cash Jodie took might get ignored, a stolen car unreported, but a kidnapped child would bring hell down on her—Amber Alerts, state police, FBI, every quick mart and motel clerk and tollbooth operator who watched the nightly news. Consent means zilch at age fifteen. Same as abduction in the eyes of the law.

Jodie stood smoking on the walkway outside their motel room, second floor, unit door open a crack between her and Cal where he lay above the covers watching a rerun of that show they filmed in Cape

Fear. Teens whining at one another with rapid-fire talk like a Shakespeare play. Off I-95 north of Richmond, Virginia, even the McDonald's arches just across the street lost their luster this late. Inside the room, the thermostat stuck to a stifling eighty-five. She might've complained, but she didn't want to make any fuss that would get her noticed.

She also couldn't admit to Calvin that she didn't expect to get all the way to New York. The more likely future was her slumped stomach-down over the Celica's hood, mouthing apologies to Cal through the windshield as a Virginia or Maryland or Pennsylvania state trooper bent back her wrists and clamped down handcuffs.

Tried to resign herself to the shitty odds, but the idea of ending their time together that way was more unbearable than death. Crossing over into New York would be even worse. And there was no going back to Atlanta. She could maybe turn around and hit Cape Fear before dawn, drop Cal off and forget the whole dream. She could try to convince him to go back home, but she'd know every minute of that backward drive that she was denying him what he wanted. Better to have buried the idea in the first place, better for them both, except that Jodie never would've tossed away her mop-and-broom life just to find him and refuse him.

I got so much to tell you, Calvin, but I don't know how.

She waited for a commercial before she asked, "Is that one of the episodes you're in?"

"No, but anyway, they're blink-and-you'll-miss-me cameos."

"It's a famous show. Even I heard of it, but I didn't know they made it in Cape Fear."

Cal let loose a vicious sneeze that shook his bed and cracked the headboard against the wall. Skittish Nero leaped off Jodie's empty bed and broke for the open door. She stuck her foot in his way and hissed at him. He arched his back and ducked under the bed ruffles instead.

"You getting sick?" Jodie said. She worried that the seams were working loose already. Good moms buy disinfectant gel and Airborne tablets when they make their kids sleep on dingy motel pillows and sheets.

Cal said, "I didn't want to tell you, but I'm allergic to cats."

"Oh, God—I'm sorry—I didn't know." She stomped her cigarette out, closed the door behind her. When she sat on the edge of her own bed she saw up close how the rims of his eyelids were tinged red.

Cal said, "All I need is some allergy pills and I'll be fine."

"How come you didn't tell me? We could've stopped for something before."

"You said we needed to make good time, and I thought maybe I'd be all right."

"There's an all-night drugstore we passed. I can walk over there right now."

"In the morning, and anyway I need the Sudafed kind," Cal said. He headed for the bathroom, and when they weren't talking the hiss of the radiator sounded like a bomb fuse. All she could do was what Cal asked, knowing how wrongheaded, but holding back her worry for his sake. Suck it up, Jodie. Deal. You can't bear to quibble and besides you got no clout. Open up your veins if this boy asks you because that's what he deserves from you.

Cal came back with a handful of toilet paper shoved against his face. He blew a wet gust through his nose and left his mouth slack so he could breathe through it.

"All right, I'm gonna go get those pills right now," she said. "Seriously, Calvin."

"It's okay."

"Forget it. I'm going. Was there anything else you needed?"

"Maybe you—

—drugstore so late, pushed carts with kids asleep inside them, chattered in Spanish. Jodie kept hearing her own name in the mix:

That's her, the bitch who stole the car from Hector. She wanted herself out of sight, get back to Cal in the motel room, and what kind of mother are you anyhow, leaving your kid alone?

She grabbed orange juice from the cooler and found a plastic pet carrier in the household aisle. Nero would hate it, howl even worse than he did already, but at least the carrier would keep him and his dander confined. A man pulled a case of Bud Light from a promotional endcap and leered at her from under the rim of his baseball hat. He smelled like diesel fumes from an aisle away. Especially him, but really everyone here, looked to have the worst at heart.

In the medicine aisle she picked up a box of Claritin and read the back label, blinked to keep her raw eyes from burning. She took the box to the attendant on duty in the overnight pharmacy, a hefty Latina in a green smock.

Jodie asked, "Does this one got decongestant?"

"We stock the pseudoephedrines back here."

"You need a prescription?"

"No, but you need to sign for it. Federal regulations." The attendant pushed a logbook across the counter, and the sight of it made all Jodie's nerves throb at once. The other signers names, license numbers, and addresses were scrawled in handwritten columns. She glanced at the black half-globe on the ceiling and decided it was a security camera. She could just drop the OJ and the cat carrier and book it back to the motel, load Cal and Nero into the car, haul ass till dawn nonstop, span as much distance between her constant mistakes as she could manage.

With her left hand, Jodie grabbed the pen taped by a length of yarn to the logbook. She wrote out the name Mary Roja with the awkward jitter of a right-hander faking left. Then she panicked at how many digits were in a license number, scanned the prior entries to get a count.

"I'll have to see your license, ma'am."

"How come? I mean, if you don't need a prescription, then why?"

"I don't know. People use these drugs to make other illegal drugs."

"I didn't bring my license with me."

"Sorry, those are the rules." The attendant offered her a smirk as she arranged some empty bottles on the desk. Jodie dropped the pen and hustled her purchases to the front counter instead, anxious to leave before anymore ugliness—

—dark dirt-road shoulder seeped with oil. The powerlines moaned like the charge they carried was just too much. Each passing pair of headlights smeared her long shadow across the scrub grass. Like a vagrant, and maybe that's what you are, girl. She walked, smoking a cigarette, gripping the pet carrier by its handle, orange juice and the wrong kind of Claritin inside it.

The leering Bud Light guy from the drugstore walked the same roadside a minute ahead, shifting from shadow to solid as he crossed under the streetlamps. He popped open a beer can and slowed his pace like he knew she was following. Men alone, brooding angry men glutted with beer and amphetamines—they're what you find off exit ramps. Jodie walked half as fast and realized she should've taken Calvin's new bowie knife, the one she had no business buying him. Calvin was the legal son of decent people who wanted nothing to do with Jodie Larkin, people who flew thirty thousand feet over motels like this one where she brought him.

She stood like a woman waiting on a bus till the creep moseyed his way out of view. Either he lost interest, or he'd be waiting for her back at the motel, drag her into a vacant room and breathe beer against her skin, slit her throat with some glass shard. Alone in the night she prayed for a voice that would tell her just to get Cal to New York, then she'd understand how everything—

—past eight o'clock but Cal still slept with his fitted sheet torn from the corners and his bedspread balled on the floor, pillow clutched between his legs. Tissues on the nightstand told of his allergy attacks.

All night he'd hit the bathroom every hour to splash his face and stifle his coughing enough so that he must've thought she couldn't hear. But before dawn Jodie's mind was already made. She left him a note to say she went for doughnuts and was coming back soon.

Nero howled in his carrier on the passenger seat. She shushed him but he would not be shushed, and she couldn't blame him for his fear. A snow dust fell from the gray above. The speed limit dropped to thirty as the road dipped into a town so full of phone wires that they seemed all tangled on themselves. The strip malls offered local diners, a pet clinic inside a double-wide trailer on the edge of a parking lot. She pulled into a slot reserved for dollar-store customers because it was not within eyeshot of the clinic. On foot she hauled the pet carrier two-handed toward the trailer. Nero cried and reached a paw through the grated metal door. Jodie shut her eyes like she could dream herself someplace pleasanter.

She rang the vet-trailer doorbell and set the carrier down on the front stoop. A woman in a white lab coat answered the door. She didn't open the screen that separated the clinic from Nero in his carrier. She said, "We're not open until nine-thirty."

"I know, but I'm just driving through. I found this stray on the road last night—"

"Ma'am, we're not an animal shelter."

"Please, I got to be moving along."

"I'm sorry, we don't have the facilities."

"Please," Jodie said. She backed away from the stoop. Every time Nero meowed, her throat tightened more, and now she could hardly breathe. She turned away and rushed back to the car and refused to cry because Nero was just an animal. He wasn't a human boy she could love in clearer ways—ways like this, sacrifices. She'd been cruel enough already, torturing him with days of driving and strange alien places.

"Ma'am," the veterinarian called after her. "You can't just—"

Jodie watched over her shoulder to see if the vet followed, but whorls of lightweight snow were all that trailed her. In the Celica she cut across the parking lot, out of view of the clinic when she pulled back onto the street. Her eyes darted at the rearview and the silence in the car was uglier than Nero's worst—

—thumbed four quarters into a vacuum drum. The tube sucked with such force that the floor mats stuck to the nozzle, but Jodie scrubbed every seatback and headrest. The timer kicked off during the backseat cleaning, but most of Nero's fur was already gone. She sat in the driver's seat and laid her head on the wheel. Maybe she could go back and rescue her cat, maybe find someone, somebody like the Bud Light man from the drugstore, who'd sign for the stupid pills Calvin needed. But how could she face that veterinarian again, and strange men who help women expect—

—*because* the Nowaks wished Calvin no further distress, *because* they preferred he had space to grow—even though Jodie's time with him in Atlanta was rare, a weekend visit maybe once a month, all they would allow—*because* she was afraid to call and ask *because* they'd lecture her on the phone like they were her parents and not just Calvin's, twist her motivations into something worse than simply that she'd grown this child in her stomach and loved him, *because* truthfully they hated her *because* when Calvin was two she filed papers to challenge the adoption and *because* she'd just as quickly dropped her claim on the lawyer's advice *because* she didn't even care enough to follow through, just making trouble *because*—

—half a dozen in chocolate-covered, jelly, and cream-filled. She bought herself a large coffee with double cream and sugar, and Cal a large hot chocolate she wasn't sure he'd like. Jodie took a chair at a café table underneath the awning outside the doughnut place. She set down the drinks and the doughnut box, pulled a cell phone from her pocket, flipped it open. When she turned the phone on, the T-Mobile chime introduced a display screen. It was a headshot of an actor Jodie recognized from that Cape Fear TV show. After a minute, the phone sang again to announce new voice-mail messages.

She pressed the mail button and held the phone to her ear. Ten new messages, the first from 4:49 P.M. yesterday. It was his adoptive mother's voice—"I just got back from running. What's this note you left on the refrigerator? It doesn't make any sense. Please call me back—" and it proved what Jodie already knew, that Cal lied about asking the Nowaks' permission to leave for New York. Of course he lied, just like Jodie pretended to believe him, a pact they couldn't speak out loud or it would lose its magic.

Cal hadn't answered any of these calls or listened to the voice recordings. She closed the phone on those nine unopened messages and threw it into a nearby trash bin. No choice, unless she wanted to chance getting flagged by some satellite system, or however it was people's cell phones were found. Calvin had belted himself into the passenger seat and Jodie had to match his commitment. He would have to understand how her every single move was for the sake—

The teletherapy machine looked like a giant microscope with Jill's bare head on the slide. She couldn't move, and her stillness looked too final for Sam to bear. He left Radiology and found an *Us Weekly* in the hospital waiting room, sat down to browse pointless paparazzi shots of celebs without makeup. Three silent elderlies sat across from him, shivering and dozing off.

On TV a mobile reporter from Buffalo begged Sheriff Olin to release information about the overnight double murder in Lyme. It was a two-minute tape of Olin standing in the snow outside Cassadaga County Public Safety telling the reporter he couldn't tell her anything. Down the hall Jill lay stretched out on a table with a heavy bib across her chest. The machine thrust an invisible beam into her skull, adjusted itself at intervals as it pounded its rays against the glioblastoma buried deep in her brain.

The pharmacy bag in Sam's pocket contained three refill bottles, all steroids to combat the radiation side effects. A hundred dollars over what insurance covered, once a week. For years Jill stalked their bank account like an online guard dog, checking refunds and overcharges, cross-referencing receipts. She didn't do it anymore. Already too much grief to juggle all at once. Their priorities were: medical, Erika's tuition, and to hell with whatever else. Costa Rica would be funded by Visa, ten years of high-interest repayments clipped from Sam's salary alone. The house wasn't his to sell. And the funeral—

Sam's hands wet the folds of Us Weekly. He studied the bags under
Teri Hatcher's eyes and wondered why celebrities never got sick. An
orderly wheeled Jill out of the hospital exit and Sam fell in behind
them, shrugging on his winter jacket. He took over the handles and
thanked the orderly away. Out in the pale sun Jill touched her neck
with her fingertips and arched her chin skyward. She exhaled a long,
hot breath and watched it steam away. They both watched it.

"Let's stop at Gracie's before we go home," she said. "I want to see if
I can manage a bacon slice before the nausea hits." Her face was so
gaunt it set Sam's heart to wailing. She stood up from the wheelchair
with only a slight wobble and refused the balancing arm that he offered
her. She was the very shape of her own skeleton, but he could still imagine her as she'd been six months back, twenty pounds overweight, lush
hair spilling over her shoulders like scalloped frosting on a cake. No
wig could come close, so at home Jill wore a handkerchief on her skull,
called herself Rosie the Riveting. The wool cap she wore outside was
knitted for her by their daughter, a Christmas gift.

Gracie's was a ten-minute drive and Jill was still steady when they
parked the Nissan. Inside they took a window booth with a view of
Central headed down toward Gulliver Bay. The diner was across the
Erie and Central intersection from the courthouse and the Public
Safety Building, so it catered mostly to uniformed cops, attorneys, and
court clerks. Sam knew most of the cops, colleagues who'd contributed
days to his vacation fund so he could get a month off with his wife. Jill
knew the clerks because she'd been Andrew C. Bannister's paralegal up
until the end of December. She could've asked to eat somewhere else,
to avoid the familiarity, but the Pig & Chick Breakfast Basket was just
two bucks, had been since forever.

"You're keeping it bottled, Sam," Jill said from opposite him in the
booth.

"I'm not hungry this morning," he told her. He grappled a black coffee with both hands. Jill had a large ice water and a breakfast basket,

though she'd only eaten the bacon. The sunny side of her egg leaked its liquid shine along a sliced edge of untouched toast. She couldn't seem to gauge her own appetite anymore, caught between the nauseating radiotherapy and the ravening steroids she took to quell the edema.

"I mean those murders," Jill said. "You're not talking it out with me like you should."

"You don't want to hear about it, plus there's not much to say. Brother and sister shot each other point blank, simple and stupid as that."

"You said you were the first on scene, right? You found them?"

Sam nodded into his upraised coffee cup. Two uniformed cops sat together at the counter over Jill's shoulder, but they were out of earshot, bantering with a waitress.

"So talk it out, Bozo. You forget our debriefing routine?"

"Honey, this kind of stuff is standard by now. Not murders, obviously, but I'm saying car wrecks and elderly shut-ins. You see it often enough, you know?"

"So you're immune all of a sudden? You're the rock-upon-which-we-can-stand?"

"What's wrong with that?"

"I'd like to think—" but she cut herself short, laid her napkin over her breakfast as if to cover the goriness of it. Their legs were laced together under the table, though she seemed not to realize she was clamping his calf with her shins.

Sam said, "These are strangers. I don't have time to brood over their bad business."

"I'm sorry. You used to want to talk about it, that's all."

"And you appreciated my griping?"

"If it helped you deal with—"

"Well, you need to learn to deal with it on your own sooner or later."

Jill squeezed her own left wrist as if to steady it. She said, "I'm feeling sorta puke-ish."

"I'm sorry," Sam said.

"Well, Mom and Dad are headed back next week, I guess."

"Flying? Did they ask you if you wanted them around?"

"Out of Phoenix, and I didn't have to ask them anything. They already decided. They rented out the trailer for the rest of the season, even before they told me. I just—I wish they'd have said something before they came up here again. I don't want them wasting all that money on plane tickets, I just don't want to screw up everybody's plans with my stupid—"

"Jill—" Sam said. They were already sliding out of the booth, Sam with the check and a ten-dollar bill in his hand. He hurried her toward the exit, like a lawyer guides a client through the press gauntlet. Strangers could probably read them easily, this couple caved in upon themselves, eking life out of months instead of decades. A sharper wound than anything Sam could've dealt to himself, or Dwight or Cecelia Kopeck or anyone he'd ever sparred with.

They paid, and Jill plucked a peppermint wheel from the bowl before she beelined outside. In the overcast light her face was ashen. She vomited in the row of bushes beside the Dumpster while Sam rubbed circles across the back of her padded jacket. When she stood, he pressed his handkerchief against her chin. Her cheeks were flushed the same shade as her hair had been. She squeezed the mint from its plastic cell against her teeth.

"What a goddamn spectacle I am," she said.

"Nobody saw."

"I don't want to go home right now, Sam. I'm tired of lying around there."

"You don't have to."

"I do have to. Everybody's standing around waiting for me."

"Nobody's standing. Nobody's here yet."

"They'll be here. Everybody's going to come by and watch me." She bent her head back and sniffled. The few stray snowflakes flittered against her eyelids while she watched them descend.

"Tell them not to come," Sam said.

Jill scoffed and reached into his jacket pocket for his key ring. She unlocked the car with his remote, started across the lot. For a moment Sam didn't follow her. Sometimes his thinking—he knew no better word but *constipated*. Nothing he could dream to say would comfort. It was all static when he tried, or rash notions he wouldn't dare speak aloud, like asking if Jill's parents were in contact with her sister, if they'd told her Jill's prognosis. He kept quiet, jogged ahead, and held the passenger door for her while she settled inside.

They sat together as the car warmed and Sam said, "Erika's focused, on school."

"She's always focused. At the moment she's withdrawn."

"From you, too?" Sam asked. "I thought it was just me."

She gazed out her passenger window at the county jail wing of Public Safety. Some guy stood at the chain-link fence out front with his hands pressed against the wire like he longed to get inside. Sam had a mind to drive over and chase the idiot away.

Without looking at Sam, Jill asked him, "What did those people look like last night?"

"What people?"

"The ones who murdered each other," she said. "I don't mean the gruesome details."

"That's all there is."

"I just want to know what to be that close is like. What you see if you're looking."

"I think whatever's there to see is gone, Jill. That's what's so tough to look at."

"Let's just drive," she said, "but not home. Take me out into the country."

"What country?"

"Out where you patrol, I don't know. I want to know what you see every day."

"You're throwing up," he said. "Don't you want to lie down and rest?"

"I don't care about that. All I want—

—where the creek bed crossed under the road, pair of thin iron rails to mark the bridge. The limit dropped to forty past a housing enclave before the country route dipped back toward the wooded southward stretch and the Pennsylvania border. Out here the yards were cluttered with snowbound construction equipment, the open-air porches used mainly for junk storage, tarpaulin to keep out the drafts.

"This place is . . ." Jill said.

"Mainly a dump," Sam said. "I do yard citations out here more times." He didn't know why he'd brought her here, like offering a confession he couldn't put into words. He slowed the car and pointed at a house upcoming on the left. The paint on the siding was chipped like a puzzle with missing pieces, buckling porch beams and a boarded second-story window. "There," he said. "Those two kids that died last night? That's where they lived."

"My God," Jill said. She grabbed the door handle and squeezed her fingers over Sam's thigh. Her touch jolted his foot against the brake and the car skated for an instant on a sheet of compacted snow before catching.

"Watch it there," Sam said.

"I'm sorry!" She was almost gasping.

Sam eased the car along the roadside. Exhaust fumes licked white plumes across the driver's-side window. A man at the head of the Kopeck driveway stood full-garbed for winter, face tufted with a beard, shoveling snow like a caretaker breaking ground. Sam figured he was probably the father of the deceased, the victim of an early-morning death notification visit from the CCSD, now ten hours past.

Jill asked, "Sam, what are you doing?"

"Give me a sec, while we're out here," he said. He left her inside the car and straddled over the snowbank barrier to get across, stepped into buildup high enough to bury all the eyelets on his boots. Anchored himself on the steep driveway with each new footstep. Above, the shovel scraped, and Kopeck grunted with it. Sam had his badge clip out of his back pocket. He said, "Mr. Kopeck, I'm with the Cassadaga County Sheriff's Department."

Kopeck quit his labor and propped the shovel handle upright and leaned his elbow against it. He said nothing, but his blank regard made clear that Sam had his attention. In a downstairs window the curtain drew aside and the woman behind it was mostly obscured by the frosted glass. She might've been a ghost for all Sam knew. He'd served death notice news to near a hundred families, chatted with pederasts still stoked on the their rape thrills, won staredowns with drugged Neanderthals, but the Kopecks stonewalled him like the cold, blank slab bearing God's final judgment.

"I'm here about the—"

"The police been here already, you know," Kopeck said. "Right this second I'm getting my driveway cleared 'cause I got to go down to Weymouth and identify them. I'm just trying to do what you people already told me to, Detective. What more do you want?"

"I understand, sir," Sam said.

"So's this a change of plans or what? I'm not eager to go down there. I'll be honest."

"No change," Sam said. "I just thought I'd take a minute to run— some of the details."

"It's my gun that's missing," Kopeck said. "Chief's Special. Dwight took it from my bedroom yesterday, but I didn't see until after you was here this morning. That gun is licensed if you need to look at the papers, but I can tell you it's mine. I had no goddamn idea, or else I never would've had it where he could get to it."

"Can you say—do you think he left with the intention of harming your daughter?"

"Kid's intents been mystifying me for ten years, so *you* tell *me*."

"You're not surprised by what he did, then?"

"It ain't hit yet. I guess it must hit when you get down there and you see for yourself."

Sam caught the scent of hard liquor as Kopeck sneered down at Jill in the Nissan. The man had to know Jill wasn't a fellow *detective* sitting out the interview. She looked much too sick for the role. From this perspective, Sam realized the starkness of her cancer more sharply than ever, a chill all the way down to his soul, and urge to total confession. But if Kopeck was suspicious, he didn't ask for Sam's name or credentials, didn't ask since when plainclothes meant ripped jeans, hiking boots, and a flannel jacket.

"Did Dwight and Cecelia have any mutual friends?" Sam asked.

"What's that?" Kopeck said. He puckered a cigarette in his lips, cupped his hands around it, but the match wouldn't light in the wicked wind.

"Did they share any of the same friends?"

Kopeck looked toward the house, but his wife wasn't there in the window anymore. He said, "You know the both of them ain't been around here too much. I don't know where they been staying lately, honest to God. Celia 'specially. Dwight come around for dinner sometimes, maybe once, twice a month, does some laundry or gets me to tune his car engine. What'll happen with that vehicle of his, anyhow?"

"It's evidence now. Afterward, it'll revert to you, I assume."

Kopeck nodded like it was more bad news. The unlit cigarette twitched between his lips.

Sam said, "This'll hit you as a strange question, but we've got reason—"

"Shoot," Kopeck offered. "I don't got nothing to hide from you or nobody."

"Were any of Dwight's friends you know of, any of them fond of

Cecelia? Maybe an old boyfriend of hers, somebody you could say had romantic feelings toward her, or somebody she had feelings toward?"

Kopeck stiffened, tossed his head to the side and grimaced at the audible crackle his neck made. He said, "Christ, everybody loved her," like he was knocking down an ugly rumor.

"I understand that," Sam said. "But romantically is what I'm getting at."

"No, I don't think. See, Dwight and Celia ain't really run together since they was kids."

"How about anyone from back then, when they were younger?"

"Hell, I don't know. I work six days a week. I frankly couldn't tell you."

"Maybe your wife?"

Kopeck rubbed his sleeve under his nose and sneered again. "She don't want to talk."

"I understand that, Mr. Kopeck, and I'm sorry to be bothering either one of you with all of this. Maybe you have a school yearbook? Senior yearbook, Dwight's or Cecelia's? If I could take a look at it for a minute, it'd be an incredible benefit."

Kopeck gazed at the house across the street where shimmering silver insulation boards were nailed to beams already blackened by fire. In the car, Jill was reclined with her eyes closed. Kopeck said, "What's this to do with anything? The guys who came here this morning told me my two kids killed each other, which is hard enough to think about without all this shit about who's got what feelings. They had me to believe the situation was pretty much the situation, and there's nothing else. So are you here telling me something different?"

"I think someone might have information on a motive, Mr. Kopeck."

"Motive? They was a brother and sister who hated each other. Dwight stole my gun."

"I'm not trying to tell you something different, Mr. Kopeck. All I'm saying is that there were some other people involved last night, people who ran off when they weren't supposed to, and those people need to be held accountable for what they did, too."

"What'd they do?" Kopeck asked.

"It's what they didn't do, mostly. They didn't try to stop it."

Kopeck eyed Sam like he was steeled by a sudden doubt. He held the shovel at his hip by its neck and strained his faltering grimace. His nod was weak at first, but it gained momentum. He said, "Whatever you think'll help you, I got no objections."

Inside, the kitchen linoleum crackled under Sam's boots. In the stairwell hung two shadow portraits of boy and girl children, just black silhouettes on white paper. Sam waited in the upstairs hall while Kopeck rummaged through a spare storage room. The furnace heat forced through the vents with a roar, but Sam could still hear a television shouting somewhere.

"This what you wanted?" Kopeck said. He handed Sam a thin volume with a school seal embossed on the cover. The binding was filmed in a fine green mold that preserved their fingerprints as it passed hand-to-hand.

"It is," Sam said. "Got a light up here?"

Kopeck thumbed a push-button switchplate at the head of the stairs. Sam opened the yearbook to the inside leaf where a few other students had scrawled notes to Dwight, most of them obscene. One in careful feminine script read: "Your a great guy Dwight. Have fun this summer!!!—Emily." Someone else had added "fucking me" as an addendum to Emily's note, smack between "fun" and "this."

Sam flipped to the senior-portrait section, a mere two-page spread for the entire graduating class, fewer than thirty kids. Dwight was bottom row on the first page, unshaven and unsmiling. The portrait was probably taken the same winter Sam arrested him for possession. This could've been the mug shot, if not for the gauzy studio glow. Nothing but years between this disaffected punk and the guy with the runaway sister he desperately wanted to find. Nothing different about the Dwight Sam spoke to in church, except the trace of an awakened soul. But Sam now felt himself alone in noticing the change—alone, or else flat wrong.

He recognized someone else on the same yearbook page, a kid with the expression of a knifepoint robbery victim. He was the one from Dwight's car, though his hair was cropped much shorter in the photo. His name was Wynn Johnston—block letters that couldn't be any clearer, any easier. Sam glared at his picture for a moment, committed name and face to memory, then shut the book.

Kopeck sat on the edge of the staircase landing and smoked his cigarette for real. He sat, aware of what life on the other side of a loved one's death was like, but Sam didn't dare ask him to describe it. He didn't expect Kopeck could give a meaningful explanation anyhow. Maybe on the day when the truth about Sam's involvement spilled out into the city like a toxic leak, Kopeck would let him know exactly how it felt to grieve.

"All set," Sam told him.

"Get what you were looking for?"

"No. Just a hunch that didn't have much merit. Appreciate it, though."

Kopeck didn't respond, but he took the yearbook back and made room on the staircase for Sam to get by. The steps creaked enough to make Sam wince, and halfway down he turned back toward Kopeck. The man was still seated on the landing, holding onto his bony knees with the cigarette jutting between his knuckles, frowning at the black silhouettes of children mounted on the wall.

"You headed down there now?" Sam asked.

"Near about. I'm just trying to work myself up to it. Hell, maybe it ain't even them they got down at the morgue, just some mismatch. Cecelia's right now probably drinking margaritas on a beach in Mexico for all's I know."

"You all right to drive? I could bring you down there," Sam offered.

"I got to get the truck shoveled out anyhow. I'll be sweated off by then, Detective."

The step under Sam's feet weakened as he weighted it, and the handrail wasn't much steadier. Kopeck stood, and Sam's sense of balance was thrown reeling. When the heat vents kicked off, the cheers and electronic pings of a gameshow took over. Sam wanted to tell Kopeck what he knew about Dwight, wanted to sugar the guy with lies about sensitive information and the need for secrecy, especially when speaking with other departmental personnel, but explanations and evasions wouldn't make—

—through the wraps of her knitted scarf, "Maybe this wasn't such a hot idea." The wind on the shoreline surged in violent gusts, though the lake stretched flat and listless while it gurgled on the slate beach.

"Come on, winter just gets a bad rap," Sam said.

"I'll take this over nothing. Not to mention in two weeks we'll stroll better beaches."

Sam pressed Jill against his ribs as they swayed their faltering rhythm on the pebbles and grit. They hadn't made love in fear of that same bad rhythm, though Sam choked a weird urge to make love to her right here in the freeze like they were still teenagers. He knew he'd reach for her hair, forgetting, and when he touched her scalp she'd flinch away and remember how she didn't feel like the same person anymore, and that would be the end of it.

They passed boulders fit for sitting, but the chill kept them on their feet. The beach was a tier below the ground above it, broken by a bank of eroded soil and jutting roots. It went on this way for three more miles, northward toward Gulliver Bay and the energy plant beacons pulsing in the haze. Two weeks, and their view would be coconut trees, palm-thatched cabanas instead.

"I messed up," Sam told her. He lifted a rock, tested it in his palm before he hurled it at the lake. Jill's tumor was smaller than that rock and just a few inches inside her skull. If his fingers could pass through matter he'd reach inside and rip out that mass by its roots and then none of its awful pressure could change them anymore. He said, "I held back last night because I was afraid of what the news would do to you, and I realize that was wrong. I just didn't want you to have to deal with anything else right now."

She pulled the scarf away from her face and said, "Sam, what are you talking about? We're not supposed to have any secrets."

"I know, I know—which is why I'm telling you."

"Telling me what?"

"Those two kids. One of them was Dwight Kopeck."

She furrowed her eyebrows at him. "Who?"

"Dwight's the guy who's been coming to church lately, praying about his sister."

"Oh my God," she said. "The one you were talking to? The re-formed guy?"

"Yeah. It was him and his sister who got killed."

"God, I feel horrible for joking on the phone last night." She eased herself onto the rocky ground, slow enough to hide the ache he knew she suffered. "But why did you think I couldn't handle that news?"

"I don't know. We were praying for him to find his sister, and then he does, and this."

"So, I think I get it. You didn't want this news to shake my faith in prayer?"

"I guess. And he was a member of our church. You get to know people."

"How's your faith in prayer holding up?" she said, and dug her bootheels into the bed of flat gray slate. A sudden gust caught a length of her scarf and wrung it midair.

"I don't know, frankly," Sam said.

"If you don't tell me the things I need to know, you might lose your chance, understand?"

"Yeah," Sam said.

"We've never been through worse shit than this, and we've had some mighty loose stool in our day."

"I know. I'm sorry, and I should've knew you'd be a hell of a lot stronger than me."

"Help me up," Jill said with one arm raised. She was much too easy to lift, but her legs wouldn't assist her effort to stand. Sam pivoted around to face the lake, crouched with his arms turned backward and his hands on the insides of her knees, too fast for Jill to resist him. She squealed when he hoisted her piggyback, squeezed her arms across his collarbones. She said, "You're going to throw out your spine."

"I'm fine," Sam said. He found his footing and marched them back toward the car.

The warmth of her body shielded him, even through all their clothes. She brushed her lips against his ear and said, "You better not hurt yourself because I intend to take you zip-lining in a cloud forest, and I don't want you crippled. It's my wild fantasy, so I dictate. And if you lie to me again, I'll cripple you myself." She pecked him on the neck with a kiss to punctuate her threat, and Sam dreamed them soaring over a lush canopy in a sinless paradise without any horizons. Two weeks he needed to get them on that flight, and nothing past that moment—

You're a liar but so am I. Calvin Nowak and Jodie Larkin, who claimed—no, who *was* his mother, plain enough for anyone to see. In the mall outlet where they stopped to get Jodie a winter jacket, just off the highway in a D.C. suburb, the cashier said to them "your son" and "your mother" when she addressed them. Cal noticed how the assumption made Jodie slouch and shoegaze, as if their resemblance to each other was an embarrassing fluke.

Cal grit his teeth against the bitter wind as he crossed the outlet parking lot, settling for his grandfather's peacoat that was supposed to withstand any bad weather. Inside the car they ate takeout McDonald's with the waxpaper wrappings spread open on their laps, streaked with gory gobs of ketchup. Jodie watched everyone who drove or slogged past the car. The species of snow hitting the windshield was like nonpareil sprinkles.

They'd spent hardly three hours on the road, a late start after the Nero fiasco. Jodie had claimed the cat darted through the open door earlier that morning when she went to get breakfast. A plausible story, except that the pet carrier was also AWOL, except that she noted wistfully how Nero's escape was just as well, considering Cal's allergies. Calvin apologized without knowing why. She stepped out every few minutes for a cigarette, and together they carried out a charade in which they pretended the cat really had run off. They waited till noon checkout for Nero to come back, but nobody was surprised when he didn't. For Cal's sake, she had abandoned Nero, and Cal did nothing in return except pretend that he believed her explanation.

On the road they talked ninetie's bands—vintage for him, nostalgia for her. Music Cal loved was once the soundtrack for Jodie's teen angst, and so it seemed that he grew an ear for The Cure and Ani DiFranco while still in the womb. They could chat music forever, but after hours together in the car she'd still cleared up none of the discrepancies that dogged Cal's mind. He felt he knew her less than when they escaped Cape Fear the day before. So now, over a McDonald's lunch, he said, "I know Nero didn't run away."

Jodie drew a long sip of Diet Coke through the pinstriped straw. He knew his question was a sucker punch with kid gloves, but he could've accused her of much worse—like how she'd obviously ditched his mysteriously missing cell phone, how this car she supposedly borrowed from an Atlanta friend had North Carolina plates, how she'd settled for the allergy pills you didn't have to show your license to purchase.

"You got rid of the cat because of my allergies, right?" he said.

Jodie set her unfinished hamburger down and wrapped it back up. "I brought him to a vet who promised to take him to the shelter. Cal, he hated being in this car all that time, and I don't got nowhere to bring him when we get to New York."

"So you weren't planning to take him back home?"

She shoved some French fries in her mouth and chewed them down before she talked. "Well, my lease ran out. I don't even know if I'll be going back there. My job—they want me to call next week to see if they still got work, but I doubt it. I didn't leave on very good terms."

Cal couldn't bring himself to ask her about the car and its alleged owner. Less than halfway through a long northward trip and already the truth felt less vital than the myths that would get them there: A woman on a week's vacation takes her son to revisit their hometown with the permission of both his adoptive parents, all documents and licenses valid and accounted—

* * *

—broke the D.C. rush-hour sludge somewhere past Rockville, then shot northwest across the Mason-Dixon with no more fanfare than a pavement downgrade. In darkness they skirted the battleground where thousands died and where a president spoke words Cal had to memorize in eighth-grade social studies. He wondered what he'd missed in school all day. He wondered also how desperate his parents had gotten by now—whether Dad cancelled his classes and Mom her marathon training, whether they went to the police, how long they took to deliberate the reasons before they guessed that his deadbeat birth mom might be to blame.

The Nowaks' worry beset Cal like it was carried to him by satellite. He could find a pay phone, but nothing he might say would calm them down. Give Dad two minutes and he'll boomerang you on a guilt trip straight back home. Cal was vulnerable to their persuasion because he loved them, though not so much in terms of emotion. He was a stray they'd taken in, and his every warm memory had their homey glow about it. Just one day behind him and already his refrigerator Post-it felt like a cruelty his parents didn't deserve. They'd done nothing wrong that they could've grasped the injustice of.

Roadside signs urged ice-conditions caution. The sticky, wet snow-fall built slush on the borders of the windshield. Jodie drove with hyp-notic focus, leaned toward the wheel like a daredevil psyching herself for a ramp jump. Every moment they didn't speak was a waste. She exited just north of Gettysburg at seven o'clock, just past a car that had jackknifed against a guardrail. The accident scene was cast with spin-ning blue cruiser lights, and it seemed like enough warning to con-vince her to get off the road.

She bypassed the name-brand motels for a local dive with dim lights and a fleet of pickup trucks in the parking lot. She didn't do this for the bargain, Cal understood. It was because she didn't want them logged on databases or caught on surveillance tape. They had a dire need to stay nameless, meaning they had been on the run since the minute they left Cape Fear, or else she'd maybe already been running before she found him.

He waited in the car while she checked in. She came back from the main office and stood by the passenger door, gesturing for him to open his window. The knob wouldn't budge because the window was frozen shut. He pushed the door open and a tuft of snow collapsed against his knee. Snowflakes drove down at a steady slant. It looked to be a storm, but with none of a storm's sonic barrage. It was silent, creeping.

"They got all king size. One big bed," Jodie told him.

"That's okay," he lied, and worried Jodie might decide in some maternal fit to spoon him in his sleep. She hadn't touched him yet, not even a hug. He supposed she never would, or that he'd cringe and squirm from her grasp if she tried.

Their room stank like ashtray. Brown water stains rippled across the ceiling, darker stains piddled the carpet, but the bed looked clean enough once Jodie ripped away the paisley comforter and shoved it into the closet. The fiberglass flooring in the shower bowed under Cal's bare feet. He kept thinking any second he'd fall through into some cellar space where gorilla men in butcher's smocks would rend his limbs with cleavers and sell the meat to a local takeout.

When he came back out with a towel around his waist, he saw that Jodie had their dinner laid out on the bed, Chinese food in paper boxes with generic Buddhist temple prints. They were in a room with the deadbolt locked and the curtains drawn.

"Feel better?" she said.

Cal fumbled for the pajama pants he'd packed inside his laundry bag. To see her on the bed sitting Indian-style with a box of chow mein cupped under her mouth, to see her plastic-cup cocktail of Coke and coconut rum. Something obscene about the food, the booze, and Jodie's communion with it all. He didn't want to stand bare-chested before her, so he retreated to the bathroom and pulled on the pajama pants and an Interpol band T-shirt.

When he came back out she handed him a box of sesame chicken with the tabs already open. He knocked the saucy chicken chunks around with chopsticks. She said, "You ain't allergic to Chinese, are you?"

"No, I'm just no good at chopsticks."

"Neither am I," she said. She leaned across the bed and grabbed the plastic cup, took a gulp from it, shuddered, and said "yikes." The rum seemed to make her aura lighter. She didn't twitch quite so much, didn't tilt her ear toward the noise of every car passing on the road, every voice in the room next door. Even the winter storm warnings crawling on the TV didn't faze her.

"We might need to hunker down for a day," Jodie said.

"Bad timing."

"It's fine. Sucks it ain't summer or we could go to Hersheypark. It's pretty close."

"Can I have a sip of your drink?" Cal asked.

"Oh—it's got rum. I got more just Coke—or, you can have some of this, I guess."

"I won't tell my mother," Cal joked.

"Well—here—" Her drink cup was actually two cups packed together. She laid down the empty cup and poured in a shot of rum, splashed Coke over the top, mixed it with a chopstick. She handed over the fizzing—

—wet handful swiped from the buildup on the windshield. Jodie ducked behind the Celica's trunk as Cal's snowball sailed into the white expanse that stretched across the lot and merged with the street. They were both in hysterics. Cal's hobbled consciousness took slow orbit in the inch of ozone around the surface of his skull.

Jodie burst from hiding and lobbed a shot that clouded into snow dust before it reached him. Bad balance sprawled him backward across the hood of a nearby sedan. His arms flailed a disfigured angel as stars sprinkled down low on a visit for the night, and Cape Fear and its inhabitants blackened off the border of his map.

"You okay?" Jodie asked. She shoved her face into his. Her drunk eyes were marbles dipped in oil. She grappled his arms with both her hands and lifted him off the hood. Everything about his mother's electrical current and her motion fascinated him.

She said, "I can't believe I got you drunk. You ever drink before, or did I corrupt you?"

"Beer sips, somewhere—a party. Nobody noticed."

"I'm the terrible mother monster menace," she lamented.

"No," Cal said. He put his icy hands against her cheeks. He wanted to press his fingers through her flesh without any pain. She hissed at the cold and contorted her face and knocked her forehead against his. They stood together like that, teetering like exhausted dance marathon contestants. The white steam from their lungs came together. The world's entirety was the space between their faces.

"What is—what you want to find so much in New York anyway, huh?"

"I think I'm there, I want to meet everything."

"Don't you dare say father because that's too much—"

"You don't know him?"

"—I know him too much, see? That's why we're always quiet and far away. Tell me—"

"I don't know why. I want to look in a mirror I never saw before."

Somewhere close was muffled music and voices, laughter from another motel room. She said, "We can't go backward to Atlanta. I took money and this car—"

"The car has North Carolina license plates, I saw," Cal said.

A harsh light cut between them, and the music clarified into a rap-rock snarl that wrenched Cal's teeth all out of whack. Others stood nearby, four or maybe five men and the blinking cursors on the tips of their cigarettes. One of them said, "Don't let us spoil your little shindig." He was a shirtless shaved bear, and he blew a puckered kiss.

Jodie hunched over and scooped snow into a pile. Something was happening, but Cal couldn't figure what, except that these hefty men were pressing all the gravity back into the night. They spread themselves out like a football team on the line of scrimmage.

"Let's go back inside," Cal said.

Jodie grunted as she pitched the snowball, arm in a wild pinwheel. It burst bull's-eye on the shirtless man's naval. The men around him guffawed, and Jodie joined in with such glee that she leaned forward and propped her hands on her bent knees and puked a liquid that splattered at her feet, and then nobody was amused anymore. Cal laid his hands on his mother's shoulders.

"Your girlfriend's a real class act," said somebody.

Shirtless already had his own snowball prepared. He flung it with a sideward arc and it smashed Jodie across the top of her head. She kept her face lowered, though she slapped the slush from her hair and grunted, either "thank you" or "fuck you." There was more cackling than could possibly hail from the number of men Cal counted.

He helped Jodie upright and urged her toward their room. Another snowball detonated against the back of his jacket. A third slapped itself against the doorframe, the unbroken half of the ball still perfectly round. He fished through Jodie's coat pocket for the room key, then steadied his hand to get it into the lock. Once inside he drew the chain lock. Snowballs barraged the door. Jodie was on the floor covering her ears with her hands. She tucked her knees up against her face and knocked her forehead against them and said, "I'm sorry I'm sorry I'm sorry."

Someone called out in a mock-kid's voice, "Can little Johnny come out and play?"

"We're calling the police!" Calvin yelled.

"Little pig, little pig, let me in. Not by the hair on my ten-inch Johnson."

The door creaked with the weight of several men—Cal was sure of it, like he knew the chain lock would snap like a costume necklace if one of them decided to shoulder the door. There was a peephole but Cal didn't dare set his eye against it. He sat down on the bed instead.

"Do it," Jodie said, "call the police."

"I can't. You stole that car, and my parents—"

Just outside there were tattooed men with handkerchiefs on their heads who could break inside any second and beat them both, hold Cal down and rape him, and the demented, dizzying threat made his nose flare up with fresh pain from the damage Gene's slap had caused.

"No wonder your parents hate me," Jodie said. "Look at this mess."

"I'm the one," Calvin said.

"I'm a grown-up. Put you in danger. What am I doing?"

She slid woozily along the wall and brought the telephone handset against her ear, managed to press nine before Cal lunged over and tapped the switchhook tabs.

"Please," he said. "I want to keep going."

"This snow is for a reason," she said. Her eyes were swollen raw.

Cal said, "Snow doesn't have reasons."

"I can't understand," Jodie said. "Tell me why."

"It's a pilgrimage, that's all."

"You're talking circles on purpose. New York is nothing, no difference, but I want what you want. What kind of mother is that?" She slapped both palms over her face. Cal was relieved to have her grimace concealed. Outside the men's grunting had quieted, but still the tension that choked Cal's body persisted. Jodie rolled across the bed and crushed the empty food cartons they'd left there. He touched her hair with his fingertips and thought—

* * *

—pay phone under a streetlight in the China Express Kitchen plaza. Cal had to brush the snow off the unit before he lifted the handset. He typed a number and a robot voice asked for two dollars in change. Cal fed the coins and watched the road where only his wavering shoe prints marred the solid expanse of snow. Across the invisible street, the cars in the motel lot were all white mounds like a row of fresh burials.

"Who is this?" The bleary voice of someone just awakened.

"Mom, it's me."

"Calvin, God—where are you?" Her stupor turned sharp at an instant. Cal heard the click of light switches, caught his father's nearby mutter.

"I just wanted to say I'm fine. I'm not in any danger, so please don't worry."

"Calvin, your father—"

"I'm sorry I worried you, but I'm fine. I'm alone, but I can totally take care of myself. I'll be home probably in a week," he said, then he eased the phone back down on the cradle. His change shimmered down into the return slot like he'd won some gamble.

He despised his own tactics, but he knew how the call would've played if he kept on the line. Dad would take over with a prepared plea that would slice clean through the façade. Cal would be at his mercy, homeward bound on the next Greyhound.

The silent blizzard had already softened his shoeprints into divots. Cal cleared the lingering drunk from his head and thumbed his return change right back into the machine. Punched another number he knew by rote, this one with an Akron area code. His best friend Burt Dwyer answered his cell phone on the second ring.

"I didn't recognize the number," Burt told him.

"Because I'm calling from a pay phone."

"Where the hell are you, man?" Burt whispered like a conspirator.

School night, so Burt was probably in bed already, his parents asleep.

"Have you heard from anybody—my parents?" Calvin asked.

"Yeah, you could say that. I'm supposed to call them if you try to contact me. They thought you were coming here for some reason."

"I didn't tell anyone that."

"Well, they wouldn't believe me that I didn't hear from you. They thought we hatched some secret plan or something. What's that about?"

"Just because you're my friend, I guess," Cal said.

"Nobody believes me. The freaking police even showed up randomly this afternoon to interrogate me, man. You got everybody scared shitless. So where are you?"

"Jesus," Cal said. "Relax. I just talked to my mom a minute ago. They know I'm okay."

"But do they know where you are?" Burt persisted.

"I'm in Pennsylvania," Cal said. His teeth chattered when he tried to talk. A regretful bile of Coke and rum and Chinese food surged into his throat. He imagined Burt perfectly toasty in his bedroom under blankets, floor vents issuing furnace warmth, and he wished he could be there beside him without all the complications.

"Are you by yourself?" Burt asked. His voice was deeper than two years back when he left Cape Fear, hardly recognizable. But hearing it now, Cal supposed all his current angst was traceable back to Burt's move.

"I can't talk about that now," Cal said. "But I'm close to you—not far."

"Why didn't you tell me you were coming? It's cool you're this close, but. . . ."

"I didn't know. It's just this crazy—forget it. What're you near that's in Pennsylvania?"

"You mean like Pittsburgh?"

"Come meet me in Pittsburgh. How far away is it?"

"I don't know—like a couple hours, but how the hell am I supposed to get there?"

"Take a bus, easy enough. I can meet you at the bus station tomorrow night."

"I have school, Cal. It'd take like four hours."

"Forget school. You know it's been two years?"

"This is seriously nuts."

"So you're not coming?" Cal said.

"I didn't say that. If I can figure out how to do it I'll be there."

"You don't know how important it is—what I need to tell you."

"Like what? You sound like you're drunk or something, man."

"I need to tell you in person." Cal yanked at the ringed metal phone cord. He wanted to tear out the phone unit and hurl it onto the motel roof, dropkick the glass from all the windows. Don't tell me again about that Akron debutante you kissed at the school dance, Burt, or I swear I'll slit my own neck and drop dead at your feet. I brought myself into this blinding snow for you, and no other reason matters.

Burt said, "You just spring this on me, dude. I'll try to see what I can do, but everybody's interrogating me and giving me the stink eye. This is seriously nuts."

"Promise me."

"Dude, don't start—"

"Goddamn it, *promise* me."

Burt scoffed over the phone line. "That's so convincing I can't even believe it."

"All right, all right. Sorry. Just please try. Tomorrow night, okay? Just be there."

"How come you're not answering your cell phone?"

"It's gone. I'll call you tomorrow afternoon and we'll make plans for sure."

Cal hung up before Burt could cast around his doubt again. Give Burt some time to mull and he'd see that they were magnets dragged too far apart. Cal sensed more loudly now than ever that relentless drag. Resisting it had led him into such rash acts, if only to distract from—

The ice glistened on the coiled razor wire. Wynn laced his fingers through the chain-link and watched the lot behind the county jail, spiny weeds grown waist-high in snowbeds. The jail was a brick façade no different from a dorm hall. Behind him in the municipal lot, prowlers and unmarkeds were parked among civilian cars.

A woman deputy came out from the station, and Wynn took his hands away from the security fence. She ducked into her vehicle and sat for several minutes, punching keys on her laptop. There was a shotgun mounted on the cage behind her head. She might've been downloading a description of him even then, the perpetrator in the Kopeck killings.

How it might unfold: The cop rises slowly from her open door frame, gun already drawn. She tells him to lie down on his stomach in the frozen sludge, and a sudden overwhelming ease sets him down like anesthesia. But it didn't happen that way. After a few minutes the deputy drove her patrol car out of the lot and past Gracie's Diner across the street.

Wynn pressed a fist into his churning stomach. To quiet his mind he divided his own birthday by Cecelia's, carried it out by five decimal places. He could march himself into the public safety building and lay his bare wrists out on the counter and say, "I'm the one." He had leverage on a crooked cop and a self-defense excuse. He had an overdose of remorse. But when he stepped toward the entrance, a suit stormed out pumping a briefcase at his hip. Wynn turned away, watched the suit cross Erie Street and shuffle up the steps of the courthouse where fates like Wynn's were decided. It would be no better inside that jail. Dwight went to county lockup once and said the inmates smelled like they were already dead.

Downtown Weymouth, Central and Erie and the square brick buildings—the Polish club, the veterans' post, the Greek restaurant. Gulliver Bay boardwalk was one block away, all the food stands closed down this time of year, the lake rimmed with ice to the far edge of the pier.

Cecelia was on that pier in cutoff jeans and a bikini top, doing cartwheels over the planks while a swing band played tunes on the Ricardo Seafood's lawn to the smell of beer battered fish fries. While Ce-ce danced, Wynn held her mint-chocolate-chip ice cream sugar cone and let the green strands melt over his fingers because he didn't dare—

—class already done. Students slung backpacks over their arms and filed out with their cellphones open, tapping codes into number pads. They dialed for help, but only for themselves.

Wynn sat with his textbook spread open to the Romantics. He circled the numbers in the margin, the lines of poetry counted off by fives. The poem in question had fourteen—a sonnet, a bout of wild worry tamed with meter and rhyme, Keats's "When I have fears that I may cease to be."

Across the room, Erika slid her book into her messenger bag. They were the only two students left in the room, them and the professor wiping his markings off the board. The hum in Wynn's chest spiked, but it formed no words he could speak aloud. She hugged her bag to her chest and left the classroom.

Wynn followed her down three flights and through the exit where smokers clustered with their cigarettes. He closed the span as she crossed an ice-crusted parking lot. This was not the direction of his dorm. The distance between them was the length of a railroad car, and she turned once and saw him as if she'd sensed his attention somehow. Then she slipped on the ice, crashed on one hip and two hands. Her satchel skidded away from her and underneath a parked car.

Instantly she scrambled upright, brushed snow dust and salt from her petticoat. She stood tightfisted with her eyes clamped shut, like she wanted to will herself somewhere else. Wynn was already there on one knee, braced against the car's back bumper while he fished for her bag.

"You all right?" he asked.

"Yeah—stupid," she muttered. She took back her bag without meeting his eyes.

"They need to salt these lots better. I slipped five times this week already."

"Embarrass. Ing." She squinted skyward as if trying to decipher a word in the clouds.

"Don't be. It's these lots. They don't salt them nearly enough."

"I'm not—I'm—okay. Okay?" She stepped over the curb, onto the public sidewalk that was only partially plowed. She wore a knitted hat with tassels, matching mittens. Her cheeks were flushed from the cold and Wynn was scared that he wanted to touch them, because she looked hardly older than thirteen in all that yarn, and because she was Sam Hartwick's daughter.

"Mind if I walk with you a little?" he asked, though he was already matching her pace.

"Where are you going?"

"I don't have any more classes today," he said.

The cars passed in their white clouds of exhaust. Erika said, "Your headache is gone, and you learned to tolerate the Romantics." She knelt and adjusted the Velcro strap on her boot, stood up, and then quickened her stride. It was like every few seconds she forgot Wynn was beside her.

"If I'm making you uncomfortable—"

"No," she blurted. "Probably the opposite."

"I'm making you comfortable?"

"I meant you—I'm making you—"

"Okay, but that's not true, either."

She heaved a long sigh that died fast in the cold. "I liked what you said back there."

"Back where?"

"In class. That Keats used poetry to prepare for death, and memorialize it even before it happened. The first comment you've made all semester, I think. Granted, he called you out."

"And how many have you made?"

"A million in my mind," she said. Another smooth ice patch carried her right boot through a sudden glide, but she grabbed Wynn by the crook of his elbow. He anchored himself in the crusted snowbank to keep them both from slipping. His bones shivered where she gripped. He wasn't wearing anything worthy of this frigid cold. She righted herself, slipped her hand away. She said, "Sorry."

"Nothing to be sorry for."

"These boots—there's no traction. I can't even walk."

"How old are you?" Wynn asked. "It's not related to what you just said."

"Twenty. Believe it or not."

"I wasn't trying to insult you or anything."

"All right, so—good-bye," she said, and she cut away from him across a driveway.

"What?" Wynn said. It was a white Cape Cod with blue shutters, pristine compared to the damp and sagging student apartment houses across the street. He didn't understand what this place was supposed to be. He'd let his bearings lag.

"My house," Erika explained. "So what happened to your ear?"

"Piercing mishap," Wynn said, touching the bandage with his fingertips. The impulse to blurt out some confession itched around the interior of his skull.

"Ouch." She stood on the topmost porch step of her house, her father's house. Two cars in the driveway, one of them a Maxima wiped clear of snow. On a night-shift schedule, Deputy Hartwick would be off duty in the early afternoon, so he was most likely inside the house, maybe even watching through a window at what his daughter dragged home. The winter sun glinting off the glass wouldn't let Wynn see for sure. If Wynn stood long enough on the threshold, then maybe Hartwick would appear in the doorway behind his daughter, and then what—

—felt himself falling through on endless repeat, molecules dissolving, electrons flinging and skittering in bodiless freefall. On his cell phone, Wynn listened while Cecelia's voice told him again to never take it seriously, never get hurt. He left no message for fear his howl would ricochet against the void and strike him back with tenfold intensity.

Among the stacks on the second floor of the Paulson Library he rushed the aisles like a father in search of a lost child. The shelves were on runners with digital controls to spread them apart or crush them together, the breadth of human knowledge in numerical code. He wanted to be caught inside it all forever.

The last aisle stopped him at a mezzanine balcony that overlooked the lobby. Banners hung from the high ceiling, replicas of medieval tapestries, monks inking their illuminated manuscripts. Erika Hartwick came through the library entrance turnstiles. She slid her student card and pressed her hip against the bar and she was cranked through.

She raised one hand as if to take an oath, and some sector of Wynn's brain tingled in response. She was waving up to him and he was oblivious. He'd been staring through her like some scavenger bird on a high branch, but now he hurried toward the main staircase, careful not to run because the speed would propel him beyond his own control. He had no place in this quiet collection of pure reason arranged numerically by subject, spine-to-spine and onward ad infinitum. His underarms dripped and his eyelids stung. His hair was erect, like the arch of a tomcat cornered in an alleyway.

She was at the circulation desk feeding books into the return slot. Wynn's heart seized. He unzipped his jacket and pressed his knuckles against his sternum and this seemed to help set the beat right again. She turned and saw him and threw her glance at the floor and then chanced another look at him again.

"Three Wynn sightings in one day," she mused. "You're getting kind of weird."

"I saw you," he said, "but I was zoning, and I didn't wave back. I'm sorry."

"I figured." She fussed with her bag strap, thumbed it off her shoulder an inch.

"I'm sorry if—it looks like I'm stalking you."

She shrugged. "You were here first. Although technically I'm here pretty much every night, before play practice."

"*Alice in Wonderland*? You're in it?"

"Costume designer, makeup artist, actor psychiatrist. Nothing glam."

Even though their talk was hushed, it carried in the quiet. She squirmed and still wouldn't look him in the eyes. She took a tentative backward step when Wynn didn't seem to have more to say. He wanted to tell her anything, that Lewis Carroll was a mathematician, but whatever he could think was inane.

She said, "Well, see ya."

"Okay, yeah."

She headed up the stairs he'd just descended. A crescent of snow fell from the heel of one boot and melted on the carpeted stair. Wynn felt a weight in his hand and it was the Chief's Special revolver. He stood in that cramped trailer room and he shot his best friend in the chest, brought the gun to his own head. Maybe this time he squeezed the trigger hard enough, and this was death.

In this death Cecelia took the form of another girl Wynn could touch no more than he'd ever touched Ce. Ideal forms like the shadows of things cast by flames, untouchable abstractions at the root of all matter. At the source of creation, everything the creator imagines, is. Who dreams who in the looking-glass world?

He considered an open computer among the clattering of keys. The *Weymouth Post Online* would give coverage of his crime, probably even *The Buffalo News*, but at this moment of reckoning he wanted to see none of it. He knew what would happen if he looked. He'd notice a code, like every sixth letter in the article text would spell out his name: W-Y-N-N-J-O-H— Or in the classifieds would appear a veiled message from Sam Hartwick: *Keep your mouth shut, surrender, stay away from my daughter.* So he turned away from the computer lab.

Upstairs, Wynn found her again by the sight of her rainbow leg warmers and boots. She was seated at a study carrel screened on three sides by a divider, so he approached and peered over the divider lip. She studied an open textbook with a silver flask on the corner of her desk, cap off, like an inkwell. Whiff of vodka. Wynn's shadow cut the fluorescent light from the paneled ceiling and overlaid her book.

"You scared me," she said. "I thought you were the library police." Her eyes were liquid enough to prove she had already been drinking from her flask.

"Are there library police?" Wynn asked.

"I don't know." She scrunched her nose to keep her reading glasses from slipping. She was huddled inside her private space like a caged rabbit, and she wanted to be left alone. Looming over her like this was wrong, he knew.

"I was leaving," Wynn said. "Back to my dorm. Just thought I'd say bye."

"Okay," she said. She offered the flask toward him. "Nightcap?"

"No, thank you."

She flinched like her usual self.

"I don't have anything against it," Wynn explained. "I'm just not—" He couldn't explain this sharpened state of his. The overhead light had an electric smell and the vodka fumes rippled like heat waves across Erika's face. The library silence crawled around in his ear canals.

She sloshed the contents. "It helps me concentrate. As of late."

"It's a cool flask, anyway."

"My dad's. He really is police—but for the county, not the library."

"He let you have it?"

"Oh, *let* is too technical a term. He lost it when he found Jesus, and hasn't been inclined to search ever since." She pushed her book shut and it was just another anonymous library volume with its dust jacket removed. She stood and slung the strap of her satchel over her shoulder. Her reading glasses had slipped down to the end of her nose, and she was nothing like Cecelia, nothing at all.

"When is your birthday?" Wynn asked.

"September. Why?"

"The date, I mean."

"September twenty-first, nineteen eighty-eight."

Wynn imagined the string of numbers—09211988—and what could be done with them. Lows and highs on the ten-scale and nothing in between, like peaks and valleys. They resisted his urge to reach to their square root: 3035.1256975 and onward beyond what his mind could contain at one stretch.

"It might be a surd," he said.

"Okay, what's a surd?"

"A voiceless quantity. It's another word for an irrational number."

"I'm pretty much a math retard," she said.

"An irrational number is one you can't actually explain because it doesn't have an end point. You'd be saying it forever. Inside of every tiny little space between rational numbers are an infinite amount of surds, like the dark energy that flows between particles of matter. The Greeks were afraid of surds because they were signs of unimaginable chaos, but almost everything that exists or potentially exists or can be imagined is made mostly of surds."

She said, "Yikes. You're into numerology? Like kabbalah, Jewish mysticism stuff?"

"No. I was just interested. Some people think math is the language of God."

"Which is exactly why I can't make sense out of it." She walked with one finger pointed at the literature shelf as she mouthed decimals, cross-referencing the call number on the book she held. Wynn followed and watched the numbers emerge from her mouth.

She slid her book into the space where it belonged, and its presence brought the books around it back upright. She said, "I was afraid you might try to tell me my fortune, but I already know. That's why I bear the flask."

"You know?" Wynn said.

"Well, medical prognosis. My mother has terminal brain cancer. Lucky her, lucky me."

"Jesus," Wynn said, and he felt the thought of it bloom outward from the center of his own brain, pushing the soft gray maze against the skullplate. Though she didn't move, Erika seemed to drift away from him.

"Yeah, I'm trying all I can not to crash and burn with my classes and life in general. That's why I liked what you said about Keats fortifying himself against death with poetry."

"There's no actual justice," Wynn heard himself say.

"I appreciate you, Wynn. You care to know my numbers. I've had too much to drink and I've said too much, and I don't think I'm going to be any sort of delight to be around—even though I'm flattered by your semi-stalkerish—well, I thought you should know. Balls—I sound like a bitch."

"No—"

"Please don't take me too seriously, okay?"

He watched her mouth move while she talked, the upper-lip snarl at every stressed syllable. The smell of books and the proximity of so many imagined realities. The cold sharp fact of her mother's mortality—it was more than Wynn could bear. Flashes of Cecelia's blood-soaked towel, Dwight's shirt with his name stitched on the breast pocket, all of it red-stained.

Flashes of Cecelia years ago in the baseball dugout as she leaned over to kiss him. The strain through time, like a trail of lit gunpowder running from kiss to kill to kiss again. He had Cecelia's face in his hands, kissing her mouth even as it moved to speak. His own lips pursed and closed, but hers were loose and unresponsive. They tasted like vodka.

"I didn't expect that," Erika said. She stepped backward against the shelving. Her reading glasses were still on her face, but tilted where he'd pressed his cheek, smudged on one lens. She was watching herself slide her mittens back onto her hands.

"God, I'm sorry. I got confused," he said.

"I didn't expect that," she repeated.

"You don't have to leave," he said. "I was going. I didn't mean—" but his mouth was too dry. He backed away from her and she would not regard him. He scampered down the steps to the first floor and the way out was through—

—huddled in the elevator eleven floors high. He was in some tower halfway to God. In the dorm room, Parker sat upright on his bed, his girlfriend beside him. They were clothed but reeked of sex. Their faces went static for an instant, like a glitch on a television image. Wynn dropped a bag at the foot of the bed. The curl he'd twisted into it bore the imprint of his fingers.

He said, "That's a six-pack of Foster's. Enjoy." Conscious of himself wheezing from the bite of cold air. He'd jogged straight across campus from the StopGap gas station on Central.

"What's the occasion?" Parker said.

"I need your car. A couple hours, tops."

"Aw, damnation. For starters, it's low on fuel."

"I'll fill it—all the way. All I need is a couple hours and I'll owe you forever," Wynn said. He scratched furiously at his neck, along the carotid artery that ran from—

—abandoned, police tape across the door, no cops in sight. The Beetle heaved through potholes and Wynn bit his lower lip until he tasted a coppery tang. The CD in the player was a John Lennon collection, and the song was "Working Class Hero." Three doors down from the trailer, the park lane circled back on itself, and as Wynn passed around again he saw from this approach the window he jumped through the night before, the woods he disappeared inside.

He kneaded the steering wheel until his hands cramped. The frost crept in from the corners of the windshield, and what seemed to be the truth was just one variant. What seemed like time was a relative curve of the always already. Wynn listened for the gunshots because he could conceive another view of himself outside the center, a witness. He watched for the muzzle flash in the bedroom window. He waited for the killer to drop from the sill and stagger toward the cover of pines.

He flinched at the blast and saw Dwight's name patch printed on the insides of his eyelids. The two thugs rushed from the front door—that bald-headed bouncer with the wine-stain face, the one with lip sores. The Beetle's headlights caught the doubled scars on the ground where spinning tires had sliced through the snow and spread wet mud. They were gone already, those men who murdered Cecelia.

Wynn saw her in cutoff jeans with the pale pocket bottoms peeking out below the seam. She could not be made to sit at a classroom desk. Senior year she forced him to watch underground animal-cruelty DVDs. She was suspended from school for spray-painting the FFA conference lounge with *meat is murder* in dripping red. There was someone else in her skin when she died.

He knew he could find those men. There were places he could go where their names and whereabouts threaded together with scents he could track. He saw a blood-soaked towel twisted and wrung till it was thin as rope and dribbled its liquid no more. He was sure he saw them shove Cecelia into the backseat of their car. They carried his love because they weren't done with it yet, never done until—

She plucks bits of broken glass from her face while she holds a newborn with its bald head tucked under her chin. As gray smoke billows from some nearby forest fire, she rushes through the woods. Roots snag her toes and oak propellers spiral down from treetops. She chokes on smoke-poisoned air. A stern voice booms the weather report— snowstorm approaching, in some areas two-foot accumulations. The baby's a pillow and Calvin's a tree trunk shifting in the dark. He stands bedside in the blue television glow chanting "wake" and Jodie obeys. Where is?—a hotel room in Gettysburg, Pennsylvania.

"What time?" she asked.

"Like two A.M.," Cal said, "but we should get moving."

She was clothed and sprawled above the covers on a motel bed. The last clarity before sleep was men pelting snowballs at her skull. The balance of her brain wasn't right. The rum had done that. She'd gotten drunk alongside her son. She poured his drinks herself like some lousy chaperone, some shit mother, and she was. Bile on her tongue and bright hangover hurt dawning across her brain.

"Where's my . . ." but she couldn't think what.

"Everything's packed. If we leave now, we can hit Pittsburgh before the storm."

"But it's already bad." She sat up and the ache pulsed through her sinuses.

"It'll be worse tomorrow, and we can't stay. And—I called my parents."

"Jesus," she said. "Can't they trace the number?"

"Probably. You don't have to drive. I have my permit and I practiced stick shift before."

"But we drank too much. If we get pulled over—"

"I'm fine now. It's all burned off, trust me. We get pulled over we're screwed anyway."

Jodie pressed her knuckles into her eyes and considered Pittsburgh. The last time she was there, her trip shot her straight southward through West Virginia, down into Georgia, all those years back when she found a place in Cobb County north of Atlanta and took a grocery-store job, when she broke the news to the Nowaks that she was staying long-term. Watched their welcoming warmth go suddenly cold. *We tolerated your visit, but we never said you could stay, young lady,* their faces told her. You don't cross people like that because—

—poor Nero in a pound somewhere tonight. Jodie guessed she'd be caged herself before long, somewhere like the Albion Correctional Facility, where all New York's most dangerous molls wound up. Or maybe she'd be shipped back to Georgia or North Carolina when they caught her. She didn't know the workings of the law in such matters.

What she knew was riding shotgun in a stolen car with an unlicensed kid at the wheel, stuck behind a dump truck as it plowed snow onto the shoulder and rained salt in its wake. The salt crackled across the Celica's windshield, and Jodie could almost taste it on her tongue. The road flanked the edge of the frozen Susquehanna and the factory stacks jutting up from the far opposite bank. Radio-tower red lights blipped behind the white static snowfall. She thought: *nuclear winter.* Hadn't heard the term since school, but here it haunted her, here where Three Mile Island was someplace nearby, close enough that the End of Days never seemed nearer.

"Pittsburgh's way off," Jodie said. She had a road atlas folded open on her lap, but she could read it only in split-second spans when they passed under streetlights. The Pennsylvania map was so vast that Harrisburg and Pittsburgh were on opposite pages, and none of the routes between them were major.

The car fishtailed around a bend and shuddered over roadside gravel before righting itself. Calvin shot her a guilty glance but kept on driving. The slip reminded her that only a guardrail and a breakable sheet of ice kept them from the river bottom. She caught her breath and said, "We hit any unplowed roads, that's gonna happen worse."

She hated doubting him out loud. Learn to put faith in Calvin or else all my choices this week are moot, put faith in him because my own senses are all dead, put faith, since cops are probably already searching the motel room we just ditched, and if not for Cal they might've caught me there drunk on the bed dreaming of babies I never raised. Faith, because I join this boy after five years apart and there must be a reason we're skidding ice tonight. Cal had pulled her back from the living dead—not because he was hers, but because he was hers raised by others to turn out right and without resentment.

"Tell me something about yourself you never told anybody," he said.

"That's everything, because nobody ever asks."

"I'm asking."

"You go first," she said.

Cal pulled the tab that sprayed fluid onto the arcs of salt residue and the wipers spread across the windshield. The road ahead went clear for an instant, and then flecks started to mottle the view again. He said, "I've told you pretty much everything about me already. It's a short story."

"You got a girlfriend?"

"Ha. Go for the throat, why don't you? What about you?"

"I don't got a girlfriend. Not much time for dating men, either."

Cal pretended confusion, tilted his head at her like a pup thinking through a command.

"I was joking about the girlfriends, in my case," she said. "I don't got anything against people like that. There's a lot of them in Atlanta, and couples from different races, everything."

The snowplow truck routed down a sideroad and its rumbling trailed away from them. Now the Celica drove alone, the heater on high to keep the cold from creeping inside. The dashboard lights flickered dim as if the electric was eager to stall, maybe twenty miles up the road when they would be totally snowbound outside town and no place to go.

"This is a problem," Cal said. The unplowed street hid itself under the flat white stretch between reflective roadside markers, cut only by a single pair of tracks. The car that made those tracks was just twin taillights cresting a distant hill ahead.

"Just keep it slow and steady," she said.

"But what if someone in your family really was a lesbian?" he asked her.

"Let me tell you I'm nobody to judge. I'm like the worst person of all to judge."

"Why's that?"

"Somehow we're back to this whole tell-me-something-about-yourself-you-never-told."

He kept his hands at ten and two and drove with an unbroken focus. Jodie pressed her fingers over his wrist and said, "You're doing great." She was thinking no chance they'd be trucking all the way to Pittsburgh tonight. Worrying how to break the news to Cal, where else to weather the storm instead. But for the moment she just wanted to listen.

"I'm not saying I'm the most normal person in the world," he said.

"You don't buy your coffee at Starbucks?"

"Not exactly. The in-crowd eludes me."

"That's all right. Fuck 'em," she said, and forced a chuckle.

Cal didn't seem to get the joke. "I'm trying to tell you. It's more than just a cultural thing. Granted, I don't flow with status quo, but this is deeper than that. On the molecular level."

"What do them Nowaks got you into? Do they worship the devil?"

"It's got nothing to do with them. Or Satan."

"So tell me," she said.

"Maybe—" he started, but the back tires skated across an ice patch and drifted too far right. He throttled the wheel to set the balance right, but the Celica went into a spin and aimed its headlights across the river and the smokestacks beyond.

"Calvin!" she cried. The coils in her ears went haywire. She pressed her hands against the dash and locked her elbows so that her arms were the spinner arrow in a kid's board game whipped so hard the blood rushed to fill her fingertips and then when she couldn't think beyond the topsy-turvy outlines the passenger window burst and something brought the car full-stop at the finish of its three-sixty spin.

"You okay—Mom, you okay?" Calvin pleaded. He popped his seat belt, he pawed at her face, and his pressure was too much. He said, "God, I'm sorry—I'm sorry."

She touched pulp where her cheek should've been. It was instant stone-cold sobriety. She said, "We need to get out of this car. Right now, we need to go." She popped her doorlatch but the mechanism was busted from its impact with the guardrail. One headlight was dark and the other burned under the snow that swallowed them. She said, "Cut the engine, Calvin."

"I'll drive it out," he said. He cranked the gearshift into reverse and stomped the clutch.

"The car's stuck," she said. "Open your door."

He wasn't hearing her bid to swipe back control. He spun the tires and they screamed inside their divots, then lurched the car into deeper snow. He said, "Jesus, come on!"

Jodie twisted around, reached toward the backseat. She grabbed the nearest luggage and hauled it close, but her wrist sent out bright flashes of hurt. She tucked her arm against her chest while white, woozy static sizzled across her body for an instant. She was alive—maimed and bleeding, but alive.

"Come on, come on," Cal demanded, revving the engine.

"Stop it," Jodie told him. Headlights and a swirling caution light glinted in the rearview mirror. "Next person who drives past—we're gonna end up caught. You want that to happen?"

He killed the engine and thrust himself out into the snow. Jodie tossed his bag and then her bag and he caught them both. She crawled into the emptied driver's seat where her son's hands came to guide her through the door. The wind rocked the car like a gang of vandals but Cal was there to raise her upright.

Her right arm throbbed from fingertips to elbow. She wanted to drop to her knees and quit, but the oncoming plow was targeted to bury her in its swash where she stood. Cal slung both bags and grabbed her uninjured left wrist, dragged her across the road through the approaching headlight beam. Their footsteps dragged against the dense snow while the plow razed across pavement toward them with its diesel chug.

The roadside opposite was a slope climbing into a stand of pines. Cal was wrenching her toward it. Flush beside them the truck halted with the hiss of brakes, and the driver loomed in his open window, nasal voice and wool hat leaning outward. He said, "You guys all right, for Chrissake? Anybody else in the car?"

"We're fine," Cal said.

"I radioed dispatch—" Driver cut himself short the instant Jodie straddled the guardrail.

"Come on," she grunted at Cal, but he was already past her, trudging upside the hill.

Behind them the driver yelled, "Hey, hold up!" He beamed a high-powered flashlight against their backs, just kept the beam on them like they were a spotlighted circus act.

Leaf beds slick under the snow caught her steps and slipped them backward. She clutched for roots to keep from sliding back to the road. The wind was so ruthless it widened her wounds. Her bad elbow dragged across bark, and the pain of it wrung her ligaments into knots. Hair in her mouth and her mouth tasting blood and Cal nowhere she could see, though he said from above her, "Jodie, I hear a siren. We're almost at the top."

She groped for branches and brush that could help her onward. Even the flashlight beam was losing its fight, cut apart by trees and distance. Finally the treetops drew their jagged border along the skyline. The slope eased flat and the ground carried them more gently, enough that they could break into a run, at least until the snow sunk deeper and the dark blocked their sight.

New lights glittered up ahead, but they seemed miles off. She lunged toward a cluster of boulders, found the largest, wiped the snow away, and planted herself there. With a crooked finger she swept the snow from the lips of her sneakers where it numbed her ankles.

"They can follow our tracks," she said.

"What?" Calvin said. He hunched with his hands on his knees, heaving steam.

"I can't. Hold on. I can't breathe."

"God, I'm sorry," he wailed. "I don't know what happened."

Snowflakes pattered her face and bit into the gash torn across her cheek. She scooped fresh snow and pressed it to the injury. "It's not your fault," she said. She tucked her right arm against her stomach, denied the holy hurt it was doling out.

"Who else's could it be?" he said. He paced a clearing in the snow. "Never mind, never mind," he said. "We need to keep going. The police'll find us if—"

"You can go back. You didn't do anything wrong," she told him, but Cal turned his back on what she had to say. Too much cold air inhaled and her windpipe was swelling, forcing her to cough, but at least her pulse steadied. She lifted her duffel bag from where Cal placed it on the rocks. She nodded onward toward the lights and he fell into step beside her, laundry bag hoisted over his shoulder like he was out delivering presents, or else burglarizing neighbors.

An unpaved access road brought them against fenced backyards, a suburban tract rising up like a mirage of the neighborhoods she haunted as a kid—townhouses packed together, rusted fire escapes and empty clotheslines like stripped umbrellas. They crossed an alley between two chain-link fences and came out under streetlamps yellowing the snowbound cars with light.

The street was freshly plowed, so when they stepped onto pavement the long trail of their footsteps was finally broken. Cal's shoulders eased like they'd made their escape. From here they could stagger like factory linemen headed home after the last-call bell. They could relax, she wanted to believe. But then headlights sliced around the corner and the panic refueled. She whispered, "Hide." They rushed back to the sidewalk and ducked together alongside a minivan.

The car crawled toward them, and passed with the crackle of a police radio. One beam split from the others and washed through the windows of the parked cars. It was a searchlight, and it was looking for two refugees from a nearby car crash, had to be. Jodie said "shit" too loud and regretted it. Cal tucked himself up against his legs, laundry bag at his feet. He shivered like a child. He was a child. It would be so easy for them to stand and make themselves known. She'd let him quit if he wanted, but she wouldn't end it now herself—not while she still hadn't done the only thing he'd asked her to do.

The cruiser passed once but it was no relief. A hundred yards up, that beam would spot their tracks coming down the trail, and then who knows what happens?—the police cavalry arrives and lights this place like a major-league night game. The cops must have already run the Celica's stolen license plate, put it all together, so they knew the nutcase broad they were after by now: thief, carjacker, kidnapper. She wondered how much her head was worth, what trouble they'd go through to find her—and it was not knowing the answers that scared her worst.

"Let's go," she told Calvin, and pointed the way. The closest porch was unspoiled by footprints, the driveway empty and without car tracks, interior lights still shining this late—all clues that the resident was either away or a housebound insomniac. It was a risk, but it seemed more hopeful than wandering streets, begging to get caught. So she hunkered low and rushed along the sidewalk while Calvin came up panting behind her.

She urged him forward, said, "Take big steps by the edge of this house."

Cal paced so wide she could hardly sink her own legs inside the holes he made. She hoped the edge of the house would hide their tracks. As they slinked, she peeked through a first-floor window, but the frosted glass and the curtains spoiled her view inside.

A chain-link fence blocked their way, but Cal tossed his bag around the corner onto a raised porch, grabbed Jodie's, and tossed it, too. He used the porch's rails to hoist himself upward, stood on the fence's crossbeam for a second before he vaulted with a grunt onto the porch, which shivered its bolts but held his weight. The racket was enough to wake nosy neighbors, but it was too late to dwell on all that.

Her own climb seemed more than she could dare, but she gripped the same rail one-handed and Cal reached down to hook his hands under her armpits. Her injured arm burst with pain so fierce she had to slam her eyes shut. Nerves fired warnings across her body. Tires crackled on the icy road, the police radio muttered, the cruiser was coming back around.

"Hurry," Jodie begged Cal. She worked through the agony just to get herself bent over the porch rail and hooked there by the lower ridge of her ribs. Cal grabbed the backside of her jeans by the belt loops. She tried to stand on the fence crossbeam like Cal had done, but the chain-link spokes wouldn't let her shoes find balance. Behind her, the searchlight beam filled the narrow corridor they'd just crossed. She slumped onto the porch before the light was full, but couldn't be sure if they'd caught the shadow of her scissoring legs or not.

So they waited. The pain surge made Jodie's heart want to quit, but Calvin squeezed her while the bashing died down. They shared the porch with their bags and a snowy lawn chair and hibachi. They squatted out of sight and the beam kept moving, shining through the empty corridors between the houses on its way down the road.

Their hill now sloped behind them, down toward the river and the emergency vehicle and police cruiser lights and the factory smoke plumes along the eastern bank.

"We're gonna get in this place," Jodie said. They were leaned against a sliding-glass doorway. She dragged her duffel bag closer and un-zipped it, yanked out a sweater she'd packed so fast it was still slung over a wire hanger. "Pull that hanger off," she told Calvin, because she couldn't deal anymore with the pain in her right arm.

He did as she told but asked her, "What if somebody's home here?"

"I don't think so—no car, no shoveling."

"But if somebody is?" Cal wondered. "What if somebody spots us?"

"Then we're Jehovah's witnesses," Jodie said. "Pull the wire out straight."

Cal cracked a smile and the sight of it warmed inside Jodie's chest, even as he untwisted the hanger's wiring from its hook and bent it out straight. When he had his instrument prepped, she pointed through the glass pane to the wooden dowel that kept the slider from moving along its track, explained how he should shimmy the wire between the sliders and hook the dowel, lift it out of place.

"You did this before?" Cal said. He worked the wire through the rubber insulation strips.

"Watched a neighbor do it once when I locked myself out of my old apartment."

"So it's not like you're a cat burglar for a living?" he said. Even with the hurt and the chase they were both giddy on adrenaline. Jodie supposed they should've knocked first to be sure nobody was home, but she swallowed worry and let Cal work.

He gritted his teeth as the wire tipped the dowel but wouldn't hook it. The endorphins in their blood diluted, and when the dowel finally rolled away it was more like relief than victory. Cal stood and pushed the sliding door, but it wouldn't budge. The door itself was locked. "Fuck," Cal said, and tossed the useless wire into the backyard.

All Jodie's agony struck back double-time. The two of them together on their tiny life raft.

Cal swore again and kicked the glass door with his shoe. She knew the Nowaks wouldn't let him act this way, and she felt privileged to see it, even in a grim moment like this. What bothered her was whether the feeling was right for a mother.

"What do we do now?" he begged her.

"There's a window," she said. It was at least two feet off the edge of the porch, but Jodie figured if the boy could reach it well enough to force it open, if the inside latch was unlocked like she hoped, then just maybe—

—flicked the lock and slid the glass door open. Like a bellboy he lifted the bags inside, offered his arm to her. He said, "Madame," and they both laughed a little because their other reactions were all bled dry. Standing, Jodie remembered she was still a bit drunk, but slipping inside was the easiest thing in the world.

They were in a darkened kitchen. An iron radiator wafted heat over her skin with such bliss it felt sexual. She pulled her arm out of her son's grasp. They didn't dare flick any switches, so the corners stayed in shadow except where the light cast from down the hall.

He set the bags at the foot of an upward staircase. Jodie tried again to touch the pain in her wrist but the pressure scrambled her head. She didn't dare think about the gash in her face. Hobbled instead toward a digital thermostat in the hallway, and the readout said fifty-five, meaning those who lived here were likely gone at least for tonight. She tapped the temperature gauge until it hit her seventy-five-degree target.

The floorboards under the rugs creaked where they stepped. The living room decor was milk-glass lampshades with floral etching, quilts on the backs of sofas with lion's paws for legs. On the mantle were frontier dolls wearing knickers and bonnets, the kind with eyes that shut when you lay the dolls down. A calico cat was coiled on an ottoman. Jodie thought it was fake, but then it raised its head and blinked at them blandly.

"Wonderful," Cal said.

"We could ask for a room without a cat," Jodie said.

"Mom, Jesus. Your cheek."

The kitchen phone rang out. Antique bell and clapper. They stood ramrod through five rings until the phone went silent. There was no answering machine. Maybe a neighbor calling to see if the Winslows or whoever were home early—*because we can see your silhouettes*—or cops on the line to alert Jodie and Cal that they were surrounded. The possibilities—

Maybe they could stay forever in this mausoleum, a single mom and her full-custody son, spied on by ghosts in mounted family photos dating back to daguerreotypes. Calvin on the love seat petting the decorative gold tacks that lined the armrest. Morning light broke in through the blinds and tinted the airborne dust. Jodie sprawled on the sofa with quilts she'd pulled from a closet shelf. While she slept, Cal borrowed her paranoia. He glanced out the window every odd minute, snowblinded every time, but there were no more police patrols as far as he could see.

He knew they couldn't stay. The cat dander made a stuffed and leaky mess of Cal's nose, swelled his eyes half-shut, and sent an itch down the back of his throat. Someone else lived here. No telling how long they'd be gone. Burt would be waiting for him in Pittsburgh tonight, and the thrill of that meeting charged Cal so hard it felt like shock therapy.

On the coffee table were Cal's snotty tissues, Percocet and Valium bottle nicked from the upstairs medicine cabinet, water glass Jodie used to down two pills, bandage wrappings, cigarette pack. Her arm was bashed bad enough to remind Cal what a traitor to their cause he was. He was the one who hurt her, his driving—because he was desperate for a Pittsburgh rendezvous she knew nothing about.

Her eyes fluttered and she said, "What time is it?"

"Can I ask something?" Cal said.

"Can I grunt the answer?"

"Why'd you steal the money and the car?"

"To see you." Her head lolled along the edge of the armrest.

"But why'd you risk all that just to see me?"

"I didn't want it no more, where I was."

"What is it exactly you want?"

"To see you—to fix—" She grabbed for the coffee table but caught empty air.

"What are you trying to fix? Did I let you down somehow?"

"No. Nothing—you didn't do nothing to let me down, Calvin."

"But you don't know me, really. I might still disappoint you."

"You won't, Cal. It's me."

"You want to fix yourself?" he said.

"I want to . . ." but she trailed off. She had her dented cigarette pack in her hands now. When she tipped it, the last cigarette fell out and rolled into the folds of her quilt. The gauze on her cheek, stuck there with medical tape, was soaked dark red, edged in rusty orange.

"We were talking just before the accident," he said.

"I know it. You were gonna tell me what makes you so different from everyone."

He pressed his fingers into the armrests and felt himself in a tailspin he couldn't break, the crash all over again. He said, "You're the only person in my family that I can possibly imagine wouldn't be devastated, but I could be totally wrong about that."

She sat up and took a long draw from the cigarette. He wanted so badly for her to intuit what he didn't want to say. Then he wouldn't have to know the exact instant she understood. The truth would be there, already processed. But she said, "Try me."

"I don't think I'm straight."

"I don't think straight, neither," she said.

"No, I don't think *I'm* straight. Okay, I'm pretty damned sure I'm not. Sorry."

"Wow, Cal. That's . . ." She tried to grin but winced instead and cupped a hand over her wound. "But what are you sorry about it for? I'm the only person who knows?"

"Basically. You and a few anonymous Internet friends."

She grinned despite the pain and shook her head deliberately. Over-tired, woozy from the painkillers, or convinced he was bullshitting her—something to explain why she seemed amused, like she couldn't care less about the way he loved. She said, "You know damn well your parents are gonna blame me for this somehow. Genetics or whatever."

"We've already established that you're not gay."

"Obviously," she said, sweeping her open cigarette hand at him. Smoke danced like a magician's diversion.

"You're not disappointed? Not going to tell me I'm too young to be sure?"

"Who am I to say? I been dealing with it since you told me, before. You didn't tell me exactly, but you were going to. Anyways, I knew what you meant, so no surprise."

"But you made me say it anyway."

"I figured you needed to, for yourself," she said, and Cal felt resusci-tated. His mother, that languid wreck, who saved him when he didn't even know he was drowning. He breathed like for the first, but the air was laced with allergens. His sinuses rioted and he lunged for a fresh tissue, brought it to his face just—

—who wander aren't always lost. Through the kitchen, up the backstairs, a surprise find: a bedroom actually outfitted for the current century. TV/DVD combo, draftsman's desk with PC, and a collection of movie-soundtrack CDs. Pink-curtained windows with cataracts of frost on the glass. The wall hangings were motivational kitten posters, tackiness that made him think of his own bedroom, how the nerdy alien landscapes he'd painted were hardly better than these kitty candids.

Nothing he discarded from his Cape Fear life seemed vital to him now, not even the artwork he'd thought was self-expression. It was all just the same ache for escape rendered twenty times over—a search without a hint of a solution.

Cal sat down at the desk, pressed the computer power button, and waited while it booted. He double-clicked the Internet Explorer icon. The prompt showed the login and password fields already filled, thus came automatic dial-up at a pace that gave him too much time to ponder the irony of seeking remote access to the life he kept wanting to convince himself was false. The modem screeched like the theme song of his angst.

He considered the chance that all his activities on this computer could be traced, that police were still prowling the neighborhood, door-to-door canvassing. Even as he tapped the URL of his e-mail login, he lamented the fingerprint evidence here and on a dozen other surfaces around the house. He could speculate forever on how the cops might track their criminal duo, how committed the pursuit would be, but he knew for sure he'd crossed a threshold now. Not just the victim of a child-snatching, but an accomplice since the moment he fled the wreck scene and breached a town house window.

His inbox screen appeared, e-mails read and unread. A dozen new notes from friends and from his father's college e-mail account gave Cal a displaced sense that his life continued without him. The subject lines grew more shrill and desperate as they laddered up the page—*u sick 2day? where r u? whut th HELL Cal?* His father's first few message headings read *[no subject]*, then *please call*.

His throat seized from another allergy wave, or from a realization: Only his father's e-mails were still labeled as unread. All the rest, including mail posted since the last time he logged on, had lost the virgin bold lettering. Worst, a string of six recent apology messages from Freez, from bullshit artist *Gene*, were all clicked. By someone who'd guessed Cal's password, or had some technology to bypass it, like police or even federal agents.

They wanted him to know they'd been rooting around, since they could've easily reflagged the messages as unread. Surely each e-mail was already printed off, ten copies apiece, already pored over by parents and authorities. A month's worth of messages rife with fag smut and ugly need.

They knew everything—his unsuspecting parents and smug cops who probably thought they now had the whole shebang under wraps: *Sorry, case closed. Your queer kid went off on a cock-suck escapade with his online homo joe. He'll come back in a week, walk a little lopsided—but you two seem pretty bleeding-heart tolerant, so I'm sure you'll make amends. Let me show you the way out. We've got real work to do.*

Cal wanted to cry, but his sinuses were too raw for tears. In a fit he tore the comforter and sheets from the bed he sat beside, the pillows and stuffed animals, threw it all to the floor till the mattress was bare. Should've deleted those goddamn e-mails the minute he read them. Should've wiped his browser of all those graphic ass-fuck Web sites, but instead the Nowaks were picking through his history files, hands to their shuddering mouths as they subjected themselves to one atrocity after another.

His hand scrambled the mouse around the pad. He settled the arrow on the *sent* file, clicked on it, and saw what he was afraid he'd find. The topmost post was sent to "Freez" at five in the evening yesterday, more than a day since Cal last accessed the Internet, meaning somebody else wrote it. Cal opened the message: *I'm real sorry, too. Let's meet again ASAP, okay? When and where? I'll be there. Reece.*

Cal returned to the inbox, knowing Gene had fallen for the bait. Stupid and so fucking eager, the perv actually believed underage "Reece" would agree to repeat their disastrous first meeting. When you have a hunger that can never be met, you're the easiest prey to trap—because you'll ignore all the alarms, you'll build ridiculous illusions, you'll resign yourself to the risk of getting caught.

Gene's response was timed five minutes after the fraudulent Calvin Nowak's. Dumb bastard didn't stop five fucking minutes to ponder whether the message even read like Cal. Potbellied slouch assumed on faith that Cal was desperate enough to accept him as a substitute for the Freez Adonis that Gene pretended to be online.

The text of Gene's e-mail detailed the terms of their reunion. The same pier on Wright Beach. Tuesday evening, seven P.M. It was Wednesday now, so Gene was already arrested the night before and had surely spent the last twelve hours in police custody. Cal imagined him slumped over a table in a police-station interview room. His computer would've been confiscated, his alibis dissected, his wife and children apprised.

"You stupid bastard," Cal said aloud. He lifted a desk phone from its cradle. He didn't know who he meant to call and didn't care whether it could be traced. But when he pressed the talk button the modem squealed and pinged like it was pissed at the interruption. He turned off the phone and erased the browser's history while he waited for the Internet to disengage.

The resident cat came into the room and swiped its body along his shin. The computer hum died. Somewhere downstairs a clock chimed a bird chirp, and then a sharp metallic snap, a deadbolt disengaging, the vacuum rush of an opening door. A female voice called out, "Shakespeare!" The cat darted out into the hall with its tail upraised. Because someone was calling him.

Cal's chest imploded. He couldn't catch his breath. The front door to the town house opened onto the living room with an unobstructed view of the sofa where Jodie lay, so she'd be noticed right away. Someone's been rifling through my medicine cabinet, someone's been sleeping with my quilt, and she's still here. He listened for the inevitable scream, the clatter of boots retreating down the porch steps, but what he heard instead was muffled voices.

Afraid his footsteps would be heard, he didn't dare move. He lifted the telephone again, laid his thumb on the number pad, and wondered where his instincts would guide him. He could call the police and surrender, call his parents and beg for help. Ten seconds passed and the dial tone went dead. He set the cordless handset down on the desk, left the line open and inoperative.

He slipped off his sneakers and hooked the heels with his fingers, crossed the upstairs hallway on his damp sockfeet. Stepped sideways down the stairs, leaned one hand against the wall to disburse his weight. His subconscious was running maneuvers Cal never could've mapped with his own right mind. He held back a sneeze and strained to hear what finally clarified:

"Maybe if I just called them—because they didn't mention anything about you."

"But that's the thing," Jodie said. "I didn't tell them I was coming."

The stairs opened on the kitchen, where their travel bags were still on the landing. He stepped down onto the linoleum, slipped his feet back inside his sneakers but did not tie them, leaned slightly forward to peer down the corridor. A teenage girl stood in profile, facing the couch. She wore jeans and a hooded sweatshirt, a wool cap with earflaps, strings dangling from the flaps.

She looked like any odd kid, probably just someone from the neighborhood put in charge of feeding the cat, watering the plants, keeping an eye on the place while the owners took a Caribbean cruise.

"Maybe I should just—" the girl stammered as she backstepped toward the door.

"All right, okay. Go ahead and call them," Jodie said.

Cal quietly unzipped Jodie's duffel bag. Didn't want to hurt the girl, but he didn't want to go down like this, caught off-guard by a cheerleader doing her chores. He got hold of his sheathed bowie knife. From between lumps of clothing, the dark round eyes of the gas mask stared up at him.

That mask was war and poisoned air and cacophony and suffocation and alien and insect and dust and mold and weird sex. He took it from the bag and slid it over his head with hampered vision and the reek of old rubber. His own breath rushed back to his ears along the contours of the mask. He slipped the knife out of its sheath.

The girl was near the entrance, ten feet across the room. She squawked at the sight of him and dropped the cell phone she held open in her hand. She pivoted and misjudged her distance from the door, threw herself against a wall instead. The dolls on the mantle blinked their dark eyelashes. The girl fell to her knees and wailed, completely overcome, like Cal had leaped straight out of some recurrent nightmare of hers.

He wanted to tear off the mask and laugh—*look, I'm just a kid like you— no worries*. But there was no call for such mercy anymore. He shouldered the front door shut, pawed for the deadbolt till he found it, twisted the bolt in place.

The girl scrambled across the floor toward Jodie on the sofa. Cal said, "Shut up! Keep your mouth shut!" He crouched for her cell phone and folded it into his pants pocket.

Jodie lay prone and petrified on the couch. *Mom, it's just me.* He didn't say it out loud, and she couldn't hear his psychic projections, but she had to know, had to realize he was doing this to save both their asses.

"Please, please," the girl was whimpering. She crossed her arms over the back of her head as if bracing for a blow. She expected to be stabbed, and her trauma was all Cal's fault.

"Quiet—keep quiet and you won't get hurt!" Cheap B-movie quotations, but the girl wasn't in the mindset to notice. He aimed the knife at his mother and she recoiled. She knew him but she didn't know him. She couldn't catch his intentions. He said, "You, grab the bags in the kitchen."

"What are you doing?" Jodie asked.

"Shut up!" he demanded. The anger was supposed to be an act, but he felt the real shock of it radiating upward from his groin. At this moment Jodie was despicable—this woman who claimed to be his mother, cowering on the couch, stoned from pills. She'd offered him nothing yet that carried any worth. She was a failure at her life, and Cal had stupidly bought stock in the same sad venture.

A violent urge shot through his nostrils and he sneezed inside the mask. The aerosol spit spattered across the lenses. It must have sounded to Jodie like a threat because she threw off the quilt and stumbled toward the kitchen.

Cal crouched beside the girl, and when he laid his hand on her shoulder, his touch made her cry out. He said, "Calm down. Listen to me. We're going to leave here in a minute. We're going to leave you alone. I'm taking your cell, and I cut the phone lines so you can't call out from this house, you understand?"

She nodded and held back her sobbing but kept her eyes clamped shut. She couldn't see that he held the knife harmlessly behind his back. Jodie rushed in with the luggage. She carried most in her left arm, dragged the rest along the floor. She tucked her injured arm against her stomach.

When Cal turned back to the girl, her eyes were wide. She extended one arm and aimed something at him like she was warding off a vampire. Through the debris on his lenses Cal saw it was a pepper-spray canister, just like the one he'd borrowed from his mother. The girl pressed furiously at the nozzle, but nothing was emitted.

He wrenched the bottle from her hand and chucked it behind the radiator. "Don't pull that again!" he said. The ribbed respirator tube hung from his face like a long limp dick, but the girl nodded furiously, eyes shut.

He said, "Listen to me this time. Nobody's going to hurt you—*unless*—you call the police, or anyone else. Understand? I know you live in the neighborhood. When we leave, we're going to see your footprints in the snow, and we'll know which house you came from, right? I also have your cell phone, so I can figure out who all your friends and family are. You call the police, and maybe they'll catch us. But if they don't, then you're in a shitload of trouble because I'll know, and I'll know where you live."

For months, maybe years, she'd probably hear the echo of his ugly, hollow voice. He was cutting up bite-sized morsels of his own char-coaled soul and feeding it to her, but there was no other way. He said, "You understand me? You sit here for half an hour and you wait. Then you can do whatever the hell you want. Call the cops, who cares. You never hear from me again. But you try to stop us and that's it. All right?"

The girl nodded, whimpering. Cal wanted to tell her the game was over. Just a game, no harm. But instead he was forced to leave her roiling in terror until—

—hothouse breath left a film of moisture on his face that chilled to a sting in the arctic air. Mother and unmasked son hurried down the sidewalk, both of them expecting any second to get nabbed. Kids doing snowsuit gymnastics in their yard, a man in padded flannel shoveling his squat driveway, none of them paying Calvin and Jodie any regard. That the girl would run screeching from the town house seemed less likely with every parked car they passed.

At the first intersection they hooked left into an enclave with a corner convenience store. Cal paused at a blue postal box and dropped the girl's cell phone inside. The phone hit bottom with a resounding clang, no mail inside to buffer. He'd forfeited his chance to head home unscathed. Might as well have scrawled his name in Magic Marker on the front door as they left.

"They can track those?" Jodie asked.

"Maybe. I just wanted to get rid of it."

She was nearly asleep on her feet, slurred in her speech, and she hadn't said a word about what happened. Her silence disgusted him. He wanted her to denounce what he'd done. Their hot breath polluted the air, but they said nothing because they were trapped together and yet an ice floe sluiced between them. Cal was blank in his heart in regards to—

Sleet spackled the Beetle's underside. Wynn's jacket was shed, draped on the passenger seat. The sweat wouldn't quit drenching out. The headlights kept him aimed at the infinite vanishing point. Out here hills crested and dived like white waves, pine trees for shipmasts and guardrails for gunwales. These were the woods where, local myth claimed, sullen teens came at midnight to hang themselves high, death-metal lyrics on their lips. Half in love with easeful death.

On joyride summer nights Dwight took along his dog named Howl, a gray half-wolf mutt with a sharp snout and oversized paws. It paced the backseat between windows and growled at the Amish horsedrawn carts Dwight passed. Stowed in the Lincoln's trunk was a keg Dwight stole from the reception hall where he bussed tables. They were headed for the muddy hillside where bonfires raged, the ravine where kids chucked beer-can empties. *Rumspringa* Amish always crashed such shindigs, talking with an accent like those colonists who used to damn witches to burn. Howl always stalked beside his master, until the night he charged a deer and kept running forever.

Dwight had installed a stereo, subwoofer, played Slipknot, Eminem, Black 47—nothing else.

"Hold the wheel," Dwight said, and held his Bic flame against the wick of a cherry bomb. Tossed the charge at the gravel roadside ten feet north of an Amish cart. The horse reared, kicked its hooves mid-air, *blam*. The cart swerved toward a ditch, missed it by a wheel's width. Dwight cackled and the wolf growled and Wynn had already lost his taste for the game. His gut clutched over the airborne hilltops. Tried to imagine himself elsewhere. But there was nowhere else to—

—parked curbside fronting an apartment house. Wynn sat alone in the Beetle awhile with his hands in his face. This was a dead-end road in Philpot, a Cassadaga County village of maybe five measly streets and a grocery store, a couple bars, rental row houses. Dwight had forged connects out here because he liked the southbound spin from Weymouth, how the roads into Philpot were never speedtrapped. You could bury the needle with only the worry of wildlife and corkscrew turns to wreck your speed-freak rush.

Wynn got out and headed for the second-story unit, reached via a staircase in a makeshift enclosure along the east side of the house. The winter crept up the first few steps. Wynn tripped on a bagged phonebook, frozen in place. Halfway, pitch darkness, and the rail wobbled in Wynn's grip. He knocked where he thought the door might be. The woman who answered was backlit, so she had no face.

"We're looking for Frank," Wynn said.

"Who's we?" the woman said.

Wynn clamped his eyes a second. His sense of time was overlapping itself like a double exposure. He divided the one occasion from the other, the now from the before, and found some clarity in the quotient. It was winter, Wynn was alone, Dwight was dead. He said, "I mean me."

"Frank doesn't live here anymore."

Behind her were three more souls: a baby in a playpen, a piggy gal in a kitchen alcove, and a guy in a lawn chair watching TV on a cinderblock stack. The guy was dipping his tattooed arm inside the playpen to thrill the baby, but the baby couldn't care. The guy was also unmistakably the same Frank that Wynn had come to find.

"That's Frank right there," Wynn said.

"Yeah, right. He's visiting." She turned toward the kitchen, bored with doorway talk.

Ultimate Fighting on the tube featured two men so tangled with each other that they fought in near-perfect stillness. Down the hall was a bedroom with someone inside, but Wynn couldn't see who. Her bare legs draped over the bedside. There were too many squatters here, and their relationships to one another were vague. It had always been that way.

"Frank," Wynn said.

Frank drank the dregs of his beer can. He said, "I remember you, but your name I forget."

"Dave," Wynn said.

"Dave, right. You're here because of the Kopecks?"

"I want to make sense of it."

In the kitchen area, the two women hunched around a stovetop pot and prodded it with mixing spoons. Cecelia came down the hall from the back bedroom. She was stark naked with a drenched red towel wrapped around her head. The slope of her hips as she moved brought to mind pure desert dunes. Wynn pressed himself against the doorframe to keep from falling over. A pain was sucking through his chest where the bullet had bit him—or rather, bit Dwight.

Frank said to Wynn, "Outside." He grabbed his jacket, shoved his feet into unlaced—

—memories of Frank and Ce-ce mashed together on the couch, her legs crossed with his. Frank was ten years older than her, a louse and a scum, son of a local butcher. Secretly Wynn had always wanted to spread Frank's fresh blood on a canvas, call it art, like all envy was. Slice him up to see what the goddamn hidden prize inside was supposed to be, anyway. Worse, Wynn could never dare to ask Cecelia why—why date this pothead petty dealer skunk who smelled of feet and barbecue potato chips? It was the cosmic injustice Wynn couldn't shake. If only she grazed lips with some other—

*   *   *

—old scabs, torn off in sheets the size of shingles. Hurtling across time and space like this made Wynn's heart atrophy. Only his determination kept it bashing.

Frank stood out front and said, "What people're saying is they offed each other."

"That's how it was supposed to look," Wynn said.

"Fuck," Frank moaned, like poured molasses. He rubbed his stubble with both hands, pushed his hair around his head. He drank Wynn's news like he knew already and only wanted it confirmed.

"You and Cecelia had some of the same connections," Wynn said.

"I realized just then that I loved her, while you were talking," Frank said. His voice doubled, the echo a register below the sound. His teeth chattered and his skin blued, and Wynn thought this waste of consciousness might just die out here after all.

Wynn said, "Help me out."

"I don't know no murderers."

"Help me out, Frank. Bring me to the molten core. Throw me into the center and run. You don't have to be seen or—or witnessed by anybody. The police are way away from what I'm doing, I promise you. I'm alone and I have to get inside something soon or or or I'm gonna split down the middle, Frank. I'm gonna fucking bifurcate."

"Who are you?" Frank asked in earnest.

"You remember me," Wynn told him.

Frank pumped the slow pistons of his mind. His boot tongues lolled stupidly. Wynn couldn't look at the man anymore, knowing he'd been inside Cecelia with his turkey-neck prick. Wynn's mission was getting confused, he knew, a shattered mirror showing him his own face ad infinitum—but he'd keep going as long as someone led him somewhere. She kissed him in the dugouts, in the library, on the earlobe, and she died, and her kiss was fading.

Frank howled and kicked an icy snowcap. Wynn slapped his pockets in search of the car keys but they were nowhere. "Find them," he

begged himself. Frank, down on his knees, gouged at the snow bare-
handed, helping with the search. Wynn shoved him in the face with
the sole of his sneaker. Frank groaned and drooled congealed strings
of blood. They were getting somewhere now. Unbalanced from the
kick, Wynn reeled and banked his entire fall on one jutting elbow.
The impact warmed him through one shoulder and across half his face.
He took the keys from the snowy walkway.

Frank's knuckles cluttered across Wynn's jaw because they seemed
to be fighting. That woman from upstairs, she tromped down the steps
with her arms wide like a preacher speaking in tongues. She damned
their outdoor brawl and exiled Frank and Wynn, both of them, to the
far—

—past numbers on route signs he didn't recognize. Lost in the
wilderness over the Pennsylvania line, north into Erie County, through
a transdimensional warp—all options equally plausible. The snow-
tufted trees were all the same. The gray shades of men haunted the
roadside and Wynn recognized them all.

From the backseat Frank thrust his finger into Wynn's headspace
and said, "Right there."

It was a windowless warehouse of concrete and corrugated tin,
neighbored by nothing.

"What is this?" Wynn said.

"Pandemonium," Frank said.

Snow dust whorled like low-visibility fog. Closer, Wynn saw cars
and pickups in the lot. They might've passed a sign that might've offered some explanation, but Wynn had already forgotten what it said.
Somehow Frank led him straight off the map, was all Wynn could—

—black-lit from ultraviolet tubes installed around the ductwork. Pandemonium. The dozen shadow patrons at their tables knew
well enough not to wear bright clothes. House speakers played "Closer,"

that old Nine Inch Nails hit on animalistic sex and self-deprication. There was a disco ball and clinical close-up smut on a widescreen. Peanut husks on the concrete floor, smell of oil spills and cat litter cleanup. Frank led him past the performance onstage.

"Did Cecelia come here?" Wynn asked him as they walked. He had to shout to be heard.

"No—no deals in here," Frank said.

The lone dancer braced herself against the pole. She was hairless between her legs like a child, sexlessly thin. Even her feet were nude. Slow night, she wandered offstage out of boredom, song not yet over. She might've been a ghost herself. Her soundtrack claimed she could get you closer to God.

Frank pushed through a door with rubber lining. Behind it was only a damp flight of stairs headed downward. Wynn's resolve was fading fast. He feared what his own search would show him. Feared Frank, who might want him dead, who might've been among the men who murdered Cecelia and Dwight.

"It was you," Frank said.

"Who?"

"I said: 'If he's here.' I don't know if he's here."

A hallway, a rusted door like the door to a high school boiler room. There were hushed voices down here, and the cavernous drip, and the deep churning fire of a furnace somewhere close.

Frank knocked, and the man who answered was an aging midget in cowboy boots, forked goatee and Hitler hairdo gone silver. He bared his teeth at Frank, took a sip of something fizzy and tan from a highball glass. Inside was an office space with a spread of grainy video screens that monitored the main showroom and the private lounges, all of them empty.

"What, Frank? Seriously: what?" the imp said in a voice too baritone for his body.

"A friend of Cecelia," Frank explained.

"Who's Sicily?" the imp said.

"She died last night," Frank said. "She was . . ."

"The murder?" the imp asked.

Frank's nod was solemn.

The imp grabbed Wynn's hand and said, "Runt. My handle. It's meant to be ironic. I'd offer you a drink but we don't serve booze in the pandemonium as a legal compromise for the sweet sight of white-trash snatch. I've got cashews, couple cans of seltzer in the mini fridge."

"This is Dave," Frank said.

Runt led them inside. Wynn sat beside Frank in a combo seat straight out of a clinic waiting room. Everything else looked culled from flea-market sales. The midget who called himself Runt got behind a sheet metal desk and climbed into his own office chair. The photos propped on the desktop were the default ones that came with the frames when you bought them: kids in vintage grown-up clothes, a cat stalking a goldfish, prices printed in the corner.

"Dave here came by my cousin's just now, where I happened to be staying for a couple days. He's looking into the Cecelia situation. I thought I'd help, thought I'd bring him here."

"That was thoughtful," Runt said.

"I'm pretty shook up myself because of Cecelia, I gotta tell you. I'm having difficulties."

"You some kind of private detective, Dave?" asked Runt.

Wynn said, "I was a friend of theirs—Ce-ce and Dwight."

"Who's Dwight?" Runt said.

Frank said, "Cecelia's brother. Looks like they creamed each other, her and him."

"I'd like to rewind back to what Frank means by *looking into,*" the imp said. "You're not police, are you, Dave? You look way too strung out for a badge, but I seen some train wrecks."

"I loved Cecelia," Wynn admitted. He was scraped too thin for evasive talk.

"That's touching," Runt said. "Wish I knew who this chick Cecelia was."

"Did she work here?" Wynn asked Frank again.

"I loved her, too, once," Frank said. "Maybe a little bit still. I'm pretty broken up."

"One of the guys had a tattoo on his hand," Wynn said. "He was a big bald guy."

The imp took a hard swallow of his drink and arched his brows. "One of what guys?"

"Other people there, at the murder," Wynn said. On the main monitor behind him a glowing blur of a woman jerked about on the stage. Her panties were the color of highlighter ink. Around the edges of Wynn's vision came flashes of white light like the symptoms of a migraine.

"I find myself wondering how you know about these Other People," Runt said.

"I saw this guy before, with Cecelia," Frank intervened. "He's all right."

"And what happened to your ear?" Runt asked Wynn.

Wynn touched his wound and found it was exposed, scabby, the bandage lost. His fever smoldered. He felt himself reduced to paper, like a body outline on a gun-range chart. His throat ached for liquid. He said, "A dog bite."

"Pit bull?" Runt inquired.

Wynn's seat ceased to hold him and he was falling backward but not truly falling and then again it was happening, this sensation of falling but not, again. His reason for being here was lost in a panic of fractal thought. They expected a confession from him, it seemed—Frank and the imp.

"I tried to tell him how pointless," Frank said. "Them guys are long gone."

"I don't know any guys," said the imp.

"I tried to tell him," Frank said. "This isn't your area, Runt-man. These guys—"

"Your friend seems a little sick. Emergency-room sick."

"I didn't mean to hurt her," Wynn said.

"But you weren't there, were you?" the imp said.

Cecelia danced naked on the stage, the same languorous sway as the others. The monitor screen pixilated her finer features. She could've been any other woman, but Wynn knew it was her. He pinched his ear and tugged till he felt the fresh blood flow. His lungs wouldn't open themselves for air again. His heart hummed but didn't beat. A wall of fabric slipped down over his face, shrouded his head. He blinked through off-centered eyeholes, smelled dry saliva and his own dark memory. He was wearing a ski mask, the one he left—

The bus engine strained to get the whole crowd trucking, rocked Jodie's forehead against the cold window glass. Sliding back and forth from dreams about her sister and babies to the truth of being on a Greyhound bus headed to Pittsburgh. She dreamed lost summer and batted her eyes and then the trees were all spiny and no birds perched on the power lines. Streets of gray slush and the sky the same. The valleys past the guardrails were blank as erase marks.

Calvin was somewhere close, but not sitting right beside her exactly. On another part of the bus. Something about keeping apart so they wouldn't get spotted, but Jodie's worries rooted way deeper. You watch your son in a monster mask threaten to slice some poor girl with a knife, and you have to chalk it up to survival. He admits his love is wired all wrong and it's just a shame you're forced to shoulder with a laugh. But you worry his sickness traces all the way back to that wicked game that brought your child to life—your fault, always your mistake.

The bus stopped in mountainside towns and picked up stragglers, one with a pair of skis he jousted down the aisle as he boarded. If Jodie raised her eyes over the edge of the seat back ahead, she could see the skulls of the other passengers. Everyone here seemed alone. She saw Calvin's shock of red hair sometimes, sometimes not. He seemed to be changing his seat every—

—toddler niece in a christening dress. Jodie is fourteen years old, sits on her heels in the front-row pew wishing the ceremony over already. Sis used to take Jode to backyard parties, drink beer at eleven and watch the volunteer firemen's hardcore band thrash out to Misfits covers in somebody's garage. But then sis had a typical townie fling: plus mark on the pee stick, marriage, baby carriage. Her and her groom in their Sunday best, both of them twenty years old and blindsided.

Jodie loves her niece all right, babysits twice a week after school. Kid sure likes to rock out, flails her stubby little arms in the playpen every time Jodie spins her old Violent Femmes CD. Maybe this baptism will drive the dance demon out of the pretty little one. Shame—

—jolted awake as the bus broke through into a mountainside freefall. She grabbed the seat back and bashed her shoes against the wheel hump. Her right wrist flared with pain. But they were safe on the highway and concrete pylons blocked the lane beside them. Fast-food and gasoline road signs reared up higher than the overpass. Jodie breathed inside the flap of her jacket to keep her panic checked. She wanted her son beside her, but she didn't dare call out to him.

If the police came to get her now, if they pulled the bus over and entered from both ends with rifles and K-9 dogs, where would they take her? She tried to think what she'd say to prove Cal wasn't to blame for what happened back in Harrisburg. But her brain was downright cottony. An old woman across the aisle glared at her like she knew the score, pulled her travel bag into her lap to keep it safe from the likes—

—Calvin said.

"How far are we?" asked Jodie. The sky darkened after just one blink and her stomach churned its hunger. The pain pills and the sleep still laced through her blood. Dreamlike memories like they never really happened. This woman who is not Jodie goes around inside her body while Jodie sleeps, and this woman who stole her life could say anything with Jodie's mouth or even find a way to die without Jodie's ever knowing.

"I asked, what's my father's name?" he said again. He was sitting beside her now. She wondered if there was a seat belt he could wear to keep him from drifting up through the roof of the bus and leaving her forever. They were headed through junctions, overpasses and under. Streetlights passed across their laps as they came into the city.

"Are we here?" Jodie asked Dad from the backseat. Sister Jill in a Hersheypark T-shirt. Headed home from vacation late at night with the windows rolled down, and the wind threw Jodie and Jill's orange hair all blazing wildfire.

"Why won't you tell me?" Calvin asked.

"We're gonna see," Jodie said.

"Is that what we're doing? We're going to see my father?"

"My sister."

"So we're going to see everybody, but we might not ever get there?"

"Is this Pittsburgh?" Jodie said.

"We have to switch busses at the station."

Jill's husband, in his Goodwill blazer and tie, tilted his little girl toward the minister's ladle. Two years later, his hands would cradle Jodie's head while her bare backside smacked the hardwood floor. The scale would tip and it would be all tumbling unstoppable sin. He'd wince his eyes and moan and turn to concrete inside of her body. "Not like that," she'd blurt, but her hips would keep seeking up for him. He'd pull away and his liquid would dribble across her stomach. Weird how fast it went cold, how quickly they both regretted.

"Sam," Jodie said.

"That's his name? What's his whole name?" Cal asked.

"Samuel Hartwick. It was—fifteen—almost sixteen years—but—"

"He lives in Weymouth? The same city where your sister lives?"

"They live—we can't go back there," she said. She reached for the wire to signal her stop but this wasn't that kind of bus. Plush seats and little white paper pads to lay your head against, the same clinical paper as what they laid on the birthing table the day Calvin—

* * *

—women's room she doused her face in water. She peeled away the damp bandage, and the slice through her cheek was scabbed and puckered. With nothing else to clean it, she used soap foam from the dispenser. She applied a Band-Aid from a packet she just bought at the bus station concession. Had to lay the wings over the edges of the wound to cover it whole.

The meat of her left forearm was bruised from wrist halfway up to her elbow in radiating circles of browns and yellows and blues. Pain bad enough to deserve another pill, but the last ones still hummed too loud in her head. She could hardly remember where these injuries came from. It seemed almost like they were always there.

She set the duffel bag across the countertop and scowled at the gas mask that eyed her from an opening. She couldn't even touch it to throw it away, so she zipped it out of sight and unzipped the side pouch instead. The leftover bills were scattered inside. She wanted to tidy them and count what was left but worried someone would see her. Maybe try to mug her. She zipped the money away, lifted the bag. She reached for a wall to steady herself but the wall wasn't there. A woman entering the bathroom wore a dark padded jacket, miniskirt, and heels. She clicked her tongue and sang, "Girl—you messed up."

The bus terminal was rows of fresh-painted chairs and sparkling sky-high windows, not a squared corner in sight. Muddy footprinted floors and signs that warned about slipping in English and Spanish. The sliding doors kept opening and closing, though nobody walked through. Out in the garage deck, the busses parked slantwise, digital destinations scrawled above the windshields like the latest breaking news.

Calvin now stood where he hadn't been before. "Buffalo's that one," he said. The driver waited outside with the undercarriage open for cargo, but Jodie and Cal both held their luggage as they boarded. The driver sneered at them.

"Do you think he recognizes us?" she whispered.

"Why would he?"

"Maybe we're on *America's Most Wanted*."

"We're not," Cal said. "He just thinks we won't tip him if we handle our own bags."

The overhead lights were dim, the passengers in shadow. Small children seemed brighter than the rest. Jodie took a window seat and Cal took the aisle. While he settled their bags on the floor by their feet, Jodie nuzzled the headrest and watched the dark windows of the bus alongside them, wondered where the people inside were headed so late at night, what was driving them away. Her eyelids were too heavy to keep open. Her brain was already considering strange senseless flights.

Beside her Cal said, "I have to hit the bathroom. I'll be right—

—phone booth awaiting the Buffalo bus departure. Cal held tight the laundry bag full of all his shit and shivered from a chill that was more than just weather. According to the terminal clock, the departure time had come and gone, but the bus still idled in its slot. In the inside pocket of his peacoat was close to two thousand dollars he'd pawed from Jodie's bag just before he stepped off the bus. She'd forgive him because she'd have to, but now he was party to her crimes for certain—fully versed, fully complicit.

Any second Jodie might come wandering off the bus like a bleary escapee. She'd call his name, search the terminal, rush about with mounting panic. Cal didn't want her to feel that pain of abandonment, even if she'd done it to him, and to Nero, and to this man Samuel Hartwick she said was his father, and God knows who else. He wanted her sleep to carry her all the way to Buffalo, where she'd wake and accept his absence like she had for the past fifteen years.

Because Cal didn't want to meet those people in New York. After what he did to that poor girl, left her terrified and crying on the floor, he was sure his father would be some brute, contributor of a colossally defective Y chromosome.

The Buffalo bus driver ushered the last passenger on board and folded shut the entry door. An unexpected strain crawled up through Cal's throat. He tried to suppress it, but as the bus backed away he clenched his teeth and sobbed like he was the deserted one. The bus rumbled and surged up the city lane toward a bus ramp that curved behind a luxury apartment building.

He was alone in downtown Pittsburgh.

Up came a vagrant dressed in grimy denim with a rucksack on his shoulder. He smelled of motor oil and urine and he said, "Got any change on you, man? It's cold out here like to make you cry like that. Them shelters is brutal else I be bunking there tonight, gnome saying? Lookit." He lifted his coat and pointed to a spot above his groin where a puffed, inchwide scar was on display. He teetered in place, scrawny as an anorexic. "That a year back, shelter up Homewood, fucker knife me good. I won't go them places no more, gnome saying?"

"Don't you have family who can help you?" Cal asked, though he didn't want to be talking to this man anymore. He didn't want to be here, but he couldn't just head somewhere else. He didn't know where anywhere was.

The vagrant knuckled some moisture out of the corner of his eye, said, "Man, I got a cousin over Philly. She it, but she disown me, gnome saying? Get this here: she a psychiatrist. Be twenty year last time we sit, her and me."

"Maybe you should go visit her."

"Maybe so, man. I hear you."

Cal dug into his pocket and took out all the money that was rightfully his, the fifty bucks in small bills from his bedroom peanut-butter-jar bank, none of it yet spent. He said, "This might get you most of a bus ticket."

The man reeled back, palms up and mouth agape like Cal pulled a gun on him. It was all part of the performance, along with the winter-weather sob story and the appendix scar. Cal knew the play, but none of it changed his need to offer up his cash. The vagrant said, "Naw, man, I can't take that." But then like magic, the money disappeared into the folds of the man's clothes. Then he also vanished, nothing left of him but his stale reek.

Cal grabbed the pay phone, dropped quarters, and dialed. Burt answered on ring one.

"It's me again." Cal's voice wheezed. He tried to hide it, didn't want to sound anxious, the fortune wheel of his life spinning on this call. "It's late, but I'm here."

"Jesus," Burt whispered. "They were around again, you know. The police came here asking me all kinds of questions." Irritated already, like Cal had been calling him nonstop for days. It wasn't the secret celebration Cal had hoped for. It wasn't co-conspiratorial Best Friend answering his cell on a bus already en route from Akron to Pittsburgh, arrival time any minute.

"Did you tell them you were coming to meet me?" Cal asked.

"Meet you where?"

"In Pittsburgh." Cal sniffled his running nose, worried it sounded like crying.

"I told you I can't go to Pittsburgh, man."

"You didn't tell me. I'm here already. We can go pretty much anywhere from here."

"Even if I wanted, there's people breathing down my neck. My parents. But I don't want to go anywhere. There's no good reason to be going all the way over there."

Cal didn't want to admit he was alone in a city and he would stay alone because of his own delusions. He'd brought himself to this point, and hated his idiotic faith that Burt would care to make this work.

Cal said, "Did you tell them I was here? You didn't, right?"

"I said you and me haven't talked, which if they check my phone records or whatever they know is a lie. I lied to the cops, man, so what the hell is going on? They were talking weird shit about some guy you were supposed to meet somewhere down in Cape Fear."

Cal felt like he had to vomit, though his stomach was empty, not a morsel of food all day. The Akron police had asked Burt about Gene, they had suggested things. Cal said, "He doesn't have anything to do with it. It's not about that sick asshole. You tell them that. After this, you can go ahead and tell them I called you and said to forget about that guy, all right? He has no relation to what I'm doing. You don't have to fucking lie about anything for me."

"You know what else they asked me? You know, don't you?"

"They asked if you were a faggot," Cal said, ruining the punchline to a tired old joke.

"Tell me why the hell they're asking that."

"I don't know. Maybe you give off a vibe."

"This is total bullshit," Burt said, and the line disconnected. Cal lowered the phone and stared into the pinprick holes that had so efficiently transmitted his sentencing. Something Gene had said came to mind— about being condemned by the nature of your love. He slapped the phone down on the hook, lifted it, slammed it again. The thick black plastic was unbreakable.

This is what it was to be a vagabond, almost. He could use his ticket to catch the next bus to Buffalo, some time before morning. He had a contact name and a city—Sam Hartwick in Weymouth—but all his fears about what he'd find there hadn't changed just because of a three-minute disastrous phone call with Burt. Only difference now was Cal didn't want to be—

—drool on her lip she wiped with her thumb. Outside passed the billboard: WELCOME TO NEW YORK: THE EMPIRE STATE, like it was waiting on cue to greet her. Snowfall again, a flurry that hung mid-air as the bus passed through it. Beyond the roads were black fields meeting black skies and the dim reflections of other riders inside the bus, most of them asleep. The woman beside her was all jacket, zipped up to her nose. She held a paperback open in her lap, except it was too dark to read. Jodie couldn't see if the woman's eyes were opened or closed.

Jodie was alert with fear and the fiery itch from the wound in her cheek. Her memory shuffled the day's incidents all out of order. Another seat, another part of the bus, or maybe a different bus. Calvin sitting beside her sometimes and sometimes not. She craned her head and looked, but people were shadows. She remembered Cal getting up to use the bathroom. There was one in the back of this bus, but the VACANT sign glowed green. And if the bus was just now hitting New York, they'd been driving for almost two hours.

At the Buffalo terminal the lights would come on, and there he'd be, fast asleep, not two seats away. It was just that this woman stole his seat while he was in the bathroom, that's all. Still, Jodie's heart was thumping alarm. She could call his name, get up and search, but the others would think she was crazy or suspect. Trapped in her seat, but no need to fret because Cal—

—wandered alone in the Strip District, a few blocks east of the station. Old factories with walls of dark windows stretching a full city block. The ground floors were bright with neon and awnings— boutiques, restaurants, Asian markets with their aluminum mesh gates pulled down for the night. Pittsburgh Steelers gold-and-black plastered everywhere, and the welcoming smell of fried food drifting in the cold. A paper posted to a telephone pole warned him to stay sober and pure or else the Devil would come and drag his whole family into hell.

At a diner he ate a soggy hamburger and a substitute Caesar salad instead of fries. When the waitress filled his Coke glass for the second time, she laid the check facedown, like she wanted him out before the half hour was up. The others in the diner were old black men huddled over coffee cups. There was nothing to watch, nothing to think except Jodie on the bus, the Nowaks back home, bitter Burt over in Akron—everybody Cal betrayed. The Burt thoughts ached worst of all.

"Can you break a hundred?" Cal asked the waitress at the register.

She held the bill up to the overhead light, conferred with a linecook. For a while it looked like she might call the cops. Cal had to wait five full minutes for the woman to gamble on accepting his money, but finally, with eighty-five dollars in change, he pushed back out into the winter. Still stored underneath the booth where he ate was his laundry bag full of old clothes. He took his toothbrush, toothpaste, and deodorant, shoved them in a coat pocket. Everything else was weighing him down.

A few doors away, a nightclub's long windows showed a dance-floor panorama, ceiling lights spinning and pulsing like the party was in full swing, even through it was yet early evening on a Wednesday. Cal passed it by. He passed everything along a half-mile stretch. The cold was cutting in through his clothes. He was dwarfed by a dark, tree-lined cliffside splitting the skyline in half. He needed to find someplace, but the chances seemed dim that he'd hit a clean motel that would rent to an unaccompanied minor paying in cash.

A boy of about eighteen sat hunched on a stoop outside a Chinese market. His head was shaved except for a lopsided mohawk, and he wore a hoodie and skintight punker jeans with the cuffs folded up. His sallow face mulled Cal over. A tattoo just under his right eye was a tiny star, but it looked like a tear. He asked, "Got a light?" and showed Cal a burnt-out, half-smoked cigarette.

"Sorry," Cal said. A sudden vertigo nearly dropped him as he passed the boy. They looked nothing alike, but they were on the street together in some lonely kinship Cal didn't want to share.

Further up was a narrow alleyway hosting a nondescript club with blackened windows and a door made of pockmarked copper. Like a speakeasy, except that the name of the club, Pandemonium, was stenciled right onto the door for anyone to see. Cal might've figured it was a strip club if not for the two men leaning against the wall outside. They smoked cigarettes and clung close together, left and right legs intertwined.

Cal walked another ten seconds until he found a convenience store and ducked inside. Bought bottled water and took a swig beside the auto trader/apartment booklet rack. The spinning in his head would not subside. All of his intention was zeroed on that place, Pandemonium. It was the place he was looking for all night, maybe all week, and it scared the shit out of him. He imagined being stopped at the door by some greased shirtless bouncer who'd grab him by the crotch and toss him into a Dumpster. Or worse, getting past the bouncer free and clear.

Back outside he winced at the cold and tried to summon his nerve.

Home came to mind, but not Cape Fear. The home he evoked was fictional Cape Twilight, and he was Reece Payton, the swaggering fag molded in James Dean's image. Burst out of the closet in season three. If Reece could flame in TV Maine, then Cal could sure as hell—

—lost him. She watched everyone step off the bus and Cal was not there. Pleaded with the driver to let her back on because she'd forgotten something, and she checked every seat, even the bathroom, and he was not there.

"Find it?" the driver asked.

Jodie couldn't even bring herself to answer him. She shouldered past where he stood in the aisle and resented that his body should ever share the same space as hers. All these people cluttering the Buffalo bus station with their hot breath and bundled jackets, she wanted them all to disappear. Then she could see across the vast hall to where Calvin stood waiting for her. Because she'd missed him, that's all. He was one of the first to step off the bus, in a hurry because he had to reach a urinal.

She stood beside a bank of phones and watched the restroom for ten minutes. Only strangers came out, and when they glanced at her with their road-weary hunger they were even more alien. The vaulted space was polluted with their talk, echoed a hundred times over. All these ugly people who were dead numb to the crisis that shrieked in her brain.

Uniformed cops, traveling soldiers in their fatigues—she couldn't look at any of them because they'd see straight into her. She couldn't ask for help because she was a fugitive. She couldn't call Calvin's cell because it was at the bottom of a trash bin outside a doughnut shop north of Richmond, Virginia. She was alone, but she couldn't scream because she was not alone.

She'd come here for him and now what—

The Johnston residence wasn't half a mile from the Kopecks' house. First stop on Sam's patrol, a subdivision cul-de-sac, upscale for Cassadaga County living. Underground electric, automatic exterior lighting, tiered landscaping. Sam wondered what these people did to afford this. He pulled the cruiser into the driveway behind an SUV at the home of Wynn Kyle Johnston, age twenty-one, who had no hint of criminal history until last night.

Doubt was Sam's drive now, and the engine ran wrong every way he could shift it.

Nobody at the station knew his business here. All afternoon he'd been primed to rush this lead down, and now that he was here he idled and wondered what the fuck, what he'd do if the kid was inside, what he'd tell the parents.

When the front-porch light flicked on, Sam swore at himself and popped his seat belt. He walked the snowplowed driveway toward the porch, noted the glass on the storm door frosting up. The mother in a cable-knit sweater and jeans. A dog, some moppish thing, pressed its pawprints into the frost and yipped. She lifted the dog into the cradle of her arms, cracked the door open a bit. Like most good people visited unannounced by cops, she evinced a petrified poise, a warm-up to collapse Sam saw plenty enough, but rarely for reasons like this.

She said, because she had to, "You probably have the wrong house, Officer."

The dog's whole body rippled every time it barked.

"I'm looking for Wynn Johnston."

"Looking? He's okay?"

"Have you spoken to him today, ma'am?" He nodded into the house behind her.

"I'm sorry," she said, and stepped aside to give Sam entry. "I called him this morning but he didn't answer. I've tried a few other times but all I keep getting is his voice mail."

He entered a foyer with a view of the living room where a TV played panoramic views of Mediterranean tourist spots. He said, "You might've heard about last night's shooting incident."

"Yes," the mother said. "That's why I called him. The Kopeck kids were friends of Wynn's. Dwight especially. I don't know if he knew the girl very well. It was terrible to hear. You just don't imagine anything like that ever happens around here, but maybe I'm wrong. You know better than I do."

"Do you have any idea where your son might be?" Sam asked.

"He's at college. He lives in a dorm there because of a scholarship."

"Weymouth?"

"Yes, in the highrise. It's just you want to ask him about Dwight?"

"That's right," Sam said. "We're just checking in, see if he can't help shed some light."

"He hasn't talked to Dwight in months," she said. "Not even over Christmas break when he was home." She looped her fingers around the idiot dog's snout to muzzle it. A portrait on the wall behind her showed Mom and Dad and only child Wynn and that stupid dog cradled in Mom's arms, same as now. The dad passed down to his son his lankiness and shaggy hair.

The difference between Sam and the Johnstons was Sam already knew that his own family life was headed toward disaster. Of course, he knew theirs was, too. It should've given him a power over them, but this was knowledge he damn well didn't need. In a rush of resentment, he wanted to tell her everything.

"Any chance your husband's talked to him?" asked Sam instead.

"Dan's at work, at the power plant. He hardly ever gets a chance to use the phone there."

"Can I get Wynn's number, his address at school?"

"Certainly, but—can I ask you something, Officer?"

"Deputy," Sam said.

"Deputy. Can I ask—was this incident—was it drug-related?"

"I'm afraid I can't get into that. You understand it's an ongoing investigation."

"Yes, of course. I'm just sure Wynn won't know anything. Those boys went their separate ways after Wynn started college, as you might expect. They had different life goals."

"Sure," Sam said. "Just the same, I'd like to talk to him."

"They—they shot each other? The Kopeck kids?"

"Like I said—"

"I know, I know. I'm sorry. I just—

—lone tower splitting the gray sky with another shade of gray, concrete ledges and the blips of lighted windows. Sam watched it from hilltops two miles out of the city—a single, eleven-story college residence hall that constituted the complete Weymouth skyline. Everything else but the power lines stayed hunkered down among the trees like it was afraid.

Sam routed himself through snow-swept vineyards and along the edge of the same woods where the fugitive from Dwight and Cecelia's murder had fled. He clocked coordinates, wondering why the kid trekked miles back to campus in blizzard cold when he could've just cut across a state highway and hit his permanent residence in twenty minutes flat. Maybe he wanted to avoid his parents' questions, avoid being seen so close to the kill site. Maybe he was delirious with what happened in that trailer.

Sam stopped at a SuperFuel pay phone to call Wynn's cell. He wanted to leave no records of the call on his personal cell phone. Wynn's cell flipped to voice mail after one ring: "You've reached my phone but you haven't reached me."

He hung up, called the dorm room number, got an answer after two rings.

"This Wynn Johnston?" he said.

"Wynn's not here. It's Parker."

"Parker, when do you expect him back?"

"Couldn't tell you. I think he's in class. I'll tell him to get you back if—"

"Don't worry about it," Sam said. "This is just one of his professors."

"Cool, cool. If you—"

Sam hung up before the roommate could finish his sentence. He stood and let the wind assault him. In the SuperFuel lot, snow dust blew in whorls the size of hubcaps. The cabbage fields were smoothed over with last night's snow. The trees ached in the wind, tapped their stripped limbs on the power lines like coded distress signals.

The residence tower in the distance was unreachable because it was university-police jurisdiction. He could park his cruiser off-campus, but his uniform alone would draw out campus cops and their smarmy, territorial piss-wars and interrogations. Safer to keep his distance yet. Even off duty in civilian clothes he'd be stopped at the dorm entrance and asked his business and ID. He'd maybe run into Erika between classes, his shit luck. What brings you to campus, Dad?

There was always Erika to think about, but Sam couldn't push his thinking past Jill's death. Couldn't even think the death itself. Almost as if keeping this Wynn business burning was a way to hold off that cancer spread.

Back inside the cruiser, he peeled off his gloves and threw them atop his thicker set on the dash. Unfolded a business letter from his jacket pocket, a Weymouth Hospital return address, spread out the letter inside and reviewed it while the wind rocket the Impala. Speed-dialed Fortuna Health Services and leaned back to wait out the prompts. Scratched his dry, itching knuckles with the fresh stubble on his chin. An India-based rep named "Adam" came on and fished for the usual numerals and IDs.

The letter had arrived in the mail that afternoon, but Sam pocketed it before Jill could notice. He didn't want her to consider the expenditures because the stark heartlessness of a hospital bill was like an argument against God. Out here, alone, Sam could take the burden as his own. He said, "I've got a bill for laboratory services from my wife's radiologist, but the coverage amounts don't seem right. They've got us paying a couple thousand straight out of pocket."

"I understand your concern, sir, and it is my sincere wish that we may assist you to your satisfaction. Please be advised, however, that any official . . ."

A Subaru Forester rounded the bend at fifty-one, according to Sam's radar. The limit here was thirty-five. Sam flipped shut his phone and lurched onto the road behind the speeder, flashing lights. The Subaru slowed and banked right, full compliance. A SUNY Weymouth parking decal stuck to the back window, color-coded faculty red. Fucking SUNY Weymouth. There was a buzz in Sam's marrow that couldn't be quelled.

He radioed in the license plate, then got out into the miserable night. The Subaru driver's door popped an inch. Sam laid a hand on the butt of his gun, but then he saw that the driver's auto window tab must've been frozen shut. Sam pulled the door wide and already the flustered driver tried to surrender a handful of documents. In the back, a snow-suited toddler slept in a booster seat. There were stockpiles of books on the seats and the floors.

"Sorry, the window—"

"You work at the college?" Sam asked. "Your parking pass?"

"Oh—right, right."

"What do you teach?"

"English. I teach English. But I'm just an adjunct."

"My worst subject in grade school," Sam deadpanned.

"Ha," the professor said, pulled his seat belt, snapped it against his chest.

"Do you know why I stopped you today?"

"I don't know. I don't know. Is my windshield obstructed?"

"That, too." Only a small aperture had been scraped out of the snow crusted on the glass. "Maybe if you brushed off your car you'd see the speed-limit signs."

Back in his prowler, Sam ran the license and wrote the ticket, headed to the Subaru to hand it off. The kid in the back was awake and whining when he got there. He told the professor, "You have a right to contest this ticket in city court. The instructions are on the back."

"Thank you," the professor said.

Sam said, "You got an ice scraper in there? You're obstructing your registration sticker."

"Oh, I didn't even realize."

"Why don't you get out and finish up the job."

"Right now? Here?"

"You need me to teach you how to do it?" Sam said.

"No, sir," the professor said, exactly like he was saying *fuck you*. Sam smirked and left the egghead to his task of shearing off sheets of solid ice with a scraper the size of a pocket brush. The thought that this could be one of Erika's professors doused Sam's fire only—

—heat blast from the air vents to warm Mom's chills, tucked under a goose-down comforter in the king-size bed. She wore a bandanna over her scalp and a pair of hoop earrings that together made her look like a pirate, but Erika didn't mention it. Erika sat above the covers on Dad's side of the bed, still a little drunk from the vodka. To hide the smell, she'd brushed her teeth first thing when she got home.

"Your show is on," Mom said. *"Cape Twilight Blues."* She hit the channel directory button on the remote and there were two teenagers bickering in a library. Reece Payton and some new actress Erika didn't recognize.

"I haven't watched this show in years, Ma. I'm way lost on the storyline by now."

"Who cares about storylines," Mom said. "They don't ever actually end anyway." She lifted her Big Gulp cup of Sprite, chockful of ice, and drank from the straw.

"Let's watch *World's Awesomest High Speed Chases,*" Erika suggested.

"Makes me worry too much about your dad."

"How's your stomach?"

"Actually, pretty good."

"You want me to make up some of those pizza rolls?"

"Maybe later," Mom said.

Erika hated talking as if her mother had come down with something that a little TLC could mend. In the last few weeks Erika had taken over the laundry and the dishes and the few meals her mother dared to eat. Erika herself subsisted mostly on coffee, McIntosh apples, and bottled water, maybe an occasional granola bar. She tried to tell herself these were all temporary states, but she knew better. She said, "A funny thing happened at the library today."

Mom was back on the channel menu screen. Erika felt sometimes that the cancer was in her own brain, too. It could have happened just as easily to her. They had the same genes, her and Mom, drank the same water, lived not a mile from the same Superfund site where a block of homes had been bought out by the power company and boarded shut. Like a cranial fetus it enlarged, it crowded out the matter that made her.

"Do you or do you not want to hear the funny thing that happened at the library today?"

"Yes, I'm sorry," Mom said. Sometimes their conversations cut in

193

and out like a bad connection. Sometimes Mom didn't hear, or forgot what she'd already heard. Sometimes she seemed to be answering with somebody else's perspective.

"A guy just hauled off and kissed me, out of nowhere," Erika said.

"Kissed you? What guy?"

"He's in my literature class. I've only talked to him once or twice, you know, for school. I thought his name was 'Wind,' like he had hippie parents or something, but it turns out his name is Wynn. So he just smacks me one right on the lips, no kidding. In the library."

"That's bizarre. What did you make of it?"

"I made lemonade. Boys are icky."

"Oh, knock it off," Mom said. "You've had boyfriends."

"Friends who were boys, yes—but none of them ever sucker-kissed me."

"So he expresses himself nonverbally. Is he handsome?"

"In a shaggy, hangdog manner, I guess."

"You were already born by the time I was your age—do you realize?"

"Are you suggesting I try to get myself pregnant?"

"Absolutely not. I'm just doing some mental scrapbooking."

Silence for a minute afterward. Even the television was muted. She wanted to tell Mom how the poet Keats, who died when he was twenty-six, harnessed the fear before he ceased to be. She wanted to tell Mom about the nightingale and what its birdsong meant. But she worried it would sound like a joke in bad taste, and humiliate them both. They were people, not poetry.

"Your father had a double murder last night," Mom said.

"He didn't tell me, when he picked me up. But I heard about it later and assumed."

"He doesn't like to talk about stuff like that."

"He hardly ever has to. When I heard they were my age, I wondered if I knew them. But it turns out they were from Lyme. Same place as this Wynn guy, the library kisser. I'm going to start on those pizza rolls, all right?"

She slid out of bed before Mom could respond, made her way down to the stairs, still a little cockeyed from the booze, and turned toward the kitchen. Her school bookbag was still on the counter where she'd left it, and tucked inside the front pouch was the flask. She untwisted it, took a big gulp, and stamped her foot on the linoleum to pound out the burn.

The buzz scribbled out thoughts of her mother's cancer for a few minutes, but the cancer always pushed through stronger and bigger. She turned on the convection oven and pulled a cookie sheet out of the cupboard, the bag of pizza rolls from the freezer. Activity was its own sort of salve. She poured the frozen rolls onto the tray. They looked like two dozen freezer-burned thumbs, and the sight of them made her want to gag.

While the oven preheated, she unpocketed her cell and dialed the SUNY Weymouth student directory. The automated voice asked for her prompt and Erika said, "Search." She waited, slipped the tray into the preheated oven, and said, "Johnston, Wynn." She gripped the stove handle as hard as she could and took long, steady breaths. The voice asked if she wanted to be connected directly.

"Parker here," somebody said. It didn't sound like Wynn, and that was a species of relief. Gave her a few more seconds to decide how to tell him that she'd overreacted because her life was a mess and because she had zero social skills, but so do you, so let's get together and—

I'm a twenty-year-old virgin because the thought of any intimacy give me hives, which you should know from the start if you think we should screw. Look, my mother is dying and that's why I'm not worth the trouble, so I don't want you to think that in some better time and place, with more forewarning, your bumbling love might not've actually worked.

"Is Wynn there?" Erika blurted.

"He just took off in my Volks. Is this another professor?"

"No, I'm Erika. I'm in his lit class."

"Cracking," the Parker guy said in a fake brogue. "I can give you his mobile digits."

"No—no, that's all right." Her thumb shivered against the button that would cut the call.

But Parker cleared his throat and got serious. "He have your number?"

"No, he doesn't have it, but—"

"I'll just save it on the caller ID. I'll let him know you called, fair enough?"

"Yeah—yes. Thank you," she said. She slipped the phone into a pouch in the skirt she was wearing, the one she sewed for herself out of her dad's old neckties. It wasn't yet so late at night, and she'd have to walk back to school in an hour for practice. Back down the rabbit hole.

She headed back into the living room, toward the stairs, but lingered in the foyer with a sense that something was out of place, empty air occupied somehow, a presence. She reached to the wall for its reassurance. A spear of light from the porch lamp cut through a breach in the window curtains. She held her breath and heard nobody else's, but there was a shadow of somebody outside.

Erika hunched low and pressed her hand over her cell phone to be sure it was there. Dad was number two on speed dial, though he was farther off than Weymouth city cops. She waited out the shadow, but nothing happened.

Could be Wynn Johnston stalking her again. Or just somebody from church checking in on Jill Hartwick and her poor daughter. They'd come before, and sometimes they lingered on the doorstep, building up their resolve before they entered the House of Creeping Death. They came to offer prayers that didn't work and casseroles that nobody ate.

She eased up the steps far enough that her view angled down through the three small windows in the door. The visitor wasn't Wynn, and she wasn't anyone Erika recognized from among Mom and Dad's church friends. It was a woman in a wool cap. She had a bandage on her face, one eye bruised, her lip split in the middle, like somebody seeking out a battered-women's safehouse. The woman had the storm door open, but she was standing there petrified.

The knock at the door was so faint Erika wouldn't have heard it if she'd been anywhere else in the house. Now she hardly hesitated: Flipped back the deadbolt and drew open the door, let the cold inside and stood at matching height with her visitor, who held a duffel bag against her thighs with one hand, pressed the other arm against her stomach.

"I'm sorry to bother you—" the woman said, and it was genuine sorry.

"It's okay," Erika said. She fixed her posture and resolved not to seem drunk.

"I didn't even know if you'd still live here, but you're Erika, aren't you?"

"I know who you are. You're my aunt. You're Jodie." A sudden urgency made her want to cry out to her mother. Nobody had said Jodie was coming. Nobody had said a word about her in years, not to Erika.

"This is completely out of the blue, I guess, and it's already so late at night."

"My mom—she's upstairs."

"I'm gonna be a sort of shock for her, I think," Aunt Jodie said. She shuddered and sniffled and apologized again. Erika tried to remember the number of years since she heard anything about Jodie Larkin, but it was like flicking on a light after long darkness—too bright to see anything just yet.

"It's okay, really. She'll be glad to know you're here," Erika said as she took the duffel bag. She told her aunt to come inside, flicked on the foyer lights. It opened onto a living room with the usual inherited furniture, orphan wires on the floor where the TV stood before Dad moved it to the bedroom. The fake Christmas tree was still in the corner and still ornamented because nobody could bring themselves to take it down.

Erika wondered if they were going to hug, but Jodie stood in a defensive slouch with her arm still tucked, timid of the walls and the doorways around her. This house had belonged to Jodie's and Mom's grandparents. Erika knew it was where the sisters spent holidays and school vacations and odd afternoons growing up. Even her own memories of Jodie were all set in this room—videotaped improv talent shows and loud music and roasting marshmallows on chopsticks over the stovetop. All those videos were stored in the attic somewhere, or thrown out, or Erika didn't know what.

Jodie drifted over toward the framed photo arrangement on the mantle, zeroed onto a picture of Erika's grandparents standing outside their retirement home in Arizona. None of the pictures had Jodie in them.

"Mem and Grands are supposed to be coming back next week," Erika said.

Jodie said, "In the middle of the winter?"

"Because of Mom," Erika said. The liquor in her system made her throat clench.

A step on the staircase creaked. Jill was there at the top of the stairs in her bathrobe and bandanna, twenty-five pounds underweight and hollow-eyed from the radiation and the steroids. There were ghosts in the house for certain.

"Jill, I'm sorry," Jodie said. "Jesus, I'm sorry. I should've called first, but, God—" She collapsed into the old recliner that she must've known was going to be there. It was older than Erika and hadn't ever moved from beside the front window.

Mom came down, both feet settling on each step before she tried the next. She held the rail and watched her own progress. Sometimes the tumor pressed portions of her brain that brought on moods, but tonight it was zero affect. You couldn't know which of her emotions were genuine or induced, or whether it could be said to make any difference which.

Mom came into the room and said, "What happened to you, Jodie?"

"There was a car accident—yesterday or two days ago, I don't remember."

"How did you get here?"

"I took a bus, from Pennsylvania, after the accident. I drove there from Atlanta first."

"Did you go to a hospital?"

"I couldn't," Jodie said dreamily. Her wet wide eyes were fixed on her sister.

Mom seemed to understand that she was on display, so she pushed away her bandanna and exposed her pale, bluish scalp with the patches of dried skin and the radiation rashes and the few tufts of resilient hair. The thing that was killing her lived inside of there, under just a few inches of bone and brain. She walked with it, slept with it, but it was completely unreachable.

"What is it, Jill?" Jodie begged.

"It's a brain tumor," Mom said as she eased down onto the couch. Her head was at a tilt. A muscle in her neck seized on occasion because of the tumor or medication or hours in bed.

"What does your doctor say?"

"They don't know yet," Mom lied. "They're still running tests." She drank Sprite from the cup she carried, sucking from the straw at an angle. Her eye settled on Erika while she sipped, deliberate and severe. The glance meant Erika had to play the edited version too, and it seemed all the more suffocatingly unfair—to know your mother is soon to die, and to be bound and gagged with that knowledge.

"Jesus, I can't believe it," Jodie said.

Mom asked, "Did they tell you, Ma and Dad? Is that why you came all the way up?"

"It's like a long while since I talked to them. Not since before I went down there. I'm saying I just seen you, just now, and I didn't know before that second when you came down them stairs." She pulled a tissue from the stand near the window and blew her nose deeply. She said, "I'm in a lot of trouble and I ended up here and I'm not even sure anymore how it happened. I just know I don't have nowhere else."

"What kind of trouble, Jodie?" Mom said. "Is it something illegal?"

"I stole a bunch of money. The car I wrecked wasn't mine, either."

"Jesus," Mom said. She coughed out a cynic's laugh. "You don't have any idea what Sam does now, do you? You know what he is? He's a deputy with the Cassadaga Sheriff's Department, for years now. How about that?"

Jodie filled her lungs and said, "Then I guess I'm gonna turn myself in." She looked at the tree and surely recognized some of the ornaments hanging from its boughs. Erika felt this woman's suffering bridging not only across the room but over years, launching outward from that family rift that faulted back when Erika was five, the design of it so suppressed that Erika had never before known any reason to wonder or wish to cross it.

"What's that burning smell?" Mom asked.

Erika hurried into the kitchen, yanked a towel from the drawer and pulled open the oven door. The pizza rolls were charcoal briquettes spilling black cheese onto the cookie sheet. She flapped the towel at the smoke roiling out of the oven, clicked on the air vent, but the alarm wailed anyway. She stood on tiptoes and swatted at the air around the alarm so it would shut the fuck—

Steel tables gleamed sterile like the layout of a morgue, inlaid wood surfaces distressed with a thousand knife cuts and dark animal stains. Concrete floors slicked by brackish water, laced with thin pink streams that spiraled into a drain. Men's shadows on the tiled walls, and the men themselves were much too vivid to look on straight. Meat grinders and cobalt industrial band saws, a corkboard display of knives and tenderizers and hacksaws. A meat-locker door with the pull-down latch, and Wynn's dull reflection shifted and bulged on its silver face.

He knelt in nothing but his briefs, hands twined behind his back with plastic snapcuffs. His face was a black blotch with wide eyeholes just a tug off-kilter. It was the skimask Dwight gave him, the remainder he'd left behind with the dead, returned to him again like everything. Like this butcher shop where he'd been before. It was in Philpot, Frank's father's place:

Frank hits the lights and there's Cecelia clutched at his waist, all addled on Crazy Horse and laughter. Dwight admires the rack of chopping implements while Wynn hangs back and broods. Dwight's half-wolf Howl sniffs along the floor and whines at the sense-overload of carnage wafting through his snout. Band saws and hacksaws, same shit as at their high school workshop. Sharp silver tools on a wall display.

A blow to the ribs crumpled him and broke the tape on his mental film reel. Somebody's manhandling hoisted him back into position. A clout to his face struck with a concussive jolt, tolling through the woolen membrane. A hose sprayed him at intervals like a cold set of razors dragged across his torso. His tongue touched a gummy slot where two teeth had been evicted. Each breath he heaved with suffocating trouble. Convulsions so bad he wanted to burst free of his body and its pain.

Vortex of voices like a toilet flush. Mostly Spanish talk. Cecelia's exboyfriend Frank said only "Christ, Christ." Wynn laid his broken face on the floor and watched from a remove as a hiking boot kicked his chest. The pain sought to explain itself but it made no—

—consciousness. A Mexican squatted nearby in a suede Carhartt jacket and gloves, navy blue sailor's cap, looming inside Wynn's blurred view. Jowls and a rounded belly, wire glasses, a thin moustache tinted slight gray. He looked to Wynn like a doctor, here to check vitals and revive, but he wasn't. He patted Wynn's cheek with his glove and said, "Can you hear me?"

"My ribs," Wynn said, but they burned brighter when he mentioned them.

"Yes, yes—let's not worry about that," the doctor said.

Wynn floated in a bed of weightless particles the size of kidney beans. They clung to his face and shifted beneath his body. He was shrinking into the microverse, soon to be small enough that he could drift between molecular orbits and collisions until the dark energy inside which everything drifted finally swallowed him down its infinitesimal void. Already the hornet electrons buzzed in his skull.

"Can you tell me something, my friend?" Doc asked. "Tell me your name."

"Dave—"

Doc winced like a game-show host on a contestant's dead-wrong answer. He said, "Can you tell me maybe the truth instead of this Dave business?"

Inhalation was pain with clotted nostrils and a hot putty nose. Consciousness sharpened, and thus the particles surrounding him were not the essence of life but simply Styrofoam packing peanuts. Wynn was inside a slatted crate with the dimensions of a coffin, cold as the outdoors.

"Maybe Ween Johnston is more the truth," the doctor said. He displayed Wynn's own driver's license, Exhibit A. Wynn's Cassadaga County Public Library Card, Exhibit B. He tossed Wynn's wallet into the crate with him, sprinkled the cards in after it.

"Let us be honest together, is okay, Ween? So now please explain why you come yesterday with your good friend Dwight Kopeck. This trailer you visit belong to my friends, so I want to understand why you come there for them, okay?"

"I loved her," Wynn said. "Cecelia."

The doctor winced again. He muttered something Spanish with the name *Cecelia* in the mix. The backlight shone too bright for Wynn to see the doctor's fellow confidants. It was a portable mechanic's light encased in an orange caging. It hung from a vacant hook on a track built into the stainless steel ceiling. They weren't in the rendering room anymore. They were inside the meatlocker.

The doctor asked, "Why does Dwight Kopeck kill his sister?"

"He didn't," Wynn groaned. He wanted to vomit. His hands were still bound and the plastic tore at the flesh on his wrists.

"They shoot each other. You are there to see this, no?" Doc clicked his tongue. He tossed something else into the crate with Wynn, and it flopped against his bare chest. The ski mask. Doc said, "Your superhero disguise. My friends find it last night after you leave. Maybe you are the one who shoots them, Ween Johnston? Yes or no? I am having difficulty to understand this."

"Your friends killed them," Wynn said.

"But this is not the truth, my friend."

Wynn coughed a metallic tang across his tongue. A mist of it speckled the doctor's glasses. Doc frowned, pulled one glove off with his teeth, found a tissue, removed his glasses, wiped the lenses. Wynn heard nothing but the freezer-fan hum and the bubbling of molecules surrounding him.

"Can I show you something?" Cecelia says. She unzips her jacket, pulls aside the collar of her blouse to expose a pale patch of skin just below her clavicle. She has carved a Christian cross there, the beams formed of a dozen wavering razor lines scabbed over like wood grain. She says, "If I told you it felt amazing, you'd know what I meant, wouldn't you?"

Frank leaned over the crate like a mourner and held a rifle to Wynn's head, contorted his face into a frozen flinch.

"Not so close," the doctor said. "You could have magic bounce bullet, okay? Here you go." He eased a gloved hand over the gunstock and inched it back from Wynn's skull, like a father showing his son how to best fix his aim on a quail in the brush. The doctor said, "You see? You will not have the, uh—ricochet."

Wynn tried to talk, but his throat was clotted. He arched his back and thrashed his feet against the crate that confined him. The foam particles crawled across his chest in electric trails. The rifle shuddered in Frank's grasp. It was a hunter's gun with a magnifier scope. Every instant was the instant Frank pulled the trigger.

"I owe them so much money," Frank whined. "I'm so fucking sorry, Dave."

"They killed Cecelia," Wynn whispered. He twisted his arms until the binding almost snapped his wrists. His hands were not his to control. His feet jammed against wood slats and even his bones creaked like the planks of a ship. Wynn was on that ship. He walked that plank. He thrashed and the crate tipped backward. He rolled with its momentum and the particles dispersed and the harsh mechanic's light swam and the rifle disappeared.

"Shoot, shoot, *puta madre*!" the doctor howled.

Wynn found his knees and he lunged himself upright. He stood within a crowd of cold meatslabs, hooked like old suits in an attic space. Grizzled muscle and white slices of rib. The odor of raw meat rode on shards of cold air. The slabs were giants, but he shouldered them as he moved. They swung, they shoved, and he stumbled among them.

A shot rang. The impact caught deep cold muscle, but it wasn't Wynn's. He burst through the beef line, hit the frosted-steel wall. Someone wailed like a smoke alarm. When Wynn's lungs were emptied, he realized it was him. The beef still swayed on its hooks. Wynn slinked along the wall, hands bound behind him. The cold fired vivid blue shocks down his spine.

Spanish tirade like machine-gun fire. Wynn's foot caught an extension cord on the floor, and it snaked between his ankles and loosed with a tug. Wynn pitched but kept his footing. The light popped and went dark. A gunshot, muzzle flash, casing clink on the floor, bullet ping on steel somewhere much too close.

Wynn blinked to get the black out of his sight, but it stuck like tar. He lurched forward again, aimed for the single cut of light that was left in his view, and collided with the freezer door, burst it wide and met the rendering room all over again. He sprawled stomach-down on concrete with no leverage to lift himself again. Flipped onto his back and sat upright, braced against a table leg.

An elderly man stood five feet off in a flannel bathrobe, long johns, fur-tufted boots. His downy white hair all matted from sleep. He toted a Mossberg pump with camouflage finish and a barrel aimed square at Wynn. He was a new arrival, not one of the torturers.

"Who the fuck are you?" the old man asked, and Wynn recognized him. He was the butcher who owned this place, Frank's father. The thickness of his glasses tagged him as near enough to blind for marksman purposes. He said, "Where's your clothes?"

"They're going to shoot!" Wynn screamed. Sidelong he scraped himself across the gritty floor, away from the meat-locker entrance, strained his neck to get a look across the room at a bank of machines, at an upright saw with a serrated ribbon blade.

"You sick—" the butcher started. But gunfire muted him. His neck spat the contents of a carotid. He moved one hand from the shotgun pump to his gunshot neck. The Mossberg wavered one-handed.

A tank-topped Mexican goon came forth from the meatlocker brandishing a handgun, the one that shot the old man. At the sight of him, the old butcher backstepped and sagged and fired a shell that burst a cone of buckshot across the tabletop and tore splintered wood. The Mex caught the outer arc of pellets in a red-tipped pointillist's canvas on his shirtfront.

The butcher knelt. He laid the shotgun on the floor beside him, close enough that Wynn could nudge it with his corpse-white feet. The butcher pressured his hand against the blood pump that was delved into his neck.

"What'd you do?" Frank whined. He came from the locker with his rifle at ease. He stood on tiptoe to peer over the table lip to where his father knelt. Up behind Frank came the doctor, who lifted a handgun on the back of Frank's head. If there was anything to hear, it couldn't penetrate the firearm scream in Wynn's ears. Wherever the killing bullet went, it found no exit. Frank's forehead bounced the table ledge before he floored. The doctor dived behind a meat grinder and after an instant he burst out from hiding, rushed through into the storefront.

The butcher leaned against a cabinet and regarded Wynn. The blood rush had already drenched to the flared sleeve on his bathrobe. He gave more blood and shallower breaths. Wynn's heart was another engine winding down. The fluorescent lights sputtered. Blood trailed into a drain where so much blood had gone before.

After a moment Wynn was still alive, and then still. He struggled upright, found his knees. The muscles in his thighs spasmed like electric shock as he tried to stand. But he rose to his senseless feet and stepped backward against the band saw machine, touched the safety guard with his fingertips.

He craned his neck to get a look at where the saw teeth snagged against the plastic of his snapcuffs. The sight of his own raw wrists nearly stole his consciousness. He scraped the plastic over the saw. It snagged, slipped, tore slivers in the bands. He eyed the power switch, but his shivering arms would not keep him steady enough to risk those high-speed teeth. White stars sizzled in his vision, but he kept at his work. The old man looked on, though his eyelids were drooping shut. He had the cast of death already. Then, like nothing, the binding—

Sam passed his second hour typing his report alone in a sheriff's department substation in the Lyme boonies, nothing but a drafty porch attached to a DPW station where they kept silos full of road salt, just off the interstate. Mud-caked floors and mildewy walls, old coffee cups with science-project sludge in them. A bunch of mug-shot dirt-bags stared down at him from the wanted board, mostly Mex traffickers and probation dodgers with a Ku-Klux vibe in their eyes. Seemed a good enough purgatory as any for the likes of Samuel Hartwick, penitent.

The write-up was his full-detail FOS report of the Kopeck double-murder scene, supplement to the summary report he wrote on his patrol-car laptop the night before. Investigators and Drug Task Force were already demanding copies.

He checked the printer and it was out of paper. He'd have to e-mail the report to himself and print it back at Public Safety in Weymouth before his shift was up, but he couldn't think that far ahead. He could barely track the half-lies and omissions that peppered the report.

His cell phone buzzed in his breast pocket. The display screen told him it was Jill.

"Where are you right now?" she asked, edge in her voice that put him on alert so bad he stood from his seat and kneed the desktop.

"I'm at the Lyme substation—why? What's wrong?"

"Can you come by the house? I think you should come by."

"What's the problem?"

"Just, please, Sam. You need to come back." She didn't sound unbalanced, but it was just this kind of stress that roused her worst troubles, her mental fugues.

"All right, okay. Give me fifteen—

—expecting Sheriff Olin's unmarked in his driveway, maybe a backup prowler in the street. Irrational: because if they were going to bust him as accessory to murder, they'd just call him into the station. No need to hit his house and use his wife as bait. But then Sam Hartwick was never before involved with the arrest of a crooked cop, so he didn't know the protocols they'd follow.

He came through the front door and got a whiff of putrid smoke. Saw Jill first, then Erika beside her on the couch, then a bleach blonde seated in the recliner as if the cushion was studded with nails. She had the look of a war refugee, but Sam still recognized her. Fifteen years collapsed like a snapped suspension bridge, and nothing but the abyss stood between then and now.

The radio on his belt crackled and he felt himself jolt. He turned it down and searched his daughter's face for any sign of apprehension, but she still looked as innocent as she ever was. Nobody'd told her, not yet, which meant there were still a pretense left to uphold, for Erika's sake.

He cleared his throat and said, "Jodie. I didn't know you were planning to visit."

She bowed her head like a scolded child. Last time he saw her, she was a child.

"Sam," Jill said. She stood up and moved toward him, crowded him out so he was forced to make his way up the stairs like she wanted. Her head was naked, and Sam supposed that stark display was for Jodie's benefit. She ushered him upward and into the bedroom, closed the door. He had to sit on the bed because the ceiling slope bore down on him. The TV was tuned to a local-news broadcast, sports recap.

"What the hell happened to her?" he asked.

"She was in some kind of car accident yesterday."

"You weren't expecting her?"

"No, Sam. Did I mention I was expecting her?"

"I don't know—I figured maybe you didn't want me to know."

"I don't keep things from you," Jill said. "She just showed up at the door, just out of nowhere. She didn't even know what was going on with me. I had to tell her I didn't know the prognosis yet because I couldn't just . . ."

Sam smoothed out the comforter next to where he sat. He wanted to touch her while they talked. But she needed to have this leverage over him, and he wasn't about to deny her. He said, "Well, this is a little crazy. I mean, where's she been? What does she want from us? I come in, the house smells of smoke—"

"Never mind the smoke, Sam. Jodie's here because she's in trouble. The car that she wrecked yesterday, down in Pennsylvania apparently, it didn't belong to her. She borrowed it from a friend of hers without asking."

"You mean she stole it, is what you're getting at," Sam said.

Jill's hands flittered against the folds of her bathrobe. She looked like she wanted to pace, but there wasn't enough floor in the room. He wanted to hug her calm, but constriction would set her off twice as fast. Jill said, "She says she was working as a maid in Atlanta, and she came across some money in a house she was cleaning, and she took it. She stole it on a whim and she panicked and that was it."

"Did she say how much money?"

"Five thousand dollars."

"Aw, Jesus, that's a felony. Along with the stolen car."

"She wants to turn herself in. She's confused, and ashamed."

"What else is new," Sam said, and regretted it immediately. It struck him by surprise, that he hated Jodie Larkin for showing up, for throwing her weight on the wrong side of the precariously balanced scale.

But Jodie wasn't any monster, now or before. Back then she was a sixteen-year-old girl stupidly seduced by a drunk in his twenties who couldn't keep his dick limp. Those were Sam's worst days, and all the faults were—

—empty egg with Santa's face crayoned on its surface, red felt hat and cotton-puff beard. Jodie had made the egg Santa ornament for a second-grade class project, blew the yolk out through a hole until it was hollow, and here it was with its shell still intact, when nothing else seemed to be. She cradled it in her fingers where it hung from the tree.

She expected within an hour she'd be locked in a county jail cell where she could mull through the muck of these last few hours for as long as she needed to get it all straight. Sam Hartwick would take her there. She'd seen him come through the door and felt that leap in her chest, that awful emotion she'd thought was killed.

Erika sat on the armrest of the sofa. A woman, but last time Jodie saw her she was hardly five. Her sudden adulthood seemed all wrong, like when Jodie saw Cal after so long—both of them, cousins, still wearing kid freckles but grown into bodies that were mature too soon.

"I remember watching you play Super Mario, when you babysat," Erika said.

"You loved watching," Jodie said. "I tried to get you to play, but you didn't want to."

"I was afraid of Bowser," Erika said.

Jodie didn't want to sit anymore, but the standing made her too anxious, too light-headed. The throbbing in her arm and her face seemed quieter when she relaxed. She said, "You used to love to dance to my music, though."

"I remember," Erika said. "I still listen to Jane's Addiction."

Jodie lifted her duffel bag onto her lap and unzipped the side pocket. In the Buffalo station she'd checked the money, saw that half of it was missing. She knew Calvin took it. Anybody else and it would all be gone. Knowing Cal had money to spend to keep himself safe—

—crisis pushed its roots all the way back to him. The clarity was as pristine as the face of God. Sam corrupted everything. Even Erika, who didn't know the truth but was still raised in its shadow—the cold, hesitant forgiveness that defined her parents' marriage. Even Jill's tumor, it had grown from where his betrayal first implanted in her brain like some demonic zygote.

Jill reached for the remote tucked under her pillow and upped the volume on the TV. She kneeled on the bed next to him. Put her hands on the butt of his holstered Beretta. He saw the weird glaze coming over her eyes, but he didn't stop her. Whatever she wanted, he would allow.

"I want to know something," she said. "I want to know if we can help her, so she doesn't have to go to jail. She told me something, Sam. She said that the car she stole belonged to a Mexican illegal, that she purposefully stole it, because she knew he couldn't report it because his papers were all falsified anyway. Do you hear what I'm saying?"

"I hear," Sam said. "You think she can get away with it. But five thousand dollars—"

"Right, but what if they didn't report it?" Jill moved her hands up his arm, throttling his biceps like a tourniquet. "Jodie said the people were multimillionaires, and they just had it laying around like spare change. What if they didn't even notice—"

"Nobody doesn't notice five thousand dollars, honey."

"I know—I understand—but what if they noticed but just shrugged it off, you know, chalked it up to stupidity on their own part, just leaving money around to tempt the maid service. They have a social conscience, right, and they don't want to get anyone in her position in trouble. You see what I'm saying? They just sweep it under. In that case, there's nobody looking for her. What good will it do if she turns herself in then?"

"She wants to," Sam said.

"But, see, I don't think she does."

"If she did this stuff she says, we can't get ourselves—"

"Goddamn it, Sam!" she cried.

"Jill, you're not being clearheaded. You know that language doesn't do us any good."

"Language?" She stood with her open palms pressed against the side of her head like a child trying to block loud noise. Her eyes bulged and she wasn't herself anymore. She pulled her hands apart and made fists and then smacked them back against her temples. When Sam reached out to stop her, she spun away from him and brought her fists together against their full-length mirror on the closet door. Spiderweb cracks wound outward from where she slammed, and their panicked reflections divided into—

—set the duffel bag underneath the tree like a belated gift. Too late now to dispose of it, pointless to bring it to jail. She'd let her lost family sift through it later, decide for themselves whether they wanted to deal with what it contained.

She offered over the stack of money, the two thousand dollars that was left. Erika looked into her face and then back at the cash. She was sitting on her hands.

"Go head, Rica," Jodie said. Her own secret nickname for the girl, fifteen years ago.

Erika said, "What's this?"

"I want you to take it," Jodie said. "I'm not gonna need it anymore."

"I can't—"

"It's the last two thousand of the money I stole. It's nobody's money because it's never gonna get back to where I took it from. You know that, right? I got about a hundred bucks in change in my pocket, and it's gonna be easy to believe I spent the rest."

"Why do you want me to have it?" Her hands slipped out from under her thighs.

"Because we used to dance," Jodie said. "And I used to call you Rica. And I owe you in a whole bunch of ways you don't even know. I owe everybody, but nobody else is gonna be able to do nothing with it. Hurry up before they come back down, all right?"

Jodie shook the money to emphasize her point. Erika took it delicately in both hands like some rare family heirloom. Upstairs, Jill was screaming. Erika held the money and listened. A few seconds later came the shattering glass and more screaming. Erika stood and crammed the money down into her left bootcuff just before she rushed—

—reeled back, slapped him across the face with her open palm and the impact was wet with her own blood. Sam grabbed both her wrists. They were thinner and drier than they ever felt before. He tried to hold her steady without harm, to wait for the synapses to find their proper pathways again. She bared her teeth at him, and this could be the time she wouldn't recover.

"You're having an episode," he said. "You could have a seizure if you don't relax."

"Don't you dare blame me for this mess. You're the one who made her go away."

"I'm not blaming you." He tried to move her back to the bed, but she fought him.

"We need to help her, Sam."

"I understand your feeling, but it's against the law."

"What do you think law means to me anymore? I couldn't care about law. My sister is here, and I want her here when our parents come back next week. I didn't think I'd ever see her again, and I hated myself for that, and you. I want her here, and I deserve that."

"What if she's wanted, Jill?"

"Then they can wait till I'm gone to take her, how about that? We owe her. *You.*"

Sam wiped his face with his jacket sleeve. It was his wife's own blood he absorbed. The awful reckoning in her expression, the wounds on her hands, the shape of her pale scalp, all of it brought him down to his knees.

Erika in the doorway asking why the noise, gasping when she saw the blood. He didn't want to subject his daughter to this, but she was their child. She couldn't be witness to anything else and still be the girl she—

Nobody stopped Cal at the door, and he stepped into a space pulsing with red light like a school-hall fire alarm. The layout was straight out of art-history class. A medieval church with the blueprint of a cross: bar at the altar, guitarist where the sacristy would be, curtained private booths along the naves, and Cal standing in the vestibule. Whiffs of dry ice and clove cigarettes. Mounted speakers amplified the acoustic cover of "Wicked Game."

He crossed the aisle under scrutiny of the men swaying slow on their feet where the pews were supposed to be. Not more than ten patrons in all, a slow night, but they peered at him with the black, unblinking eyes of sharks.

"Rum and Coke," he told the bartender in the muscle shirt, and then he held his breath. Cal couldn't move his eyes from the bartender's fluid routine—grab a glass, scoop ice from a bin, set the glass on a rubber pad, tip in the rum, press the Coke fountain spout.

Someone slinked up beside Cal and said, "Better ask for his ID."

Cal's throat clenched. It was a long way back across this chapel to the exit, but it was another shock altogether when Cal faced the man who'd spoken and saw that he was a dead ringer for Freez. Not Gene the Imposter, but Freez the Adonis surfer boy in the online avatar.

The bartender arched his eyebrows, set down a cocktail napkin. "You of age?" he said.

"Sure he is, aren't you?" Freez said. He raised a highball of something clear and bubbly.

"Yeah," Cal croaked.

"See," Freez told the bartender. "My guess is as good as gold."

"Uh-huh," the bartender said, then to Cal, "got an ID to prove it?"

"I don't have anything on me," Cal said.

"The city send you in here to test me?"

"Spoilsport," Freez told the bartender. "Pittsburgh's got no jurisdiction here."

The two men shared a laugh. Cal's drink sat on the bartop, unattended, but nobody moved to renege it. Cal lifted it and took a sip and tried not to wince when it bit back at him.

The bartender gave a clown frown and said, "Nobody said you could take that, kid. For the record. Plus you didn't pay for it—"

"That reminds me," Freez interrupted, slapping down a ten-dollar bill. "Here's the tip I forgot to give you earlier." The issue was settled, so Freez turned to Cal and asked, "First visit?"

"Here?" Cal said, with a hitch in his voice. Across the room, the live performer dissolved "Wicked Games" into "Fast Car" with barely a tempo change, but it tipped Cal's soul upside down and poured it out slow.

"Never Never Land, where none grow old. Or Pleasure Island, without the ass faces."

"It looks like a church." The ice in Cal's glass shivered. He took small, constant sips.

"And yet, Pandemonium is a place in Hell, reserved for me and mine." Freez flirted every word and his tone warmed Cal faster than the alcohol. Cal tried to remember what he'd said to the fake Freez so he could say it for real this time. Once, he'd been stupid enough to believe this unicorns-and-leprechaun shit could actually happen.

Soon the live guitarist was gone, replaced by Eurotrash dance on the sound system, and in sacred spaces men danced slow steps in twos or threes, dry-ice fog roiling at their ankles. The drinks squeezed tendrils beneath Cal's skullplate.

The nave booths were half-circles with velvet cushioning, velvet curtains, and velvet art on the walls featuring a stalking tiger, Marilyn Monroe, a sad hobo clown pinching wilted flowers. Every time Cal looked down at his drink it was full. The techno rhythms made his eyelids heavy, and each time he blinked ten minutes passed and new guests were at his table. He seemed to be the host, seated in the center with men smoking and swallowing cocktails all around him.

Sometimes the Freez lookalike was there, sometimes it was the mohawk boy in the black sweatshirt, the one with the star/tear tattoo who Cal saw begging on the street. Nobody thought anything was strange, so Cal didn't, either. Somebody held his hand and whispered into his ear that what he did to that girl was justifiable, that she'll recuperate, and you must always do what you must to survive. Cal nodded into his lap.

"I was in the navy, too," said a gentleman in his fifties with a mustache that looked like some starlet's plucked eyebrows. He seemed more amused by Cal than hungry for him—nothing like slobbering, fraudulent Gene. The navy veteran brushed the lapel of Cal's coat between his fingers and pursed his lips.

Cal heard himself talking, ". . . mostly paintings of places I imagine, like fake landscapes. One I made with my blood because I knew it would dry the right color, the color of dirt on Mars, or somewhere even further."

"Positively primeval," the navy man said. Beside him, the mohawk kid brooded with a domestic beer in his hand, tore swigs off its mouth like he was unimpressed with Cal and this whole circus sideshow.

"But my stupid art teacher," Cal said, "she turned me in, to the school counselor. They put me on some kind of watch list, and they confiscated my journal I was doing for English class. All the teachers were pussyfooting around me like I was a bomb ready to blow. My parents made me go to a psychiatrist, and he wanted me on Zoloft. I wouldn't take it."

"Well, they deleted your disease from the DSM," Navy said. "Doesn't count anymore."

"*Ready to blow,*" someone sang. Chuckles all around the table. Cal couldn't keep account of how many, or where Freez had disappeared to.

Mohawk hiked his chin and said, "Where'd you get it from? The blood?"

Cal pulled up his jacket sleeve and showed the thin white scar on his wrist.

"There's serious attempts and then there's cries for help," Mohawk said.

"I never said—" Cal started.

"Pay no mind to Mr. Doom 'n' Gloom," Freez said, right beside him all along.

A thin piece of silk fluttered around Cal's face, brushed the back of his neck, though he couldn't see it exactly. Christmas bells were ringing in the square, and there was no such place as Pittsburgh—only here, where everyone's face was bathed in Valentine red and it was all so delightful and borderline perverse and nothing was cold and nothing—

—about riding at night when the dark and the road are both an excuse not to look at your passenger. They were in Sam's prowler, skirting Erie along Lake Ave, past the pier and the war memorial park, the pizza parlor and used car dealers, all of it Weymouth Police jurisdiction. Sam drove and Jodie rode beside him. The February roads were sludge and salt, and the curbs were two-foot snowbanks gone brown from exhaust fumes and mud.

"I never would've guessed," Jodie said, gesturing at the radio equipment. "This."

"Yeah, well," Sam said. "People change. People stop drinking, for one thing. And you didn't used to be a car thief, from what I can remember."

The backseat behind the cage was empty. Jodie's wrists were uncuffed. She hadn't brought anything to the car with her besides her jacket, and Sam saw no need to ask why. Jill was back home, Erika on watch for signs of a seizure. Sam was left to deal with the prodigal sister, left to stew in the shame he felt sitting this close to her.

"Back at the house," Sam said. "Jill just gets like that sometimes. It's the cancer."

"I know—and I'm sorry I had to cause—anything."

"She's not angry like it seems. She's not angry at you. She forgave me, she can forgive you a lot easier." A set of train tracks jostled the prowler's shocks and marked the edge of Weymouth's limits. Trees replaced streetlights and ushered in the black wilderness that was Sam's usual beat. Here he didn't feel any more in control than back across the tracks.

"Can she come to visit me?" Jodie asked. "I still want to see her again."

"I'm not taking you to jail," Sam explained.

"What?" Her face was distorted by surprise and by the shadows of the dash glow. There was a fresh bandage on her cheek from his own medicine cabinet. He felt himself free-falling through the center of his body.

"Here," he said. He turned into a roadside lot with a wing of rooms detached from the manager's office, a motel called The Enchanted Angler. The walls were fashioned with lake slate and pine crossbeams. Sam had visited here once or twice on domestic calls and found them tidy by comparison to some of the biker flops farther outside of town. This place was on his watch, clean, mostly safe, isolated from almost everything, and not somewhere you'd waste much time snooping around because the rooms were generally vacant.

"Here's where Jill wants you to stay, for the time being." He pulled around to the back lot where a parallel row of units stood against the woods. Just a few parked cars back here, out-of-state plates. Back here, no passersby would see his prowler from the road.

"Jill wants me here?"

"She wants you out of jail till we figure out what's going on."

"You don't believe what I told you, about what I did?"

Sam cranked the gearshift into park. He said, "If I didn't believe you, I would've brought you into the station so you could make a fool of yourself with a false confession. No skin off mine. But—since I believe you—bringing you in is something I really can't deal with right now."

"What about what I think?" Jodie said.

"Jodie, way I look at it, you came to us because you needed help, and this is the help."

"I'm not sixteen years old," she said.

"Right, because people change. Where's the money you stole?"

She leaned her head against the passenger-side window and her breath fogged against it when she spoke. "I spent most and lost some, so it's all gone. I have maybe seventy, eighty left."

"What do you mean lost?"

Jodie said, "Somebody stole it off me when I was sleeping on the bus."

"All right," he said. "I can get you a fish-fry or something and bring it back."

"I'm not hungry."

"Look, we're doing this for Jill. Everything is for Jill from here on in, all right?"

"Yeah," she said, and she popped open the passenger door. She didn't break out running toward the woods, or back toward the road. Instead, she leaned against the biting wind and headed straight at the rental office. Her hair was short and blond, but it used to be the same as Jill's, vibrant orange coils like a hot range on a stovetop. He'd watched his wife pull clumps of that hair from her own head, standing before the bathroom mirror, until it was all but gone.

Sam sat in the prowler and wished for his old flask brimming with sour-mash whiskey. He squeezed the steering wheel until his knuckle joints popped and wished for God's resolve instead. When that cancer took possession of his wife's head, it mocked every truce they'd settled between each other. They had made a clearing, but now the wilderness was pushing itself back upon them and the prophets were already proclaiming doom. He wanted Jill back, more than booze and more than God.

Jodie came out of the office and hurried along the walkway under the awning. She stopped halfway back to the car and pushed a key into the lock on Unit 6. Sam glanced at the dead quiet Sentinel 911 program on the laptop and wondered if all the county's sleazebags were hibernating tonight. They were giving him too much time to brood.

He questioned why he would've ever had the urge—because they were much the same, these sisters, and Sam couldn't think what he would've wanted from this woman that his wife had not provided. He wanted to lock her up in that room and never let her out. He wanted to toss her back out into the world and tell her to stay gone this time. He wanted to—

—boots fit, but much too loose, laceless boots that belonged to Frank. Dead Frank, and Frank's father the butcher was also dead, and some anonymous Mexican in a shotgunned wifebeater. Off of Frank's corpse Wynn had stolen the pants and even the underwear. If he could've peeled away Frank's tattoos he would've taken them, too. He'd have become Frank the butcher's boy so that Cecelia would love him despite all his wrongs. Cecelia, who was also dead—and Wynn who should've been dead twice over by now. He could hardly remember his name or the reasons why he should still be alive.

The warp of the line toward the unsayable pi is the simplest proof of an infinite God, the endless irrational slant. The horror of the innumerable spaces between all matter is a darkness we cannot bear because it stands for the chaotic void from which all things sprang, the mind of God that cannot begin or finish. Every dimension, every whole number, every clean square root is a barrier we raise against that limitless black vacuum, and a bowl we construct to contain it. We teeter on the edge at every nanosecond, we suffer lifetimes of vertigo, the desire to leap, though we can never quite fall into that chasm.

Wynn crossed the back lot of a quick-change tire shop, watched through the garage windows as a first-responder county patrol car sped with lights and sirens down the main road. They'd soon be standing in their uniforms among slaughtered bodies that were not meant for meat. One of the dead was the old man who'd saved Wynn's life.

He measured his distance at two blocks from the butcher shop, bearing the agony of every step. No chance of running, because aerobic lungs bent his tender ribs to their snapping points. Shallow breaths kept him going. He wore a dead man's clothes and a Thinsulate jacket he'd found dangling from a peg beside the meat locker, a faint vapor of blood on one arm. He wore no shirt because each of his three options was splashed with too much carnage. Where his own clothes went was a mystery, and where the Mexican doctor fled was another.

Wynn found a pay phone in the restroom hallway of Paulie's Italian Emporium. He drifted on a whiff of baked dough and the wafting pizza oven heat. He wavered punch-drunk, and a kid exiting the men's room slid along the far wall to avoid him. Wynn's fingers were swollen past use, one eye squeezed shut, and his whole damaged ear felt deformed. It occurred to him without much concern that he was a walking suspicion not half a mile from a massacre.

Couldn't remember now why he fled the scene at all, except that he wanted to go home. Not home where his parents lived, but home where his dorm room was, where his slow train away from this place departed from. Graded math test to retrieve, Moscow Semester paperwork to file, MIT application to fill. He wanted all his past aborted and replaced with the clean future he had worked toward. Should've fled much farther in the first place, to an out-of-state college where Dwight wouldn't have been able to find him.

It was a painstaking dial, but Wynn called collect to his dorm-room phone, and Parker accepted the charges. Wherever Wynn's cell was, it had disappeared with his clothes.

"I didn't even know they still did collect," Parker said.

"I'm in some trouble," Wynn said.

"Shit, Wynn. You wrecked my Beetle."

"No, no. It's fine. Or—I'm not with it right now."

"What do you mean? Where are you?"

"In a pizza shop. In Philpot. I got separated from the car."

"Well, where the hell is it, Wynn?" More worry than Parker ever evinced before.

"I don't know right now."

"You're saying it got stolen? Is that it?"

"No. The other way around. If I could just get somebody out here—"

"Why you asking me, dude? You took my car. *My* car."

"Maybe your girlfriend. If she just came out, we could drive over to where it is."

"She doesn't have a car. Plus it's freaking eleven-thirty."

"I'm in trouble here, Park." He wanted to sit down, but the cord wasn't long enough.

"Why don't you get this Cecelia chick to bail you out?" Parker said.

"What?"

"I said call this Erika chick, see if she'll help you."

"Erika?"

"She called here, man. Like maybe an hour and a half ago. People been calling all day. Caller ID picked up her number. Why don't you get her to come out and drive you to my car?"

"Number," Wynn said, and Parker gave it over.

In the men's room Wynn spit blood in the sink basin, grinned at himself in the mirror to assess the damage. Two empty slots where a canine and incisor should be. He put his tongue in the space to be sure he wasn't hallucinating. He held paper toweling to his bleeding ear. He recalled Erika's telephone numbers and divided them by her birth date, and it carried out over seven, eight, nine decimal places, beyond what he could hold in his mind, toward the infinite surd. The calculations pushed the pain aside.

Somebody came into the bathroom behind him, and Wynn saw in the mirror he was a biker type, bearded and rawhide, the sort that scared other men from public restrooms just with his looks. He was gunning for the urinal, hands on his fly. Wynn turned on him and asked, "Sir, any chance you have a quarter I might—

—glass shards from a dustpan into the bathroom wastebasket. Erika brushed the bandage packaging and blood-stained napkins from the counter, cleaning up after household disasters like a maid. Maybe this was why Aunt Jodie had had enough of her job and fled. The vodka was all burned off and here Erika was, her susceptible self again, with somebody else's cash in her boot. Here she was culpable, and the daughter of a deputy. Two hours late for *Alice*.

You cage your own wonderland for two decades of life, and what does it get you? There were higher laws than those her father served, laws that passed harsh judgment whether you had virtue or not. What mattered was beauty, and Erika had missed all of it. The bathroom mirror showed her opposite self, and a slice of the hallway, and her mother's bedroom beyond.

She wondered if her mother was sick in the looking-glass world. It seemed the identical six prescription drug bottles were arranged on the counter in that universe, too. She touched the flat reflection of her own fingertips, but the way out was not through there. She'd overheard Alice's lines so much she could be the understudy: "Now let us consider who it was that dreamed it all. It must have been either me or the

Red King. He was part of my dream, of course, but then I was part of his dream, too."

Mom lay on the bed with her bandaged hands at her sides. Her cuts were minor, but the cloud of her outburst still lingered thick. Erika sat on the edge of the bed, hugged her legs against her chest. Her boot-soles were on the blankets. The sorts of rules against such habits didn't matter in this house anymore. Erika asked, "How are you feeling?"

"Fine," Mom sighed. "But I don't want to lie down anymore."

"You're supposed to."

Mom turned onto her side and reached toward Erika's arm. For a moment, Erika thought her mother would reach down into the boot and retrieve the contraband cash. But she only grabbed her by the wrist and squeezed.

"Where did he take her?" Erika asked.

Mom averted her eyes but said, "The Enchanted Angler, over on Lake Avenue. She's not going to the police just yet, and Dad doesn't think we can have her staying here. He's probably right. I wish I could explain to you why we have to do this, with Aunt Jodie."

"So explain," Erika said.

"We owe her."

"You can say a lot more than that."

"I can't."

"I'm supposed to just let it pass?"

"For now," Mom said.

"Yeah, because tomorrow would be better. Or maybe next Christmas you can tell me."

"Erika," Mom said. She grabbed for the arm again, but Erika recoiled. She stood up next to the spiderwebbed mirror and felt the same urge her mother had felt to blast it to pieces and shred her own flesh in the act. A reflection of herself all out of whack, coming together unrecognizably.

"Erika, sit down please," Mom said. "I've had to forgive a whole lot of things."

"So what am I going to have to forgive about you?"

Mom tossed aside the blankets, fled into the bathroom with the door shut behind her. Erika followed, shoved open the bathroom door. Mom was seated on the toilet with her bandaged hands shuddering against her face so violently that it seemed at first like a seizure. Erika almost wished she could draw a seizure out of her mother, like exorcising a demon.

Mom said, "Please, I'm on the toilet."

"Tell me what's going on. You can't die and still be hiding shit on me."

"I'm on the toilet!" She grabbed the plastic soap dispenser from the counter and howled as she chucked it, almost cast herself off the seat. Erika held the door like a shield and the projectile cracked against the surface, spun away, clattered on the linoleum floor in more than one piece. The worst of it was her mother's animal shriek.

Erika spoke through the barrier she made between them. "You're not—you're not being yourself! You're letting it mess with you! Why don't you fight that fucking rock inside your head instead of me? You're just going to let it—" Her open palm slapped at the door and got nothing for it but the sting. She pressed her forehead into the wood, held it for an instant, then turned and barreled down the stairs hard enough to shake the old dry bones of the house.

Mom threw open the bathroom door. She was wild and ugly, robe undraped to exhibit skin that was vacuumed against her ribs and her hipbones. She said, "You want to know what I fight?"

"Yourself, and your family," Erika said.

"Your father screwed Jodie when she was sixteen years old. How's that?"

"What the hell are you talking about, Mom? You're confused."

"He came crying to me all sorry, and I hated them both, and I drove Jodie away. Your father drove her away, and I forgave him instead, a grown adult." She folded her robe shut and wrenched a knot into the belt. "That's why I owe her, and that's why I don't give a damn about anything she's done. Whatever it is, it's my fault."

"Mom—"

"That's who your mother is, and I'm goddamned sorry for it," she said, and she was already gone from her pulpit. Erika dropped down onto the step, her back against the wall and one boot on the railing. This was what it meant to have your mind invaded by something relentless and growing with exponential divisions.

She snatched her buzzing phone and saw a local number she didn't recognize.

"Is this Erika? Erika Hartwick?"

"Yeah," she said. She placed his voice, and her instant reticence surged.

"This is Wynn Johnston. Am I bothering you? Is it too late? My roommate—he said you called, so uh . . ."

"I called, yeah. Earlier. It's fine, though." She breathed a faint laugh through her nose and watched the vacant landing where her mother had been. "I wanted to apologize. In the library, I didn't know what to say. I never know what to say."

"You didn't—you don't need to be sorry."

"These things you have no way of anticipating. It's my whole life lately."

"I'm on a pay phone," Wynn said. "I don't know how long the call. I'm in Philpot. Do you know where Philpot is? I'm gonna ask you something, and please feel free to hang up."

"Wynn. I told you I'm not very good at sudden—

—dazed drunk reflection of himself that winced with every impact. Too much skin in the bluish light. The bathroom mirror was bordered with stickers for gay sex chatlines and Web sites, bare abs and stiff dicks galore, and it all hungered at Cal in three vivid dimensions.

His hands gripped the edges of the sink while the hands of another clutched his hips and mashed his flesh. Nothing like love, but each thrust was slicked with lubricated rubber and spit. A familiar blood thread darned from his nose along the edge of his lip. Nothing like love, but it pumped his tears. He whispered, "careful," but the stabbing ignored him. The backbeat muffled by the bathroom door gave his violator a rhythm to mimic.

The condom dispenser on the wall featured glow-in-the-dark and ribbed varieties. He smelled the rubber and the salted-butter scent of someone else's pheromones. He willed himself to remember this sense he'd never known, like they were the first ever to discover a fresh perversion, Calvin Nowak and whoever was—

—shift switch partner, Murph, dropped Sam home. Murph pulled the prowler into the snowless patch on his driveway where his Nissan was supposed to be parked. Sam pulled his cell to see if Erika or Jill placed a call that he somehow missed, thinking they'd rushed off to the hospital at the onset of a seizure, or worse. But no missed calls, no messages.

"You all right there, Chief?" Murph asked from the driver's seat.

"Peachy," Sam said, with as much conviction as a boxer dropped to the mat. The college kids on the porch of the apartment house next door began to make their beer cans disappear. Most of the neighborhood was owned by the slumlords who staffed the Weymouth City Council and rented out to students at maximum capacity. He would've moved years ago if the house was his to sell, but they paid low rent to Jill's parents and had saved with a plan to buy outright. Now, most of the money was gone, and nothing was certain, not for anybody, anywhere.

Dispatch hailed them on the radio, "Weymouth to eight twenty-four."

Murph said, "Eight twenty-four."

"MDT transmission," dispatch said.

"Sure, you get nothing all night," Murph told Sam. "Fucking minute I drop you off—"

"What's the call?" Sam asked.

Murph tilted the laptop screen and the LCD made his face glow blue. After a moment he said, "Talk about peachy. Gunfire in Philpot, all patrols OS to Furst's Butcher Shop."

"Maybe they had to put down a bull," Sam suggested.

Murph said, "Get the hell out of my car so I can do my job."

Sam shut the door behind him and smacked the prowler roof, his usual C-shift sendoff to Murph. It was coming on midnight and the last thing on Sam's mind was rest. He wanted to don civilian clothes and steal himself onto the college campus, track down that Johnston kid. But as Murph pulled away, the maze of Sam's mind turned him straight back to his worry for Jill.

He found her in the kitchen pouring steaming kettle water into a mug with a teabag. There was a scorched baking tray on the stovetop, cluttered with what looked like charcoal briquettes. Dirty cups and breakfast bowls filled the sink and spilled over onto the counter. Jill's bandanna was back on her head, gauze bandages on her hands. When she turned on him he was unholstering his gun.

"It's come to that?" she asked.

"Very funny," he said. "Where's Erika?"

"She went out," Jill said. "A friend needed a ride home."

"I asked her to stay here and keep an eye on you." He set the gun on the kitchenette, switched off the radio receiver, and unbuckled his Sam Browne belt, laid out the whole apparatus in the routine that loosed him from the palpable heft of his equipment. The gun would go in the safe in their bedroom closet, and the uniform would hang from its designated hook.

Jill said, "I'm okay now. I'm sorry about earlier, Sam."

"You don't need to apologize to me—but, Erika, I asked her to look after you." He opened his cell phone and pressed Erika's speed-dial number, let it ring four times before he disengaged.

Jill set her tea back down on the counter. She said, "How did it go with the motel?"

"Fine," he said. "Jodie says she's blown through the money she stole, so we're probably going to have to start shelling out for her pretty soon. She had enough to pay tonight, at least."

"Can you find out if she's in trouble? Search a database or something?"

"Not without buying myself the rope they'd lynch me with. If it turns out she screwed up as much as she says, or worse, people will ask why I was looking. My own sister-in-law, then she turns up here in town. Mighty coincidental."

She wrapped her arms around his torso, laid her head against his chest. When he hugged her back he felt the empty space around her that she used to fill. Every day launched planes to the tropics, yet the family name Hartwick appeared on none of their passenger manifests. Tickets weren't yet purchased, and the Costa Rica green hazed away like a mirage. They were snowed in deeper and deeper, and they both knew what was always unmentioned, that Jill was too weak to travel anywhere.

"I want to go talk to her tomorrow, after the radiation," she said.

"I don't think that's a good idea," Sam said.

Her embrace slackened as she said, "Why not?"

"People—I don't want nobody noticing. This isn't a huge city."

Jill stepped back and looked him in the face. She said, "We need to do something that isn't putting her in jail. If God sent her back here, I want to give her a chance."

He said, "Why won't Erika answer her phone?"

"She's angry. I was still a little—we had a fight and she got upset."

The stink from the burned food was getting unbearable. Sam broke away from Jill and grabbed the baking tray, unlocked the back door.

He set the tray on the porch and closed the door on it, but the stink lingered. He said, "What's she got to be angry about with you? It's not your fault when you get like that. She knows damn well."

"I start talking. I don't even know what I'm saying. Sometimes I don't remember."

"What did you say to her?" Sam asked. The strain was seizing his throat.

"She kept asking me why—why Jodie, why all this tension. I couldn't look her in the face, Sam. I got furious and I couldn't help it. I just blurted it out."

"Jesus, Jill," Sam said. His knees buckled and he slid down the face of the porch door until his ass hit the linoleum. He thought of his daughter out patrolling the night with a criminal on her mind, and it was him. The gun on the kitchenette was aimed level with his head, and he wished it would just—

Erika pulled her father's Nissan around back at Paulie's Italian, squeaked the right front tire against a curb because her night vision was so crap. The Dumpster was nothing but a darker patch in the night, but Wynn stepped out from the trees beside it, right where he said he'd be. He limped to the car, grabbed at the passenger-door handle before Erika had a chance to unlock it.

She hesitated, after driving all this way, yanked at her knee-high argyles. She had two thousand dollars in her pocket and an aunt in hiding and a hypocrite father and even a few bruises of her own, so she unclicked the automatic lock.

Wynn dropped in beside her and she turned down the radio. Too dim to see him clearly, but he held a compress of brown paper towels against his left ear. Even in the dark his face looked worse off than Jodie's was—cracked and swollen all out of proportion.

Erika said, "Not you, too. Maybe I should've brought an ambulance?"

"I don't have any insurance," he said. "Thanks for coming. This is your car?"

"My dad's. He's out on patrol, or home now, I guess. Was it a car accident?" She was pulling back around toward the lot exit, signaling to turn back the way she just came. An urge to tell him about the injuries she'd witnessed already, but the family secrets were hers to bear alone.

"I got jumped," Wynn said. "They took me away from my car. My roommate's car. It was two Mexican guys, and somebody I thought was a friend of mine."

"Holy shit," she said. She turned back onto the road and almost instantly a county prowler swerved around the blind curve behind her, lights whirling. She muttered a curse and swung onto the shoulder, but the siren sped past, blowing the Philpot town speed limit by at least forty over. For an instant she'd been convinced it was Dad tracking her down somehow. She'd been all ready to scream total hell at him.

Wynn turned toward the back window as if to see if more traffic would drive them off the road. He smelled like freezer-burned meat, but she willed herself to fight past squeamishness. To help her, he repeated, "Thank you for coming out here. You didn't have to do that."

"You sure you don't want to go to the hospital? Or Public Safety? You can file a—"

"I just want to forget about the whole thing," Wynn said.

They drove back through the center of Philpot, past all the shutdown businesses and the tall houses crammed at close quarters like mourners at a funeral. She didn't know anyone who lived in this elderly town. Among her friends was nobody who'd ever been beaten or even instigated an attack, so far as she knew, but she couldn't peer into everyone's hearts and know them for certain.

"Where's your car?" she asked.

"That's the thing. I don't know. I don't remember how to get to where it is."

She approached a small squadron of prowlers verged along the curb and fronting an ambulance parked in a lot hardly big enough to accommodate it. Flashers and swirlers gave a strobe show to the residences across the street and the clapboard building the deputies had strung their crime-scene tape around. Erika slowed to a crawl and read the vendor's sign posted over the entrance—FURST'S BUTCHER SHOP.

"Don't stop," Wynn said.

Light flashed in Erika's eyes and she pressed the brake. A Maglite beam came at her from the left curb, wielded by a stout deputy with his gloved hand upraised, steam chugging from his mouth. He was her father's nightshift partner, Chris Murphy, whom everyone called Murph. Her automatic window slid down, sloughing off ice.

"Erika?" Murph called out. "Heh, what a coincidence. I just dropped off your dad twenty minutes ago. I recognized his Nissan here when you was coming up, the union decal. Go tell your dad he's got to buy American before America closes down all its plants."

"I will," she said.

"Granted, a Maxima's a damn good ride, loads better than the Impalas they make us drive. I can understand why your dad shelled out for it." Murph cut the flashlight across the car's interior and struck Wynn with its wicked ray. Wynn flinched and twisted his face out of view. The outdoor cold seeped in, and in that burning bright instant Erika spotted the invisible threads that tied all these flashing emergency lights to Wynn's injuries, his earlier whereabouts.

"What're you doing all the way out here, kiddo?" Murph said.

"We were at some party. You know, some friends. I'm the designated driver."

"Ah, I see." Murph frowned at her passenger, who was slumped against his door like a drunk on a bender. Murph scrunched his raw red nose and bared his teeth, the hideous expression that lake-effect winter so often provoked. He said, "So this party is a sort of hush-hush thing as far as your dad's concerned?"

"I'm in college now," Erika said. The longer they spoke, the more her poise was bound to shudder apart, the more she'd have to question her own motivations. And anything she said, Murph could transmit in a minute flat to Dad, who'd know she was lying about her reasons for being out in Philpot.

"Sorry," Murph said. "I forget you're all grown up. My own kid just started—what is it?—fourth grade? I can't always keep track, you know, 'cause she lives with her ma now up in Buffalo." He hunched his shoulders, trotted in place to ward off the chill. "Anyways, they got me stopping cars. Yours is the first to come along. Some crazy stuff here tonight, I got to tell you. So you'll want to skedaddle back to Weymouth pretty quick."

"What happened?" Erika asked, nodding toward the emergency circus.

"I don't know the whole scoop. Some thugs roughing each other up, I guess. Looks like we're having some kind of spree lately, after what happened in Lyme. Your dad caught it last night before my shift, so tonight's only fair, right?"

"Last night? Is somebody—" Erika started.

"I better not get into it," Murphy said. "Just be careful heading home, all right?" He backstepped from the car and waved his flashlight like an air-traffic controller. He was all business now, and Erika felt herself abandoned. Wynn wasn't saying a word, and he seemed more like a ghost than some awkward boy who'd thrown her off course with a kiss only a few—

—factor in acceleration, but even the switch from thirty to fifty out of Philpot and into the wilderness wouldn't affect the infinite distance of the vanishing point straight ahead. Point A equals the butcher shop, while Point B equals an unknown factor X for which to solve. You can strip away the trees and the asphalt and all the mediating nature, and there you will see existence in its purest abstraction.

"Where are we going?" Erika asked as she drove toward the horizon.

"Back to the way things were," he said beside her in her car, but he had almost been caught. Wynn in the passenger seat with a cop at the window, shining a light in his face. After that, Wynn refused to look at her because when he looked that confounding longing flared up again. She came for him when he called, but she was the daughter of the man who tried to divide him from his future. Except there was no future because the same forms keep repeating—a traffic stop and Wynn in the passenger seat, a girl he loved though he shouldn't. The curve skirts the line closer and closer but can never strike.

She smelled like wintergreen and she'd saved him. Her bare knee-cap perched on the curve of her leg between the skirt pleats and the seam of her argyle socks hiked all the way up her shins. He tried to remember when she was younger, but this wasn't the same girl.

He said, "I can't go back there until it's fixed."

"Your roommate's car?"

"No. I have to—put things back the way they were."

"Is it about back there? Do you know something about what happened?"

"They tried to kill me, Ce . . ."

"Yeah, I see. But you got away. How did you?"

A cough erupted in his lungs and he brought a fist to his lips. Each one of his ribs sang out in shrill harmony. There was blood on his tongue and his thumb, and his wrists felt like they were studded with slivers of glass. The heater vent blasted so hard it scorched, but still he was quivering cold.

"Some people got hurt, but I swear I didn't hurt anybody."

Let Point A equal the butcher shop and Point B equal the Moscow Institute of Science and Technology. No way to drive there on a perfect line, unless through the earth. And worse was the tyranny of Zeno's paradox: $AB/2^n$. Consider half the distance, add to it a quarter of the distance, plus an eighth of the distance, plus a sixteenth of the distance, and so on ad infinitum, and you never reach wherever you think you're going. The width of an atom is an infinitely divisible accumulation of points. The span of an instant is equally impossible chaos.

They drove, but where did they drive to, and were they even advancing?

Erika said, "Am I accessory to some crime now? Shit, don't answer that."

"My friend Dwight died last night. I went looking for the people who killed him."

"Oh, fuck, you knew him," she said, hunching forward like the road had just become treacherous. It was the least he could admit, but it was already enough to make her reject him. She said, "Are you serious, Wynn? I need to know right now if you're serious."

"They think Dwight and Cecelia shot each other, but it isn't true."

"Jesus, my father was on that scene last night. You knew those people. Out in Lyme? Of course, because you're from there. Wynn, you need to go to the police and tell them about this. We can go to my . . ." Her hysteria dropped like somebody slapped her in the face.

"Your father?" Wynn said.

"Forget him. We'll just go straight to Public Safety. You can talk to the shift sergeant."

Chevron signs led them around a sharp curve, and for a moment Wynn wondered if all this insight would distract her too much, if she'd drive a perfect line off the road and out into the razed field, how far they'd go and if they'd survive. He said, "I can't go to the police. The parameters keep changing, and I don't know anything worthwhile."

They came to a stop sign on the back road they traveled, though the sign was so caked with windblown snow that only its octagon outline was visible. It was not a specific stop sign, but all of them at once, which was why, Wynn knew, she kept her foot on the brake and rested her head on the steering wheel and waited even though there were no cars in sight on the crossroad. It was a junction of flat white fields without end.

She said, "I'm not going home tonight. I can't."

"I didn't mean to ruin your life."

She snorted. "It's got nothing to do with you, Wynn. You're just icing. You don't want to go to the police and neither do I, so we're in agreement. None of that matters to me anymore. You understand that? I'm betting you do. We can just get on the highway and keep driving south, somewhere warm where we don't have to think."

"I don't—" Wynn started, but he didn't know quite the words for his objection.

"I have the money for it. We can get into Pennsylvania even before we stop anywhere."

Wynn said, "I don't know how to decide—

—hydrogen peroxide from a grocery store on a commercial strip in Erie, Pennsylvania. Wynn waited in the car. At a Red Roof Inn, Erika refused to leave a credit card on file, so she drove on farther, past the indoor water park and the usual restaurants and found a local place willing to accept cash. It was tropical themed, a lobby with fake palms and piped-in bird sounds. If not for the snow seeping in through the sliding-glass doors, she could trick herself into thinking she reached some kind of paradise. And to think her father had almost convinced her to pass this up for Costa Rica.

While she checked in, Wynn stayed with the car. One glance at his condition would be enough cause for a suspicious desk attendant to call out the local police. At least these locals weren't Cassadaga County anymore. She left their authority, crossed state lines, nothing but voice mails on her cell phone and her own aching conscience to remind her. If not for Wynn, she'd keep driving until the weather turned and real birds sang, however far a couple thousand dollars would get her.

Back in the driver's seat she said, "Second-floor room."

Wynn was seat-belted with his head slumped against the passenger window, silhouetted by a parking lot lamp. His mouth hung slack, but he didn't move, and he didn't whiten the windowpane with breath. She clutched him by the shoulder, certain he was dead. But the contact jolted him awake. He flailed, almost backhanded her in the face. He breathed like he'd been suffocating for minutes and rocked in his seat with his eyes crushed shut.

"Wynn, I'm sorry. I didn't mean to surprise you."

"It's okay," he groaned. "It's fine. I thought . . . where are we?"

"It's some kitsch carnival called Great Lakes Tropics, but they took cash."

Into the lobby, Wynn wore a black winter hat culled from the back-seat of the car, probably one of Dad's. He pulled it low and borrowed her plaid scarf to cover the worst of his visible injuries. His limp was fierce and obvious, though Erika didn't dare touch him to help. In the end their precautions were moot because the attendant was absent from the desk and the lounge was empty.

Elevator to the second floor, down a hallway with a carpet like a Hawaiian shirt, pineapple-and-surfboard motif. Erika swiped the key-card and they entered a room with a view of the strip mall across the street and two queen-size beds. It all seemed like speculation until she saw those beds and accepted that she'd be sleeping in this strange place with this boy she barely knew, who was terribly hurt and might've hurt others.

But she'd decided for certain somewhere on a county road in Philpot that she wanted to help him. She wanted to punish her father and refuse to watch her mother die any further. Somehow, she caught the call that led her away from them and their stifling home, just like her Aunt Jodie years ago. The road sang a melody into her ears, though she didn't yet catch all the meaning.

Wynn went into the bathroom and shut the door behind him. Erika set the grocery bag on the bedspread and pulled out the first-aid kit, unpacked the gauze and the tape, the antibacterial gel and the butter-fly bandages, the cotton balls. In the dark she hadn't seen the extent of his wounds and didn't know now what she'd need, or if any of these supplies would help him at all.

She turned on the TV, caught a weather report from Ohio that griped about snowstorm cleanup in Akron, couldn't find any Buffalo channels. In the bathroom Wynn ran the faucet water. For the first time in hours Erika considered her college classes, absences, withdrawals. She remembered her grandparents were coming back early from Arizona, how fearful they'd be to find that she ran off. And her mother, the last thing she said so vicious, the last thing. Her cell phone shimmied across the nightstand, buzzed three times, but she couldn't—

—in the bathroom mirror. Purple blotches on his chest, geometric shapes he couldn't name or guess the area of, fading through each other inside yellow auras. He fingered swollen ribs, but even the lightest touch recalled the pain of every punch. The flesh unwound was paled winter-white. The borrowed wool hat peeled away from the scabs on his brow and brought fresh blood. Dried blood on his neck and in the crooks of his elbows, brown in the creases of his palms. He felt the sheets of liquid and pockets of gas roiling inside his body and it was all so fallible, nature's sad shadow of perfection.

Cecelia was dead, Dwight was dead, Frank and his father were dead, but death couldn't touch their abstract forms. All of mankind wiped from the universe and fundamental truths would still exist. The living just a strange subspecies of the dead, rife with limitations. A library, a microchip, a whelk's cochlear helix—more perfectly sound than anything alive.

Wynn ran the tap until the water warmed. His hands were red and swollen and they stung like a wasp attack when he held them under the stream. The welts on his wrists could've passed for pursed lips. He didn't know the location of this bathroom, or why he was inside it, and he didn't know why there was a handgun stuffed in the inside pocket of the coat he took from the butcher shop. A dreamlike recall—pulling off his ski mask, stealing Frank's clothes, confiscating this gun from the dead Mexican's hand.

It was a Glock 9mm, black polymer with a stippled grip, simple as a toy gun. The only part that looked like a safety was a tiny lever jutting out from the trigger. The magazine was loaded, but he didn't know if there were rounds inside it, or how to check without firing. There wouldn't be a need anymore. He took a hand towel from the rack above the toilet, wrapped the gun inside the towel and placed the package deep in the drawer below the sink. If someone else searched, it would be easy to find, but he didn't know what else to do.

A knock on the door, then, "Wynn, are you all right?"

It was Erika's voice, and its sound made him wilt and remember how she rescued him. He pulled open the door. She was there with a brown bottle of disinfectant. Her hair was let down and spilled across her blouse. She stood in her stocking feet. All his metaphysical musing splashed against his instincts like a cupful of saltwater tossed back to the sea.

The sight of him caused her a sharp intake of breath, and Wynn realized he was standing only in white briefs that weren't his. She didn't know that he stripped a dead man for them. She didn't know he turned away from the sight of Frank's limp, stunted organ that had violated her body so many—Cecelia's body. Not hers.

She said, "I thought you might want . . ." and set the supplies on the countertop.

Wynn lowered onto the toilet seat, wincing as the pain in his chest gushed stronger.

She said, "My dad got beaten pretty bad once in a bar fight, just before he went into the police academy. I think maybe that's why he joined. I remember he was all bruised up—but you, Jesus."

"I want to go back to school," Wynn said.

"Oh, I wasn't suggesting you should . . ."

"People are just beasts. You can't correct them."

"I know, Wynn. Believe me. If I could tell you what I know about him now." She peeled the plastic ring from the bottle, uncapped it, and overturned it against a cotton swab. Then she dabbed the open wound on his forehead. The liquid sizzled along the seam of the cut. She said, "This one looks like it could use stitches."

"What do you know?" Wynn said.

"About stitches? That all we have here is butterfly bandages."

"What do you know about your father?" Wynn said.

"That my family's been fucked since I was a little girl, and it's all his fault." She tossed aside the bloodied cotton ball and wetted a washcloth instead, brushed it lightly over his brow. The pleats of her skirt brushed against his bare knee, and light freckles danced on her forearm as she rubbed. Her blouse raised an inch away from her skirt and exposed the strip of unblemished flesh where her hipbone shaped her waist. He set his swollen fingertips there and she flinched, but then she eased her hip against his hand.

"Your hand was cold," she said.

"I'm sorry," he said.

"No, it's . . ." She kneeled down on the floor beside him while she brushed his jawline with the warm washcloth, ran it across his mouth and then pressed it gently against his ravaged ear. The pain sent white flashbulbs to his eyes, but he could see her leaning toward him like she meant to examine the wound up close.

A wave of longing struck him, but it wasn't bodily. The tangent to the curve in the line of his sight, the trigonometric sine waves, the orbits of spheres in the microverse as he divided within it, the infinitesimal vibrations of strings along the theoretical grid where every possible reality found infinite convergence points.

But the physical still insisted. Her lips pushed on his and the terrain of her skin loomed so near that every pore and every follicle magnified into monstrous, teeming life. He turned away from her, nauseated at the sense—

—separate beds. Through the window Erika watched a pair of car headlights weaving through the strip-mall lot across the street. She watched instead of looking over at the boy on the other bed who had played some terrible trick on her, rejecting her kiss when she was finally ready to return it, and no explanation. Just the sudden jerk of his head and that strained look like he was trying not to puke. She had escaped with him, but now the fantasy sheen of it was gone. Maybe she could sneak out in the night while he slept and drive on without him, but she had no clue where she was going. It seemed ridiculous.

"Where are we?" he asked her.

The television played a VH-1 show where D-list celebrities and comedians reminisced about pop culture from the early eighties, years before she and Wynn were born. None of it made sense, but nothing in her present did, either.

"Pennsylvania. Erie, Pennsylvania, in a place called Great Lakes Tropics."

"That's impossible."

"I'm beginning to realize."

"There's gaps—in my thinking. I think I keep blacking out."

"Then you should probably see a doctor," she said. She lay under the blankets in her clothes, but still she shivered. The waistband of her skirt bit into her hips, but she'd brought nothing else to wear. Despised herself for not thinking through an impulse because she'd been drunk on anger and expectation. She didn't know what she expected. The money Jodie gave her could buy pajamas, a few changes of clothes, but nothing was open past two in the morning. Such deep night had overcome her, she didn't believe dawn would rise again.

"Are you worried about missing classes?" Wynn asked.

"I couldn't care less, to be honest with you."

"I didn't ever want to have to go back," he said. "I was studying for my math exam. I didn't want to leave with anybody, but these gaps happen without my control and I end up—I don't know how I strayed so far."

"So you're saying you want to go back. You want to forget it, right?"

"I don't think I can," Wynn said. "They keep trying to take it away from me. Do you think, because there are concepts only humans understand, all of our mathematical abstractions, do you think when we die these things fade to nothing? Like a whole ocean of knowledge held inside our six billion bowls and when we're all gone, the bowls are all dry? Or do you think because we know that nothing can ever reach zero, no matter how close we approach, do you think it's even possible to die?"

On TV people fawned over a Rubik's Cube while stock footage ran of some gaming competition where a bearded man in huge glasses twiddled the toy's shifting planes so fast that his fingers blurred. Within seconds he had all the color-coded squares aligned in perfect—

"Erika, you need to get in touch with us here. You've got everybody worried about you, honey. I know you're upset with me and with your mother, and you're a grown woman, but we need to know you're all right. Please." Sam lowered his cell phone, thinking what else he might say, but this was already the fifth message he'd left on his daughter's cell. He didn't want to drive her away any farther or longer. So he quit the call and folded the phone back into his sweatpants pocket.

The kitchen dishes were done, burned tray scrubbed with Clorox until it was silver again. He'd drenched his gullet with a full pot of coffee while he did the work, and now he was wired so hard his arteries sparked inside his chest. The caffeine only spiked his sense that the connections were all wrong from the start, and nothing had changed over fifteen years. He learned policing, he caught God, dropped booze, slept in bed every night with the approach of death, but none of it changed the fundamental sin that already defined him.

Noon, and he'd been up for two hours, fueled by less than another two of actual sleep. Three hours till his shift and already he wanted to swing by The Enchanted Angler, see if Jodie was still where he left her. He tried to figure ways to hit the campus in civilian clothes and track down Wynn. Get in the car and lurk through the city for his car and his daughter with it. Lay down beside his sleeping wife. What this all meant in practice was paralysis, drawn and quartered by his competing desires.

Upstairs, Jill lay curled like a fetus with her back to him. She didn't groan or turn when he sat down beside her, so he lowered his palm onto the back of her head. He wondered if he could ever make love to her again, if he could manage, and dreaded that one morning he'd find her cold, and often he tried to set the expectation down in his mind like a plan for disaster. This time, she was perfectly warm and his touch made her intake a breath.

He hit the remote and watched the local news out of Buffalo on mute, closed-captioned. The lead story was an apartment complex fire in Tonawanda, but the next was out of Philpot. Sam set his coffee on the nightstand and hoisted himself upright in bed. The video feed showed a cordoned crime scene in early morning light, a butcher shop Sam recognized from his patrols. The video was just various angles of the exterior, but the captions told Sam there'd been a shooting, three dead. Police weren't releasing names, no suspects held, if you have any information—the typical script.

As an addendum the reporter noted this was the second murder in Cassadaga County in as many days, "a relatively quiet county that had gone two years without a murder before this week." Subtext: there's a good chance the murders are related, and related murders almost always mean a shake-up in the local drug-traffic scene, and overtime for the sheriff's bloodhounds.

Sam's cell phone chimed its text-message tone and he opened it, knowing the sender would be Erika—just like her to text so she wouldn't have to talk. Jill turned toward him and her eyes read his face for news, alert like she hadn't been asleep at all. She asked, "Who is it from?"

The text read: URGENT HARTWICK SHERIFF PRIVATE BRIEFING 3 PM.

"It's not her," he said. "It's nothing."

Outside, the college bell tower chimed the quarter hour. Still three hours before work, before the briefing, but Sam arose and removed his sweatpants, draped them over the end of the bed. Took his two-part Kevlar vest from a drawer and strapped it on over his long-johns shirt, pulled the straps taut. Jill watched him but she didn't question. In boxers and bulletproof, he went to the bathroom, took the electric razor to the bristles on his scalp, like the last ritual shaving of an inmate headed—

—shivered awake in a strange place. Every organ was knotted tight from the booze, Cal's brain worst of all because it wouldn't remind him where he was or how he arrived. So cold here, his breath formed a cloud above his face. A high ceiling weaved with ductwork, an endless window grid emitting morning.

He crunched upright and the layered blankets folded away from his cold-puckered nipples. The bare mattress was flattened to its springs, torn in spots. There was a warm male body turned away beside him with the knuckled curve of his spine exposed, a slope of an ass cheek. No need for Cal to see his bedmate's face because the telltale mohawk draped the single pillow. The air between their bodies smelled like stale bread.

This is not my life. You are not my love.

Cal's stomach lurched but he fought the threat of vomit. He slid sideward until his legs slapped the concrete floor and the noise of it echoed wide in pockets untouched yet by morning light. He wore nothing but his boxer briefs and his socks. The mattress he'd been sleeping on was tossed into a huge empty space, a squatter's den that looked like it was once a factory floor.

Hissed at the cold and the soreness that radiated from his coccyx to his calves. His body was loath to move, but he pushed it through the ache as he gathered his clothes. A patch of dried blood crusted his boxers, and the sudden sight of it horrified. He wished the daylight could wash it away, but all the sun did was show him the bruises on his hip bones, two yellow stencils shaped like hands.

He found his jeans and slid them on, his shoes. He dressed soundlessly so not to wake the punk, whose name he didn't know. He longed for Burt instead, or even that man who looked like Freez from the

Pandemonium nightclub, but this was some kid he'd seen on the street and pitied. This was the bottom.

Sweater and his peacoat last, lifted them from where they lay on the dusty floor. Dipped his hand into the inside coat pocket to double-check his stash, and the emptiness was like an electric shock. Almost nineteen hundred in cash was gone, though his hand kept dropping into that emptiness like it was some vortex that would swallow him.

Cal felt faint. He propped one hand against his bent knees and hyperventilated—panic on the intake, anger on the out. There was dust on the floor, yellowed newspaper, faded candy wrappers. The ugly space bore down on him with its dizzying breadth.

"Hey," Cal said. He kicked the edge of the mattress. "Hey."

The punk groaned and turned onto his back. His face was too angular, too drawn, not the sort of face Cal would've ever found attractive in the daylight.

"Somebody took my money?" Cal insisted. "I had a bunch of cash and now it's gone."

"Good morning, Sunshine," the punk said. Cal wanted to kick him in his roman nose.

"Who the fuck are you?" Cal demanded. "How did I end up here?"

"Seriously? You're seriously asking that?"

"I had almost two thousand dollars. That was supposed to—"

"Don't look at me, dude. I got no place to hide it, obviously. Do a fucking full cavity search if you don't believe me." He threw back the covers and exposed himself, full frontal. Shaved pubis and his dick limp across the crook of his pelvis. There was Chinese lettering inked across the topside of the shaft, and Cal was sure he'd never seen such a dick before, not last night or ever. But then he remembered a comment in the late-night haze: *"My cock speaks Mandarin."*

"Somebody at the club," Cal said.

"Which one? I can't remember them all." The punk stood and hugged himself from the chill. Rubbed the skeleton tats along his arms. Body so thin his jutting hips gave him the shape of a girl. He was completely divorced from Cal's crisis. He approached a broken pipeline rising up from the floor, widened his stance, and pissed down into the opening. Steam rose up from the arc of his urine.

Cal kicked debris on the floor with some mindless hope that the money had just fallen from his pocket. Nothing in the garbage resembled money. That cash could be anywhere in Pittsburgh by now, split among the grubby hands of thieves, stolen and stolen and stolen ad infinitum. Somewhere, someone was probably giving his toothpaste to a beggar on the street like some twisted Good Samaritan.

"All's I know is you best have enough to spot me what you owe," the punk said.

"Owe for what?"

The punk turned, still holding his limp dick, and wagged it at Cal to illustrate.

"You're a—what are you?"

"Fun and profit. Sixty bucks should do, it being your cherry and all."

"I'm telling you, all my money is gone."

"Don't mess. I gave you fucking lodgings."

"I don't remember anything," Cal said. "You fucking took advantage of me, you whore." He eyed the pair of swinging double doors at least thirty feet off from where he stood. If he could outrun the punk to there, find his way outside, then the punk couldn't rightly follow him naked.

"Give me whatever money you got and we'll let bygones be blow-jobs."

"I don't—" but he found himself running, and just as quickly as he sprang a flurry of cold flesh tumbled him to the floor. A punch rattled his brain in its cage, and the knee in his gut made him wretch. The rough concrete tore at his cheek. There was a flash of teeth and Cal didn't know what next. The punk's breath like soured meat and it burned against Cal's neck. That star tear on his cheek. Cal grabbed a fistful of dangling scrotum and squeezed and the punk howled red rage and coiled like a grub.

Cal scuttled away, found his feet, and pushed through the heavy double doors. A dark stairwell descended one floor to where the light split a crack, and he pushed onto the sidewalk and the exhaust fumes of early-morning delivery trucks. Configurations of concrete and brick and old smoky glass he didn't recognize. He hurried around the corner, jaywalked between parallel parked cars, no notion where he was going. He kept sniffling, trying to hold back the snot and the tears. Scraped his pockets just to be sure he was truly and completely fucked, and found his unused bus ticket, folded and battered.

A corner boy spat aside the rail on his stoop and said, "Hey coke-head, your nose is—

—handcuffed kid in baggy pants with notches shaved into his eyebrows, sneering on a bench outside the interview room. The corridor was lined with photos of sheriffs past, vintage cruisers in their heyday, plaques for fallen deputies. Outside the patrol room, a bulletin board advertised taxi services for freed inmates and a vintage invitation to call Attorney General Eliot Spitzer's Complaint Hotline. Someone had scratched out *Complaint Hotline* and written *For a good time, call.*

In his uniform and tie, Sam strode the corridor toward Sheriff Olin's office. He passed the secretary's cubicle, and she said, "Go ahead." Olin was at his desk with a bevy of outdated code books stacked on the shelves behind him. He wasn't alone—the undersheriff in his shirtsleeves occupied a chair at the small conference table. A privileged view out the sheriff's office window was of the lockup yard, and the parking lot beyond.

"Sam, thanks so much for dropping in," Olin said, and motioned him toward the facing chair. He was a ruddy Scandinavian in his sixties, the undersheriff was standard western New York Italian, but both of them wore the lockjaw scowls of cigar-store Indians.

Sam sat down and said, cordial as possible, "No problem, Sheriff."

"Jill," Olin said. "How's she doing? I mean, as well as can be expected, I suppose."

"That's about right," Sam said.

"Anything more we can do for you, Sam, you just say so, all right?"

"I appreciate it, Sheriff."

The undersheriff cleared his throat and piped in. "We've got an unusual situation here."

"I heard about the shootings last night, down in Philpot," Sam said. He tried to look relaxed, no elbows on the armrests, no forward lean to his posture, rhythms steady enough to pass a polygraph.

The undersheriff consulted some paperwork and said, "Overnight we got a flagged wanted bulletin from all the way down in Cape Fear, North Carolina. A kidnapping case. Fifteen-year-old boy. The snatcher was the biological mother. Took the kid from his adoptive parents. Looked to be a simple runaway case at first—kid even called home from Gettysburg, Pennsylvania, to check in—but the dynamics are revealing themselves to be a tad more complex."

"The bulletin made it all the way up here?" Sam asked, totally adrift from the port where he thought they were going to dock him. He'd never been to Cape Fear or Pennsylvania, didn't know any kids that age or adoptive parents.

The undersheriff said, "Well, Cape Fear posted this one to us special because the case has local roots, so we need to ask around as a matter of course, follow up the leads and so forth."

The sheriff leaned back in his chair and crossed his arms over his brass. He watched Sam and the undersheriff like they were on the court in singles tennis, passing himself off as a friendly spectator. These were the same sort of gags deputies used when interviewing violators down the hall.

"You want me to get some statements on my shift tonight?" Sam asked.

"Well, the fact of the matter is that the suspect is your sister-in-law, Jodie Larkin."

Sam gripped the armrests hard enough to make them creak, and the sheriff perked his ears at the noise. If Sam showed half the panic he felt, they could nail him on a hunch alone.

"Please realize, Deputy," the under said, "we completely sympathize with your home situation right now, but you understand we have to make these inquiries, just like you would have to in our situation. We just needed to see whether you or Jill have heard from this woman."

"Not for—fifteen years," Sam said. He spun inside a whorl of caffeine and adrenaline.

The sheriff lifted a fax from his desk, donned a pair of reading glasses. "This is interstate business, potential FBI stuff, even if she doesn't show her face back here. Says she fled Atlanta after apparently having stolen a sum of five thousand dollars cash from the home of Marlon Weaver, who is, incidentally, a Falcons defensive lineman. She was in his service as a maid."

Their pursed-lip hush told Sam that these men had already shared a laugh over the details, the sort of chuckle cops share around the corpse at a fatal car-crash scene: *Well, I'll be damned. You wouldn't've expected a guy's kidney to look as much like a kidney bean as it does* .

"What's the kid's name?" Sam asked.

"The kid?" Olin said. He scanned the page and said, "Calvin Nowak, age fifteen."

The under said, "I get the sense you didn't even know your sister-in-law had a kid."

Sam shook his head once he remembered it was there. "Not a clue," he said.

"Well, if Jill's up to it, maybe you might just broach the subject with her, see if maybe she knows anything or can find anything out. Maybe her parents know something?"

"They're in Arizona. Far as I know, they haven't talked to her, either. It's been so long."

The undersheriff tucked his chin against his chest, brooding in a style that drove gangbangers and burglars and child rapists to confess, and now it was aimed on Sam. He said, "That's right. Fifteen years, like you said. Weird coincidence, that kid's age. Maybe the pregnancy had some relation to the family rift. You think that's possible, Deputy Hartwick?"

"I'm beginning to think," Sam admitted, as a blaze ignited in his brain. That grown woman passing herself as a helpless child, practically on her knees for confession and punishment, but she had lied about the worst of her crimes, omitted what she knew none of them could forgive her for. He raged against her, and himself, knowing his hate was—

—door knock. Jodie thumbed the remote power and the TV went black, and the only noise was the thrumming of her heart. Alone all night in this cramped room with its single bed and its painting of a fly fisherman casting from a spot in some reeds. The faint stink of fish in the bathroom, as if to fit the theme.

The knock came again, and an accented man's voice said, "Housekeeping." Middle Eastern, or something like that. The peephole gave a fisheyed view of the office manager standing outside her door in a jacket with a fur-lined hood. She recognized him as the man who checked her in the night before, and he had a maid's cart on wheels to prove his intent. He keyed the lock and pushed the door open two inches before the chainlock stopped him. "Pardon me," he said through the crack.

"Hold on, sorry," Jodie said. She pressed the door shut and slid out the chain. When the manager came inside apologizing, she smelled familiar solvents, the ones she'd used to scrub other people's bath-room. They hung in clear bottles from their nozzle triggers on the rim of the maid's cart, and the sight of them told her she hadn't come any distance at all. This motel room was smaller than her apartment. There was no black cat here to comfort her. Her son was in some other city without her.

"I will return later?" the manager asked without looking at her bruised and battered and torn-up face. Probably he thought she was an abused wife on the run from her husband. He'd seen a deputy drop her off the night before.

"No, it's fine. I just need maybe another towel."

He nodded and lifted a fresh, folded white towel from his cart. She already made her own bed, and there was nothing else for him to do but set the towel on the TV stand and smile stiffly at her. He said, "Checkout time is noon."

"I think I might stay another day."

"It's perfectly okay. Please pay ahead at the office before noon." He turned toward the door when a wind gust pushed it wide open against the wall. The cold air circled low around their ankles and lifted.

"So you run everything yourself, housekeeping and all?"

His eyes widened and he inched toward the door. The cart wheels shrieked as he pulled. His panic swelled him up, like he thought she was INS demanding his papers or something, but he was too polite not to answer. "Usually my wife also, but currently my wife is having a baby."

"She's having a baby right now?"

"What I intend to explain is that she is having a baby two months before now."

"So you're here all day by yourself?"

"That is correct, but it is not difficult work. I can prepare the rooms."

"There's not a lot of other people staying here," Jodie said.

He snuck a glance, and now her face was in his memory, easily matched to a police photo or a TV news report. She didn't care. She'd skittered like a cockroach long enough. All she wanted was to ward off the loneliness of this place for a minute. The phone on the nightstand worked, but she couldn't call Jill after the trouble she'd dragged to their doorstep. A few times overnight she thought to call the police, maybe run outside and hail a passing prowler like it was a taxi service. But she was done with choice, because her dyslexic hunches fucked her every time. A holding cell, worse than even this room or her apartment, nothing inside it but a cot and her million regrets. Here, at least, she was where her family wanted.

"Is your baby a boy or a girl?" she asked.

"I have a son." His first answer that didn't sound like another question.

She said, "I have a son, too. He's fifteen years old."

"Children are a gift from God," he said, like reciting from a phrasebook. "I hope you are enjoying your stay, and I hope your injuries are recovering." He nodded so deeply it was almost a bow, and then he left, shut the door behind him.

She wished she could've told this man about Calvin and what she regretted, told someone. I gave birth in a Rochester hospital, nine months a pregnant castaway, worked as a waitress, lied about my age, not even my parents knew where, or that I was pregnant. The Nowaks so eager to adopt, promised I could visit whenever I wanted, and the best I could've did was let them vanish with him so my trail of mistakes would drop off a cliff where I couldn't follow. But I held onto his ankles, I infected him, I tried to drag him back here where it started—so tell me what the fuck I thought would happen? You can't heal what's depraved from its making. Somewhere on that road he saw who I was, and him, that same disease, and he cut the cord before it could feed any more poison into him. He knew better than me what would happen, and now he's drifting like a ghost in some gray city like I did. Calvin, you're better off without me, but please don't keep yourself alone. Alone makes you want such awful things. It just keep needling till you lash out against it. You have secrets about your love like me, and when we bash them together it becomes some pain love shouldn't—

     —reverse, but an unmarked rushed in and blocked Sam's prowler like a near-miss T-bone. In the rearview mirror, a squat pit-bull man with a sheepdog haircut got out of the shotgun seat wearing splotchy tan coveralls like he'd been out collecting city trash. But that was just one of Sergeant Royce's many narco getups.

Sam left the engine and heater running, stepped out of the driver's side. Royce was already on him, a foot too short with an extra large snarl. They faced each in the narrow lane between cars while a posse of cops exited the unmarked—two ramrod investigators out of Major Crimes, and Royce's Drug Task Force partner.

"Hartwick, you got a copy of Tuesday night's FOS report for me?"

Sam cleared his throat. "It's finished. I've just been in with the Sheriff."

"You're on your way out," Royce noted, crouching to glance into Sam's prowler.

"Yeah, my shift is starting."

"That's all right—you just go ahead and fiddle while my fucking case burns. I'll take it." Sam sniffled up the snot the arctic air teased out of his nostrils. Royce pivoted himself toward one of the Major Crimes guys and said, "Shit, we got to get SUNY campus police on the phone before we head over there."

All four of these men looked like they had worked through the night on that butcher shop scene, and something had come of it. "SUNY campus?" Sam said, knowing he had just chomped the hook and swallowed it down.

Royce cupped a handkerchief to his face and blew, pinched his nostrils to get it all out. The dramatic pause. He said, "Three more murders last night, or rather some kind of OK Corral shootout in which one of Cassadaga County's Most Wanted, Ramon Ortiz, takes some buckshot in the chest. Good fucking riddance, but the other two vics are Frankie Furst Senior *and* Junior, another family affair." He eyed Sam as if daring him to dispute these facts. "Senior is local Joe Public, and Frank Junior was my *prize* fucking informant, two years running. Thing is, Ramon Ortiz would've never worked alone, so someone, or *ones*, rode off into the sunset last night, perhaps even our very own public enemy *numero uno,* low-rent Weymouth cracklord Placido Riviera, old Peaceful River himself.

"But of course we won't ever know because poor Frankie the Informant caught it execution-style. Daddy Furst meets his by way of a burst jugular, predicated by a speeding projectile. This all went down in Furst Senior's butchering establishment, mind you, which ought to go a long way toward defining irony."

"How's this relate to SUNY?" Sam asked. He might as well have had a couple sausage links hanging from his neck.

Royce grinned and wagged his finger. "Funny you don't ask a more obvious question. In the meatlocker, of all places, we found a wallet, driver's license, a couple loose credit cards—non of which belonged to any of the deceased. Talk about a Christmas present. Fella by the name of Wynn Johnston. Sound any alarms for you?"

Sam said without hesitation, "Wynn Johnston was Dwight Kopeck's best friend."

"Right answer. And how have you come to know this factoid?"

"Yesterday I talked to the Kopecks, and then I talked to Wynn Johnston's mother."

"In your capacity as an investigator for the County of Cassadaga, State of New York?"

"In my capacity as a friend of the family," Sam said. "I told you that two nights ago."

"So I assume all of this will be found in your report, as well as your crackerjack explanation for why you felt it was completely unnecessary to apprise the investigative team of your findings?" Royce said through his teeth. "Imagine my *surprise* one hour ago when Mrs. Johnston told me that she already spoke to a sworn deputy yesterday evening."

"Nothing came of that conversation," Sam said. "I didn't have the connection you do."

"Did you track down Wynn Johnston himself?" Royce asked.

"No."

"Too bad for you. Could've had the case all wrapped up in a pretty bow by now."

"I didn't intend—"

"Just get me the fucking complete report, Hartwick," Royce said, heels off the ground. He slapped the prowler roof openhanded, with a smirk like he meant it as a substitute for Sam's face. The three men behind him were all snickering against the wicked wind. But whatever Royce suspected, he didn't know the full scope of Sam's involvement. If he knew, Sam would've been taken down, relieved of his gun, handcuffs transferred to his wrists. Instead, that shame would be reserved for later, after Wynn was caught and caged and sang his birdsong. The sweat on the back of Sam's neck was freezing into—

Wynn woke alone beside an unmade bed, with the curtains drawn to keep the hotel room dark. He remembered the night before in variations, but the pain in his ribs and his face brought the right account to focus. His left arm, bent at the elbow, wouldn't tolerate straightening. He winced himself upright with a throb under his skull. The girl was gone, and he was not surprised.

In the shower he cried because the tears were the same as the wash dripping down his face. Every fourth vertebra felt wedged against the hot, electric line of his spinal cord. His knees shook violently, and Frank's hunting rifle threatened his face in staccato flashbacks. Cecelia left, and she stole pieces of his flesh as mementos. The drying towel burned against his skin. He couldn't resent her leaving. Only that she took him here instead of his home, his room in the tower, left him here alone without money or his own clean clothes.

Erika, not Cecelia. She tried to love him but some problems were unsolvable.

He tried to piss, but the knife blade sensation cut off the stream. Only a few dark red drops of urine dribbled into the toilet bowl. He wiped the steam off the mirror with his towel and stood naked with bruises in Rorschach blots. In the drawer he found the hidden hand-towel, and peeled back its folds, lifted the Glock, his finger through the trigger guard. With the muzzle he pushed wet strands of hair behind his damaged ear, held it steady, and considered his own breathing.

Naked on the bed, gun under his pillow, he watched the news on a Cleveland, Ohio, station. Buried behind weather-damage reports and arson investigations came a piece out of Cassadaga County, New York, where "suspected drug violence escalating in recent days led to a gruesome discovery overnight at a local butcher shop." The anchor read for fifteen seconds, with a graphic of police tape beside his head. They showed no video feeds or on-site reporting, and then they moved on to college basketball.

Wynn closed his eyes and saw himself again lifting the Glock against the back of Frank Furst's skull, how easy it was to pull the trigger and watch him collapse. So many of Cecelia's worst mistakes vanished in that instant.

An electric blip didn't register with him until the room door swung open. With one hand he covered his nest of public hair, and the other he pushed behind his head, under the pillow. He howled as he sat and the agony played a tune along his ribs.

It was Erika, waitressing two Dunkin' Donuts coffees in a to-go tray on her upturned palm, fat department-store bags against her thigh, room keycard clamped between her teeth. She said, "Mm my Goh," and averted her eyes.

Wynn took his fingers off the hidden gun and covered himself with both hands. "I didn't think you were—

—coming back," Wynn said.

She tried not to look, but there were mirrors everywhere, casting reflections of him with his hands between his legs, all bare skin and bruises, herself mottled red across her cheeks from the cold outside and the shame. She set the coffees on the desktop next to the Erie tourist guide. She wondered if the coffee tasted as good in that looking-glass world, if her father was a saint and her mother a survivor, if in that world she could lie down beside Wynn without any delusions.

She took the keycard from her mouth and said, "I went to get coffee and clothes. Here." The jeans and black pullover were both still on hangers, but she took them from the bag and draped them over his naked body. Cuts on his shins were scabbed over ugly, but they summed into a feeling that flitted like life inside her groin. "I had to guess on your size, but I'm pretty good at it, costume designer and all."

"Where's my Mad Hatter top hat?" he asked. "You didn't have to do this."

"I kinda did. Was I just supposed to ditch you here without anything?"

"I was trying to decide what I was going to do, if you didn't come back."

She dug out the packages of underwear and socks, tossed them on the bed. "I admit I'm a loner, but I think I'd go crazy in that car by myself."

"I'm probably not a great choice for a navigator," he said as he tore open the bag of briefs. When he stood up to slip inside them, he exposed himself like it was nothing, like she ought to be used to sharing a room with a buck-naked man. She dropped her eyes. After the stupid risks and miscalculations they'd gone through, she resented that he could be so casual.

"Actually," she said, "I seriously thought about taking off. Instead of going to the mall. I started thinking how much I didn't know about you, and it scared me. I couldn't sleep."

When she looked again he was buttoning the jeans, pulling off the tags. They were a little loose on him but she'd bought a belt to cover it, the whole wardrobe from Target for just over a hundred dollars of inherited dirty money. He said, "Your instincts—" but a bout of pain made him groan instead. He sat back down on the bed. "I don't think I can go any farther with you. I'm sorry. I have to go back to Weymouth and straighten this out."

She offered him his coffee. He held it in his lap without drinking.

"It's not drugged," she said. When she sat on her bed, their knees were inches apart. Her cell phone text-message chime rang in her pocket. "Jesus—what is it you need to straighten out?"

"I don't know is the problem. I need to talk to your dad."

"My dad is like the worst person to talk to if you want shit straightened out. He's not even anybody important in the department, Wynn. He's just a deputy. I can take you to see a detective or even the sheriff if you need—"

"It has to be him because he's the only one who can help me."

"If you think just because you're my friend or whatever he's going to—"

"It's not about that."

"Then what is it? I can't fucking go back there to him."

"I have to try to piss again," he said. He stood slowly and limped toward the bathroom with his new pullover caught in his fist. She wanted to toss her coffee at his bare back to see how much more suffering he could take, but it wasn't anything she'd do. The door closed behind him, and the bathroom air filter kicked on automatically with the light.

She hated her father for what she knew about him, and fixated on Wynn because of what she didn't. He was involved with some drug-gang shit, saw somebody killed, maybe even killed somebody, even if it was in self-defense. He lived the world her father policed, but the reasoning didn't gel anymore. It wasn't because Dad was a cop that she rejected him, threw herself on a live grenade instead. It was because of some dusty old sin.

Nothing in this room was hers that she wasn't wearing or holding, so she took the keycard and slipped out into the hallway, eased the door shut behind her. The coffee was too hot on her tongue but she drank it. On her way down the steps, in the midst of tropical sounds piped in from speakers, she opened her cell phone and retrieved the last text. It was from her father, and it read PLEASE ERIKA I CAN FIX THIS. She crossed the lobby and the sliding doors—

—vacant shopping plaza bordered by train tracks and the high-way overpass. The Buffalo-Weymouth local bus pulled away behind Cal. With nothing to stop the wind, it blasted him with wet snowflakes that weighed down his eyelashes and stung his neck. He was here a day too late with nothing left but stale clothes and a peacoat that belonged to a man who was just his grandfather by default. Look around: This was the place that made you, the home of your mother and father.

He found a service desk in the Shop-Mor grocery store, where an elderly woman sat behind a Plexiglas window decorated with dozens of starburst decals bearing the names of those who donated to cancer research. He asked for a phonebook, but there was no Hartwick listed, and no Larkin. Weymouth suddenly grew from a walkable village into a vast network of streets.

"What's the matter?" the desk clerk asked in a shrill, nasal voice.

"You don't know anyone named Hartwick, do you?"

"Nope, and I been here my whole life. Eighty-three years and I'm back to work."

"How about Larkin?"

"I knew some Larkins over by the college, nearabouts anyway, but they're long dead."

Cal pushed the phone book back through the slot and said, "Thanks anyway."

"What I mean to say is the house is still in the family, last I—"

—vending machine breakfast burrito warmed in the manager's office microwave. Jodie hustled back to her room along the walkway, jacketless. She didn't want to have to eat a damn thing, but her stomach cramped and dizziness struck whenever she stood still. A day and a half without food had passed already. Coming on a full day without Calvin. She'd rowed him ten miles out to sea and thrown him overboard without a life preserver.

Halfway to her room she saw the prowler turn the corner of the motel wing. The tires crackled across the fresh strewn salt as the car swung around and pulled alongside where she stood. Sam pushed out his door and raised himself beside it. He wore sunglasses and the face of a military statue.

"You scared me for a sec . . ." she started, but Sam flexed his jaw muscles in such a way that stopped her short and made her hunch all the more from the chill. "What's the matter?"

He pointed at the doorway to her room, cracked open an inch with a Gideon Bible as a doorstop. She took the cue and entered ahead of him, set her burrito on top of the television set. He closed the door behind him and stood holding out his arms beside the black weapons on his belt.

He sucked heavy breaths through his nose and said, "I'm going to tell you something I did, Jodie. Two days ago I took a five-hundred-dollar bribe, money I didn't even keep for myself. I took a bribe in exchange for information, and what I did got two people killed, maybe even more people now. I didn't want such a thing to happen, but it did anyway."

Jodie didn't want to sit down on the bed or anywhere because she'd feel too vulnerable. A confession like that didn't come loose without dragging worse business along with it. She said, "I'm sorry that happened, Sam, but I don't get why you're telling me."

"Want to know why I did it? Because I wanted to help some people, and the same goes for last night when I brought you here instead of jail. I don't know if I was helping you, but I was helping my wife. That kid Dwight thought he'd be helping his sister, except that he brought along a gun. He lied about his gun to me, but that doesn't matter. It's still my fault."

"I don't know who Dwight is. I'm sorry."

"Well, I'm sorrier, and I'm through with all this shit as of this minute."

"Sam, where's Jill? Why didn't you bring her with you?"

He rested his thumb on his holstered gun, and Jodie backed away until the unmade bed stood between them. He blocked the only exit from the room. He said, "I lied to my brass, twenty minutes ago, when they asked me if I'd been in contact with you."

The dizziness struck her dumb. She lowered herself onto the edge of the bed with her back turned toward him. Vulnerable or not, it didn't matter anymore—because she was on the run and Sam Hartwick was police. She said, "They know about me. I tried to tell you last night. I wanted to turn myself in and be through with it, but you wouldn't let me. I told you."

"*You* lied to us, by omission," Sam said, with a catch in his voice. "By the end of the day I'll be arrested, and it's nothing to do with you. You're much worse, when I think about it. I wanted to set a family straight, but I don't know what you wanted. Maybe the opposite. It doesn't matter. Now we're both criminals because of what we did."

"Please, Sam. What did they tell you?"

"I want *you* to tell it."

She turned toward him, expecting to see his gun drawn, but he was granite as ever.

He asked, "Where is Calvin Nowak?"

"God, I don't know, Sam," she admitted. "He split from me in Pittsburgh. He ran off."

"Why did he run off?"

"I guess because I wasn't what he thought."

"You're not," he said. "But I want to ask you one other thing."

"Sam, please—it's not gonna do us no good, or Jill. Especially not her."

He clamped his teeth like he was holding back an outburst. He said, "Don't you try to tell me what's good for any of us. You and me are the worst people to know what's right, and I'm standing here in this fucking uniform. Why did you come back here to us?"

"Calvin wanted us to come here. He wanted to see Weymouth, and . . ."

"And what? You thought that would be just a splendid idea?"

"All's I was thinking—was what he wanted. All right? I wasn't thinking of me or you."

"Why'd you still come, even after he left you?"

"I didn't have nowhere else to go."

"What made you think you had here, either?"

"Sam, just—please. How was I supposed to tell you about him?"

He broke his stance, kicked a dent into the edge of the dresser. He snatched her burrito and pitched it against the wall with a brown splatter of bean that could just as well have been shit. Jodie wanted to laugh at him, but the feeling cut off quick. He said, "I'm taking you into custody."

"I don't care what you do," she said, but she saw herself tied to a chain that led from here to the prowler to Weymouth Public Safety booking to a cinderblock jail cell. She saw herself in that government-assistance Atlanta apartment with its dungeon windows. She'd been confined in cars and busses and motel rooms for a week, and it was no kind of freedom. That's what Calvin realized, and he escaped it.

"We're gonna do it quiet, and Jill doesn't need to hear a word," Sam said.

"How long you think it's gonna take her?"

Sam unclipped his handcuffs and showed them off like they were props in a magic trick. "Don't ask me about Jill, all right? You don't just come along out of nowhere and start picking my life apart. You got no right to do that."

"You think I'm gonna resist arrest?" Jodie said, nodding at the handcuffs. She stood beside him now and the heat of his anger was on her skin. With his bald head, he looked like a bullet. He was thicker then she remembered, but he was someone she loved once, and the trace chemicals still made her shake.

She touched his face and pressed her lips against his for an instant, and she felt that they had both escaped the traps they laid for themselves. But then Sam grabbed her throat and pushed her backward on the bed. She lay sprawled and her mind was a blank. She would've submitted to anything, but now she twisted the comforter in her hands and said, "He told me he was a faggot. How do you like that, Sam? Your kid is a faggot."

He slipped off his glasses and folded them into his breast pocket and said, "What do you think that's supposed to do, make some kind of—

—rang the bell and waited on their porch, hunched his shoulders against the wind. Not enough time or focus for Cal to think what he might say to them, whether he would lie or strip himself down to the truth.

But nobody answered the door, so he rang again. A single envelope hung from the lip of a mail slot in the siding. He shifted a few steps to the left and looked through the window where a two-inch gap between the curtains showed a hardwood floor, nothing else. He raised his thumb to ring a third time, but swiped the letter out of the slot instead. It was credit-card junk mail addressed to Samuel Hartwick.

That name, here at the supposed Larkin residence, like some prank orchestrated by the Shop-Mor lady, just to fuck with his head. Cal slid the envelope back into place, hurried back down the porch steps, and stood squinting at the house from a wider vantage, hoping some new sense could be made from it.

He followed the shoveled walkway ten feet over to the driveway, and risked the icy asphalt on that side of the house until he found the backyard breezeway. He pulled the door open and stepped onto the plastic floormat. The firewood stacked inside the breezeway looked frostbitten. No curtain to block his view, through the door glass, of a kitchen. He tried the doorknob, but it wouldn't budge.

The floormat under his feet was molded with the words: GET LOST! GUN OWNER INSIDE! He pulled back the mat and didn't find the key he expected underneath, so he lifted the recycling bin behind him, flipped through a stack of old *Buffalo News* editions. He pulled the A-section from the topmost newspaper and wrapped it over his right fist, held it in place with his other hand, then punched clean through a glass panel the size of a paperback book.

The pane broke jagged, but the noise was minimal. He slapped with his newspapered hand to break the remaining glass away, reached through, and unlocked the knob from the inside. It was his second break-and-entry in a week and he felt more alive than ever. He entered the kitchen, kept his steps quiet as he stalked onward into the living room.

On the mantel a bank of portraits depicted the panorama of a marriage. A husband growing meatier and balder until his head was shaved altogether, a wife's array of skin tones and hairdos, though always the same vibrant red as Calvin's own hair. They had a daughter in ballet slippers at age ten, black-dyed hair in her senior portrait. She was older than Cal, but not by much if the last picture was recent. He hated that he should care so deeply about these people, just seeing their portrait faces, especially when not one of them knew he existed.

He stood in silence beside a fake Christmas tree two months out of season. It angered him to see it, though he couldn't think why. The house smelled of age and even a hint of sickness. Somebody had taken away the television from the corner of the room, as if house was recently abandoned, TV and all, so fast that the Christmas tree and the clean dishes in the kitchen weren't properly stored.

His forearm razed across the mantel and plowed the frames into each other and they fell facedown on the brick and crashed to the floor. His sneakers crunched the shattered glass. He turned against

the Christmas tree and yanked a plastic branch until the entire struc-
ture toppled and the aluminum ball ornaments crunched and rolled.
Birds and stars were hooked on the boughs, but he'd brought them all
down to the floor. A Santa Claus head made from a hollow egg still
clung to a branch by a loop made of yarn. Cal raised the sole of his shoe
against it, then crushed the egg into crumbs.

Nobody knew who he was. He didn't know who he was.

In the space where the tree had been standing was Jodie's familiar
duffel bag. His head spun and he sat on the fireplace hearth, wrapped
together the fingers of both hands across the back of his neck. He
swayed like a mental case and wondered if he was. Moisture dropped
from his eyes to his knees. This goddamned duffel bag, he dragged it
against his shin and saw that the side pouch was unzipped and the
money inside was gone, every last bill.

He unzipped everything. There was his gas mask with its wide-eyed
stare. That girl in the Harrisburg townhouse—she was the only one
who'd seen him for who he was, the blank black eyes and the swinging
dick for a mouth. Somewhere on the Carolina coastline, two decent
people who were not his parents believed that they loved him and understood him, but they were wrong on both counts.

"Who are you?" someone asked. The voice of a curious child, but she
was a bald and withered woman who stood in the center of the room in
her bathrobe, hands brought together to cup a handgun that she aimed
in his direction. The weapon was hardly bigger than a cigarette pack,
but Cal cried out from the suprise of it. He gripped the hearth brick, and
in that instant the destruction he caused was an outrage even to him.
The crushed eggshell—

—stink of mashed burrito. Jodie couldn't stand it, so she pushed
herself off the bed, into the bathroom for handfuls of tissue from the
dispenser. Sam didn't move as she wiped gobs of bean off the wall with
the tissues.

"I'm sorry I did that," he said.

"I'm sorry, too," she said. "This whole last day's got me totally confused, and nobody—I don't know nobody. I tried—but now I just want Calvin okay. That's all I care about."

When his belted radio crackled next, it was right behind her. He reached over her shoulder and pressed his hand over hers on the wall and said, "Let me." She slipped her fingers out from underneath his, left him to wipe up the mess. He said, "We both need to consider what's best for other people right now."

"I know."

"We're going to let the right authorities look for Calvin Nowak. We're going to go down to the police station so you can tell them everything you know to help them."

"All right."

"And we're going to do it all quiet, without any fuss. We're not going to involve Jill."

She sat on the edge of the bed and watched him clean while she tried to remember whose fault it was, the fifteen-year-old mistake that brought all this on. They had both drunk beer all afternoon watching television, and she was way below legal drinking age, but Sam didn't stop her from going to the fridge for more. Who to blame didn't matter anymore. Now, even in his uniform with his gun and Taser he looked helpless and wrong, tossing soiled tissues into a wastebasket. He didn't belong in a clean-up job any more than her. She asked, "You seen inside that jail? What's it like inside there?"

"Like you'd expect from a jail. Lots of concrete, cells you share with one or two people, a communal area to eat and move around inside. I don't know. It's just what you'd think."

"Like bars on the cells?"

"Glass windows," he said. "This is all beside the point."

"How long will I have to be in there?"

"Jodie."

"What if they don't find him? Calvin. I'm stuck in there and there's nothing I can do about it, and I'm never going to be able to talk to him again."

Sam stationed himself back at the door, shaking his dropped head like the losing team's coach. Jodie didn't think her legs would even work if she tried to follow him out to the prowler. Inside that jail she'd be surrounded by others, but they'd all be women stinking from days without baths, moaning at all their losses. They'd be the same as her.

Sam said, "Be realistic, Jodie. You know you're not going to see Calvin no matter what."

"And what about Jill? I want to see her again before she—what if I don't see her?"

"She doesn't need our problems, anyway. Try to respect that, will you?"

"But you get to be with her. She's my sister, longer than your wife."

"Yeah, Jodie. We all go home. Calvin goes to his parents, I go home to my wife."

He yanked open the door and stepped out into the daylight. Her empty stomach clenched. He'd ruined her lunch and the smug bastard thought he could ruin everything else. She wanted to rush him and grab his gun. She hung in the doorway, anchored herself to the frame with both hands and screamed into the wind, "Don't you fucking say that! I'm his mother! He's mine! I have a right you can't do nothing about!"

Sam had the door to his prowler half open when he spun on her. "You think so? Then go. Get the fuck out of here." He gestured both his arms toward the open woods behind the motel. "You've been in that room all night and half the day, and nobody was here to stop you. So go ahead and track him down. Go live happily ever after in your dream world."

Her knees buckled and she sank in the doorway, caught splinters in her hands as they slid.

Sam approached her, sneering. "Were me, I'd never've left if I knew he wasn't with me."

"He got off the bus when I was sleeping."

"Then don't sleep! That's called being a parent. If it was my kid, I'd do everything I possibly could to keep him safe. I never would've done half of what you did."

"Listen to what you just said," she muttered. "He *is* yours, Sam."

"I know that."

"Jill is your wife."

"I know. I'm sorry I said that. I messed up." He stood above where she was crouched, shivering. He reached down to help her to her feet. He said, "And I know what she's going through is my fault because of what we did. It's all—God taking her to be with him instead of me, and leaving me here to suffer for it. I understand, and I just want her safe, but I don't get it the way I want it, and neither do you."

"I don't believe in God," she said, wiping at her nose with her sleeve.

"All you need to believe is punishment," he said, and opened the passenger—

—are you?" the woman demanded again.

"I don't know," Cal answered.

"How did you . . ." she started, but she studied him with such rapture that her question was lost.

"I'm sorry," he said. "I'll clean it all up. I didn't mean to hurt anything."

"This isn't your house," she said.

Cal said, "I thought it was, but I'm confused."

He couldn't look at her because she was almost his mother's apparition. She didn't seem afraid. She didn't move toward a phone or retreat from where she stood. She even lowered her aim to the floor while she said, "You look—are you looking for somebody?"

"I was supposed to come here with Jodie," he said. "But we got separated."

"Oh my God," she said with one hand over her mouth.

"I'm sorry," he said. "I should've been here with her the first time."

"You're—who are you?"

"I'm her son," he said, squeezing the gas mask in his lap. The moment was charged with an energy that made him need to stand, but when he did, she raised the gun on him again. The barrel wavered and darted because she couldn't keep it still. Cal thought he should raise his hands but it would mean releasing the mask. All he wanted was to put it over his face and be nobody again, nobody's child.

"I know what you are," she said. "I can smell it, that lilac smell. I can see the aura."

"Lilac?" he said.

She held the gun one-handed and pointed a shivering finger at her bare temple and said, "In here, in my brain. That's where you're growing. You're mine, not Jodie's, and I know what you are. I know what's going to happen. I can smell it."

"Lady . . ."

She tossed the tiny gun onto the coffee table, pressed her hands on the top of her head and stepped toward the couch, sat down as if she were falling. Cal didn't stop her or lunge for the gun, not even when she took a cell phone from a plush pocket in her bathrobe and pressed a single speed-dial digit. The connection rang but she didn't seem to have the strength to lift the phone to her ear.

The volume was loud enough that Cal heard the voice of the man who answered.

"Sam," the woman said. "Sam, I think—I don't—some—"

"Jill?" the voice said. "Jill, what's the matter?"

Her hands worried the phone in her lap and her spine arched. She began to shudder in mad paroxysms, teeth gnashing like bricks scraped together. Cal stepped over the fallen tree and reached for this woman whose neck muscles were taut and whose eyes were stark white, this woman who was—

Wynn awoke as the Nissan came to a stop. He found himself a passenger in a car parked behind a minivan, but a few seconds passed before he recognized the Hartwick house. Erika turned the key and the engine died out, but the folk-rock music on the CD player persisted until she killed that with her thumb.

He sat upright. No police cars in the road behind them, just a woman pushing a stroller with a heap of blankets inside it. The wounds on his face felt like extra mouths yawning. He didn't want to care what they'd look like when they healed, as long as his mind stayed clear, his reason and logic.

"This is your house," he said, as if to exercise his faculties.

"I hope so," Erika said. "Do you want me to drop you off at your dorm instead?"

"Your father," he said.

"He won't be home till almost midnight, but we can call him if you need."

"I don't—I don't know," he said. The college campus was two blocks away, his own dorm rising at such an obscene height above the powerlines. He hadn't expected to see it again, and now he couldn't remember why he ever left to seek out Frank. He'd confused himself with false scenarios when the elegant truth was that Dwight and Cecelia had cancelled each other out, and Wynn was free. He'd gone searching for remainders, but he was the only one.

"I just want to say I'm sorry," Erika said.

"You're the last person who needs to apologize."

She looked pale and exhausted, like Cecelia the last time he saw her. He wished Cecelia could be gone from his memory, because under those conditions, he could've let Erika kiss him when she tried. At its root the kiss would've been a fallacy, but it also would've been an escape.

"At least let me thank you for talking me into coming back," she said. "It feels right."

"There's nowhere else we can go. Not yet, anyway." Something solid was lodged in his ribs, but when he reached inside the pullover, he touched the gun he almost forgot was there. The trivial weight of it against his bruises was agony.

"That's what I'm saying. I just freaked and took you with me." From out of her own jacket she pulled a cash fold, held it with both hands in her lap and thumbed through the bills. She said, "I'm going to find out what happened, aren't I? Over in Philpot last night? And I'm going to have to explain to my father and everybody why I helped you."

His body spasmed and he cried out. He couldn't think how to cancel out these variables.

"Wynn, what's the matter?" she yelled to him all the way from the far end of a wind tunnel. He pushed open his door and struggled to stand but the ground underneath him was a sheer patch of ice. One knee gave out and pitched him forward into the snowbank skirting the driveway. Bare hands were buried, and the crystalline cold shimmered on half his face. He crawled across the lawn, away from the car. He retched, but no fluid came with it.

Erika's boots crunched through the snow and her hands touched his back with a tentative flinch. When Wynn raised his head, he saw the prowler skid to a halt in the street. Sirens like the wails of demons that would tear him into shreds.

Someone who'd been inside him was gone—a loner too scrawny for love or violence. He scooped the white in both hands and pressed it against his face because it seemed the only way to stop the pain. He reached underneath his pullover and wrapped his fingers around—

—fifteen miles overspeed. This city where Sam lived so deeply he could drive blindfolded through the streets, but now he saw it through the eyes of someone exiled for a decade and a half. It looked the same—the power plant like a massive furnace, the potholes where the old brick street showed through, the mustard-yellow tenements with Puerto Rican flags for curtains—but that illusion was a trap.

Jodie was seated shotgun with her wrists uncuffed, not behind the cage where criminals go. He owed her that at least. The shock of her kiss was still on his mouth, and it told him just what to pity about her. He said, "You ever wonder how things might've turned out? If we just forgot it happened and went on with our lives and nobody ever knew?"

Jodie turned to watch out the window at Weymouth Hospital, a perfect rectangle of brick and crumbling mortar, and the Catholic cemetery beyond it. She said, "I think Calvin would've made us remember."

"Is that what you named him—Calvin?" He tried to mold this idea of a living person in his mind, some younger, male version of Erika, scrapped together in the same gene pool. What Jodie'd told him about the boy's sexuality reeked of slander meant to fire Sam's rage. But it could just as well be true. The kid couldn't rightly go unscathed, not after his depraved conception.

"No," Jodie said. "I didn't name him."

"What would you have named him?"

"I never even thought about it," she said. Stuck between her seat and the radio console was a book with its dogeared pages facing upward. She pulled it out, the guide to Costa Rica. Sam hadn't even realized he lost it. The centerfold featured full-color pages of poisonous dart frogs, volcano hot spring spas, and fat Americans zip-lining over a cloud forest canopy. She said, "You went to this place?"

"Me and Jill were trying to convince each other we should, but that's over. Maybe if we left last week, we wouldn't—hell, all I can think about is what didn't happen."

They were at a red light, one block from Public Safety and county jail booking, a holding cell, a black-and-white striped jumper. A process that likely awaited them both. The cell phone in his breast pocket vibrated against his folded sunglasses.

Jodie said, "You can't run away from nothing, let me tell you. Leave, you just run right into whatever's coming to get you. I know that now."

The light turned green and Sam pressed onward through the intersection, toward the modest dome of the county courthouse. He fished out his phone and read JILL on the caller ID. He told Jodie, "We do what we think is right. Even the worst of us do."

Jodie said, "You're a cop, so I know you know that ain't true."

He pressed accept on the phone and brought it to his ear. Over the line Jill said his name and something else confused, almost inaudible. He said, "Jill? What's the matter?"

Waves of static came back at him, but nothing else. "Jill!" he yelled, and his prowler sped past the entrance to Public Safety as if it were just another building on the route back home. They were storming up Central with the flashers and sirens all firing, the patrol-car readout on the radar pushing sixty in a thirty. The cars ahead of them flashed red brakes and steered against the curb, not fast enough.

Jodie put both her hands on the dash and said, "Sam, what's going on?"

"Jill! Can you hear me!" he screamed into the phone.

Someone on the line, a male voice, said, "Is this Sam Hartwick?"

"Who the hell is this? Put my wife on the line! Who are you?"

"Your wife is sick. She's having—"

"If this is Wynn Johnston I'm one fucking minute from my house, I swear to God—"

"My name's Calvin. I'm—I think she's having a seizure—"

282

Jodie's hands fluttered in Sam's face, clutched for the phone. She said, "Calvin? Is that Calvin?" and the chaos jerked the wheel left across the solid yellow twenty feet ahead of an oncoming UPS truck. Sam lurched the prowler straight and shoved his frantic sister-in-law against the passenger-side door. She howled some curse he ignored in favor of the phone.

Sam asked Calvin, "You're at our house? Is that right?"

"Yes, I—"

"I know who you are, Calvin. I'm less than a minute away. Keep her safe, all right?"

"Let me talk to him!" Jodie insisted, but she didn't strike out again.

Sam told Calvin, "I need to call an ambulance, all right? Keep her safe."

"I want to talk to my son!"

Sam shoved the cell phone at her and she took it in both hands. He stomped the brake and twisted the car onto his street, clipped his tires against the curb edge and missed a fire hydrant by inches and danced a black-ice patch before catching on the road-salt grit. Twenty years of living off Jill's spoils, his mortal sins, and God forgive the sense that he was waiting for her to die. He said, "Weymouth, this is eight-twenty-four."

"Cal, this is Jodie! Do you hear me?"

"Weymouth, eight-twenty-four."

"I need EMS, Advanced Life Support at Forty-five Chautauqua Street, my home address. My wife—" He stomped the brakes again and squealed along the streetside edge of his property, past the driveway crowded with two cars. One of them was his Maxima. Like a Polaroid just taking shape from whiteness, nothing he saw made sense. His daughter home, and his son Calvin there in the front yard with her, unaccountably.

"We're here at the house," Jodie said to the phone. "Just outside."

Sam threw open his door, flicked off the siren. A dark mass of clothes crouched in the snow, a white male in a jacket and winter hat. Calvin Nowak, Sam had decided. Erika was leaning over him like he was wounded wildlife too feral to touch. Paper money twirled and flipped in the wind, slapped against a drainpipe, a car window, danced across the surface of the snow as far as the gusts would drive it.

Too much stimuli threw Sam off-target. He tried to exit with the radio transmitter still in his hand. It sprang away from his grip on its coiled line. The image in front of him went crisp and changed his impression entirely. The young man in the snow couldn't be his bastard child because—

—somebody else's life and death. A woman named Jill. She lay on the couch still twitching with the aftershocks of her seizure. Cal sat on the cushion in the crook she made with her body. He'd hold down her arms if she started flailing again. Her face was slick with sweat. Something from health class about holding open their mouths to prevent tongue swallowing. Too late for that now because she was quiet again. Cal stopped his nose against her sour odor and looked away from the network of veins on her head. The few hairs remaining there were the same color as his.

"Hear me?" Jodie told him over the phone. "Stay inside the house."

Muffled shouts outside the window, a siren now silenced, spinning reds.

"What's going on?" he asked as he moved toward the window, lifted the curtain aside.

In the snowy front yard two people rolled together like lovers too eager for spring. The boy locked the girl's neck with his forearm and dragged her upright with some awkward wrestling move. Beyond them, Sam Hartwick emerged from his Cassadaga County cruiser in full uniform. This supposed father of Cal's looked like a brute, but he raised both hands and wrenched his face, playing the role of a victim at someone else's mercy.

"Just please stay inside and keep an eye on Jill," Jodie said. Cal could see her, inside the open cab with the phone to her ear, transmitting messages clear through the chaos. The shouting doubled itself, live on scene while split-second delayed from a radio tower, into the call.

"What the hell is going on, Mom?"

"I don't got a clue, just—"

"Who are those people in the yard?"

"I don't—she's your cousin, Erika—your sister—"

"Which is it?" Cal demanded, still in the window.

Jodie threw open her door and rushed out of the car. She panted into the phone, choking on her commands, "—out of the window! He has a gun!"

Cal saw it, a pistol in the anonymous guy's grasp, pressed against the side of Erika's head, and this precise gesture held everyone in thrall. His sister, his cousin—her identity doubled like the noises through the phone. The paradox wrung his brain.

Erika clutched the arm that squeezed her by the throat and squirmed to get loose. Cal was struck with shame, viewing this all through a window. He turned toward the woman on the couch, but she was perfectly still, her mouth gone slack. Her chest didn't drop or rise.

The gun she'd threatened him with now lay harmless on the coffee table beside his deflated gas mask. The bowie knife Jodie had bought him a lifetime ago in Cape Fear, it was in its sheath on the floor. All this was his but he didn't want it anymore. His mother was screaming his name from the phone he left on the windowsill. He lifted the mask by its corrugated nozzle and wrenched it down over his face. In its musty confines he could breath again. Through its darkened blinders he could—

—process fast enough. The attacker was a white male whose face was raw with bruises and swelling. But he was recognizably Wynn Johnston, swapped with terrible magic from one crisis in Sam's life to another. The divisions were all collapsing. Jill was inside the house having a seizure, and Calvin with her—or maybe it was all a ruse.

Wynn held a handgun to Erika's head. She slammed her eyes shut and went limp from the shock. The boy struggled to keep her standing upright. His aim scattered and bounced. Sam didn't count this a blessing, because a wild gun was always too eager to fire.

"Wynn," Sam said, palms upheld. "Wynn, don't—I'm not here for you."

"Dad!" Erika cried out, and her eyes flew open.

"Stay there!" Wynn howled. "I didn't do anything! It wasn't my fault!"

"I know that, Wynn. I just want to clear this up, just like you."

"Unbuckle your belt," Wynn said. "Unbuckle your whole belt and let it drop."

Sam wanted to refuse. His hands wavered but he kept them up.

"Do it!" Wynn said, and it might as well have been the voice of God.

Sam unclasped the buckle on his nylon Sam Browne, but the police belt was looped to his leather dress belt. He pulled the pin from the eyelet and slowly slid the dress belt out from his waistband. The Sam Browne began to drop.

It collapsed at his feet, draped half over the curb—his Beretta and extra magazines, Taser and handcuffs and baton, radio and mini-flash, everything. His only weapon was the leather belt he still held, three feet long and useless. He stood as vulnerable as if he were naked, in direct opposition to his training, but he knew what the rules did not. That his own daughter was the hostage. That Wynn was probably not the crass killer he playacted now. Sam would gladly drop his guard if it bought him a few seconds' talk and the panicked boy's attention.

"Kick it into the gutter," Wynn said.

Two feet to the left of the discarded belt was a grate with a sewer drain cut into the side of the curb. Steam from below had melted the snow around it in a smooth crescent. The sight of it was a view of the abyss. With a cardiac jolt, Sam tilted toward collapse. He used his instep to push the belt until it gathered on the grate lip and snaked down into the drain, weapons and all. He wore no secret backup gun inside his boot or under his armpit. Never had a reason, not in sleepy Cassadaga County.

Inside the car, dispatch kept hailing him. Jodie screamed something about a window.

"Wynn, I didn't come here for you. I don't even know what you're doing here."

Erika cried out again, "Dad! How do you—" but Wynn thrashed her wordless and pressed the gun harder again her head. She clawed both her hands against the arm that squeezed her. Her flushed, petrified frown threatened to be the last Sam would ever see of her alive.

"It's your fault!" Wynn howled. "You're the one! All I want is to go back and forget!"

"Go back where, Wynn?" Sam pleaded.

"I don't want to be part of this!"

"You don't have to be," Sam said. "Just tell me what you want." He dared two steps forward with no sense of what he'd do if he came within reach of Wynn and Erika. God was on his lips and a mantra of penance was in his mind.

Behind the desperate boy with the gun, behind Erika, the front door to Sam's house eased open, and some kind of rubber-faced monster stepped onto the porch with Jill's Colt Pocketlite in its right hand. Sam dropped to his knees and begged the cold gray sky for—

—wouldn't answer her call. Because he was on the porch wearing that mask and his button-up jacket, the same ghoul he became in that Harrisburg house. Jodie cried out but it wasn't any words. Everything cycled backward. She stumbled around the front side of the prowler. Her sneaker treads caught ice and threw her onto the asphalt. Sam's cell phone slapped between her hand and the cruiser's mounted crash guard and clattered against the curb. Grit embedded in the hand that broke her fall. The dried leaves flitting past were the color and shape of the money she stole, Franklin smirking on all their faces.

"Stop!" Calvin called out. He took one step down off the porch. The gas mask hid his face from everyone. Everyone except his mother, because she could see straight through it. She could see his soul inside, and it was—

—spun around as Erika fell away from his grasp. She draped herself across the crusted snow, broke through like it was a sheet of milk glass. Wynn had no resolve to hold her anymore. She wasn't his to risk. The thing coming at him from the house had nocturnal eyes and a pendulant proboscis. It was past any logic Wynn could figure, not in the lizard brain that had control of him now.

The bug-eyed beast tracked him with the gun, squeezed the trigger. Over and again, it clicked dry and empty. Wynn absorbed the imaginary bullets, then turned his loaded Glock on whatever this—

—firework ricochet across the neighborhood houses. Wynn's gun jerked in his grip so hard it knocked him one step back. On the ground, Erika twisted aside and screamed into her hands. She wasn't yet synced to the whir of her father's arrival, Wynn's attack, the figure in the mask storming out like one-man SWAT.

She propped her elbows in the snow. On the property line her kneeling father grunted back up on his feet, but Wynn jabbed the gun at him and screamed something so wild it was no human words. "No," Erika tried to say, but she had no voice, either.

Surd, Wynn had called it, the thing that can't be spoken.

The gunman in the mask dropped onto the porch stairs, leaned backward with his arms akimbo, slid down two steps until he sat on the walkway, legs spread wide. His covered head pivoted loosely and revealed the speckled red stain it had left on the snowy step. One of the mask's eye lenses was shattered.

Wynn sobbed so violently he gagged from it, and the gun looked to be an impossible weight in his grasp, pulling down his aim. "I didn't mean it," he said. "It just came at me, and I didn't mean . . ."

Aunt Jodie lifted herself up against the trunk of the prowler and rushed across the yard toward the house. She didn't have her eyes on Wynn, didn't seem to notice his gun lifting in her direction, or how simply she could die. She raved things that sounded as nonsensical as Wonderland logic. All this confusion, Erika thought she might've been shot after all, straight through the language center of her brain.

But there was no pain, no blood, at least not for her, not yet.

Jodie fell beside the body on the steps and peeled away the mask, dropped it in the snow. The undamaged lens stared out from the mask's collapsed folds. She lifted the boy against her chest and his head rolled backward on his neck. Just a boy, wet orange hair matted to his face, the stark entry wound on his brow.

Someone grabbed Erika by the shoulders. She screamed and lurched away, but it was her father. His face was swollen pink from the cold. He loomed so close she could see the burst capillaries in the whites of his eyes. He begged, "Are you okay?" but she could only blink at him like a deaf mute. Behind him, Wynn stood at a distance with his aim still wavering.

"Dad," she said. "He's going to . . ."

Her father stood and turned on Wynn, who leveled the gun at the badge on the breast of his jacket. They were ten feet apart in six inches of snow. Dad didn't raise his hands this time. Some of the bills Erika had dropped were fluttering at their feet like birds in death throes. She wondered if her aunt would be angry about the lost money. She wondered whose reckoning this was, exactly, and when the mercy would start.

"Wynn, don't threaten me with that thing anymore," Sam said.

"He came out of nowhere. He had a . . ." Wynn's dazed eyes kept drifting toward things that weren't there, and he crunched a slow circle around Erika and Sam, pivoting on the centered aim of his gun.

Just above Jodie and the boy she cradled, the storm door opened out again. Its creak broke Wynn from his daze. He turned the gun on Mom as she stepped onto the porch, hunched and barefoot, squinting at the sunlight that glared off the snow.

"Jill, don't come out here!" Dad warned, but she took another step toward her sister and the dead boy, braced herself with one hand against a support beam. She surveyed them all below her like a martyr on the stake, silent judge of the uncountable sins she'd taken upon herself. Erika saw the full breadth of it now, her mother and father, almost her entire life, that constant eggshell effort not to break—

—is he?" the shooter asked. "Tell me who he is!"

Calvin was so heavy, and Jodie didn't have the strength, but she fought to keep him sitting. She held him where her jacket was unzipped and his skin still warm. She mashed her face into his, and his skin took the shape of hers. For one minute after he was born, still slicked in blood, she held him, and it was no different now. Ambulance sirens wailed closer every second, and she let herself believe he could still be saved.

"Jodie?" Jill said. She stood on the porch above, pale like the winter around her.

"He's my son," Jodie whispered. It was only for her sister to hear, not for that killer barking his questions. She eased her child back down on the step and covered one hand over the wound on his head. He was only sleeping now, just dreaming of a better family than the one he thought he wanted. He held a tiny gun, and Jodie reached out to grab it.

"No," Jill said. "There aren't any bullets."

Jodie pulled back and stood, pressed her hand to her mouth to stop her soul from bursting out. She had to give Calvin over to be saved. It wasn't her fault they were apart again. Cal wanted to come back. He crashed the car. She didn't bring him here. She told him to stay inside, but he came out anyway. She told him Erika was his sister, his cousin, and he decided to save her. Fifteen years ago, Jodie pushed Sam away the first time he slipped his fingers across her breasts, but only the first time. There wasn't anything she could've done, but all the shame bled through her anyway.

In the yard behind her, Calvin's murderer cried hot tears and held the gun like it was trying to twist from his grasp. Sam didn't look like a cop anymore, not even with his uniform. Erika made a lopsided angel where she lay in the snow. When Jodie looked at her boy again, she saw as the others saw and understood that he was dead.

From the beginning, it was a wish to live her sister's life because her own didn't have any weight. The same curse passed down to Cal, that desire to escape. Down in Cape Fear, the Nowaks waited for a son who wasn't coming back, and Jodie realized their grief would be worse than hers. Grasping that truth was a whole other kind of loss. She stumbled up the walkway toward the Maxima idling in the driveway, both front doors still wide open, dash alarm pinging since before Cal died.

The shooter clocked her with his gun and she muttered, "Go head and shoot me."

"You can't," he said, but he didn't pull the trigger. "What are you doing?"

Sam stood like a prisoner set for execution. She couldn't look at him so defeated. He wasn't even going to stop her from circling around the car, dropping into the driver's seat, shutting the door. She put her hands on the steering wheel and considered how wrong her whims always turned her. The money in the bowl, Hector's car. She thought of Nero in a cage somewhere, like she should be. His purr when she pet him, it used to give her a flash of satisfaction, a moment to hold still and appreciate.

The shooter jumped through the open passenger door and slammed it shut behind him. He collapsed in the seat, waved the gun in her direction, and said, "Go, now!" Through the window, Sam watched them in his car like they were bad news on the television. Then he sprang, hooked both hands under the passenger latch, but the shooter pressed the automatic lock at the same instant. The door didn't open.

Jodie pulled reverse and shot out into the road, scraped the length of the car against the back bumper of Sam's prowler. One of his tail-lights popped loose and crunched under her front right tire. Her passenger moaned and smacked the sliding block of his gun against his forehead, whispered something that sounded like numbers.

She spun the wheel and righted the Maxima for a forward burst, but the face of an oncoming ambulance filled her windshield, the noise of it in her ears, and she swerved on the narrow road, burst through the crusted roadside snow before she veered straight again.

"He wasn't anybody, nobody. None of this is real!" the shooter said.

"He was my son!" Jodie screamed. She swerved through the stop sign onto Central Ave. Without her seat belt she leaned into the wheel like she was part of it, bad arm flaring from the pain. Pedestrians on the sidewalk gawked. The two of them in this car, Jodie and the kid who wasn't much older than Cal, who was just as hideously bruised and broken as her. Maybe they belonged together after all.

"No! No!" he screamed. "Stop the car!"

Her toes crushed into the accelerator, but he grabbed the wheel and cranked toward the sidewalk. Jodie stomped the brake in turn, jerked against his intent, and the car stalled in the middle of the street. A horn blared behind her.

Just as fast as he'd thrown himself together with her, the boy who killed her son was gone. The door slammed shut behind him. His shape flashed in her rearview mirror, and then he sprinted across Central, headed for a side road with a tree-lined median—Commencement Drive, the main entrance into SUNY Weymouth.

Her foot on the brake was only a glitch. There was a streetlight above her, just now red, but she tore through it as the speedometer gauge jumped like the needle on a lie-detector test. You have deluded yourself again, it told her, but she wasn't listening. She was running as far from her sentence as—

· —windpipe almost swollen shut. But it was all just body and Wynn could transcend. He rushed down the walkway and gained on the students strolling their blind paces down the Commencement Drive footpath. They turned on him and jerked themselves aside just before he would have collided against their backsides, full-sprint.

They were all faceless. They were the same essential form. Every last one of them wore the same hideous mask, and Wynn shot each through its wide black eye, one after the other, with a bullet from his conceptual gun. He'd left the real one in the car with that woman. His hands were empty now.

The campus contained him like a perfect square root. It verified his reason and his need. Nobody pursued him past its outer boundaries, but still he ran. He skirted the west edifice of the administrative hall, brick after brick in duplication by the thousands. His bare feet slipped and chafed inside of Frank's oversized boots. He fumbled because the footpaths were too slick.

Time wound down until there was a stillness about the quad, the sway of the branches on a leafless tree as deliberate as stop-motion movement, the clouds overhead all caught on pause, a gesture forever. He felt the intervals between seconds stretch out around him and fill the empty slots that had no speakable decimal place. Numbers were not the abstraction of things, but the things themselves.

Here was the entrance to his dorm hall, the patio crusted with salt and melting snow. A student pushed through the glass doorway, held it open for Wynn as he passed through. The heat inside the lobby wrapped itself around him and squeezed hard enough to warble his consciousness. He leaned against a wall for a moment to catch his breath.

Ahead was a campus cop admiring the glow of a vending machine, not five feet away, oblivious to Wynn's arrival. Wynn divided his birth-date by the date at hand to draw his mind away from weakness and pain, then he pushed himself from the wall and staggered toward the elevator banks. His wounded knee screamed at him.

The face of that dead boy with his mask off, of Cecelia and Dwight, Frank bleeding out on the butcher shop floor, Frank's elderly father. They were all piled up inside that elevator car with him, clawing and bleeding, and when the doors closed he was lifted together with them like he was just as dead. He watched the whole numbers climb from one to eleven, and believed as best he could that there was no death.

The elevator slowed on the tenth floor, a moment of vertigo. Wynn could prolong, if he chose, that last ascending instant from the tenth to the eleventh floor. He could halve the distance between through eternal permutations. He could treat time and space in the terms that best suited his own starving need, but what he needed most was to get back into that room with his books and his notes, the life he wanted that nobody would let him claim.

The bell rang and the doors drew open onto the dusty, tiled floor and the rumble of laundry machines and the splash of photo collages on almost every suite entry door. He turned toward his own, four doors down on the right.

"Hey—hey stop—" someone shouted.

Behind him, uniformed cops crowded the hallway, campus and city, some in plainclothes, a few already filing into another open elevator car. He didn't stop for the one that hailed him, even though they were always already calling him back, forcing him into the chain. Not any-more. The Xeroxed announcements tacked to the hallway bulletin board fluttered in the wake of his passage.

He pushed his door wide open, almost pitched himself onto the common-room carpet. Parker stood there beside the futon, the tails of his corduroy blazer hooked behind his hands in his pants pockets, like he'd been waiting. He said, "Wynn, what the fuck is—" but Wynn kicked aside a recycling bin to get at their bedroom, and the empty containers clattered over whatever else Parker said.

Wynn slammed the door behind him, twisted the knob lock vertical. It was his tiny square cell, with book-lined shelves and cots for the sleep he would no longer need. He was beyond that now. He was thinking of a formula, working to get the symbols straight in his mind. Slipped his *Principles of Logic* textbook off the shelf and laid it open on his desk at the Table of Contents, heaved his asthmatic gasps over it. He ripped through the pages for the perfect reason and solution that he knew would—

—tapped against the seat-belt latch on the passenger side and Jodie knew, even before she glanced, that it must be the gun, there on the seat where the shooter left it. All the cars around her swerved like they were scheming to help her pass, but it was a fire truck wide in the road, bearing down with its sirens and its horn all throwing their fits at once. The blaring red force of the thing rocked the Maxima on its axels as they passed.

She swerved within an inch of a black SUV that shuddered into the intersection in a stream of brake-pad smoke. Ice caught her in a tentative jackknife, but she righted her aim straight beneath the interstate overpass, where the road hit fifty-five past the county fairgrounds and into the backwoods.

In the rearview mirror, a dark vehicle squealed out of the intersection and rushed up behind her. It cried and Christmas lights danced on its roof. She shoved the pedal down until the gauge hit ninety and her car tore the wind into tatters as it raced. The car behind her was police—but it wasn't Sam or any Cassadaga County badge. Dark blue meant Weymouth city police.

Every driveway and crossroad threatened to spit a car at her. A Ryder truck puttered along the road ahead. She gained on it, swung into the oncoming lane with nothing but a prayer that the road ahead was empty. Her whole being shoved itself into her throat and it was too much to hold down. She bashed the steering wheel with her fists and cursed at the world turned against her. She kept driving, no will to choose anymore.

Two cop cars behind her now, side by side. She wondered if Calvin ever loved before he died, if someone else would have to grieve for him, someone she never dared to ask him about, someone out in the world with a thousand others, pockets of grief in every house along every road. It all multiplied in her gut, all this pain she'd barreled past in her car. You can't outrun it. Her speedometer told only seventy miles per hour, and dropping. She was losing the will to press. What she wanted was left behind, and nothing came ahead but a long, cold stretch of road sloping downward.

Men huddled in at every window, screaming at her with their guns all aimed. The trees on the roadside weren't moving anymore. The guardrail wasn't shivering along. A state-trooper car stabbed in at a slant and tapped her front fender with its own, like the last slow-motion bounce of the bumper cars when the electric's cut off. The gun was on the seat beside her. The police surrounding her shouted their conflicting orders: "Open your door!" "Keep your hands up!" Jodie closed her eyes and reached—

—three fingers wound together tight. The emergency medic cut the tape with surgical scissors while she knelt next to Sam on the couch. The front door was open, welcoming cold. The hardwood floor was muddy with boot prints and melting snow. Christmas tree and the family photos, all in shambles around the unlit fireplace, though Sam didn't know how or why it all had to be destroyed.

Except that this was the site of his worst sin, this room, years ago but hardly any time in God's eyes. Sam had kept bribing Him with abstinence and tithes, with faith, but Sam couldn't begin to understand the justice it brought him now.

Through the open curtain, he watched two volunteer firemen in the street smoking cigarettes and muttering at each other, nodding. They kept looking at his house like they expected it to catch fire and give them something to rescue. Nothing to do now but stand around and wonder, shiver.

Sam's three wounded fingers were swollen immobile, collateral from Jodie's last maneuver before she'd peeled away. Not satisfied just to steal his car, she snagged his fingers on the door latch while she did it, wrenched them bad enough to break. He couldn't blame her alone, because Wynn—*because Sam* stood by and watched her escape. He let it happen because she'd lost her child, and she was ruined. She couldn't be around these people anymore. Around him. He'd been the one to teach her how to fly in the first place. Another sin he could devour in her place.

He would've let her leave without a fight, if not for Wynn's sudden maneuver. For all her mistakes, she still didn't deserve that boy with his gun in the passenger seat. Sam should've leaped, but Wynn made an art of stumbling past trip wires just two seconds ahead of him. He and Jodie were at each other's mercy now, and it was just too much fresh trouble to brood over.

"This should hold you till you get to a doctor," the medic said.

"Appreciate it," Sam said, wincing from the radiating ache. But a doctor visit felt like the worst indulgence he could dream. He said, "Have you seen where my wife went?"

The medic shook her head. She shut her case and tried to offer Sam a smile, decided to make her exit instead, around through the kitchen door because the porch was a crime scene. Sam moved to his front doorway and studied the fire blanket that the volunteers had draped over his porch steps. The dead boy was underneath it. His funeral contours outlined, and the damp rubber toe of one sneaker visible where the wind batted at a corner of the fabric.

Nobody had moved him from the steps. They were waiting for the police to arrive. Other police. Something about Sam's missing belt and his snow-drenched pants and injuries threw his authority in the toilet. They treated him as just another victim—the medics, the fireman, the neighborhood gawkers lingering on the edges of his property, most of them college kids, like Erika, and like Wynn. Those analytical glares they inherited from their professors, thinking they could size up any-body with a glance and the applicable theory. Sam wished he could stuff his resentment away for once.

He wanted to sneak outside and lift the edge of the blanket to get a look at the boy and convince himself Jodie's story wasn't true. But the instant he first saw Calin, even from a distance and only for a second, Sam had been sure. It wasn't about genetics so much as God's justice, even if Sam couldn't quite parse the meaning. Why Sam should stand mostly unhurt while so much suffering went on around him—you crawl into a dark cave on faith alone, and meet the truth with its teeth.

After a minute Sheriff Olin's car eased up the road through the con-gestion of a fire truck, ambulances, and onlookers. Seeing Olin, Sam was struck with the clarity that he would soon have to face his reckoning. But there wasn't enough time, not nearly enough, to understand. He needed to see that boy alive again and speak more with him than just a few hectic words. Sam wanted more time to live an existence where he was the father of a second child.

He stepped backward out of sight. He was the only one in the living room. Only a few minutes back Calvin was alive in here talking with Jill. He stayed beside her during the epileptic fit and relayed the news to Sam. Then, he stormed outside with an unloaded gun.

Sam was still trying to make sense of the sequence. It was an awful decision Cal had made. Doomed himself, could've gotten everyone killed, and if Sam had stayed on the phone he could've talked the kid into staying put. Sam could've convinced him. What happened might not have happened. Erika might have been killed.

My child was saved. I couldn't keep her safe myself, and somebody else had to sacrifice.

The raw moods churned in his chest but wouldn't blend. His daughter saved was weightless levity, but he had lost a child anyway. Calvin was his. He had watched his own offspring die. Sam understood, even if he couldn't quite feel it yet. Saw himself in some other cop's boots, trudging up to the Nowak's Cape Fear home with his cap in his hands, pressed against his badge. I'm sorry to have to tell you—

—but from another vantage, Sam saw himself meeting a solemn officer on his doorstep, bracing for the news about his son. I'm sorry to have to tell you Calvin's abductors weren't even competent enough to keep him alive. It's a damn shame for a father to confront—

A lifetime of grief crammed into the single hour Sam knew Calvin existed before he was dead, a split-second record in his mind of the boy's voice. Maybe that was all Sam deserved. But none of this was about what Sam deserved. That was the grace that lifted him, knowing his needs were meaningless. Not his atonement or punishment. Not the unjust diagnosis rendered onto Jill. Not Jodie's wild wanderings or even Wynn Johnston's panic.

Let the law come and demand an explanation. It didn't matter that Sam had none to give.

"Jill?" he called out.

His wife's condition was checked by the other emergency medic during the first few minutes of their arrival. Sam was then too stunned to keep track of where she was ushered next, where she rested. Too stunned to do anything but watch over Erika, but even she had somehow slipped away from him.

He grabbed the banister with his undamaged hand and called up the stairs, "Erika?"

That dread of loss draped over him all over again.

He took the steps three at a time and steadied his dizzy head in the upstairs hallway. They were together in Erika's bedroom, mother and daughter, lit only by the fish tank glow and the string of Christmas blinkers stapled along the wall border. Erika slumped in her beanbag, hugging her legs. She was alive. She carried more knowledge and experience than anyone should shoulder, but she had life left enough to find her own grace from it. She was safe.

From the edge of the bed, Jill brushed fingers through her daughter's hair. She was still in her bathrobe, still wasted and weak, but Jill wasn't the one who'd have to parse out the truths and turns for years to come. She wouldn't have to consider the depths of her husband's weakness or accept the stark fact that the child born from her family's sin had somehow saved her daughter's life.

That would have to be Erika's labor.

"I didn't know where you guys were. I was calling you," he said in the doorway.

"Nobody wanted to yell," Jill said.

He said, "I thought something happened."

"Something did happen," Erika muttered into her lap, forehead on her knees.

"I know. I mean—" He sat beside Jill and put his arm around her waist, rested his chin gently on her scalp. It was a miracle when she relaxed her poise and melted against him. She wiped a balled-up tissue under her eyes.

"I can't believe she ran off like that," Jill said.

"They'll find her fast enough," said Sam.

"She's going to get herself killed. Just like that boy down there."

"I don't think he's going to hurt anyone else, Jill."

Erika said, "You knew his name. How did you know him?"

"I didn't," Sam explained. "Jodie just told me—"

"Wynn—how did you know Wynn?"

Sam breathed deep and listened to the rumble of the many engines outside. He could force himself to think about Jodie and Wynn together in his car, and what further damage they might cause or commit, but stray thoughts weren't worth the wasted time. Those two fugitives were beyond his reach. He was here with the women he loved. Nothing was worth more.

Sam said, "He was a suspect in the Lyme murder case. He knew I was after him."

Erika shook her head. The fish in her tank were bright and indifferent. Sam could only imagine how his daughter judged him—another train of thought he refused to catch. And another: where his daughter had been all night, and how she had come to know Wynn. But he let those questions drift away just as easily as he'd dropped Dwight Kopeck's bribe into the church mail slot. What mattered was what she'd remember about this moment when it ended, what convictions she'd mold out of its ashes.

Erika said, "They're going to ask me to tell the truth."

"It's all right, honey," Jill said.

"But I haven't figured out what the truth is."

"I know," Sam said. "But you will."

Erika looked at him across the crook of her elbow, hiding her expression. The part that Jill smoothed in her hair uncovered a thin strip of Erika's orange roots amid the darker dye. He hoped she'd let it grow out like she used to, but he wouldn't dare ask anything else of her. She said to him, "I don't believe you."

"I understand," he told her.

She reached for his taped-up hand and held it gently between both of her own like it was a delicate heirloom. She ran her own fingers across the overlapped layers. Jill pressed her forehead into Sam's ear and her warm, steady breath brushed his neck.

Erika asked, "Does it hurt?"

"Yeah, it hurts," Sam said. Downstairs, there were slow and heavy footfalls on the hardwood floor, men's hushed voices, and the static echo of the dispatcher muttering over multiple radio receivers. Sam curled his undamaged thumb and pinkie around Erika's wrist and offered her the surest pressure he could possibly—

—heaved the aluminum desk chair over his head. Wynn's vision spun and crackled with white oblivion as he smashed the chair through his dorm-room window. The blinds tore from their moorings and exposed a span of solid-gray sky. The glass and the chair plummeted out of view. Paralyzing wind pushed back at him, but he would not be deterred.

Nothing in the city was as high as this. Out across the campus, the twisted tree branches and endless brick, past the bell tower and the football field, through the woods toward the Town of Lyme and everything he'd rejected along with it.

"Mr. Johnston, this is the police!" They were bashing, a hundred hands slamming like a battering ram. He slowed down their tempo and the percussion dragged out like the rumble of earthquakes in underground caves. Cecelia said *come here* and she kissed him on the cheek. She showed him the cross carved into her chest. Wynn could slide himself back and forth through everything he wanted, and linger forever. He was fifteen years old, and could never dream of hurting anyone, least of all Cecelia.

Like Alice down the rabbit hole, he fell through the window in a way that was not a collapse, but a dance. He left the room behind him. Glass shards all orbited like systems of his own devising. The distance to the ground meant nothing because there was half of it to travel, and half of that, and half, and. More points in that space than he could ever pass, unthinkable spans.

The time of his flight meant nothing because he was falling just as planets fall. Winter would shift to spring, and he would watch the landscape drip from white to green in cycles upon cycles. He reached his arms out wide and spread his fingers, and even the widening of the distance between index and thumb would take centuries or more if he wanted. Some creator set him on this path. No end, sure enough, if that was how Wynn wanted, when he dreamed with the mind of his maker.

The bullet never reached the brain and they were all still alive, and he was a sinless, drifting fetus. He turned his eyes to the sun but he did not curse God. He raised his hands and reached and held everything inside of them. The tower with its hundred windows sailed along, parallel to the infinite regressing points he crossed. And he wasn't afraid because death would never reach its final—

ACKNOWLEDGMENTS

Thanks to the Chautauqua County Sheriff's Department in Mayville, New York, for their welcoming attitude and candor while I plied them with questions. Many of the sheriff's personnel offered time and expertise, but special thanks go to Sheriff Joseph Gerace, Captain Darryl Braley, Deputy Westley Johnson, Deputy Joshua Ostrander, and two clandestine guys who showed me the gritty underbelly of the Southern Tier, incognito. Once again, I thank my uncle, Officer Emre Arican, of the Rochester Police Department, for his knowledge and insight. Any inaccuracies are mine alone, and all the ugliness is absolutely fictional.

Almost all the math philosophy in this novel I derived from David Foster Wallace's *Everything and More: A Compact History of* ∞ (Atlas Books, 2003), a text I sought following the author's tragic suicide. I've twisted theories and vastly oversimplified for my own purposes and my limited intellect. I stand with many other contemporary novelists of minor talents in the formidable shadow of Mr. Wallace.

I'm deeply indebted to DHS and his Dallas crew, and the folks at St. Martin's Minotaur: George Witte, Andy Martin, Hector DeJean, Naomi Shulman, Kenneth J. Silver, and especially my intrepid editor, Michael Homler, who always steers me safely through Crime Alley.

I also wish to honor the memory of Raymond Smith, founder and editor of *The Ontario Review*, who first introduced my writing to a larger audience. He will be missed by many more than me.

ACKNOWLEDGMENTS

And, as always, my deepest thanks and love to those who give me a home life to share and a room of my own in which to write: Caroline, Gavin, and William.